STONES

A Novel by
Ruby Standing Deer

STONES
Copyright © 2014 by Ruby Standing Deer
Cover Art Copyright © 2014 by Samuel Keiser

All rights reserved. No part of this book may be used or reproduced in any manner whatsoever, without written permission, except in the case of brief quotations embedded in articles and reviews. For more information, please contact publisher at Publisher@EvolvedPub.com.

FIRST EDITION SOFTCOVER
ISBN: 1622539583
ISBN-13: 978-1-62253-958-1

Edited by Megan Harris and Lane Diamond

Printed in the U.S.A.

www.EvolvedPub.com
Evolved Publishing LLC
Cartersville, Georgia

Stones is a work of fiction. All names, characters, places, and incidents are the product of the author's imagination, or are used fictitiously. Any resemblance to actual events or persons, living or dead, is entirely coincidental.

Printed in Book Antiqua font.

Other Books by Ruby Standing Deer:

Circles
Spirals

DEDICATION:

For Aya tsi scuceblu Walksfar, for all her encouragement and insight; and for Pearl, my sweet diabetic dog who lives to guide me.

Chapter 1

River Song crouched on top the low bluff. Several unknown mustangs appeared in the distance, and men became visible on them as they neared the opening of the canyon. Four riders approached and lay off to the sides of their animals to give the illusion of there being only mustangs, but a human head bounced into sight and gave them away.

Small stones pressed into her knees and she moved to find a better spot. She turned to make sure where her son, Singing Stone, and her mother, Listens To Wind hid. One wrong movement, one sound, one simple mistake, and one of them may never see another sunrise. Her mother sat on her mustang behind the bluff, out of sight. Her son... her stubborn son! The hunters would soon notice her son.

She waved her arm. "Singing Stone, they approach. Lower yourself out of sight. Stay put this time! Listen well to me. I do not need to worry where you are." *Do they hide from the mustangs, or do they know we are here and hide from us? Why would they fear two women and a boy?*

He crouched low, but not behind the boulder. He scooted next to her. "I am good with a bow when we hunt. I can protect the Mustangs, as well as you and Grandmother."

"I need your silence now. I know you are good with a bow, but do as I say. Remember well what happened last moon." Her glare did not lower him to the ground.

He raised his head higher despite her warning. "I only wished to help that sunrise. The stones did not sing, but vibrated. You know when they vibrate, danger approaches... as now." He sat on his knees, crossed his arms and glared at her, his long dark hair falling behind his shoulders. He leaned past her, his dark eyes squinting.

She raised herself to her knees and cradled his face in her hands. "We will speak more of this when we camp." She dropped her hands and returned to the place near the edge of the bluff.

The warm breeze filled her nostrils with the smells of dirt, new grass, and the sweet scent of the mustangs. Nine animals grazed but a few paces from where they crouched. Their calm breathing swelled their sides in an even rhythm. She nudged several stones down the path with the back of her hand. The tumbling stones smacked into each other and created enough clatter that they alerted the lead dun-colored female.

The lead female's body tensed, her skin quivered, and her ears swiveled as she tossed her head into the air. Her nostrils flared as if she tried to pick up the smell of danger. She cocked one ear toward River Song, while the other pointed toward the sound of approaching hunters. After snorting and pawing the ground with her front hooves, she trotted around the small herd to alert the male. The rest of the females and their young ones raised their heads, stopped grazing, and pointed their ears forward.

They are not as alert as they should be. Perhaps they have grown too used to us?

River Song edged forward on short leggings she had made for ease of movement.

Every time, I see the scars. The hairy-faces use their spinning spikes tied to the back of their footwear to gouge the mustangs' sides, and use snapping sticks to slash at their shoulders and rumps, forcing them to run faster. Most of our people show great respect toward all living beings, and even ask before we use them to pull our drags. Never would we beat them! So why do these warriors hunt them and try to capture the males?

Heat rose to her face and anger filled her heart.

The dark brownish-red male, with four matching white legs, raised his head at the snorting and pacing of the lead female. The male's body grew tall with tension as he snorted, stomped, and trotted down from his small hill and passed beneath the bluff where River Song crouched. Most of the females had young ones two or three moons old. They were born with an alertness inherited from their mothers, but they were slower, easier prey. Many times the mothers turned to fight, to protect their young, but they could not defend their young against this kind of hunter.

River Song raised her head as the babies trotted to the safety of their mothers' sides. The first human cry sounded. Arrows whizzed past, and one young one squealed but ran on. The lead female circled the herd, her young one at her side as they raced out onto the grasslands, then veered toward the canyons. The male galloped behind the herd, moving from side to side, pushing the slower ones by nipping their backsides.

Once the mustangs were out of danger, River Song's little family would seek the security of the high red-orange walls along the bluffs, where they could watch more easily for peril. Sometimes the mustangs beat them back to their hideaway, and glanced up from their grazing as if to say, 'What took you Humans so long?' This time she would make sure they were there quickly, to see if the young one took an arrow.

She turned her head at her mother's bird whistle, which she used to call for help. She hurried to the edge of the bluff where it was not quite so steep, and peered down to where Listens To Wind held the ropes of two mustangs while the one she sat on pranced backwards.

A warrior fast approached her on his animal.

River Song's heart pounded at the man's whooping scream. She fumbled for an arrow. "Mother—" She spun around on her heels and with deadly calm, raised her bow and set the arrow.

Unaware of her, the man pulled his own bow taut, arrow ready to fly at Listens To Wind.

River Song's arrow flew and found its mark first, piercing the back of the warrior's shoulder.

Off balance, he clutched the animal's neck hair as the mustang reared and whirled. The rider barely hung on, bouncing from side to side like a hide bag whose ties had let loose as the mustang raced away.

She turned her head in time to see her mother urge her mustang behind a large boulder. River Song dropped to the ground, ducked behind a smaller boulder on the edge of the bluff, and readied another shafted bone arrow.

A second warrior shouted and started toward where her mother hid. As he raced closer, she leapt to her feet and let another arrow fly. The arrow bit deep into the man's thigh, and he jerked his head up, spotting her. He dug his heels into the sides of his mustang and forced the animal up a narrow deer trail that led to the bluff. Legs tight around his animal, he drew his bowstring taut and let the arrow fly toward her.

She ducked, rolled and came up, bow ready as the arrow bounced off a group of large stones next to her. She whooped and the man hesitated — the last mistake he ever made. She whirled around at the sound of hooves, and only dust remained of the third warrior galloping toward the grasslands. Behind her stood her son, arrow drawn.

"So, you were the reason he hesitated. I thought my yell surprised him. You saved both our lives, Singing Stone, who is growing into a man." She rested an arm across his shoulder. "This was very brave for you to do."

Listens To Wind called and waved to her from below.

River Song and her son moved forward, closer to the edge of the bluff to wave back. Sister Wind teased at her mother's thick, nearly knee-length hair that darkness had blessed with its own color. *My mother, a strong, brave woman!*

She slung her bow over her shoulder, and slid down the trail toward the man her arrow had stopped. The mustang suffered no harm and was able to turn without falling. At the side of the bluff, too steep to reach the fallen warrior, she knelt on the trail. A large branch sticking out of the side of the bluff had caught him. He was her age, probably a father.

Her son put his hand on her shoulder as she spoke. "Creator, forgive this child if I do wrong. I only wish to protect the most beautiful animals I have ever known. To have been gifted with one as a companion is more than I can ever thank you for."

She would leave the man where he fell, untouched. Even if the bluff side were not so steep, she would never send another to the campfires mangled, as some did. She was not so vengeful that she would ruin someone's afterlife. To take another's life pierced her heart enough.

A tear escaped and slid down one cheek as emotions evoked by the attack collided with memories. She longed to know her father's comfort again, her man's caresses, but they sat at their campfire together in the sky.

She raised her head and searched the cloudless, turquoise sky. "Father, and man of mine, the two of you taught me well. You both must be proud to see us protecting these animals as both of you once did."

She reached for her son's hand. "Singing Stone has passed his tenth winter. He, too, loves the mustangs, and helps protect them. Father, please help us care for him as we do this, as you once protected me. Man of mine, your son grows more into a man each sunrise."

She stood, still holding her son's hand, and lifted her other hand to her raised brows.

In the distance, mustangs had left a dust cloud. The pawing of the man's mustang at the base of the bluff caught her attention. A light brown, female mustang with black neck hair stood before them. The animal tossed her head and pawed the red ground.

Singing Stone slid down to the animal, and took off the mustang's nose rope. The female tossed her head, trotted a short ways before she kicked her heels in joy, and raced across the land after the herd.

The boy ran around the bluff to a well-used trail and climbed back up beside River Song.

She stood on top the hill, scanning the few large orange stones scattered across the grasslands. Uneasiness crept over her. It was time to turn around, to go into the canyons, the only place they had ever known. As she replaced the arrow she held in the quiver that seldom left her shoulder, worry pressed hard on her mind. They might still be attacked; she did not know where two of the riders had gone. She touched the bow that hung over her shoulder and motioned to her son.

Her mother waited with their mustangs, and they scooted down the larger deer trail, and went around to where she hid. Blood stained the lower edge of her mother's tunic and her mustang's shoulder.

River Song slid down the bluff, her son nearly on top of her. "Mother, you are hurt! Please, allow us to help you down—"

Listens To Wind raised a hand as a thin smile crept across her face. "Daughter, I am fine. Look beyond me... the blood is not mine." She nodded toward a warrior who lay on the ground. "My knife caught him across his chest, and stopped him from pulling me from my animal. I am not so helpless."

She brushed her hair from her face. The movement revealed a scar that ran from the corner of one eye to her chin. Once, she had not been so fortunate in avoiding a knife.

Listens To Wind slipped off her animal. "The man still breathes."

His bloodied chest, partly covered by his hair, made it hard to see how badly she had wounded him.

She walked over to the man on the ground, knelt beside him, and pulled the hair from his face. "Young, so young. He... he has a growth of hair on his chin! He is part hairy-face. He will live. The wound on his face is not so bad, caused by the stone he hit his head on. Where I cut him is shallow. He sleeps the sleep of one who has hit his head. It is not good to stay here. His people will come for him. I think they are the Likes To Fight people." She frowned. "Perhaps some of the hairy-faces may have joined their band."

Singing Stone knelt beside her. "Grandmother, you are skilled and I hope one day to—"

She stood and pulled him away as the warrior coughed. "Never allow harming another to become easy, little one. It bruises the Soul, leaves darkness there that cannot ever be washed away, and cannot be covered up by good deeds. Listen well to me."

She clutched the tunic at his shoulder. "We do not know why they hunt these mustangs, capture the males. This season has brought many humpbacks, deer and elk. There is no reason to hunt the mustangs. They ride them as we do, yet do not respect them."

Her mother shook a finger in River Song's direction. "You must remember your son and keep him in your mind as you do this with me. He can hunt, set fish traps, and has much knowledge about surviving on his own. Still, we must think of his safety. He rose when he should not have."

Listens To Wind hugged her grandson, and brushed the back of her hand across his cheek. "You look much like my oldest brother. He was the best in our band, brave enough to sneak in and set the mustangs free from the hairy-faces. The stories my brother told me of the cruelty stays in my mind like a bad storm filled with lightning. Everyday, as others followed the herds of the great humpbacks, our band followed the mustangs."

River Song motioned her mother and Singing Stone to jump on their mustangs. "Mother, I will trot ahead and be sure our path is clear."

***

They headed back to the canyons at a trot. They needed to hurry away from the hunter's people, who might come to find the wounded young man.

Listens To Wind tapped her animal so the mustang would come up next to her grandson. She continued her story. "We only took the mustangs we needed to ride, to help us pull our drags. Before long they became used to us and followed willingly wherever we traveled."

She lowered her head for a short span, and twirled her fingers around her necklace made of braided mustang hair and hand-made stone beads, which were woven in.

She began speaking again as she raised her head. "Your mother knows of this, but never have I told you. I speak of this so you know your blood is strong. One night, when I was about twelve winters old, hooves thundered through our camp. Everyone was asleep, as we never had a reason to have men guard the camp. I woke to loud voices and ran outside. We scattered in all directions into the darkness. My mother and my brothers were fighting, and I ran toward them, but a rider scooped me up. I bit and scratched him, but no matter. I was captured by the Likes To Fight People when I was about your age."

She pointed to her head. "I was smart. I let them think I trusted them, liked them. That took two full cycles of seasons. They stopped watching me. I went for water and kept going. Our people taught the girls, along with the boys, to hunt, so I survived."

She twisted his way and tapped her animal. "We must hurry. The young mustang may need our help.

"You show no fear. This is good. You show the strength of your mind. As I am, you are one who will live long. You are keeping the herd safe, doing what we must. That is good, to not show fear, but you must learn caution."

He gripped the off-white neck hairs of his mustang and fidgeted on her back. "I am no longer afraid as when I was only a boy. I am much older now." He spoke on, proving his lack of concern. "Tell me more, Grandmother! I wish to hear more about our family. Did you find your mother and brothers when you escaped? Did you become a band again? Where are they now?"

She shook her head, jumped down, and stepped over loose stones too big for the mustangs to trot through. Then she jumped back on.

Singing Stone mimicked her actions.

"Perhaps this night when we sit and rest, I will tell you more. I cannot say the names of my mother, or my brothers, as I never saw any of them after the attack, so I do not know if they left their names behind or took them as they crossed over... if they did. I went back to our old camp. Nothing was left but scattered burnt wood we used to make our homes. We did not use the humpback hides as we do now. There was no trail for me to follow, so I wandered for a long span. I met your grandfather as he hunted. He too, was alone. I was young, but a woman, so we became mates."

Her daughter stopped ahead and waited for them to catch up.

"Never tell me you are old." River Song's mustang pranced in a circle. "You have a motion as if Sister Wind helps you to fly where you need to go. The grace of your thirty-eight winters... I can only wish I, too, will have the same ease of motions that you have."

"Daughter, *you* will soon know what it is to look through *my* eyes and wonder why you thought me old!"

She leaned over her mustang and muttered words about young people thinking only *they* had ease of motion, and pushed her mustang to pick up the pace.

***

Silent as a stilled blade of grass, River Song flattened herself to the ground. The herd had circled back into the canyon where the grass was at its best. While the others grazed, the lead female stood stiff with her head hung over her young one.

Singing Stone breathed next to her, and she reached out to squeeze his hand. "Be still."

Her low voice caught the attention of the lead female and her young one — the young one they hoped to catch. An arrow flopped from his white and grey spotted flank, and blood seeped from the wound and ran down his leg.

The boy slid backward in the grass and moved away from his mother. His independence frustrated her and she scooted back to grab him, but he was not there.

"Son, the male is protective, and with the young, the females are very cautious! You know this." She tried in vain to call out quietly, but the sound alerted the male and he tossed his head and started to move their way. "Do not simply walk among them. They may know us by sight, and allow us to walk up to them, but the wounded baby may make the male and the mother act differently." Her heart torn, she raised her bow.

"Get back! The mother turns your way!" A raspy, high pitch replaced her whisper.

Singing Stone's voice rose on the wind, carrying a soft melody. He sang to the mother and young one — a song she could not understand, birdlike, but also like a mustang's calming nicker call. He opened the pouch of healing salve that should have been in her pack. The baby held still as he worked the arrow shaft out of his flank then smeared the medicine in the wound.

My son has fast hands for me not to see him take the medicine from my pack. What is this singing he does? The mother mustang turned and blocked River Song's view.

Listens To Wind, on the other side of the herd, rose on one knee too fast, causing panic to pound in River Song's head. *I cannot see her well enough to know what she does!* Before she could react, the mother mustang moved away exposing her son and the young one.

Singing Stone held the arrow and its shaft in his hand. Several other mustangs moved his way and sniffed the shaft and the young one's wound. His song still carried on Sister Wind as he reached for the muzzle of an off-white animal who lowered her head.

The male made no move from the small hill where he stood. He bobbed his head up and down, watchful.

Her son spoke in a soft tone. "You see, Mother? They know us well and know we would never cause them harm. How many times have we slept on the edge of their herd? Not once have we been stepped on. They know us better than you understand. Many times we have walked among them. They even allow us to pet them, and they knew the young one needed help... our help."

The boy dropped the arrow, inspected the wound and rubbed in more salve. He moved along beside the young one, and rubbed his grey-white back as he made his way to the mustang's head.

"I have never seen one of your colors." He nodded toward the watchful lead male. "He has grey on his shoulders and in his neck hair, but not as dark as yours, and you have white spots where he is painted in splotches of darker grey." He ran his hands through the young one's short neck hair. "Your neck hair shines white as snow, and your eyes.... I can see deep into them and see forever. How is this so?"

Eagles calling to one another caused him to lift his head. "The Spirits mean for us to be companions. I can feel it!"

The lead male whinnied, and the young one's mother called back, sending the herd trotting away.

Singing Stone held up a few small, white hairs in-between his fingers. "One day, one day... I will ride on your back. I call you Spirit Eyes."

***

Listens To Wind pushed her lightly star-dusted hair from her face, and walked away from her family and the mustangs as Father Sun woke. For more than a moon, Sister Wind had whispered warnings to her. She climbed up high on the old steps where some long ago people had carved images along the walls of the stone. The path, pounded by hundreds of footprints, remained even after the long passage of many cycles of seasons. She admired the faint carvings of long ago animals that another Peoples had left.

Once on top, an old camp came into view. The Peoples who occupied the area many winters ago had left most of their lodge poles. *Fish People, I think they were called.*

She turned away to look out over the canyons. The waters wound through the mysterious paths in the red-orange gullies, appearing and disappearing from sight. Greens of many shades followed alongside the river, where the land widened into colorful valleys of silvery Sacred Sage and flowering yellow rabbit brush, which stood out among the other plants.

Her mind drifted from the beauty below as chill bumps rose on her arms. Tears threatened to fall as she lifted her arms, reaching upward to the turquoise sky. "Spirits, I ask for protection for my little family. With my man and my daughter's man taken in battle with the mixed Peoples of the Likes To Fight and hairy-faces, I have much fear. I know we must decide soon about the mustangs, if we can keep protecting them...."

Chapter 2

Turtle Dove lay still in her robe as her father slipped out from under the humpback hide he and her mother shared on the other side of their lodge. The fire sat toward the back and center of the lodge, sending up tiny sparks that the stones protectively kept inside the pit dug below the ring. They gave only enough light to see shadows.

Shining Light grabbed his pack and a spare smoked deerskin, and stepped over Turtle Dove as he made his way from the lodge.

Her mother slept a deep sleep this night and did not stir, but Turtle Dove only pretended to sleep.

After her father vanished into the darkness, she covered herself and followed. White Paws stretched and followed, leaving his mate and wolf pups who slept outside the lodge on a spare humpback robe. With the night air only mildly chilled, the four pups lay on the ground next to it. The rest of the pack hunted this night.

Her bare feet made no sound as she crossed the damp grass. The smell of the night flowers wafted past her. *If anyone wakes, they will make me go back. Sister Moon is full of Power this night, and Father is always restless when she is so big. I wish to see why he leaves after Mother sleeps.*

Above her, a flock of birds called to each other as they winged their way across the darkness. Three deer bounced away through shrubs, sending other birds flying for another cover. Sister Moon exposed their silvery wings as they vanished into the safety of tall trees. She smiled at the distant, soft laughter of a couple.

As she and White Paws approached her father, the waters from above the cliff splashed into the river below. The rushing water gave her the cover she needed to move faster. She crouched behind white flowering shrubs and peered through them in anticipation. White Paws lay beside her, nosing her hand.

Shining Light knelt and pulled out his Sacred items: the pipe that his grandfather had made him, unwrapped from the feathers gifted to him from birds as they dropped them when he walked, small shells and bits of fur—items that only held meaning to him. He placed them on the robe next to him, and then raised his arms.

It was not right to watch another seeking guidance, but she needed to know why her father sought to be alone so many nights instead of sleeping. She moved the shrubs to get a better look, but as she did the wolf used his teeth on her robe, pulling her back. Flower dust floated past and tickled her nose. She cupped her hand over her nose, but not before she sneezed.

"Dove, I can hear you. And you too, Wolf! You must come and tell me why you follow." Shining Light turned and motioned for her, then packed his items away.

With head bowed and arms crossed, she approached him. "Father, I am sorry." She sat next to him, but looked down still, her arms folded across her waist.

White Paws pushed his way in between them, and put his head on Shining Light's lap. The wolf poked at his arm with a paw.

He lowered his arm and scratched the wolf. "White Paws, why are *you* here? Do you also need to know why I am here? You understand things before I do, Wolf Brother."

Her father reached past White Paws and pulled her onto his lap, rubbing her nose with his. "You are too young to worry where I go, but I will try to explain why I do this." He gathered her in his arms and stared ahead as he spoke.

"Daughter, no one can go through life without some kind of guidance. Those who try, their lives are as a wild wind with no direction. No one can live that way and be happy. All we need to do is ask Creator, the Spirits, or even a stone for help. Trees hold answers, if we listen. Watch an animal, and see how they react to things.

"It was Fox who saved my mother, grandmother and me from a bad flood. Everything in Nature has messages if you only open up to them.

"We have more than our ears to hear with. Our hearts hear also. We can feel answers if we try. Sometimes a vision or a dream speaks through us, maybe not in words, but as paintings, like the ones Falling Rainbow puts on her hides. We do not always understand as quickly as we wish, but the answers will come."

He squeezed her tighter and rested his chin on top of her head. "When I was but six winters old, dreams started to frighten me. I told no one. When I was seven winters, they became stronger. I would leave our lodge and climb to the top of a canyon to be alone. I thought I was clever to have sneaked away, but when I crawled into my Sacred place, my grandmother felt near. It gave me the courage to reach out, to allow the dreams to wash over me, just as the falling waters before us splash over the stones."

He reached down and worked his hand into White Paws' thick, furry neck. "Those dreams, with the guidance of Creator, the Spirits, and some very special people, taught me who I could become."

He moved his head back and stared into her eyes. "I have seen the blue glow in your eyes since you were born. At eight winters, it is stronger now. The glow holds the mystery of the Spirit Land, and everyone whose eyes carry it becomes a Healer. I wonder who you will become."

He raised his hand and lifted her chin. "Now, tell me why you followed.

She bit the inside of her cheek before nodding. "I had a dream this night, Father, which I do not understand. Someone called Blue Night Sky stood in a place of.... It was all misty and full of blue swirling something. She smiled at me and said I had your eyes, and then she became part of the blue colors. Then I saw mustangs and people who lived together as one band. There is a boy, a special boy I wish to meet. He says we will be mates. What is a canyon? Is it really the color of a sunset?

"Father, why do you stare at me with big eyes? And why do you squeeze me so tight? You are scaring me!" She shivered when he took in air and forced it out of his mouth.

He released his hold. "Dove, my little one, Blue Night Sky was a special ancestor of ours who held much Power. She helped me the most as I explored who I was. I did not mean to scare you so."

He untangled his arms. "Why do you ask the color of the canyons? I know it has been a long time, but stories of the canyons are in our talks so we do not forget where we come from. I was born in those canyons of beauty. Many bluffs are tall with flat tops, some connect and make long pathways with small streams, and plants grow along their edges, in the mud. Dark blue birds with long, split tails made nests from that mud and somehow, the mud clung to the walls. Some canyons have paths that weave back and forth as if maybe waters from long ago raced through them."

He reached high above as if trying to touch Sister Moon. "They grow from our Mother's body and shoot straight up in colors of oranges, reds, and the color of light-tanned deer hides. Before Father Sun woke, I would go sit on a smaller bluff that overlooked our camp, and I would watch the colors as they changed with the sunrise."

He pulled her gently this time, and cuddled her. "First, when Father Sun would wake, they would look like the spiked purple flowers that grow in the grasslands. As Father Sun moved across the sky, the canyon walls changed to warm orange-reds. You remember the flowers I sometimes bring back with me when I leave the forest for a few sunrises?"

She nodded, turned and brushed the long hair from his face. "I remember the happy face on Mother when you handed her some. You were good to bring them back to her. She did not care if they were no longer awake. She made dye from them. She is so smart! Someday I will be smart, too, and I will make dye, and learn how to paint and how to ride like you and—"

"Dove, so many words spill from your mouth all at once! Heh, my grandmother spoke these same words to me. Now I understand. She would tell me I would use up all my words and run out of them."

His laughter echoed against the trees.

"Did you?"

"If I had, silly one, I would not be able to speak to you now." He tossed his head back and laughed harder. "I have a daughter who will be like me!" He stopped laughing and squeezed her once more.

"Fa-ther. No air. Let... me go." She struggled to be free of his tight grasp. "My eyes... going to... pop out! I need my—" She sucked in air as he loosened his hold, and reached for her eyes. "Mother says you squeezed her very tight, and she laughed and said she had to push her eyes back in! I do not wish that to happen to me. What would happen if I could not get them back in? I would walk into trees and fall in the waters and walk into White Bear."

"White Bear? Little one, when have you seen her?" His grip tightened once more, but she pulled away.

"I see her all the time. She has a white baby, and the baby comes to me. I pet him and the mother sits beside me, watching us play. We are good friends. Father, have you seen her? She is all white and so nice and—"

"Dove! How many times have you done this? You must be very careful with what you do. Even Spirit animals when they walk the land are protective of their young." He tightened his lips and shook his head. "You must not do this."

"No, Father, not her—she will not harm me. I saw her in a dream and she reached out and touched me. The next sunrise I found her sitting close to our lodge and I followed her into the trees. She took me to meet her baby and we played. She is my friend."

He pressed his forehead against hers "Again, I ask, how many times have you done this?"

"I cannot count that far. Will you take me back to our lodge? My eyes are tired now."

"I bet your mouth is tired also." He stood and scooped her up in her robe.

They started to walk back to camp when a rustling noise caught Dove's attention. "There. There she is."

***

Shining Light stopped mid-stride and turned in the direction she pointed.

White Bear and her cub ambled out of the shrubs as if it was nothing to greet his daughter. She squirmed to get down and before he could stop her, she stood before the mother and her young one, and wrapped both arms around the cub.

He stepped with caution toward them, worried he might ruin the mystical Energy. When White Bear raised her head, she spoke to his mind.

'We have a different connection, your daughter and I. She will carry my message of understanding far away from this forest.'

"White Bear, I will never allow her to leave the safety of the forest without me!" Panic in his voice made his daughter turn away from the cub.

"Father, what is this you say?"

'Shining Light, you will have no choice. Her life is her own.'

Chapter 3

Shining Light carried Dove back to the lodge.

Animal Speaks Woman and her grey and black-speckled dog, Blue Waters, stood in front of their lodge, next to a small fire that flickered upward as if reaching for the campfires in the sky. She rubbed her belly, her six-moon bump pushing against her long brown-fringed tunic that fell well below the knees. A long braid of shiny raven hair lay over on one shoulder, reaching past her waist.

Such beauty, and not only her body, but from deep within. I am truly blessed.

"So, my man and my sweet daughter, where did this night lead you both?" Her face held no anger, no worry, as he approached.

"Dove, go inside. I wish to speak to your mother. Do not look at me with worried eyes, little one, everything is good." He sat on their log next to the fire and motioned Animal Speaks to sit next to him. They waited for Dove to settle in her sleeping robe and listened for her soft, even breathing.

Moon Face raised her head, and White Paws curled himself next to his mate and their five pups.

"Five this time, and only one who is like her father. The rest are a mix of the colors of fallen leaves with specks of grey and white." Shining Light reached toward the little grey and white female and scratched her head.

He nodded toward the wolves. "I still wonder why our mustangs do not shy away from them. Free mustangs outside the forest run in great fear when the wolves leave with me. We have... what? Eleven wolf packs in the forest who do not harm mustangs? And *our* mustangs show no fear the way the wild mustangs do."

He pulled the female pup into his lap. "Only White Paws, his mate, and their first two groups of pups stay as one pack while the others are scattered throughout the forest. I can no longer count all the wolves, yet they know me."

"Yes, man of mine, they do. Even the ones who joined ours when they left the forest know you. They know their Brother." Animal Speaks stood and reached for his hand. "Dove sleeps already. Her breathing is even, peaceful. Light, we need to talk about our daughter."

He squeezed her hand and stared into her deep-set, dark eyes. In the fire's shadow, the blue in her eyes danced with Power. The pup jumped down and stretched, then made her way back into the pile of pups.

She tightened her grip on his hand and took in a deep breath, allowing it to leave her slowly. "I listen to her as she sleeps. She has a bond with White Bear." She ran her free hand over her belly. "She connects with her brother. He moves when she speaks to him. Dove has much Power for one so young, just as you did, but in a different way that I do not understand."

He loosened his grip. "How is it that I did not know of her bond with White Bear? I am a Holy Man and feel all things around me."

"Only the Spirits can answer that. Perhaps mothers are closer to their children because we carry them in our bellies. We also bond when we feed them from our breasts."

Her smile warmed him as no fire ever could.

"I had no dream as I should have." He shook his head and shrugged. "White Bear's shadow crossed our lodge as I held our daughter. I thought White Bear was there as my Guide. Why did I not know then that White Bear came to be with her? Dove's Energy mixed with my own, as any new baby's might, and I did not feel any other join us."

He curled his bare toes under, pushed out the dirt from under his feet, then reached over and pulled on her arm.

"I did not understand White Bear had chosen her." He glanced up into the darkness. Distant sparkling campfires in the black sky winked back at him. "Heh, I will now learn what my grandparents and parents did about a child whose Power comes too soon."

Animal Speaks Woman wove her arm into his as she scooted closer and leaned her head on his bare shoulder. "The cool air never bothers you. Your skin is free of cold bumps, unlike mine." She pulled away and added several small twigs to the fire. Red fingers reached up and grabbed for them. "White Bear and her cub have appeared to Dove and me both. She reached into my mind and told me Dove would leave the forest one day, and that we must allow her to do so. I spoke no words to you the day Dove came to be with us. Fear raced through my heart faster than fire eats dry grasses. I... I had hoped my mind made up things. I was a new mother whose only thoughts were of the joy I held in my arms, not cycles of seasons far into the future.

"White Bear never returned, and soon my mind rested... until... until I heard Dove call out as she dreamed last warm season. She asked White Bear's cub to play with her."

"Speaks, *this* makes chill bumps rise on my arms. I brought us here for safety, and Dove will leave." Shining Light lowered his head and pinched the top of his nose, his long raven hair falling forward. "I would miss this place. I can taste the air here, not dusty as in the canyons, more like mist mixed with the sharpness of pine trees."

He raised his head and pushed the hair from his face. "But I will not allow her to leave without me."

Animal Speaks Woman stiffened. "Surely this is many cycles of seasons away, *if* it is to happen at all."

A shadow covered the small fire they faced.

Shining Light jumped up and spun around so fast, he nearly backed into the fire as he twisted to see who invaded their talk. "Wanderer, you are sneaky! How long have you listened?"

"It is impolite to listen to another's words without their permission, but Sister Wind brought them to me. So, I come to hear more unless you wish me not to hear." Wanderer put a finger in each ear and sat down on the edge of the log. Three mice jumped from his shoulder and faded into the darkness.

Speaks turned and grinned. "I will never understand how the wolves know your mice from the others."

"What? I cannot hear you."

She rolled her eyes and pushed Shining Light. "Please, do not go crazy. Promise me you will not." Animal Speaks pulled him back down. "When we left the forest to find Falling Rainbow, and Wanderer rode up just in time to save Sparkling Star's life, I was mystified by his presence. Then he yelled at you to watch over his mice who raced all over our camp!"

"I heard that. I am not without hearing." Wanderer peered at them through his loose hair, fingers still in ears.

"But, you said you could not hear." She smacked her forehead.

Fingers now out of his ears, Wanderer leaned Shining Light's way and whispered, "She still has a sharp tongue. Turtle Dove will also. She will be as you and her, all in one body."

Speaks cleared her throat. "I am not without hearing either, Holy Man."

He turned her way. "Good, you are too young to lose your hearing."

He faced Shining Light. "I hope to be nearby when a young man smiles your daughter's way. She will want the attention, but will also turn away. Heh, you may wait many cycles of seasons before you are a grandfather."

Shining Light gripped Wanderer's leg. "I am only twenty-three winters! Do not speak of us being grandparents!" His words too loud, he slapped a hand across his mouth, then jumped up and left.

Wanderer chuckled and turned his attention toward Speaks. "Many wondrous happenings are in your daughter's future, and I came to remind you that Blue Night Sky may no longer walk among us, but your mother's grandmother, my sister, walks beside Dove. Already, blue swirls around your daughter." He stood and stretched. "My mice call to me."

***

Before Shining Light made it back to the falling waters to start his quest for guidance again, White Bear and her cub ambled out of the shadows and blocked his path. White Paws sat at her side, and a golden glow appeared over both White Bear and Wolf.

"This cannot be right. Sister Moon has only reached her high place a short span ago. Darkness still claims the sky. And White Paws, why do you sit next to her? What is this glow?" He reached for his absent pack. *My pack... it still sits by the falling water.*

"Please, White Bear, tell me why you are here? I have not seen you in almost two winters. I must... wait! Why do you fade? White Paws, where are you?" A wet nose pushed at his hand from behind and he spun around. "White

Paws, where is my mind? You were before me with White Bear, were you not?"

White Paws responded with a shove to his leg and moved past him. The wolf led the way back to where he had left his pack.

"I wait for guidance from the Spirits. Why are you here?" He sat on the robe.

White Paws settled next to him, and put his head down across his Human Brother's leg.

Shining Light leaned over and hugged his Wolf Brother. "Thank you for being with me." He lit the tied bundle of Sage plants, waited for them to flame and blew them out. With Eagle's feather, he waved the smoke over his body and over White Paws, cleansing them both. With eyes closed, he prepared his mind to let go as he sang a quiet song.

"My grandson honors all with his cleansing."

His eyes shot open. "Grandmother?" He spun around and glanced up to see Bright Sun Flower's calm face. Her eyes pulled him in and held him tight.

"I wish to sit beside you. As I passed your lodge, Wanderer waved my way, so I sat with him. He told me to remind you that you may help life come into the band, but that does not mean that *life* belongs to you. He is a wise man."

Shining Light gathered his Sacred items and placed them in his pouch, then moved from the center of his robe, scooting White Paws with him. "I came here seeking guidance. Why do you wander around in the darkness, Grandmother?"

"I am full of guidance. My many seasons tell me this is so." She settled on the robe next to him, and small tinkling shells braided in strands swayed across the front of her light-brown elk dress. "A long time ago, when you were a boy, I would feel you when you were restless. This has not changed. I just do not follow you anymore. Until now."

She turned his way, her expression calm. "I now feel Turtle Dove as I did you. With two parents who have the Spirits' ears, as the both of you do, of course your children would be born with Power. You have taught her much, and you think she only understands part of it, but she understands more than you think. As you came to me, so does your daughter. She started coming to me when she was only seven winters old. You did not know that." She became silent and played with something in her hand.

"I did not. I should have felt it." He twisted his hands.

"You were not meant to. The Spirits told me not to speak of it."

"The Spirits have much that they choose to remain silent about."

"Yes, they do. It is not for us to know everything." She took his hand and squeezed it.

He took in air and held it until he had to let it go. "On my way back to where we now sit, I thought I had seen Father Sun start to wake. Before me sat both White Bear and White Paws in a light—light that only comes from sunrise. What does this mean, Grandmother?"

She shrugged one shoulder. "I know what it would mean to me, but perhaps it is not the same meaning for you. I see the light as a way of gaining attention. Perhaps it means you need to pay attention to what both have to offer."

She took his hand and placed an object in his palm. "This is for your daughter. Wanderer made the carving."

He held the blue object up to the light cast by Sister Moon. "A blue sky stone made into a mustang?" He turned the carving over many times. "This must have taken a long time." He held it up to the light again. "This is a beautiful, detailed carving! Even the neck hairs can be counted."

"There is a small hole so it will fit on the tail hair braid he also made." She handed him a thin, dark grey braid mixed with yellow hair. "It is from the tail of Grey Storm's daughter. Did you know Dove rides her? She surprised your grandfather several sunrises ago while he fished, when she bounced past on the mustang's back. She named her Fire."

He jumped up. "My baby rides a half-crazy mustang? Why did you not tell me this?"

She chuckled and pulled on his legging. "Sit, silly one. You act as your own mother when she saw you race through our old camp on Sandstone."

"I was *not* eight winters! I was... was....." He plopped beside her, still clutching the blue sky stone carving.

"Good to know you do not get so crazy as your mother did!" She leaned back and laughed harder.

"Grandmother, I am not... not...." He shook his head. "I am as my mother. Dove is young! How... *who* taught her to ride? I must have a very serious talk with—"

"Me."

"You? You taught her? On Grey Storm's daughter? She has too much Power for a very young child. Why would you do this, and not tell me?"

"You would have said no. Then I would have had to honor what you said."

He pulled up his knees and picked at the fringe on his leggings. "Wanderer would do this, not you."

"Heh, he may have helped. She came to me asking if she could ride Sandstone, worried you would say no. Most children her age already ride. Gentle Wisdom has taken her many times on her little brown mustang for rides, and you know this. You puff out your chest as your daughter rides by.

"I cannot get used to your cousin's new name, Gentle Wisdom Who Rides A Flying Mustang. Heh, I know she earned her new name through her vision quest, but I still see her as she was, not the tall, proud woman she is now. Like you, she is still silly in many ways."

"I am not silly."

"Yes, you are. Stop pulling at your fringe and listen to me. Wanderer walked with Dove and me toward the herd, and a red female trotted over to Dove. She reached out to the mustang and the animal put her nose up to Dove's face and gave her a welcoming breath, as mustangs do.

"Fire chose her as her crazy mustang sister, Thunder, chose Sparkling Star. She is gentle with her. This was meant to be, and you cannot change it. Sandstone has had fine young ones, each with their own minds. Her last one shares Sandstone's color, even her gentleness for once. I had my eye on her for Dove, but she did not respond to her."

He crossed his arms. "Grey Storm is... as different from Sandstone as sunrise is from sunset, and I have watched his daughter act much like him. She has too much Power for a little girl."

He played with the carving. "Mustang Woman. I dreamed that name when she was in Speak's belly, but I forgot until now. I promised my father's mother's Spirit I would give her name to our daughter. One day Dove will be called Mustang Woman, perhaps sooner than I wish."

Bright Sun Flower faced him and pressed her forehead against his. "When we are too close to things, we do not always see what is right before us." She leaned back. "I must tell you what the Spirits told Dove."

Bright Sun Flower took in air and forced it out. "When you had left the forest about a moon ago, Gentle Wisdom and I took Dove to a quiet place and helped her speak to the Spirits. No, Shining Light, close your mouth. There are night winged ones who may find your open mouth a nice place to explore." She chuckled when he put his hand over his mouth.

"Animal Speaks followed and joined us. Stop making big eyes, or they will pop out and in this darkness we may not find them before a small, four-legged does."

"Grandmother, I am not a child! Speaks never told me of this."

"Must *I* hold my hand over your mouth as I did when you *were* a child? I will finish and you will not make squished faces at me as I do." She held his gaze and waited for him to soften his face. "Heh, you are silent. Your daughter has your mouth. I must tell her the same thing as I do you about speaking when others do."

She raised her hand as his mouth opened. "No, we did not make her fast, even though she could have done so. Your little one is strong. In her vision, White Bear's cub came to her, but the cub did not speak. Instead, he reached out to her with his paw and tapped her leg. He then vanished. Dove told us she could see red hills and many mustangs. She also saw a young boy holding a stone and singing. We will have to see what this means."

The mustang carving slipped from his hand and he bent to retrieve it. "Grandmother, I think you already know what this means." He waited for her to answer, but when he glanced up, she had slipped into the shadows.

"Why is life not simple?" The air became still and he rubbed the chill bumps on his arm. Blue Swirls wavered in front of him, and a paw gently pulled at his arm

'*Human Brother, a simple life would soon be forgotten. It is what you do in life that remains, teaches others. They will pass on that knowledge. You chop wood, no one notices. If you chop wood for everyone, others will notice. Tell one story and it makes people listen for a sunrise, but if you continue to tell the story, they will remember —*

others will remember – and pass it on to many others.' White Paws cocked his head and stared with amber eyes into Shining Light's deep brown ones.

'You would not carry the name you do if you were meant to lead a simple life. You are the Shining Light and your daughter... she is a bright spark waiting to become her own light. You must allow her to be that light. She will walk her own path, one that you cannot follow.'

The wolf pushed his nose into Shining Light's hand then took a step back and sat. The pair raised their heads and each let go a long, soft howl. Sister Wind carried it throughout the forest.

Ruby Standing Deer

Chapter 4

Bright Sun Flower shuffled across the camp with her head low. Dove and her grandson, Shining Light, were heavy in her mind. She shared Shining Light's worry about Dove leaving the forest on her own. Since that little girl had learned to ride Fire, she rode the edges of the forest without fear.

A feeling of sickness stabbed her belly. The lower branches on a tree grabbed her and made her stop. She raised her head, and light wavered through the branches. The leaves had started to change colors.

Is Dove truly safe? What about the traders who gather at the edge of the forest seeking a way in?

The bands in the forest had missed hearing news of relatives and trading for goods they could not get within the forest. After many Council meetings, the members decided to allow some of the traders into the forest, but only as far as where the first band settled—Bright Sun Flower's people.

Over several seasons, other traders heard of the bands who lived in the Forest of Tall Trees and of their many mustangs. When asked how to find this great forest, traders would say, 'You go here, then you travel....' Yet when others came, they could not find the way in. No trader could clearly remember it. All they could say was, 'Wait at the edge of the forest and a Holy Man will come to lead you in.'

She clenched her belly as memories of one trader came into her mind. All had been well between the Peoples and their guests, until one trader had asked for more mustangs than he needed to carry back what the people had traded with him. At first, he had tried to flatter the Peoples, telling them that never before had he seen so many fine mustangs. With a look of hunger in his eyes, he promised much in trade next time he came if they would give him ten of the animals.

When the Peoples shook their heads and talked of other things, he told of how hairy-faces took great care to keep the mustangs for their own and shot anyone who tried to take them. They even sent scouts to kill mustangs just to keep the Peoples from having them. He gritted his teeth and spoke of how without the mustangs they could not hunt, nor could they be equal to the hairy-faces. When no one would willingly trade, he became angry and shouted that the bands had no need for so many animals.

Then Dove, her little Dove, had spoken up. 'My mustangs are my friends, my family and... and would you trade *your* family for goods?'

The trader glared at the adults and asked how they could allow a child to speak while adults spoke.

Bright Sun Flower's own anger had shown. No one dared speak to a child of the Wolf People with anger in their voice. Hawk Soaring, her man of many cycles of seasons, came to stand by her. One by one, the gathered people brought forth the goods he had traded to them and demanded that he return theirs.

Shining Light led him out of the forest, without the mustangs, without any trade goods, and told him to never come back.

Bright Sun Flower had followed in shadows of the trees.

The trader left with heated words and vowed to return with his sons. Yet when he had ridden only a short span, he twisted around on his old mustang and confusion creased his face.

She had left the shadows and returned to the camp satisfied; the trader had no hope of finding his way back. To him, the forest path was gone forever.

That was only six sunrises ago and worry now tightened around her throat. What if the trader lay in wait outside the forest? What if Dove should ride out alone and no one saw her?

She could not allow this to happen. A cold rain created a day for people to work on projects inside, and a story would be welcome, though it was not yet the cold season, the normal time for stories.

She made her way to the Counsel Lodge. Makes Baskets, her daughter, had become the storyteller when they arrived in the forest, yet some stories still belonged to Bright Sun Flower. This was a day for such a story.

Shining Light sat by the flap and opened it wide for her.

She smiled to see Makes Baskets' man, Flying Raven Who Dreams, sitting with her daughter and their children—Soft Breeze, now twelve winters, and Sparrow Hawk, who was two winters older than Dove.

The boy stuck out his tongue at Dove.

She leaned over her mother, Animal Speaks Woman, and tried to grab at it before he giggled and pulled back out of her arm's reach. She started to climb over her mother, but Shining Light leaned her way and cleared his throat.

A chuckle escaped Bright Sun Flower. Children were one of the Spirits' truest treasures. There would be no future without them.

The Lodge, which had been enlarged to accommodate all the Peoples from other bands, bustled with chatter and bouncing children. People moved their feet so she could pass and stand in the center by the fire pit. A fire burned in preparation for this gathering, for the stories that would be forever retold. A bundle of Sage and Cedar lay next to it.

Bright Sun Flower turned in a slow circle, motioning for the people to draw closer, and as they did, White Paws and Moon Face slipped in and wriggled their way to either side of Shining Light.

"We have a very large group this cold day" she said. "I see some must stand. Please allow parents with small children to sit. I believe Creator made special times such as this so we could gather and listen to stories, speak of good times and enjoy each other."

She pushed her robe from her shoulders, allowed it to fall, and smiled at her man, Hawk Soaring. She turned to acknowledge as many people as she could, and all chatter stopped. Only the low crackling of the fire broke the silence. She bent low to add a sprinkling of Sage and Cedar to the blue flames and breathed deep of the cleansing smoke.

With her arms spread wide to include all who were present, she continued. "So many are here this day. Some are fine hunters who keep us fed. I am proud to honor them. Without their skills, we would be hungry. We all know the elders watch over the children as their parents help bring back the meat. They, like each one of us, are an important part of our band, but they are the part that holds us together. Without elders, we would not know the stories that speak of who we are. The stories teach the children so, when they become adults, they can pass on the knowledge that binds us to one another."

Hawk Soaring took Dove and sat her on the far side of his lap, then smiled up at his woman.

She could not help but stare at the light of her life, making heat rise to his face as others turned to see why she looked so long his way.

She cleared her throat to speak. "Our children are restless, and I can also see a few adults who tease each other. We have a band of happy people this day. I welcome the small group of the ones once called hairy-faces. We all know them now by the band name they chose for themselves—People Of New Beginnings. They were told we were not good people, but they learned differently by taking time to know us." She shook her finger upward. "Too many people judge without true knowledge! They hear words from others, take those words as truth, and never try to find out for themselves. Remember this well: vever judge someone by what another says. You might miss having the friend who will be with you for life. I now wish to start my story.

"This story has two meanings. My heart was heavy with worry for those who travel away from the forest. Are they safe, I wondered. Spirit spoke to my mind and said our people learn from everything around us, even from our enemies. So it has always been. It is what makes us a stronger people. There is a story that, for too long, we have not heard. It is this story I wish to tell.

"When we lived in our village in the canyons, a greedy trader came and we sent him away with nothing. This trader waited a canyon away from our village, and when one of our young women went berry picking alone, he kidnapped her and told us he would return her only if we gave him five mustangs. Several of our warriors snuck up on him and rescued her. This is also the way it is with the greedy trader who came here to the Forest. We sent him away angry six sunrises ago. He, too, may wait in ambush outside of the forest, so we must not go out alone, but in groups, so we are strong enough to fight him if we have to. Greed comes in many forms.

"And so it was many cycles of seasons past, long before the mustang. Two warriors from different bands desired to have the same woman. Her name spoke of her beauty. 'Pretty Woman.' She had no mate and was seventeen winters old, very skilled at working colorful dyed porcupine quills into clothes and baskets. She was wise enough, even at her young age, that the elders welcomed her into their councils when they needed advice. This was unheard of! An inexperienced person in the Counsel Lodge? Pretty Woman had the knowing since her first words.

"She loved the children of her band and told them stories her grandmother had passed onto her, and not just in the cold season. Whenever a child asked for a story, she would stop whatever she was doing and wave to all the children to come hear the story. She was loved by all.

"These two warriors were always at her parents' lodge offering gifts. Each man would hide to see what the other one brought, then hurry off to bring something even better. If one warrior brought three humpback robes, the other would bring four. One brought his humpback robes and a beautiful quilled shirt for her father. It was quilled on a very soft, smoke-tanned elk hide that must have taken a woman the entire cold season to make.

"Not to be outdone, the other warrior brought many fine gifts—quilled baskets and the finest spear points ever carved. He brought well-trained hunting dogs, which no hunter would ever be without.

"The other man, frustrated, brought all that he owned, even his lodge. He stood before Pretty Woman's father wearing only a breechclout. Even his feet were bare.

"'Great father of Pretty Woman, I give you all have. Here, I give you my bow and all my arrows.' He placed the bow before her father and stepped back, but not as a humbled man, more as a man full of pride and vanity. His smile was like that of a fat bear who had gorged himself on fish.

"Pretty Woman's father did not look upon him in favor. He glared at the young, selfish man. 'Where will my daughter sleep this night? What food will fill her belly? Where is the humpback robe that will keep her warm? This night brings cold, and someone without shelter, food and warmth would have a very unhappy night. And what of sunrise? You have no lodge in which to start a fire to cook the food you do not have. You have no bow, no arrows to bring food to a home you do not have. You have not chosen wisely with your gifts.'

"The warrior's eyes widened. 'I have offered all I have and more. I went to another band and sneaked in after darkness to bring you many fine gifts from there also.' His arms spread wide to show knives, animal skins finely tanned, and many colors of porcupine quills. 'I spent many sunrises to show you my worthiness.'

"'What you have shown me is you can steal. You have not shown me your hunting skills. You have not shown me how you will provide for my daughter. Not once have you come to my fire and told me of your desire for Pretty Woman, how you would make her happy. Gifts do not always show worth, especially if they are stolen. This shows cunning, yes. Shows bravery, yes. All good things a man must have, but I see no love in your eyes for my daughter. I see a bad hunger, a man who only knows his own desires.'

"He turned toward the other warrior who now raised himself high and stood with his chest puffed out as if he had won the competition.

"Pretty Woman's father turned toward him. 'I see no reason for you to stand with pride. You may not have given all you have, but you have thought this a contest to see who could please me the most. All I see is greed.' He turned and stared at his daughter, who looked down at her feet.

"'Daughter, would you have one of these men as your mate? If so, speak up.'

"Pretty Woman slowly raised her head. Her beautiful face had turned into a scowl. 'No, Father. Both of these men are good to look at, strong, but both are full of pride with no humility. They want what they see as a prize, a 'thing' to possess. Not once have I heard the word love spoken. Or caring. Or desire. But I have seen much greed before me. No, Father.' She again looked at her feet. 'The mate I wish for will not only be good to me, but to the band also. He will be a good hunter, a warrior who would give his life to protect our people, and a father who would put his children's need before his own. He will be poor in things, but rich in knowledge, and willing to give the last bite of food to a stranger who starves. I choose... I choose....'

"She pointed to a man who sat next to his father and mother across the camp. The mother had carried him in her belly late in her life, and both his mother and father were past seventy winters. His parents wore fine clothing and he wore a nice, but worn, tunic that was unadorned.

"Pretty Woman turned toward her father and the gathered people who waited to hear her words. 'This man has played his flute for me and whispered in my ear of his love. He has given freely to his parents and to the other elders in our band. He offers hides and meat when he has none for himself, and has never asked for anything in return. He had the right to the best pieces of meat. Did he take them? No. He gave them to the elders. Yes, he lives with his father and mother, cares for them. He only has what he needs, not what he wants. He has compassion, understanding, and a deep love for all of the people. He even makes sure our dogs are well fed. Could I ask for more? Yes. But why would I when he is truly a man of the people, a warrior? I do not need fine clothes. I do not need more robes or more furs. I do not need to wear many adornments when one will do. I choose love. I choose this man, Sun Shines Bright, for my man for always and forever.' She walked toward him as he stood and smiled. His parents stood beside him and nodded in agreement.

"Everyone watching nodded and spoke of their approval. Her father's smile lit up her heart. He called for the Holy Woman to do the binding and make them mates.

"The two who had tried to impress her father gathered their gifts, but instead of leaving with them, placed them at the feet of Pretty Woman and Sun Shines Bright.

"They had many children who grew up with the same kind hearts as their parents, and the band prospered. When Pretty Woman and Sun Shines Bright were very old, the band placed their lodge in the center of camp where everyone who passed by would leave food at their flap, and children, many their own grandchildren, would come and sit to hear their story.

"And what became of the many fine gifts given to them from the warriors? They passed them out to everyone, and there was a great celebration that lasted for sunrises until everyone's lodges could hold no more.

"My story is finished. But we must remember, unlike the two warriors who were greedy but learned a lesson, the trader who became angry with us did not learn. Still, he and others like him prowl outside the forest and seek a way in. No one must allow a young child to leave alone." She stared long at Shining Light, and he squeezed Dove close.

"The other thing I ask is that all of you remember what is important to you, and what is simply something you have, but could do without. If you have three robes, maybe you should give one to some other person.

"In my heart, I feel it is time to do a give-away. Clear out what you do not need and your mind will feel cleaner. Too many things make you want more.

"Soon your mind becomes heavy with worry, with a hunger that cannot be filled. Your belly hurts. If your mind feels full of useless things, but you cannot let go of them, maybe you need to think of the reason. Why do you need these things? Do they make you feel safe? Do they make you feel better than others because you have more? If so, this is not good. No one is better than another.

"Go off by yourself and ask for guidance, and when you receive this guidance, think long and hard about what you can do to make things better... for you and others as well. Never only ask how you can better yourself. This is wrong.

"Once you have cleared your mind and your lodge, joy will live in your heart. You will find no time to complain because you will be busy thanking the Spirits for the little things that are the true joys—like the laugh of a child, the newly hatched birds as they make their first sounds, the sweet smells Sister Wind brings. Remember well, you will find joy not in what you have, or who you are, but in what you do for others."

She stood for a short span to allow the group to soak in what she had told them. Nods and whispers told her that many understood. Ordinarily, a story would be told several times with different words. She would tell this one many times as the cycle of the cold season approached.

"I wish to add more. Even though some of it has not much to do with the story, it is still connected.... The Sprits asked me to do so. One thing you must remember well: if you see someone in need, offer your help, even if you must give something up. It will come back to you. A Holy Person never turns down someone who is sick, who needs help. If they did, they would not only lose their Power, but their way in life. We all have gifts and they are to be shared, not hoarded. The one who has a gift and will not use it will shrivel as an old, prickly plant when it receives no water. If you have no gift to give a healer, this does not mean they have the right to refuse you. They should embrace you more, knowing you came to them for help.

"I now leave the stories to my daughter and anyone else who wishes to speak."

Bright Sun Flower left the lodge. She had some things in the back of their lodge that needed to go to someone else.

***

Shining Light walked with Dove toward their lodge, leaving Makes Baskets to speak to others who wished to visit. "Daughter, you must never leave the forest alone. You should not do this at your age, but I know you have done so."

"Father, I am not afraid. I—"

"You need to be very afraid." He stopped, pulled her to him and raised her chin. "You cannot stop a grown person from harming you. You know this." His eyes bore into hers. "Listen well to me, little one. There are dangers you know nothing about. We are safe here in the forest. No one can come in unless we invite them. Outside, it is very different. You have heard the stories from others about the dangers. No one who tells these stories speaks with a dirty tongue. They speak only the truth."

He hugged her hard against him. "Promise me you will never leave the forest without someone who can protect you. Ever, for any reason."

"What if Singing Stone—"

"Daughter, promise!" His body shook.

"Father, are you afraid?"

"I am very afraid, little one." *Very afraid you will leave me.*

He turned away.

She did not need to see to know of the tears forming in his eyes.

Chapter 5

Sister Wind pushed against the lodge. Dove twisted in her sleep and moaned. "Stone? Singing Stone?"

Shining Light sat up, rubbed his eyes and squeezed Animal Speaks Woman's shoulder. "It has been a full cycle of seasons and she still dreams of that boy." He nodded their daughter's way.

The girl tossed in her sleep. "Mustangs... help you." Her body relaxed and her breathing became even as she slipped into a deep, quiet sleep.

Speaks wiped her tear-wet face on Shining Light's bare shoulder. "She is too young to carry such weight. And this boy... my heart knows she desires him." She pulled back from her man and dressed. Then, she scooped up their baby son, now considered a winter old, and left the lodge.

Shining Light soon followed. The campfires above sparkled. "Speaks, it has also been nearly a full cycle of seasons since she started following me out into the darkness. She always sits in silence, but I see her lips move. When she speaks, it is about White Bear, who tells her the forest will always be her home, but she will have many homes and know many people. She is anxious to meet these people, and then it is me who sits in silence.

"I had hoped our short rides outside the forest would calm her. I have seen no traders in moons to bother us. She always wishes to go further as she dreams more of the boy." He rubbed the chill bumps on his arms and looked up at Sister Moon's bright light. "She is just past her ninth winter, still a child, but she already tells me Singing Stone will be her mate. *Her* mate! She told me the boy wears braided mustang hair worked into his own. He hangs strands from his tunic, and... and understands these animals' words. How is this so? I reach Sandstone and the others through my mind, but she tells me he walks up to them and understands them without that connection!"

Speaks held her baby tightly to her breasts, rocking him as she cooed him back to sleep. "Our son, Hawk Feather... his eyes follow Dove. You remember my telling you she sang to him, talked to him while he was in my belly? She spoke of the canyons and their colors. Sometimes when she dreams, he wakes. I wake when our son moves, and many times he watches her movements as she sleeps.

"She refused to leave the birthing lodge the night I waited for him to come to us. She held my hand and comforted me. *She* comforted *me*! How a child so young understood...." She moved farther out into the darkness. "He came so much faster than Dove. I had no time to send someone to find you. Dove told me to surprise you instead, and she laughed when she spoke of the joy Singing Stone would feel when she, too, would carry a baby in her arms." She shook her head and began to walk away.

"Speaks, do not leave. Please tell me what you know, and I will tell you what I know. The Spirits are not open to me about her. When I ask, they tell me to watch and wait. Only when the Spirits decide will I know. Used to think all I had to do was ask to receive my answers. I only boasted to myself."

Animal Speaks slowed and waited for him to catch up, then continued walking and picked up her pace. "Man of mine, I worry for our daughter. Dove does more than dream of this boy. You have heard her. She laughs with him in her dreams and, when she wakes, speaks of sitting with him on a large stone near the canyons. When Hawk Feather came to be with us, she told this boy of her little brother. I have heard her speak of you and me to him. She has even told him of the place we live, in the Forest of Tall Trees. She is living with him in her mind and her heart.

"She wanders by herself more often. I wish for you to tell me why she follows you in the darkness. You say she does not speak, but you must feel something."

"My sweet woman, I have said nothing because there is nothing to tell. Dove follows me, yes, but it is only to sit next to me. When I have asked her why she follows me, her words are always the same. She says, 'I only wish to be near you.' She smiles, looks up at me and says, 'I love you, Father,' and speaks nothing more to me."

"Light, I see something in your eyes. You hide something from me." She adjusted her baby sling.

He cleared his throat and bowed his head. "She asks when we will see Singing Stone." He ran his thumb across his fingers on one hand and made a fist. "She tells me his family protects mustangs from harm and she wishes to meet him. She wants to be with him."

Speaks stopped walking and her voice cracked as she sniffled. "For now, man of mine, tell her when she is older that perhaps we will find him, or he will find us. Say we must wait for you to have a vision to show us the way."

"I have had no vision of this boy, nor has he shown himself in my dreams." He sighed and looked away. "The air is chilled. We need to go back."

***

Shining Light spun Turtle Dove in circles. Both giggled while White Paws ran around the pair. "Father, my eyes are going to fall out! I see too much all at once." Her head held back, she squealed for him to stop, but when he did, she wanted more.

He tossed a robe down on the mix of yellowing grass and moss that grew along the falling waters and stream they played by. Late-season flowers swayed white, yellow and orange in the soft breeze. He pulled her on his lap. "Daughter, will you ever get tired of this? My head needs to catch up to my eyes."

"Here, let me hold your head so your eyes will stop looking crazy. Mine are younger and stop faster than yours."

"Dove, I am not so old. I have only lived twenty-four winters, a very young man!" He allowed her to hold his head. "See? My eyes have stopped being crazy." He rubbed noses with her and squeezed her little body close. "Little one, you have grown so fast. Where have all the seasons gone? How is it that you are nine winters old? Soon another cold season will pass and you will gain another winter."

A few green-yellow leaves fell and floated to the ground. White Paws dashed past, scooped up a leaf and raced off. Moon Face and four nearly-grown pups ran after him.

Animal Speaks Woman dropped her robe next to Shining Light and Dove. Surprised, Shining Light jumped up, and Dove rolled off him onto the cold grass, squealing in shock.

"Speaks, where did you come from? You are as a mother fox sneaking up on her prey!"

She laughed and placed their son beside her in his furred clothing. "Man of mine, your eyes must still be silly, and maybe some of it went into your mind. I called out to you before I approached." The fringe on her soft, tanned deer-hide dress hung two fingers long, settling near her ankles.

"Dove, my little bird, will you go find your cousin Soft Breeze for me?"

"Why, Mother?" She stood and rubbed her legs. "You sure scared me good!"

Speaks chuckled and leaned closer. "Child with eyes so bright, so full of silliness, it is because I ask."

"But why do you ask?" Dove leaned closer to her mother's face and grinned.

Shining Light pulled her back and wiggled her shoulders. "You are not to question when an adult asks you to do things for them unless you have worry." He put his hand up to her mouth. "And you have no worry. When Mother asks something of you, always say yes, not why. Understand?" He pulled her brown deer hide dress down below her knees, and wrapped her robe around her.

Dove played with her fingers and raised her brows. "No. But I will go, even if I want to know why." For a brief span, she stared at her mother. "Fine. I will ask Soft Breeze why you want her."

Dove called to White Paws and Moon Face as she skipped away through the grass, dodging the rich colors of the many wildflowers while singing to herself.

Shining Light nodded toward the three. "Outside the forest, White Paws and Moon Face would have gone to the campfires in the sky by now. They are a part of my child times and I wish to never lose them." After Dove and the wolves disappeared into the dense shrubs, he added, "Why did you send Dove away?"

"Light, we need to speak of her dreams. You have asked her about them as I have, and she does not wish to talk. She says she does not remember them.

She may not remember all of them, but she is getting closer to that boy. She speaks to him more, and I worry.

"One sunrise as I rose, I heard her speaking, and stopped to listen. She said they needed help protecting the mustangs that others wished to harm. Light, we may have not seen any traders for some time, but I still worry that traders may be pacing outside the forest seeking a way in. I need to know you will not allow her to wander outside the forest without you... ever!"

"Speaks, she is only a little girl. She goes nowhere without an adult, and now I will make sure it is with only Gentle Wisdom or me. Do not worry so. If we must, we will tie the flap shut at night so she cannot get it undone, and I will tell her she must ask us, or my parents, before she rides a mustang. She is a good daughter and will listen."

Hawk Feather gurgled and Animal Speaks bent over his little face as he lay on her robe. His tiny hand reached up, and he twisted his fingers in her hair, clasping the shells braided into it. "I see a gentle smile in his bright eyes, and yes, the blue glow such as shines in Dove's eyes also. I feel the same strength about him as Dove." She leaned up and reached out to touch Shining Light's face. "The same Energy you have."

"Why is it every time I see you two, you are making big eyes at each other as if you are new mates?" Gentle Wisdom Who Rides A Flying Mustang jumped off her animal, Brown Dog, and sat beside them.

"How is this so, Wisdom, that you find us every time we are making big eyes at each other?" Shining Light wrinkled his nose at her. "And why do you still ride that little mustang when you could ride any in the forest?"

"Brown Dog was my first mustang. He may not be fast, but we know each other well." She stuck her tongue out at him and scooted in front of him and his woman. "Cousin, you and I are linked. I feel your Energy no matter where you are. You too, Speaks, because we are as sisters. As I came toward you, I heard you speak of Dove's dreams. I, too, know of them." She wore a quilled white headband with the natural black tips woven in, creating a jagged line across the middle. Her hair fell loose over her fur-lined tunic that had the same skilled decoration around the collar and alongside the fringed sleeve edges.

Shining Light raised himself on his knees, his mouth open. "Who speaks to you of our daughter's dreams?"

"I followed Dove one sunrise as she went to the waterfall that you like to visit. She stood, raised her arms, and asked Creator to tell her more of Singing Stone. She stood for a short span, sat on the soft grass with her head bowed, and waited for an answer. She called to me, told me to come out from behind the shrubs and sit with her. I asked how she knew I was there. She chuckled and said 'I could feel you, of course.' I hugged her and said I should have known. I told her she is special, Sacred.

"Dove told me she was no more special than the waters that fell, no more special than the stones, no more special than any other being. Your little one has much wisdom for one so young. It was then that she laughed and said Singing Stone was the special one. I asked her what a Singing Stone was, and she said not what, but who. Dove curled into my arms and spoke to me of her future mate."

"Mate! She is but a baby!" Animal Speaks Woman grasped Shining Light's tunic, and pulled him down to the grass next to Hawk Feather. "Our daughter will not leave the forest. I, her mother, will not have this." She pushed him away and sat next to the baby on the robe with her head in her hands.

Gentle Wisdom wrapped her arms around Speaks as a bewildered Shining Light looked on. "Sister of my heart, surely this is many, many cycles of seasons away for your little Dove.

"You must remember how much you wanted my cousin, your man, even when you were very young. Remember this. When Dove seeks a mate, she will need both of you to guide her, to show her the way. Do not fear what is to come."

Shining Light reached over and squeezed his cousin's shoulder. "My cousin has grown much in wisdom. Perhaps Blue Night Sky gave you the name Gentle Wisdom before she left, knowing *Gentle* had to be part of your name after all. Even if you are still a pain in my backside." He dodged her flicking finger as it came toward his nose.

Animal Speaks flicked Shining Light's nose for her. "She is a true teacher. Children gather around her to listen to her words as they do your mother and grandmother. Light, we too must listen."

Sadness filled Shining Light's face as he chewed on his lower lip. "I go now to prepare my body for a vision. Do not worry so—all will be as it is meant to be. One thing I have learned is I must accept the visions that come, the answers I am given. If I try to bend them to my wants, the Spirits fall silent." He leaned forward and pushed himself up.

Animal Speaks reached for one of his leggings to hold him in place. "Your eyes are troubled. What vision have you wished to change?"

"I have seen my family follow me back to the canyons. I know sometimes visions do not always mean exactly what they show, but they put me on the path I am to follow. This is one I beg not to happen." He turned at Hawk's call. "I need to leave. There is urgency in his call."

Ruby Standing Deer

Chapter 6

Singing Stone eased up to the young mustang he called Spirit Eyes and offered him yellowing leaves from the branches he could reach. Spirit Eyes still followed his mother even though he no longer nursed.

"The seasons move so fast, Spirit Eyes! Within the next four or five moons, I will ride you, if you allow me."

Breath rose from the mustang's nostrils as the animal nodded and munched the leaves.

Singing Stone admired the many-colored mustang. No other in the herd looked like him. The young male's body had changed from dark grey to light grey, but splashes of red and brown now showed across his body. Even his face had a brown splotch around one eye and one ear. The neck hair was a mix of grey and white and the tail was pure grey.

"Your mother shows some white and grey through her red-brown hair, but nothing like you." He wrapped his arms around the mustang's neck. "I am happy we are good friends. Mother did not think I would ever get a rope around your neck. Now, you carry a small robe on your back... well, for a little bit anyway."

He leaned on Spirit Eyes and scratched the animal behinds his ears. "You will help me find Dove. She says they have many mustangs, and no one hunts or whips them as Grandmother said the hairy-faces did to your mother and the others. She speaks of a land of tall trees and much grass, and says rainbows dance down falling waters! I would like to see this."

River Song, his mother, approached. "Son, your mind is full of visions of this strange place. I no longer wonder if it is real. I know it is." She moved slowly and looked down as she approached so the mustang would not run away. "I still wonder at your Power with these four-legged ones. You carry a stone, sing, and they come to you—a few steps closer each time. Even the male allows you to approach."

Her eyes shined with pride as she turned to Singing Stone. "And now you have even removed the ropes from the old ones! I am so proud of you that my heart overflows. I could not have a better son. Always you have been helpful."

"Mother, you honor me with your words of praise, but it is all of us who do this. I only use my gift from the Spirits, as do you and Grandmother. You listen, feel the waters, and know if we are in for a calm day or if a storm comes. I have watched you do this. I know the water tells you things just as my stones do with me. And Grandmother, each day she raises her head and feels Sister Wind, listens to the whispers and knows before we do if we need to prepare ourselves for any danger that may come our way."

She reached out and stroked his hair. Multi-colored braids of horsehair hung from the sides. "The waters tell me things by the way it flows and the sounds I hear as it splashes over stones. The Holy Woman who called you Singing Stone knew much that I only now learn about you. I am thankful you can hear stones. You, too, have warned us many times and saved not only the mustangs, but also us from the hunters. You truly do have Sacred Powers.

"How it is that you reach the Mustangs as you do? I walk up to them, yes, but with you it is different. They accept you as part of their herd."

He leaned his head against Spirit Eyes and stroked his neck. "They let me walk into their world. Did you know they hear and feel danger long before we do? They hear storms, other mustangs that are far away, and even those who hunt them." Singing Stone nodded. "These mustangs have a special gift we humans do not. They can hear the songs of trees, grass and so much more. They hear our Mother, which we walk upon, and know her changes.

"Spirit Eyes spoke to my mind. He says the Mustang Band knows of the bad ones' approach before we do, but do not panic. They have grown used to us letting them know when to run."

He hiked himself up on a low orange-red boulder and stared across their campsite. Grasses had yellowed and shrubs hung heavy with red berries. More gold leaves than green hung on the trees. Clouds made up most of the turquoise-blue sky, and Sister Wind chilled him enough that he rubbed his arms.

His mother shook her head and smiled as the young animal trotted toward the grazing herd. "When you talk to the one you call Spirit Eyes, he nods his head in understanding. You are a true brother of the Mustang. Your grandmother says this also."

"I feel them. We are part of the Mother we walk upon, but can only feel her through our movements. A mustang feels each grain of dirt. It is as if our Mother is deep in their minds, part of their Soul."

He pointed at the puffy clouds. "We see those clouds, but mustangs feel them, know them as brothers, sisters, as if they themselves are the clouds. They are the grass they eat and the air they breathe."

He reached out and ran his hand over the rough surface of the boulder he sat on. "I feel the stones as they do the clouds. I am the stones. They, too, hear the stones as I do."

"This is good. You have found the connectedness that will keep you and the mustangs together always." She slid herself up on the stone. "I am the river, the river's song. To be away from the waters too long makes me feel empty inside. Each of us is connected to something that gives us Power. Some people go their whole lives and do not feel connected because they never listen to their inner being. It is simple to do if you understand how animals do it."

She took his hand into hers and scooted sideways to face him. Her thick leggings protected her legs from scrapes. "Son, somehow you have always understood this. When I was young, I only thought of playing. Even as I grew older, this understanding escaped me. I would take long walks and allow my mind to go where it wished. I decided to go off by myself for a few sunrises. High up on a rocky overhang, I asked for the Spirit's guidance, prayed to the Great Mystery, and asked for understanding. I stood and danced with my arms raised, and sang so the Spirits could hear me."

She looked deep into his eyes. "You must never tell anyone of my vision. Grandmother knows because she watched over me. Understand? I have a need to share it with you now."

He nodded.

"I had a vision, a vision of much water. Many animals came and drank from the waters. A young mustang came to drink. After she drank, she crossed the waters and stood before me—beautiful, with light and dark brown stripes on her legs. I stood and reached out to her. She walked behind me and pushed me towards the waters. I knelt down and drank, and the water filled me with Energy. I turned to thank the mustang, but she was gone."

She reached for the dark brown carved mustang that rested at her throat and caressed the stone. "Not only was I connected to Mustang, but also the waters. Mustang guides me, and the waters give me a connection to our Mother. I am twice blessed, as are you. Mustang is also your guide. Yes, I know this, even if you do not yet. And the stones keep you connected to our Mother. Mustang guides even Grandmother, and Sister Wind keeps her connected. You have given me much to think about, and I have spoken much your mind needs to swallow and understand.

"Perhaps it is time to go for your walk and find out more about who you are. You are young, yes, but not so young in your mind. The season changes and the herds move into the grasslands farther every day so they will find more to eat." She held out a hand to catch drops from the light rain. "The air feels cold now. Perhaps you should wait—"

He took back his hand and scooted off the boulder. "Mother, I have already packed my Sacred items to do this. I have been ready for two moons. I have not left for worry over you, Grandmother, and the mustangs."

He puffed out air and put his hands on his hips. "You are too stubborn to ask for help. The band who lives not far from us, the Big Sky People, are good people, and one man smiles much when he passes by us as he hunts.

"I would maybe like a new father. We need to wait until we are all one band before we move out much farther into the grasses this season. I know because the stones tell me this by the Energy I feel from them." He rubbed the side of the boulder. "The Energy feels as a tingle and flows through me.

"Perhaps his whole band will come to us. There are only ten of them in his band, but I hear there are really three bands of people who live separately, so it is easier to find food. They are good to their mustangs and dogs."

Singing Stone's face scrunched in thought. "We should join his band and the other two, their sister bands, when it is time to move to better hunting grounds. That way when Dove comes to be with us, there will be a Holy Person to bind us."

"Son... binding? And you wish for a father?"

He grinned at his mother's big eyes and ran off laughing.

***

River Song crossed her arms and pounded her feet against the stone she sat on. "How is it that he knows so much about these people and that man of the Big Sky People?"

Listens To Wind came dragging a log behind her. "You make too many words when you are alone. We need to *make* a few new logs for our lodge." She grunted. "Singing Stone knows, silly daughter, because he talks to the hunter every time he rides by, and he has been to his band as well as to the other two. You do not see this. You are as a girl who will not look up when this young man passes. Now help me with this log."

***

Singing Stone wound along a narrow, red-orange canyon and enjoyed the fresh smells after the short, cold rain. The wet sandstone smelled so old to him. The Spirits of the ancient people wrapped in animal furs spoke words unknown to him, as they had before when he chose this same path. The Peoples' women laughed and sang as they picked berries from shrubs long gone. He passed through them and their Energy. Here was home. He belonged here just as the ancient people belonged. Even as cold as the small stream was, tiny fish darted along the sides as they moved from one hiding place to the next.

Noise above him grabbed his attention. The branch of a tiny pine tree struggling to cling to the canyon wall bobbed as a squirrel chattered and scolded. Someone from long ago had painted a large, long-haired animal with things coming out of the sides of his mouth.

A tail on either side of his body! He stood on his toes and tried to reach it. *Too high! It is as if someone sat on another's shoulders to paint that high.*

The squirrel tossed a pine cone at him, then another. "Okay, I leave now!" He laughed and ran on.

The pungent smell of pine mixed with wet plants comforted him. Fear did not block him, as curiosity about things always pushed him forward. He carefully stepped over stones, picking some up to speak with while leaving others where they lay.

Some do not wish to be bothered, yet others want me to touch them, hold them and feel their songs.

The sound of a breaking stick made him turn around, and he spun to face one of the ancient people. *Grandmother said not to fear them, and I never have.* He stepped forward and offered his hands, palms up.

The Spirit pointed to a stone, then vanished.

He bent and picked up the stone the ancient one had pointed to, and it vibrated in his hand. Goosebumps came alive on his arms and climbed up his neck. "Perhaps I am not so brave. What is this that I hold?"

The stone became hot, too hot to hold, he dropped the round piece. "Stone! I did not mean disrespect, my brother."

He picked up the stone again, and the vibrations continued. This time when the stone warmed, he held tight and the vibrations moved into him, through him, and stopped.

'Why do you come this way? The other way... you are turned wrong.'

"Who speaks to me? Who is there?" He shielded his eyes and squinted.

'Who do you ask? Did you not come seeking?'

"Yes, yes I did, but I have not reached where I wished to go. There is a cave up high—"

'Why do you need this cave when I am right here?'

"Right where?"

'Silly one, you hold me.'

"Hold?" The stone vibrated again. He stepped forward and the stone stopped vibrating and turned cold.

'You walk the wrong way. Turn around.'

He turned and walked a few steps. The stone's vibrations entered him again. "What does this mean, Stone?"

Only Sister Wind answered him with a warm push. When he turned back, Sister Wind responded with a cold blast.

"Yes, okay, I understand. Some of it." He continued the way Stone had told him. "What is happening? Why must I go this way?"

Nothing. Not even the ancients fogged the canyon with their Spirit forms. He continued to hold the stone until his hand burned. He shook his hand and dropped it in a newly formed puddle, splashing his leggings.

Heat rose to his face. "What? What am I to do? That hurt, Stone! Never before has a stone spoken to me, only sung the sounds of humming."

Small pebbles fell from the top of the canyon wall and smacked his head. "Hey! Why is this that I am hit by—" He jerked his head upward. "Paintings? What is this?"

He stepped back and stood on his toes. Above him a story unfolded of a people called the Fish People. Pawing sounds from behind him drew his attention, and when he turned, Spirit Eyes stood there.

"Where did you— I did not hear you behind me."

'At last, you found your way, little one who is Human.'

Chapter 7

Instead of seeking solace inside the hidden cave of his favorite falling waters, Shining Light rode into the grasslands on Sandstone. The pull of the grasses had become too strong to ignore. Even Sandstone pranced and wanted to trot. The air had cooled and his breath turned into a fog. White Paws, Moon Face, and their grown pups ran ahead and hunted in the grass, dancing about.

Behind him Dove followed. He had tried to make his daughter understand that he needed to go alone. It did not work the first four tries. At least she was where no traders prowled nearby, or he would have turned back to take her home.

Too cold now for traders. They know we do not allow any to stay the cold season with us.

"I should have taken Fire," he said to himself, "but after Dove's big, round eyes and quivering lips pained my heart, I agreed to leave 'her mustang' behind. Never did I think she would be able to ride her as she does. No nose rope! She must have watched me, and learned the body language I use with Sandstone. Smart girl."

"Yes, she is."

He twisted around so fast he nearly fell from Sandstone. "Wanderer!"

"Why, Shining Light, it looks as if you are trying to see both ways at once. You are not Owl."

He cocked his head. "Why do you follow, Fox Medicine Man?" He tried not to disrespect the Great Elder, but a glare escaped his eyes.

Wanderer's mustang trotted ahead. "I am in front of you now, boy, so *you* must be following me."

"You Fox Medicine people need to wear shells that make noise when you move. You and my woman are both sneaky!" He glanced around to search for Animal Speaks Woman.

Wanderer raised his chin. "You are lucky to have such a good mustang. Another we know would have maybe thrown you to the ground."

"Thunder has a young one and now leaves Sandstone alone. Thunder is—"

"Crazy. She has not changed at all. She still leads mustangs away from their own herds deep into the forest, and now she has turned them toward the grasslands. For sunrises she trots across the grasses, and then just as quickly turns the herd back to the forest."

A mouse jumped out of his pocket and sat on Wanderer's shoulder. "My mice wish to go search for new mates... if your wolves have not eaten them all.

They will not tell me why they do not like the ones in the forest. I, too, need to go ride out on the grasslands, but I do not know why. My mind keeps secrets from me."

"Secrets from yourself? How can you do that? You make my mind crazy!"

"I do not always know what I am to do. You are no different."

"What? I always know what I am to do." He pinched up his face. "Maybe you are not so crazy. I do admit that, this day, my mind floats in the clouds at times."

Wanderer's eager mustang bounced in place as he tried to keep him still. "Listen well, young one. Allow your daughter to be with you. Your father will watch over you both. I will be a few sunrises gone. Maybe more." He tapped his animal into a fast trot and left Shining Light in a cloud of dust.

"Wait! Where do you go?" Shining Light scratched his head as the Great Holy Man vanished over a small hill. "Always he leaves me wondering what he has said!"

Sandstone tossed her head and called to the approaching mustang.

What are we to discover together? No one has a vision together. The stone necklace that Wanderer made Shining Light many cycles of seasons ago felt warm against his skin. He wrapped his fingers around them and they vibrated. As he held them, the vibrations penetrated his body.

What is this? How can this be? Stones I have worn since Dove was only a baby have never –

"Father, I am happy Wanderer made you stop." She shook her finger at Sandstone. "But you must learn to ride better as I do! Maybe I need to teach you."

She passed him before he could remind her that he rode mustangs long before she came to be with the band.

The humming vibration from his necklace entered deeper into his body. It startled him and he jumped off Sandstone. She started to trot after Dove as he clung to her neck hair. With a wide sweep, he swung onto her back as Sandstone raced to catch up to Fire.

"Sandstone! Never before have you been so full of Power, or maybe silliness, as your daughter, Thunder."

***

Sandstone slowed down as she approached Fire.

Dove sat in the grass near a small stream, her neck arched back. She watched Eagles drift through white puffs in the cornflower sky. "Father, Fire stopped here, so I decided this was a good place to sit on my robe. Is it not beautiful? The waters may have a thin ice on them, but they are full of fish. And look at the humpbacks wandering across the grasses in an endless herd."

She inhaled deeply and nodded at the four Eagles drifting across the nearly cloudless sky. "Never will anything change. How could it? Life could not be better." She stretched and yawned.

Shining Light hopped off Sandstone. She barely gave his feet a chance to touch the ground before she trotted up to Fire. The pair of mustangs rubbed noses and wandered off together to graze.

"Why, Daughter, did you name her Fire? She is as grey as her father, only with a few white spots on her back."

"Her name came to me when she jumped over a campfire."

"You let her jump over someone's campfire?"

She twisted her lips. "Of course not! She did it on her own." She pointed toward the Eagles. "Why can we not fly? I would like that! I could find Singing Stone, and we could fly back together. His mother and grandmother could fly with us, and we could all be together and—"

"Daughter, the sky would be very crowded if humans flew also. Sky belongs to the winged ones. Creator made sure all his children had a place to live. If we humans could fly, maybe we would become greedy and take more than our share. Maybe some would fly to other lands and cause trouble for the people who live there already. People who have plenty might fly away with more than they needed, so they did not have to share."

He sat next to her and pulled her close, wrapping his arms around her. "Grandmother once told our band about a band called the 'Never Needs People.'"

Dove pulled away. "I remember that story. They had much in fine things and refused to help on the hunt at a gathering. They expected others to give them the meat they hunted simply because they came. Grandmother's band gave them the meat so they would go away."

She was quiet for a short span as she stared toward the mustangs. Fire nickered to her and she smiled and waved. "If the Never Needs People could have flown as birds, they would have gone to many bands and taken what was not theirs, and other people would have been very hungry. Maybe they would have taken everything they had and left them poor. I am happy our people share all we have. Not one person in the forest is above another. We are equal, and no one has more than anyone else. When the hunters come back, the elders who cannot hunt are always given plenty. Wait, how did this story change from humans flying to greed, Father?"

"Because they are connected. You helped to connect them."

She bounced up and ran a circle around him, laughing. "I am smart!"

She became still and stood before him. "We, too, are connected, Father. You, me, White Paws, Moon Face, Sandstone, Fire, and Singing Stone. Others, too, but I do not know them yet. I saw people in my vision that I will know one day. Did you know I had one? I wish to have one with you. It is like an awake dream, only everything is brighter."

"I have never thought about what a vision is. Yes, you can call it an awake dream. I feel more part of a vision than I do waking life sometimes. I—"

She took in air and continued to speak without waiting for him to finish. "Singing Stone told me in a dream I could reach him through a vision, and I did! We saw each other. He is funny. He told me he lives with mustangs, that he was part of the herd. How is this so, I asked him. I wanted to know if he was part mustang, and he laughed and said he was part of everything."

Her voice changed. "Father, you said we are connected to every being upon our Mother. How is this so? Do we have invisible ropes I cannot see?"

"Little one, slow your words!" He laughed, reached out and pulled her onto his lap. "Grandmother used to put her hand over my mouth so she could speak to me." He pulled on her single braid that lay across the front of her shoulder.

"Your eyes are bright, so full of life that they sparkle. When you smile, you light up the land as does a sunrise. Father Sun must have given you a special brightness, because when you walk past someone they stop whatever they are doing and smile at you. You are full of life and joy and —"

She put her hand over his mouth. "You say too many words at once. My mind cannot keep up with all of them!"

He leaned back and roared with laughter. He pulled her with him and they fell over. White Paws rushed out of nowhere and pushed himself in-between them. Soon, grown wolf pups covered them both. Moon Face tried to wriggle into the pile and Dove squealed.

Shining Light pushed on the wolves so they could sit up again. "You, my sweet one, are a joy in my heart and Soul. I wish this to never end." He rubbed noses with her as she giggled.

She jumped up and ran in a big circle, the wolves following behind her. "Singing Stone and us. We will all be together."

"Daughter, how do you know? And why have you not spoken to me of you going on a Vision Quest? At your age!" He chased after her and grabbed both her arms. "I wish to see no wounds from cutting."

He pulled her close. "You are too young for cutting. The cutting helps us focus on the pain, go beyond it and go deep into a vision, yes, but my eyes would spill rivers down my face to know you had been cut."

"Father, you know I have been taught since I was a little girl what we do on Quests." She puffed up. "I was not afraid, and if Grandmother decided to cut my arms, I would have sat proud."

He glanced around them. *No wolves. Where did they go? Usually this means they wait, but for what?*

He held a hand to his eyes and searched for White Paws. Instead, his father and grandfather came into sight.

Why has so much been hidden from me?

Chapter 8

Shining Light left when his father sat next to Dove and waved him away, preparing to take Dove to where she needed to go.

Shining Light rode Sandstone far out into the grasslands, where a group of seven large grey-brown boulders rested, and climbed to the ledge of the largest one. At one time, Eagles nested there. Small feathers remained entwined in the large twigs used to make the round, flat nest.

From up here, the land looks endless. Four sunrises have passed since I climbed up here. I thought Dove was to come up here. How can we share a vision when she took a different path with my father?

He pulled his robe up tight around his face. *It gets so cold when I sit and do not move around. I thirst. Does Dove thirst? Where did they go? I have prayed and sang and danced and prayed even harder. Does Dove do the same?*

These boulders, how did they get here? I see no others piled. It is as if Sister Wind pushed them together. Of course, Wind could not have had the Power to do so. So why —

'*Your mind chatters, boy. For four sunrises, I have listened to your silliness. Even as you raised your arms pleading for guidance, you were not focused.*'

"Blue Night Sky? I hear you, but your voice is far away. Where are you?"

'*Stop thinking. Stop worrying about your daughter, about the boulders. Your mind races as a mustang across open land.*'

"She is too young to—"

'*No, she is not. Her mind grows. Yes, she is a child, acts as a child, but she grows as you did.*'

He hung his head. "Why can I not find the answers I seek?"

The boulders warmed and vibrated as Blue Night Sky continued. '*Stop trying so hard to receive answers you already have. I sound far away because you are the one who is far away. Bring yourself into your body. Seek inside, not out where you are. Your mind searches for Dove and she does not need your interference.*'

"Interference? I am her father. Why do the boulders vibrate?"

'*The boulders are alive, so of course they vibrate. Dove does not belong to you. You know no human can own another. She belongs to herself and will share what she wishes. Her visions are her own, as yours belong to you and you only... until you decide to share.*'

Brilliant blue colors swirled before him, and Blue Night Sky appeared within them, her long hair wrapped around her. '*Now you are where you belong. Someone wishes to take you somewhere.*'

"Someone? Who?"

'I, Hawk, wish to show you something. Look into my eyes, Human. Feel my wings become yours....'

Sister Wind greeted Shining Light as his hair fell away and flawless, rich brown and off-white feathers took their place. His body fell away and red-orange tail feathers stretched out behind him. He breathed deep the smells Sister Wind brought him through his beak—rain, smells of deer, mustangs, humpbacks, feathers. As before, when he flew with Hawk, speed ate up the land. He passed a herd of humpbacks that would have taken days on a mustang to follow.

A familiar winding river came into view. "I know this place, Hawk. My old home as a child. I thought I did not miss it, but I was wrong. Many large trees grow along the waters. Beneath the trees, deer and elk lay together. The colors of the red-orange stones bring back so many memories. The beauty pains my heart, and such a longing I feel.

"I remember the fun I had then." He breathed deep. "It was here the Peoples sought me out, but not all believed me. I will forever have a heavy heart, for dreams have shown me what happened to some of them. They have gone to the campfires in the sky, battling for what they could not hold onto. I never told my people. Some of those who now watch from the campfires are relations of those who live in the forest."

'What once was in your heart, which you think you have pushed away, always finds its way back from the depths you placed it in, young Holy Man. Nothing stays buried forever. Nothing. Remember this well. Every emotion, smell, taste, and thought is within you. All you have ever done, be it right or wrong, is with you, even beyond your last breath. Let them not be regrets. Regrets will never allow you to grow beyond where you are now. They become hardened as in stone and make your heart heavy. One day you will sink and drown in that regret, and your Spirit will not be able to move onto the campfires in the sky. No one can choose for another, nor make them follow where they do not wish to go.'

Mustangs came into view. The small herd grazed in peace, and people wandered through the herd.

"Hawk, what is this you show me? Who are these people?"

Hawk dipped through clouds and dove closer. 'You see Mustang People. Not far away is a band they will soon join. Look at the boy running with the young mustang. He is Singing Stone.'

Hawk flew closer as the boy shielded his eyes to look up. He waved and shouted something Shining Light could not hear. "Singing Stone? The boy my Dove dreams of?"

'Soon the band will follow the paintings the boy found that your people left to show where you traveled. A human who is called Falcon Storm In Clear Skies will lead his people and Singing Stone's family. We return.'

"Hawk, what do I need to do?"

'I cannot tell you what to do, only show you what you need to see. I now bring you back. Others of the Spirit Land wish to speak to you.'

Far in the distance, a herd of mustangs appeared. "Thunder! Does she lead mustangs toward them, Hawk?"

'I am Hawk, not Mustang. I do not know the minds of the four-leggeds. Perhaps your young one knows.'

Once again, the land soared past. Turquoise sky turned light blue, red-orange bluffs laced in off-whites faded into light purples, and waters winding along the land with many trees were replaced with hills and grasses. The moving herd of humpbacks blended as one wide, long, brown blur.

The boulders came into view, and Shining Light and Hawk parted. Emptiness filled his body where once two shared a common body. He sat against the same warm, vibrating boulders as before. Several hawk feathers lay about him.

"My water bladder." As he reached for it, it bounced down the boulders and splattered onto thirsty ground. He leaned over and stared as the water soaked into the ground. "Why did this happen? I thirst!"

'You thirst, Human?'

Blue fog surrounded him and he jerked back. White Bear's voice surprised him. "White Bear, I have thirsted many times as I sought your guidance. I cried out for you, cut my arms to show I was worthy, yet you never came. Why, Great Bear, why did you not answer me? Am I not worthy?"

White Bear lay in front of him while her cub played with his mother's tail. *'You have always been worthy. I had no answers to give. You asked for knowledge of Dove's future. Her future belongs to her, as I said before. Ask about your future, not another's.'*

"I know you have watched over me as I left the forest to wander. I felt you and Mouse. Always Hawk flies above me, and many times, Grandfather Wolf has whispered advice."

'You answered your own questions.'

"Ahh. I am shamed. Because I do not always hear answers to my questions, and you did not fulfill my needs, I thought you were not there. I understand now. You waited for me to find my own way."

'If all your wants and needs were given to you, you would become weak. Expect everything always to come your way, and you would miss the stones in your path, the large hills in your way, which force you to discover why they are there. Never would you walk another way, see other things. You must walk many paths, cross many rough waters before you truly find your way. Some things are just what they are.

'Listen well to me, young Human. You gain in Power each time you seek guidance. You may not feel it or understand it, but it happens. You do receive it, even though you do not think you do. You never walk alone, not even one step.'

Mouse appeared between Shining Light and White Bear. He licked his paw and cleaned his ear, taking much time. Finished, he crawled closer, and as Shining Light held out his hand, he sat in it.

'You will learn much from children in the seasons to come. Open your ears and hear what they do not say as much as what they do say. Children of all Peoples, be they Mouse, Bear, Hawk, Wolf or Human, are born with knowledge passed to them by their ancestors. Some adults think it is made up as they play, but you know better, do you not? How many listened to you before Blue Night Sky opened their ears?'

For the first time, White Bear's cub stopped playing with his mother and turned his attention to Shining Light. His midnight eyes sparkled with bits of intense blue as he spoke.

'Children bring knowledge with them, but they do not know this until someone asks a question. It becomes clear to them, yet an adult does not hear the words right away.

'Always stop and listen to the children, even if you think they speak nothing of importance. You brought much knowledge with you, yet it took a Great Elder to make others listen to you. Listen to your daughter, Light That Shines.'

"Little Cub, you honor me with your words, and I thank you for them. All I hear, I will pass on. Even those with dirty ears surely must hear some of it for the sake of their children." Shining Light's mind pulled back and the fog dissipated as his head cleared.

"Here, Father. Drink."

"Dove, where... how did you get up here?" He reached for the water bladder and cooled his parched throat with big gulps of water.

"Silly, I have been right here. I went for a ride with you and Hawk. I needed to make sure he showed you Singing Stone. I went inside the pretty, blue color with you and heard White Bear and her Cub speak to us. Even Mouse spoke! My mouth did not work as I tried to ask questions. I am thinking I could not speak because it was your vision, not mine. Do not look at me with big eyes. I would be sad if they fell out and you could no longer see with your outside eyes."

"Dove, how? How did you follow me *in* Hawk? How did you make sure Hawk took us to see the boy?"

"I followed Grandfather up here, and he put two cuts in your arms and you were gone somewhere in your mind. You have many scars on your arms. Will mine be that way one day? I sat holding your hand so you would not leave me behind." She shrugged and smiled. "My heart is filled with much love for you, Father. One day soon we will ride mustangs together in the canyons."

Before Shining Light could ask her more, she hopped up and ran down the hill into Flying Raven's arms.

"I am a Holy Man and cannot even understand my own daughter." *I will stay up here until I at least understand her message. I will stay for sunrises, if I must, until I do!*

Flying Raven put her down and took her hand. They left as ravens flew and cawed to each other before them.

My father, the greatest Holy Man of the Wolf People, I love you.

The elder Holy Man stopped, turned, and glanced up at him.

***

Singing Stone jumped from a tree branch and ran to his mother, nearly knocking her into the hide she scraped. "Mother, Grandmother, did you see Hawk? He brought Dove and her father here to see us!"

River Song raised a hand to shade her eyes. "Little one, I almost found myself on the ground from your push! How do you know this? All I can see is a hawk flying away from us."

His grandmother, Listens to Wind, chuckled. "Our little one is growing in so many ways. He sees through his inside eyes unlike another I know." She stood and dropped the coiled bottom of the basket she wove.

"Mother, this is a Sacred Happening and you talk silly. Singing Stone has Sacred Powers I can only wonder at." River Song pointed toward Hawk as he became a small dot in the clouding turquoise sky.

"Grandmother is right, Mother. You do not see so well with your outside eyes either. Falcon Storm In Clear Skies has ridden past us four times this day, and he did not carry any meat back to his camp. I do not think he even hunted this day. He again passed by a short span ago and you never looked up from scraping your deer hide. He even asked his mustang to rear and dance in circles, yet you only cleared your throat and kept scraping as if nothing of importance had happened. I think he wishes to make a Sacred Happening with you."

River Song dropped her scraper and spun around in a circle, loose hair flying in her face. She slapped her hands to her sides. "Falcon Storm In Clear Skies. Is that all you two can speak of? For days now he has ridden past, and the both of you do the waving for us all!"

Thunder rolled in the distance, and the herd of mustangs gathered closer to the orange-red bluff's overhang.

Listens To Wind became silent. She put her face to the breeze as it picked up. "Sister Wind says you two should be happy I made you help me put up the lodge last sunrise. Hard rain is in the air. Look at the mustangs. We can speak more about Falcon Storm In Clear Skies and Hawk in the safety of our lodge. We have a short span before the rain comes our way."

River Song took her hide down, rolled it up and pushed it in the lodge, while Singing Stone grabbed the wood next to the lodge and ducked to climb in past the two women.

His mother started the fire, pulled out humpback robes to lie on the bare ground, and pulled out smaller elk hides to roll into pads so they could lean back, sit and face each other.

She stretched forward and tied the flap shut. "Now tell me, son, about Hawk. I have heard much already but will listen."

Singing Stone added a piece of wood to the small, waking fire. "I forget that you do not see as I do or hear as Grandmother does. You hear the river's song and can tell us when fish pass by, when the waters become too big to stay inside their path. You have a wonderful gift. Creator gave each of us our own gifts to help us keep one another safe and happy."

"Yes *and* we will never need another to complete our family." She stared with lowered brows as if she knew where he would lead the talk. "Tell us more about your Dove. I wish to know more."

He reached for an arrow shaft he had started that sunrise. "This one will fly true." He admired it, twirled it, then put it down and clasped his fingers together. First, he looked at his mother, then his grandmother.

"Many times Dove and I have met in our dreams. I really do not understand how this is so. It began when I fell asleep while thinking of how it would be nice to have a human companion my age to explore the canyons. In my dream, I walked the canyons. The walls felt warm and I heard them sing as I went deeper into my dream. Before me stood a girl, and as I walked closer to her, she giggled and ran away. I chased her, caught her, then let her go. We ran and laughed. Then I woke up. That was the first time.

"Now she and I sit on the stones and talk. Not talk as we do, but the air vibrates, and sometimes she fades before we are very far into speaking. A few sunrises ago, we touched each other's hands. Dove will one day be at my side!" He grinned, picked up the shaft again and twirled it. He began to wrap his arrow point to the shaft.

His voice changed from a happy mood to one more serious. "I see the ancient ones more and more, and they showed me—"

His mother's jaw fell open. "Son, what is this you say? The ancient ones? Why do the two of you look so calm?" River Song reached out and took the shaft. "Speak to me."

He nodded toward his grandmother. "She knows."

"That my son holds secrets and tells me nothing?" She reached for his hand. "You will speak."

The rain picked up and Listens To Wind cocked her head. "Hard rain. We must stay inside until it passes. We have much time for speaking."

Singing Stone continued. "Um... they are very old, but do not look old, and wear animal skins not as we do, but with the fur attached. Some wear animal heads on their own heads. They do not speak, but I understand them. Their people left long, long ago, but these Spirits stayed behind to watch over the land instead of going to the campfires in the sky.

"The day I left to go on my walk they found me. I never did get to sit in a cave I know about on top of the bluff. They pointed toward another way, where stones fell from above and hit me on the head. I picked up a stone they pointed to, but it was so hot I dropped it. One of the ancients pointed up the canyon wall, and I looked up and saw paintings—many of them. They told the story of a band called the Fish People." He leaned forward on his knees. "Mother, they showed the way to Dove. Her people are the *Fish People*! I want to follow where they say to go. We can all go! The cold season is here and the mustangs are restless—"

"May I enter?" a loud male voice called out. "The rain has turned hard, and I am being beaten by it. My mustang ran to be with yours and I saw you had your lodge up."

"Falcon Storm In Clear Skies?" River Song shivered.

"Mother, it is *he* who must shake from the hard rain. Why do you shake?"

"Will someone please allow me to enter? I may be beaten badly by these hard circles of ice while you who are inside try to decide!"

Listens To Wind undid the tie on the flap. "Yes, enter! Forgive my silly family who sits in here unmoving." She offered her robe to him as he crawled through. "Here, wrap up and I will add more wood to make it warmer in here."

Singing Stone watched as his mother looked into the man's eyes.

Never before have I seen her face redden. She did not even try to turn away. Her eyes hold a sparkle and her lips part, not squeezed tight as they do when she usually sees him!

He grinned and looked away. *Soon... soon I will have a father, and we will belong to a band. I will show my new father the paintings and we will go to Dove.*

Dove. We are only children in the eyes of adults, but in my heart, the warmth of deep feelings increases my heart's beating.

A cold wind howled through the flap, and Singing Stone shivered as his grandmother's eyes widened.

Sister Wind spoke to her, but of what? She never shows any fear or any worries. Her eyes always remain calm, even when we fight to keep the mustangs safe.

Now *he* shivered.

Ruby Standing Deer

Chapter 9

"Shining Light, how long are you going to sit up here?"

Gentle Wisdom Who Rides A Flying Mustang pushed on her cousin's shoulder. She sat eating freshly cook meat and blew the smell his way as she teased him. "Mmmm, so good. Sparkling Star is good to me. She is better at making food than I ever was. Her sons... our sons grow fat with all her food. They need an adventure, one that will take them across the grasslands. When do we leave, cousin?"

Startled, he whipped his head around. "*I* am not leaving the forest. You must make your own adventure."

She shifted sideways and pulled on his long, shimmering, loose hair that fell below his waist. "Light, it has been three days. You sit as still as an unmoving blade of grass. What can I do to help? I will do as you ask, and you know that. Dove told me Hawk allowed both of you to join in a vision. I have never heard of this before. This is more than a Sacred Happening. It is a new way, and you and your daughter were part of it!" He grinned as she pressed her face closer to his. "Wisdom, I could not ever imagine you not being with me. You have helped me to understand myself. You have helped me to find my way into the Spirit Land. You loved me even before I knew we would always walk together."

He reached out and took her hand. "I have this to ask of you. I have an empty belly and have had no water this day. I ask you help me enter the Spirit Land. Yes, I know Dove and I were there only four days ago."

She pulled out her obsidian blade without hesitation. "I brought the one always set aside just for this, just for you. I have Sage and Cedar as well. I will Sage the ledge, then you and me, to take away any bad things, negative Energies. The Cedar will cleanse your thoughts. There is tobacco for your pipe so you can send your prayer to Creator. Heh, why do I tell you this?"

"As always, we need reminded. Even a Holy Man who sets up a Sweat Lodge reminds everyone what they are to do, what to expect, to push away everything negative. This way, we already start to think only good thoughts. Someday, someone maybe would forget to speak as you have, then someone else would forget, and soon no one would remember. It is as the stories we tell our children. We must keep telling them so they remember to pass them onto their children." He raised his chin and smiled. "I am that child."

She waved the Sacred Sage over the small hillside, him, herself, and White Paws, who refused to leave. She lit the Cedar and passed it over the three of them, then disappeared to give him time to prepare himself.

Shining Light stood, arms raised, and sang the song in his heart, a private and very personal prayer song, one that Spirits taught him in a dream and told him not to share. He sat and loosely draped the robe his daughter had left for him sunrises ago over his shoulders, closed his eyes, withdrew inside himself, and continued to sing his prayer under his breath.

His cousin came up beside him, but already his thoughts had moved away. Only his mind picked up the brush of her blade on his skin.

Sunrise turned into sunsets twice, combining them in his mind into one. Colors of the sky turned from cornflower blue to... nothing. No campfires in the sky, only blackness.

Sounds of a crackling fire turned his head. Beside the fire sat several children of the ancient ones. Their eyes shined from the flickering firelight.

The oldest boy handed Shining Light a round stone.

He hesitated.

The boy shoved his hand toward him until he took it. The other children nodded encouragement as he turned it in his hand.

"So smooth. I can see the fire dancing across it." He glanced up to smile at the children, but they had vanished, leaving the campfire behind.

The stone vibrated, catching his attention. He held it tight as the fire grew. Children danced in a circle, holding hands.

'Listen to the wisdom of children, young Holy Man. Have you forgotten the story your grandmother told about how special children are? They have much wisdom, and you must remember this. You once had it, but as you aged, you questioned what you knew and it faded.'

A young girl, who reminded him of Dove, sat and held a fawn in her arms. A blue mist encircled her body and the fawn's.

"I have never met a child Spirit before. Why did you cross over so young?"

She ran her hands over the fawn and smiled. *'I have never lived in your space. I have always been who I am.'* She lowered her head as the fawn raised hers. *'Ah, Fawn wishes you to know that perhaps one day I will live in your space, when there is a need for me.'*

"A need for you?"

'Yes. One day, my wisdom will be needed, when adults become lost and need to hear the words of a child. Like you, Feather Floating In Water who is now called Shining Light.'

He bowed his head and spoke soft words. "I am no longer that boy."

She cocked her head. *'I know, but yet you are. Inside you, he still lives – his wisdom, his knowing, his desire to be heard. Listen to that boy. Become Feather Floating In Water again. He still has much to tell Shining Light who is a man. Do not forget to be a child. Free yourself of the bonds the adult has placed upon you. Dance in Sister Moon's light. Set Feather free.'*

He opened his eyes and squeezed his hand. The stone was gone. The girl and fawn had vanished.

He stood, raised his hands, laughed the laughter of a child, and danced around the Spirit Fire, enjoying its warmth on this cold day.

Chapter 10

The hard rain quieted and the air had become cold. Sister Wind found her way into the lodge and chilled everyone.

River Song stumbled past Falcon Storm In Clear Skies to secure the bottom of the lodge outside. She tried to ignore him, but his smile sent heat to her face.

"Woman, allow me to help."

Before she could stop him, he stood outside with her, brushing away the icy balls along the edge of the lodge with his worn footwear.

"Your woman is lazy to allow you to wear footwear with holes that your toes poke out of."

"I have no woman. It is me who is lazy. I can make my own footwear, but not as nice as a woman can."

"You must practice and learn to do better. Even our children practice to make their skills stronger. Perhaps you need to find a woman." She slapped her hand over her mouth to catch words that had already escaped. She dropped her hand and pinched her lips together. Words once spoken could not be unheard. "Surely there are women in your band who must fight over you."

"Oh, perhaps one or two smile my way. Our band is small." He shrugged and stood in her way.

She shoved past him to scrape away the balled ice from the lodge sides. "You are not so worried about being bold!"

He pulled her back and dropped his hand. "I have desired you for moons, yet you look away each time I ride by, as a shy girl would. I see how much you care for your family, how hard you work. Stories of how you and your family fight to keep the mustangs safe have crossed over our campfires at night. Your bravery is known among my people." He lowered his head. "Perhaps I am not so good to look at. Maybe my arms do not have strong muscles and you think me a poor hunter." He turned away, but not before a grin spread across his face.

"I guess you are good enough to look at, if I was looking for a man. I am sure you are a fine hunter... when you do hunt. I seldom see you with meat across you mustang's back."

"So, you do watch as I pass."

Sister Wind quieted down as if to hear their conversation, and Father Sun peeked through the thinning clouds and shot a beam of light down on them. Whispered giggles came from inside the lodge.

"River Song.... Why are you called that? It is not so cold now. A ride on our mustangs would be a nice way to learn more about each other." He smiled.

"Your mouth has many words that it cannot keep inside of it." She scrunched her brows.

The lodge flap flew open, and Singing Stone jumped out and whistled. Several mustangs turned his way. He handed her two nose ropes. "You know how to ride without them, but maybe Falcon Storm In Clear Skies does not."

"Falcon. Call me Falcon. My mother called me Falcon Storm or Clear Skies. She has gone on to the campfires in the sky to be with my father. They were elders when my mother found out I was in her belly. I took great care of them. I may not have had a woman and children, but I do know how to—"

River Song huffed, causing him to stop, and put her hands on her hips. "Do all your people waste so many words on people they have never spoken to?"

"I—" Falcon Storm slapped his thighs.

"Daughter, you were never taught to be so rude!" Her mother did not attempt to leave the lodge. Instead, she slapped the side of it, sending slushy ice balls flying.

"Mother! Now my leggings and shirt are wet. My footwear was already soaking up the melting ice balls!"

"Falcon Storm, you have my permission to take my daughter as your mate." Listens To Wind came part way out of the lodge and turned her head. She held her hair back so it would not get wet as she stared at them. "Ha! Good thing you dress as a man or your legs would be freezing."

She waved her free hand. "Go. Go riding and speak of sweet things to each other. I tire of watching a man sick for love being ignored by my daughter. Singing Stone, come inside and help me."

"Help you with what, Grandmother?" The boy still held the nose ropes, grinning.

"Stone, you are not to ask questions. Now. I need you now, Grandson. Hand the nose ropes to your mother and stop being so silly."

"I wish to go with them."

Both River Song and Falcon Storm spoke at once. "No."

Singing Stone chuckled and dipped low to enter the lodge.

***

Falcon Storm stayed a couple mustang widths away from River Song, a simple show of respect for her. She sat tall and stared ahead, waiting for him to speak. Even though the mustangs tried to be closer to one another, he pulled his animal away from hers.

Why does he not speak? I see him watching me from the sides of my eyes. What does he wait for? I am not a first-time woman who must have another to speak up for me. I do not have a man relation to offer gifts to him either. He now acts shy or maybe angry, and looks away. Did I anger him when I told him he spoke too many words?

River Song twisted around and turned her head to look his way. "You grin! Do you find me silly to look at?"

"I did not look your way." He leaned over and rubbed her mustang's neck hair.

"Perhaps not, but in your mind maybe you think this!" She tapped her mustang into a trot.

Before she made it more than a few strides, he raced ahead of her and turned, blocking her way. "Woman, I do not seek to anger you, but to make you see me. I ride by every sunrise, every sunset, and when you do not know it in the darkness—"

"Darkness?" She jumped down and tried to lead her animal toward a small stream that branched away from the main waters, but the light brown mustang balked and pulled the leather lead from her grasp. As she reached out to grab the lead, the animal backed away, turned and trotted back toward the herd.

Falcon Storm laughed and jumped from his mustang. His animal followed hers. "You know, I think your mustang must know my mind. I wanted to walk beside you. Mustangs must have more understanding because they see more, feel more than we do. I am sure they are better connected with the Spirit Land than we are. They live in both worlds as a Holy Person does. Heh, mine always made sure we went the same way every sunrise, right past your sleeping robes. It did not matter if you slept outside or in your lodge, always every—"

"I was right."

"You were? You knew this also?"

She sat on a large stone near the stream's edge and made sure to take up the middle of it. "I was right about your mouth. More words come from it than my mother's at night when she tells stories."

He sat on the ground and tossed small pebbles in the trickling stream. "My *mouth* only makes up for the silence you create when you are around me. I only wish to know you better, but you find ways to be busy as I ride by. Many times you find great interest in scraping hides and find reasons to turn the other way as I raise my arm in greeting."

He stood to face her. His eyes held a depth of compassion.

What secrets does he hold? His face holds no scars, no lines of stress. Most people carried their past across their features, but his face tells no secrets.

"You will never find the answers you seek until you set your heart free." He tossed a pebble in her lap. "Do not use the stones to create a wall around you. You cannot see over the ones you have in place now."

She turned away from him, but he reached out and pulled her chin back his way.

"Falcon Storm In Clear Skies, I am not ready."

"Falcon, or Clear Skies. The woman I am to be mated with will use the name my mother called me."

She jumped up and turned back toward the lodge. In her rush, she slipped on a rock and cried out.

He was beside her before she hit the ground. "Why are some women too stubborn to allow a man into their life?" He helped her to sit on the bank.

"I am not stubborn. I have been alone for a long time." She lowered her head and whispered, "I am afraid to give my heart again. My man took a big part of it with him. It is protection from pain I seek."

Pounding hooves sounded behind them.

"Mother, Falcon Storm, I need help!" Singing Stone led their two mustangs behind him. "Hurry, Grandmother is alone!"

Falcon Storm reached out to grab him. "There may be danger. You must stay away until we call for you."

Chapter 11

"Bright Sun Flower, why are you my grandmother and yet my father's grandmother?" Dove danced in circles around her as they made their way through the forest. Squirrels raced after each other, spiraling around trees and trying to steal each other's food to put in their own storages.

"Why would you even ask?" Bright Sun Flower smiled at the young girl's boundless energy. "Every elder is your grandmother or grandfather, even if they are not by blood. I am Grandmother to all the people. I am Grandmother to all children, mine or not, because I am an elder."

The warm season had ended in the Forest of Tall Trees and the cold season made itself known. White Paws danced after them more in play than hunting. He tried to grab for Dove's grass-and-leather doll, but she raised it up in time. She scolded him and he raced off, only to turn back and try again.

Bright Sun Flower grinned at her granddaughter as she held the doll over her head. "You are connected to everyone in our band as you are connected to the birds, squirrels, even the trees."

"Father told me you taught him these things. Once, you showed him a seed, then planted it. He said when it grew an animal would eat it, then pass the plant out onto the Mother." She skipped around, waving her arms up and down. "It would nourish the ground so another seed could grow!"

She stopped, the expression on her face serious. "Father took me for a walk, to show me how flowers grew in circles and that the trees were round." She could not stand still any longer and twirled around, her arms once again flung out as if to embrace all she could see. "Spider makes her web round, too! He told me you taught him much when he was little. Now he teaches me the same things. He told me that we all do things for each other, making us connected! My mind fills up with so much I worry it could run out of room. Grandmother, could that—"

Bright Sun Flower bent in laughter, her long hair falling forward. Her elk teeth necklace tinkled as she swept her hair from her face and straightened her back. Her brown deer hide dress fell about her ankles, barely exposing the tops of her yellow- and orange-quilled footwear.

"You are so much like Shining Light. When he was young, I called him my little Feather. You are very much your father's daughter!"

Dove stopped and her jaw dropped. She let go of her doll and took the elder's hand. "Of course I am my father's daughter. Who else's daughter would I be?"

She turned. "White Paws, you bring back my doll!" She shook her finger at the wolf as he dashed through the smaller trees.

Bright Sun Flower squeezed Dove's hand. "White Paws only plays. He will not harm your doll. Little one, let us sit by this wonderful tree. He is so wide the whole band could lean on his body. He is on the edge of this place of much grass where we can watch animals play. See the mother deer and her grown baby making their way through the thick shrubs?"

They sat in the deep yellowing grass against the tree. The colorful rainbow of late season wildflowers gently swayed in the breeze.

Bright Sun Flower nodded up at several blue and grey birds. "The baby birds, now the size of their parents, still beg for food, but their parents pay them no heed. They must learn to find their own food. Even as the land prepares to sleep, life must go on."

White Paws trotted back and dropped Dove's doll into her lap. He lowered himself to the ground and looked toward the deer as if to say 'you are safe.' Two rabbits stopped, eyed the wolf and moved into the underbrush. He scooted closer to her, and she laid her head on the big wolf and stretched her legs out across Bright Sun Flower.

She rubbed Dove's bare legs, then tugged her dress down. "The air chills *my* legs, girl, and your bare ones make me shiver. It is time to wear warmer clothes."

"I am not cold. I do not get so cold as elders do."

"Dove, you only *think* I am old! I feel as young as a weaned fawn. I am—"

"Grandmother, will I have another name soon?"

"Granddaughter, your thoughts change so fast you confuse my mind. Perhaps someday you will have another name. I know you saw many mustangs in your vision with hawks, flying above them. Sometimes a name does not come in a Vision Quest the first, or even the second, time. You are young yet, very young to have even gone on a Quest."

"I hope it is a good name! Do you know what it will be, Grandmother?"

Bright Sun Flower patted her legs. "Perhaps, but you will know when you are meant to. Some women and men never change their names."

Dove shifted sideways and pulled herself up so she could lean on her grandmother. White Paws rolled over and faced the pair. "I think White Paws is listening to us! Look how his eyes glow with a blue in them. Blue and deep yellow. What is this blue I see? It is in your eyes, mother's and father's eyes, and even Wanderer has it. Sometimes, I see the blue in my dreams. Singing Stone... he has the blue color." She touched her eyes. "Do I have it too?"

Eagles called, and Bright Sun Flower raised her head as they drifted into the trees with their young ones behind them. "There is much for us all to learn. Yes, Dove, you have the blue in your eyes. It is a blue not found in our space. It is a Spirit blue, such a color as I have never seen anywhere except in the Spirit land. Everyone has this blue around them, yet sometimes it is much brighter around others, others who have a special way. Those people can see what others are blind to. They dream deeper than others and feel another's being in ways even the person themselves cannot."

"Is this why I can live with Singing Stone in my dreams? We talk to each other in the way I speak to you. Well, most of the time. Sometimes I reach out but he fades, and I find myself alone, or his words fade before we are done speaking. He has a mustang called Spirit Eyes, and Spirit Eyes has many colors, more than the mustangs here. He showed me the herd his family watches over. Why would anyone wish to harm a mustang? They are fun companions and take us across waters so we do not get wet. Fire and I play chase!

"Singing Stone tells me of the canyons, the ones Father says he grew up in." Dove's eyes widened and she gasped. "I can feel something from you. I see the canyons in your head! How is this so?"

"Oh sweet, sweet little one, you can feel the emotions in my mind. Many children can do this." She ran her hand over the top of Dove's hair. "I hope it never fades for you as it does most children."

She sighed lightly. "I grew up in the lands near the canyons, and when your other grandfather, Hawk Soaring, took me as his mate, we went to live within them, with his people. The canyons are full of colors not seen here."

She squeezed Dove's legs. "I knew you understood more than others thought you did. Girl, you really *are* your father's daughter." She pulled her up and hugged her, a little too tight.

Dove spoke with a muffled voice, in her grandmother's arms. "What I do not understand is the grey dust storm I see. Sometimes, my dreams are full of people and animals running away from it."

She shivered.

Dove must have felt it. "Grandmother, are you cold? This day is only cool."

Bright Sun Flower rocked her. "Many long cycles of seasons ago, I too had this vision. It was then your father started dreaming. He saw the same things when he was a little older. A Great Elder came to us and gave him the guidance I could not. She was called—"

"Blue Night Sky. I know." Dove pulled away. "She is my relation who now lives in the Spirit Land. She is beautiful and has those blue sparks flying around her. All she would say to me was that I would one day find my life very different from what others wanted it to be. I wonder if it will be what *I* want it to be."

Bright Sun Flower pulled her close again. "Little one, life... life has many stones in our path we never dreamed would be there. We must step with care over each one so we do not lose our way. Each stone offers challenges, and we must be ready to face them."

Worry shadowed Dove's eyes. "I am scared for Singing Stone and his family. I think they have a big stone in their path. I think they may be in danger because they choose to protect the mustangs. I wish to go find them, but Father says he has yet to have a dream vision of where they are. Grandmother, I know where they are. They are near the old camp of our people. He told me our old name: Fish People."

Chapter 12

Listens To Wind jerked upright from the almost finished basket and dropped it. Her pulse quickened as Father Sun neared the tops of the canyon walls. Soon, darkness would take the land. Already the turquoise sky showed darkening peach-orange in the clouds above her.

Chill bumps on her body rose and she rubbed her arms. The small fire she leaned over offered no warmth. Cold crept in, but it was a different cold... a cold that settled into her mind, not her body. Fear crept into her thoughts.

Coyote howled early.

Very unusual. They call to each other after darkness, not now. There are no other sounds, not even the last of the crickets who still seek mates before the cold takes them. She rose and slipped into the deepening darkness, hands cupped to her ears.

A mustang in the nearby herd nickered and pawed the ground.

She spun around to see the lead female standing with neck arched and ears pricked forward. Listens To Wind turned back around and moved farther away from the campsite and mustangs. With it still light enough to see, she cupped her ears again and moved in a circle. Her feet vibrated when she became still. Long ago, her parents had taught her to feel through every part of her body.

Her voice low, she called out to her grandson. Then she remembered that she'd sent him to find his mother and Falcon Storm In Clear Skies when she'd felt danger earlier.

Gone too long. I did not listen well enough when Sister Wind whispered at sunrise.

She had sought to ease the want in both her daughter's heart and the warrior's, but now she felt the danger growing.

She hurried back toward camp to retrieve her bow and quiver of arrows. The silence grew too loud. *Where are the night birds?* She pressed against the side of a boulder, forgetting her weapon as the feel of danger thickened like a dense fog around her.

Mustangs whinnied to each other, gathered and trotted through one of the passages that led out of the canyon. A male snorted and pushed a slow female with his head. The female picked up speed and ran past Listens To Wind.

She whistled for her animal. *Where is she?* Always the animal stayed nearby, but the mustang did not respond this time. Sister Wind whipped passed her with such a force that she lowered herself to her knees and wrapped her arms around herself.

Such a cold wind, and I am without my robe. Why do I smell smoke? She peered around the boulder. *Our lodge... it burns! Those men, they are warriors of the Likes*

To Fight People! They must have shot it with fire arrows. They come to our camp when it is this close to darkness? I must hide better.

She stayed low, crawled toward a dry wash and rolled into the center where the grass grew longer. Hooves rumbled past, slowed and turned away from the burning lodge. Sister Wind quieted and sounds of the mustangs faded.

They did not chase the mustangs! Do I move? Our lodge, I smell it. Sweet Mother! Everything we have must be gone. Sister Wind, why? I do not even have my bow, and Snow does not come to my call. Creator, let nothing bad come her way!

'Reasons, Human sister... reasons that will create your future.'

"Sister Wind, what do you mean?"

No response, just a cold breeze whipping the branches in the nearby trees.

She leaned up on her knees and crawled out of the dry wash as the lodge and most of what it contained smoldered. The blackened logs remained, as if still holding their home together. She pulled out a humpback robe, stomped the embers, and searched for anything else that may have not been destroyed.

Sounds of mustangs sent her scurrying for cover behind the sandstone boulder next to what remained of their lodge. Boot knife in hand, she crouched and waited.

A man's voice rose on Sister Wind. "No one is here. I do not understand. They never leave the animals alone. It is near darkness and we must leave. We come back in two sunrises with more warriors to capture the mustangs and be rid of these women who harmed my son! We go back now."

The warrior yanked his animal's head around and slapped his legs against her sides. She jerked at the rough treatment and raced away.

I remember their words. They are the Likes To Fight! His son... the one I wounded. Now we have no choice but to find a new place, and somehow make the Mustangs understand they cannot return here. Two sunrises! My daughter and grandson, where are they? Darkness now takes the land. Do I stay hidden or use my birdcall as I try to walk the way they went? No. The warriors will know it is a human who calls, not a bird.

Voices and nickering mustangs returned.

Listens To Wind eased up and peered around her hiding place. Her grip tightened on her knife as the sounds of running animals came closer. If they had decided to return yet again and give the campsite a better look, they might find her. The Likes To Fight People would not consider taking a woman her age alive. Past her time of giving a baby to a man made her as good as the old worn robe that lay in the mud in front of the once-warm lodge. Snow started to fall and gather on her hair and clothes.

So cold! She stayed crouched for a long span. *Is my family safe?*

The sounds of mustangs rose again, and fearing the warriors had returned, she crouched in the cold grass. The sound of hoof falls stopped and she strained to hear. Sister Wind brought the whisper of clothing to her ears. She shivered and prepared herself to die a brave death.

"Mother!" River Song hissed.

Another quiet voice joined her daughter's. "Listens To Wind, it is Falcon Storm. Where are you?" He had the only bow and readied it to fight.

She stumbled out of her hiding place. Blood seeped down her leg. "I am here." She placed her knife back in her boot.

"Grandmother!" Singing Stone flew from his mustang and darted to her, stomping through the mud. "Why do you bleed?"

"Blood?" Her hand swiped her thigh. "It must have happened when I rolled into the dry wash. It was muddy and I must have scraped myself on a stone. I am fine. There is no pain."

The mud churned around the camp and spoke to River Song. "Mother, what... what happened? Did the lodge catch a spark from the fire? Where are the mustangs?"

Listens To Wind limped toward what was once a lodge. "Warriors came. I understood part of their words, and they sounded as if they were a band of mixed hairy-faced and Likes To Fight men. Their leader...." She raised her eyes to River Song's. "It was his son I wounded moons ago, and for some reason he seeks revenge now."

Falcon Storm stood in front of Listens To Wind and stopped her from picking up muddy wood. "There is nothing left. Come. We go to my people. Jump on with your grandson, who I asked to stay behind for his own protection."

Singing Stone looked ahead, not facing Falcon Storm. "We cannot leave the mustangs. The warriors are coming back in two sunrises to take them. I will not leave them. Never! I am as much mustang as I am human. The animals will return when Father Sun wakes, as they always do."

"We will come back. I, Falcon Storm In Clear Skies, say this is so. We will find a safe place for the mustangs and us. I will ask my people to follow. If they choose not to come, we will gather everything from my lodge and find another place that is safe, then we will return for the animals."

Singing Stone nudged the robe in the mud with his toe. "They will never stop attacking. I say we go find the Fish People."

Falcon Storm kicked mud over a dying ember that tried to come back to life. "The mustangs always move out into the grasslands in the cold season to find more food. Singing Stone, can you try to make the animals understand that we need them to follow us until we find some place safe for them? If they move out onto the grasslands, they will have protection from the hunters but we, ourselves, will be as helpless prey. For a short span, we must remain in the canyons."

"I can try. How will they find food?"

"I will ask that someone be sent to our two sister bands to ask for help. We are small bands, but together we will be stronger. We have all lived together in the cold season before to share our food. We are never far from each other. The Likes To Fight people are our enemies as well."

Listens To Wind nodded, shivering as Sister Wind picked up and blew scraps of burned hide and ash past them. All that remained were burnt clay pots and parts of the lodge poles. They had nothing left, no reason to stay.

As they turned to go, a single ragged piece of hide flapped against a charred lodge pole.

The pounding hooves of a single mustang turned everyone's heads, and Falcon Storm readied his bow.

Snow stopped in front of Listens To Wind. She hugged the animal's neck. "I knew you would not leave me. I do understand why you did not come when I whistled for you. Had you, the enemy would have seen me."

Chapter 13

The Counsel Lodge held the combined three small sister bands of Falcon Storm's people and River Song's family. Many wrapped themselves in humpback robes, sat close to the center fire, and whispered among themselves.

Their Holy Woman stood so she could speak her words. She cleared her throat, and everyone stopped whispering and sat tall. "When our three bands combine, we are a strong people of forty-eight. We should not separate into our smaller family clans for now. The Likes To Fight People grow strong with their decision to be part of the hairy-faces. This has been a long time coming. Already we miss many mustangs. To go back to the old way, before the mustang, would be a life none of us wish to return to."

Her withered face held the Power of wisdom. Everyone could see her dark, bright eyes sparkle. Her wispy star-dusted hair fell about her elbows. Water Lily did not show any weakness as she stood. Her body did not shake with age. Even at seventy-two winters, she stood strong.

"Combined, our bands only have twenty-three of these four-legged big dogs, the mustangs. The Big Sky People separate and we weaken. This can no longer be so." She shook her head and many people nodded.

"We have heard the words of Listens To Wind. She may not be a Holy Woman, but she has her own Power, her own knowledge. I, for one, have never met anyone who can hear Sister Wind as she does. We all know to pay heed to Wind, but to understand her words? If more of us could do so, we would be fortunate indeed."

She allowed her robe to drop, exposing her muscled body. Hard work all her life made her respected, admired by all her people. "I know the cold season is upon us. We are a *strong* people. Living the life we have has made this so." She waved a hand, palm up. "Even our children are strong. We can, and have, endured much in our travels. We are wanderers and will remain so. This is *our* Power.

"Why not welcome these new people into our band? They, too, are wanderers. This is not the time to be on the move, but to settle in. I say we have a reason to help these people. Our mustangs are our relations just as the trees, the animals who share their bodies with us, and the air we breathe. We are all connected and to remain connected, we *must* help one another. I will not leave my people, but I ask that my people consider my words. I wish to follow this family who has lived much hardship to protect our four-legged relations.

"My words are done. Now all of you must decide." Water Lily nodded toward Falcon Storm and sat next to Listens To Wind.

Falcon Storm In Clear Skies stood and cleared his throat. "I wish to take River Song as my mate. She has not agreed yet, but I still choose to go with her and her family. They call themselves the Mustang People, and I will call myself this also. What they do is a good thing, Sacred. To save another, be they human or animal, is Sacred.

"Last season when we hunted, and found the mother doe whose leg was caught in old vines, we did not take her even though we hunted. Her two young ones stood without fear as we helped set their mother free. She, in turn, walked up to one of our hunters and licked his hand before leaving with her children. This was a Sacred Happening. The next day, we had a good hunt. We had enough food for all of our bands for some time. That allowed us to stay together for that cold season. We were blessed by the Animal Spirits for our kindness."

He pointed to Singing Stone. "This boy speaks to mustangs as you and I speak to one another. He also has a gift, a very special gift, even more so than making words with the mustangs. He shares his being with stones. Somehow they speak to him, tell him of danger, of when all is calm and safe. His dreams are full of Power.

"I know many of you feel the old ones in the canyons. Singing Stone has communicated with them. Even though they never speak words, he understands them. They showed him the old paintings left by the Fish People and pointed the way to them. We all have heard the stories, and some laugh while others know they left to find safety in a new land guided by a boy's dreams. I say Singing Stone is one who, one day, will be a great leader. I would be honored to follow him.

"His mother, River Song, is a warrior, as is her mother. Both are strong women with much courage." He lowered his head and smiled at River Song. "I know she does not need a man. It is I who needs a woman. I ask you, River Song, in front of all my people, to be my woman. I will follow you forever and always."

She stood and took air deep into her chest, but said nothing.

"Mother, it would be good for me to have a father." Singing Stone stood and turned his gaze on Falcon Storm In Clear Skies. "I accept you as my new father."

Falcon Storm's faced reddened. "I would be glad to have such a son as you." He shifted his gaze to River Song. "Will you accept me as your man and your son's new father?"

Singing Stone pulled a braided mustang hair rope from around his waist and held it out to the Holy Woman. "I offer this as a binding rope for my mother and my new father."

Water Lily solemnly accepted it. "What say you, River Song of the Mustang People?"

She bit her lip and slowly nodded her head.

***

The Big Sky Mustang People, their names now combined, moved their camp near the burnt lodge of River Song's family after the mustangs refused to follow the people deeper into the canyons. With the larger group of people, River Song no longer needed to be wary of the Likes To Fight People as she gathered wood. Her mustang held still as she added more wood to the bundle on the animal's back. The air smelled of the promise of snow, which would slow the enemy down for a time.

Together, the three bands of Falcon Storm's people—her new people—were a large group, and with warriors guarding the camp, she relaxed. They had little fear from the Likes To Fight People. Twice they fought off the enemy and chased them back. The last time, several warriors of the Big Sky Mustang People followed and found them. They pushed them farther into the land of the setting sun, where her people knew they would remain until the warm season came around again. No one wanted to cause trouble as the deep snow came.

Her new people followed the mustangs deeper into the grasslands. They needed to find more to eat and start the search for the Fish People, which kept creeping into her son's dreams as well as his waking life. More and more, the people felt the pull to move forward. Their new band loved to wander, to explore, and they too were eager to see what lay ahead. In spite of the cold season, they moved deeper into the new lands, as meat was plentiful.

Her moon time had come and gone. *Do I really carry a baby?* So much time had passed since Singing Stone kicked in her belly. No longer did fear tighten her gut as she thought of bringing forth a new life. They were safe among a large band for the first time since she was a child. A smile made its way across her face. To be a new mother after so long would bring much joy into her heart.

She waved to her son as he chased Spirit Eyes through the people's combined herd. Spirit Eyes and her son were seldom apart. The young man even slept next to the herd as they had always done.

Listens To Wind helped River Song make him a lodge so Singing Stone had a warm home. He was a man now at eleven winters old, no longer a boy in many eyes. He had earned the right to be called a man the day he rode Spirit Eyes into the herd of humpbacks and brought one down with only three arrows. He gave most of the meat to the elders in their new band, keeping only enough to satisfy his hunger.

She led the mustang back to their lodge, unloaded the wood from his back, and sent him back to the herd with a tap on his rump. Another sunset crept across the grasslands. In the distance, only the tallest walls of the canyons jutted up from the land. The darkening sky had changed from turquoise to a lighter blue, and the colors of the coming night held much beauty as deep orange blended with dark pink and yellow. The smoking campfires rose in trails of white and grey. Children chased one another and dogs raced after them.

Such joy filled her heart.

This night, the people sat in front of campfires, shared stories of their Peoples, and shared food. River Song sat with her mother and quilled the sewn clothing they both had worked on since the beginning of the cold season. They hoped to give back some of the generous gifts their new band had willingly given when they had come holding nothing in their hands.

She leaned into Falcon Storm and smiled. Her family belonged to a band who loved mustangs as much as they. They cared for their dogs and allowed them to sleep snuggled in thick robes next to their lodges as well.

Her son had welcomed three into his lodge, and many people shook their heads, telling him dogs belonged outside. He said all beings were welcome in his home. Even if Bear or Mountain Lion came seeking shelter, he would open his flap to them.

Everyone had laughed, but no one knew her son as she did. He would indeed welcome any animal to sleep with him. He once cared for two orphaned wolves until they left to join their own kind.

Her mother already had two men ask after her, but she stubbornly refused both. She took all her belongings and moved in with her grandson so the men had no excuse to visit Falcon Storm late into the darkness to speak of lonely nights.

River Song grinned and pushed Falcon Storm's shoulder as a man shuffled his feet near their son's lodge, which sat next to theirs. "I never thought to be so happy again. My son was wise in choosing you for his father. I had decided to be stubborn and not love you." She took his hand. "That did not work so well. Your songs at night as you held me in our lodge melted my heart."

She rubbed the new boots that he surprised her with that night. They were finely stitched with a brownish-red and white mustang painted on the upper part of each one. Inside, rabbit fur kept her feet and legs warm. He had rubbed them with bear grease, which did not allow water to invade them.

How did he do this and I not see it? He must have worked on them as I slept.

"I sleep well next to you, a deep sleep that was unknown to me for a long, long span."

"The air chills me, woman. I am in need of some warmth." Falcon Storm tossed the stick he used to stir their dying fire with and crawled inside their lodge.

"Oh? And you think I will just follow?" She crossed her arms and raised her head to look at the campfires in the sky, then squealed as a hand pulled her inside by the back of her robe.

Listens To Wind, who still sat outside their lodge sewing, cleared her throat.

River Song wrapped her arms tighter around Falcon Storm's body. "My mother knows something you do not."

Listens To Wind cleared her throat loudly. "I leave now, Daughter. Someone I know perhaps has a warm fire burning inside our lodge."

Chapter 14

Dove pulled her robe tighter around her. The light late season snow did not bother her, but the chill of Sister Wind pursued her and pushed her. She allowed Wind to guide her through the winding paths. The First People led her father when he and his cousin felt the pull from their Energy through these paths, but most people did not follow these ancient paths. They were Sacred, and only when someone felt an invitation did they come this way.

Animals, plants and the Energy—they were unlike any in other parts of the forest. Her body tingled as blue sparks swirled around trees and shrubs. Her mind held strength, Power unknown to her. For one so young, the pull, the urge, the need to know more, gave her an inner knowing that had taken her father cycles of seasons to understand. Her woman time would be soon—sooner than most.

"Soft Breeze came into her woman time when she was eleven winters. Will I do the same? Or sooner? Why did she not get the Power as I have? We are from the same family. Father could not tell me, nor could grandmother."

'Girl, Spirit chooses who will be needed.'

A shiver ran down the middle of her back as she stopped and glanced around. "Who are you?" She whirled in circles and smacked into White Paws. "White Paws, where did you...?"

The wolf shook himself, raised his head, and pushed her with his muzzle. His amber eyes shined when he looked up at her, and blue sparks circled his body.

"You are so special. You follow me and I do not always know it." She squatted to hug him. "I feel so connected to you. Father must wonder where you are. I left before sunrise. A dream showed me this old path, and I needed to find out why. Did you dream of it, too?"

The wolf jumped up and licked her face, then moved on ahead of her and disappeared into the shadows of the trees.

"White Paws, wait for me!" She pulled her robe up to her waist and ran ahead. "White Paws?"

Why do I feel warmer? It is the cold season. What is this?

In the distance, a howl answered her. She stepped through a small grove of saplings into a meadow clear of snow. Small circles of budding flowers protested their imprisonment and pushed upward in the grass. She turned around in confusion and readied to run, but stopped.

"No. I am guided here. I will not turn back. There is nothing to fear. Nothing to fear."

Sister Wind tickled her ears. *'Nothing to fear.'*

Father Sun broke through the trees and lit up the meadow. Birds sang and emerald moss along the trees sparkled with dew. Tiny white flowers rose above the moss.

The air brushed against her skin. She tossed her robe to the side of the path on a large stone that stood alone. Eagles above called and she walked on. White, orange, and yellow flowers mixed in the green grasses, and bees danced in circles around bright purple-spiked flowers.

Nearby, a small waterfall with rainbow colors gently splashed into a pool. Fish jumped clear of its surface and caught creatures that darted and skimmed across the waters. Shrubs bloomed with white and pink-red flowers that swayed in the soft, warm breeze. The cornflower sky was alive with birds calling to each other. A white doe lay with her twin fawns and slept in peace.

Dove glided across the meadow on bare feet toward the doe. The deer's ears twisted, but she made no move to leave. As Dove came close enough to touch the doe, she held out her hand, palm down to show she meant no harm.

"This land is seen by few, Dove."

She jerked back and turned toward the voice, her eyes wide. "Who... are... you? Are you a Spirit?"

The young woman laughed and the air vibrated. "Child, I am of a band who came here long, long ago." Her thick white hair fell about her hips.

"You are young, yet your hair is white, and... your eyes! Are they red or purple?" Dove stepped back and into White Paws.

"I am an odd one among my Peoples. Like a white Buffalo, a rare one. I am called White Cloud."

"Why have I not seen you before?"

"I live here, among my own people. I have no need to wander. Come." She held out her hand.

As Dove took it, the woman vanished. "Wait! White Cloud?" She put her hands to her face. "Do I dream? I feel real."

'Sometimes we dream-walk, little one.' White Paws stared up at her, his eyes sparkling amber-blue. He turned and trotted toward the sounds of wolf howls.

"White Paws, wait! I am coming."

Out of breath, she stopped. "White Paws, I am lost! Do not leave me."

"He has not left you, little one. He merely guided you where you needed to go." White Cloud sat atop a white mustang who pranced in place. The fringe on her knee-length white dress hung down to the middle of her calves. Pieces of blue-green shells made into beads sparkled in different places on the fringe.

"You have beauty I have never seen, White Cloud."

"Child, beauty does not come from the outside, but within. Too many only see with their outside eyes. Humans shine when Father Sun is awake, but when the darkness sets in, their true beauty is seen only if there is a light from within." White Cloud jumped down from her mustang and he trotted away, kicking up his heels.

"The smell of rain is beauty. The whisper of Sister Wind. The laugh of a child. Watching a butterfly find her way out of the cage of winter's sleep. Father Sun on your face. The shade of a tree to relax in. The first snow after a hot summer, and so much more we do not give thought to.

"Beauty is when another gives away their food when they have little left to eat themselves. An elder treated with deep respect for all the wisdom they carry in their minds and hearts is as much a treasure as a new baby. When a child cries and the first person to pass by picks them up and offers comfort, this is not only selfless, but also beauty.

"Beauty is when a child cries for the *first* time, and when an elder smiles for the last time as they pass from this land into the Spirit Land.

"When you look into the eyes of the one you know will be your mate. After a rain... the sweet smell. Beauty lies in every living thing, Dove."

Dove lowered her head. "Too many times I forget. I see maybe too much with my outside eyes. I will learn from your words. They hold their own beauty. Mouse taught my father to use his inside eyes. Perhaps Mouse will come to me someday." She raised her head and smiled. "Are you going to take me to your people?" She sat in the tall grass, mimicking White Cloud.

"You are here with us, Mustang Woman." She waved her hands in front of herself. "This is our home, and I welcome you. You may come back any time you wish."

Dove twisted her head about. "I see no one but you."

"Do not look with your eyes. Close them."

Dove started to close her eyes, but instead leaned forward. "Wait. You called me... Mustang Woman? I have been called that name before! I am not a woman—well, not yet—but soon! I have had the feelings, you know, the feeling of changes. You knew I was called Dove? Your mustang, never before have I seen one so white. Why is he so white and why is his neck hair so long? Why do you call me Mustang Woman? Why do I see fawns and flowers? It is the cold season, is it not?"

White Cloud's laughter vibrated in the air. "So many words! It is the warm season where we are. It always is. One day soon you will have the answer to why I call you Mustang Woman, sweet child."

A fog took over the land, and the woman faded with the fog.

Dove stood. "White Cloud?" She sat up in the darkness of the lodge. "I did not get to see your people! White Cloud, take me back. Please? I wish to meet your people." She leaned down into her hands. "Why are dreams like this? I thought I was awake and walking."

"Daughter." Her father's whisper floated across the space between them. "What did you dream?"

"Father? I am sorry I woke you. A woman with white hair and red-purple eyes called herself White Cloud. I thought I was there! It was warm and flowers bloomed. Then I woke up here in the lodge and it is cold. Maybe I was there and not here. She said I was in her People's land deep within the forest, and she called me Mustang Woman. Who is she?"

He cleared his throat. "Red-purple eyes? White Bear and her cub also have this color in their eyes. Are you sure she was human? We need to go outside. We do not need to wake your mother and brother."

***

Animal Speaks Woman lay holding their son snuggled next to her breasts. When she had first come to the forest, this woman of white hair and skin came to her. She never told Shining Light what the woman told her.

'One sunrise you will wake and see white doves flying over, and they will land on a pole that comes out of your lodge. You will know it is time to follow your man and your family out of the forest.'

One day we will leave this place. I have known this since we came here. He brought so many people here to safety, and yet, I will willingly follow him wherever it is we are to go.

Chapter 15

Father Sun warmed in the early season of newborn animals. Sparkling rainbows scattered themselves across the grass. Half-asleep buds poked out on shrubs, and along the small stream, the thin ice coating the edge of the water melted. The sky started to turn into a gentle rose color infused with the cornflower blue, and the sunrise songs of many birds greeted Shining Light and Dove. Evergreen needles sprayed the air with light snow as the winged ones landed on branches. It melted as soon as it touched Shining Light's robe. He tilted his face to the sky to enjoy the warmth.

The soft crunching beneath their footwear made Dove laugh. She tangled her hands in White Paw's neck fur, but as he ran ahead, she lost her hold and fell on the grass.

"Girl, you are not so little anymore. You have grown too big to hang on White Paws." As soon as the words left Shining Light's mouth, the truth of them weighed upon him. He scooped her up and swung her in circles. "You are not so big that I cannot swing you!"

"The air is chilled! My teeth sound like a squirrel chatting in my mouth. My robe, it flies away. I need my robe!"

Their laughter brought White Paws racing back.

"Father, White Paws has new pups, and Moon Face needs food. Is there enough in the forest to feed them all?"

"We have much here in the forest. There is no need to ever leave." He stopped, spread her robe on a large stone, and sat with his robe open across his shoulders to share with her.

She held up her hand in a push-away gesture and raised her face to Father Sun. "Time to give thanks, Father, or have you too many heavy thoughts on your mind."

Shining Light stood, raised his own arms and started to sing his morning song. His voice carried high into the trees and Hawk answered.

Beside him, Dove's song blended with his. With her arms raised, the light-brown fringe on her long dress sleeves fell back and reached her face. Her beauty had begun to show the woman she would soon become.

Shining Light spoke part of his prayer. "Great Mystery, I am blessed beyond many who dwell outside, and even within, the forest. Please let it remain so for my children and ones yet born. Allow my grandchildren to grow up in this place of plenty."

A small pebble hit him on the head. Above, a raven peered down at him.

Raven cawed and flew off when another raven answered him. A small mouse climbed up Shining Light's leggings and, when he reached his tunic, clung to the edge for a moment before squeaking and jumping off.

Dove laughed, then twirled and danced, her arms waving up and down as she sang. She stopped and sat next to her father. "I am dizzy now. I saw Raven and Mouse both. Are they trying to tell you something? I wonder what. I know Mouse sees and understands things we do not see as important until much later. And Raven is Grandfather's—"

She put her hand over her mouth. "I did not mean to say what I should not. To speak of another's guide is wrong."

"Little one, everyone knows who guides him. He wears Raven's cloak of feathers. Yes, it is not right to speak of another's Guide to someone, but I do think he would not be angry with you. And you are right. The Spirits are trying to tell me something. I must think about why Raven calls my attention."

"Father, it is something you have hidden inside, something you fear. Raven can give you the courage you need." Her wide eyes welled up and she whispered, "No matter the future, I will always be your little one."

Water filled his eyes too as she took his hand, and he looked away. "You are too wise for your winters."

"I am all grown up inside, Father, and understand things that I have not shared with you. I may not understand many things about being an adult, but I do know my life will belong to others, just as your life does. Perhaps White Cloud will help me understand. Perhaps I will understand a little bit as I grow, become who I am meant to be. Mustang tells me—"

"Mustang?" His head jerked back. "Mustang speaks to you? You never told me—"

"Can I speak of it to you? I would like to. I met her during my Vision Quest."

He wiped his eyes and squeezed her hand. "Yes, my daughter, if you wish to share, you are welcome to do so."

***

Her chin high, she stared ahead, took in air and allowed it to go free. "I smell sweet air, full of so much joy for the new season. Soon baby animals will become part of their Animal Bands." *How can I tell him one day soon, very soon, I will belong to another band?* She cleared her throat and turned his way.

"When Mustang came to me, she trotted toward me in the orange land, the land you said you came from. Behind her, tall red-orange stones grew from the ground and many had...." She let go of his hand and made hers look like a pointed lodge. "Like that. The sky had more of a green color than ours.

"Mustang was a light red-brown color, like the colors of some of the stones. She came across the waters and stood before me. I stood to reach out to her, but she backed away, turned and went back across the waters, so I followed." Excited, she danced a few steps away, came back, and stood before him.

"Father, she took me to see the peoples I will belong to! As I approached them, I heard Sister Wind say, 'Mustang Woman!' White Cloud called me that too, and—"

"People you will belong to?"

"You and Mother can come too, and Grandmother and Grandfather. Everyone can come!"

"My sweet little Dove, this forest is a good place. I wish never to live anywhere else. Why would you?" He raised his hands in the air. "Look about you. We never need fear any enemy here. This is a land of plenty, where the beauty of the falling waters spill into streams filled with fish. Many animals live among us without fear, which is why we decided only to hunt within the forest if we have to. We have found many healing plants that do not live anywhere else, and the cold season is not as harsh here. Of course, you have never seen the lands as I have. I can tell you this is a good home."

She stepped close to him. Her voice sounded much older. "It is my future, Father. I wish to be with Singing Stone."

He reached out and grasped her hands. "Then we will go get him and his people. We will bring him back... when you are older."

She let go his hands and wrapped her arms around herself. "I am cold now. I wish to go sit by our fire."

***

Wanderer stood behind a tree and watched as Shining Light and Dove walked back toward their lodge. His lips pinched and a frown gathered his brows.

Though we may not wish it, the seasons move just as they do outside our forest. It does not matter that in the forest time is just a word. Still it reaches out and touches our lives, forces us to move forward.

Even the mustangs are restless. They feel the Energy shifting, as I do. I can no longer bring them back to the forest. Like Dove, Thunder is growing in Power and is now a lead female. She must go where the Spirits lead her.

Ruby Standing Deer

Chapter 16

Mustangs grazed on the new rich grasses, moving only to find another mouthful. New babies rested in the warmth of Father Sun or pranced about with other young ones. The lead male kept his head turned toward his grown son, Spirit Eyes. The young mustang stayed at the edge of the herd most days, but his father did not try to drive him away. The lead male had gentled down some in his older years, but he still stood tall and watched over his females and young ones.

When Singing Stone rode Spirit Eyes past, the older lead male only nickered. "I wonder if he runs off his daughters for a reason. Maybe he does not wish to breed them. Has he accepted you, or will he soon chase you away, too? I know you both have worked together to chase off more than one danger." He patted Spirit Eyes' neck. "I have tried to make him understand that you and I are companions.

"Several men from our new band cut many of the young males the way the hairy-faces do to stop them from breeding. They told me the lead male would accept them as part of the herd without challenges from his cut sons."

Singing Stone had stood his ground when they came for Spirit Eyes. No one dared to touch his companion. He told them that they, too, might lose something!

He had stood away from the others as they traded young females from the herd for females from another band. His heart lay heavy with sorrow. Always before, every other cycle of seasons, the male would chase them away, but they were always nearby with other herds.

A sister band of the Big Sky Mustang People would lead the females away and leave ones in their place, a fair trade. The lead female had snorted and bobbed her head as she approached each one, defending her role, and none of the new ones challenged her.

Falcon Storm rode up to his new son on his dark red mustang. "You wonder if the lead male will let him stay. He will. There is much we still learn from the mustangs, but this I know to be true: a lead male can be friendly and live together with a son, sometimes two. What little I understand, and have seen, are that there can be two lead females and two or even three males in the same herd. They may break away, but may also stay together for many cycles of seasons. Males will sometimes even share females.

"When we first found our own mustangs, there were two brothers in the same herd, and their father allowed them to stay at the edge of the herd and make their own small herd of four females. They lived together without fighting. Once, a male came to challenge their father, and the two brothers came and helped him to chase away the unwanted male. Not long after, we lost all but five mustangs to the hairy-faces." He glanced away.

Spirit Eyes nickered as Falcon Storm's new female stretched her neck and sniffed him. Her brownish-red neck hair and tail sparkled as he allowed her to move around the young male.

Spirit Eyes made soft sounds as she moved around and danced in circles with him. Singing Stone held on and grinned.

"Heh. I had better pull her away. Spirit Eyes may find himself in some trouble with his father yet. I know he favors the young one I ride. Males have favorites, and it is better to not allow Spirit Eyes to like her too much."

Singing Stone pulled his animal away and nodded toward his mother and grandmother, who scraped and tanned humpback hides near the lodge. "We have not moved in nine days. We will not find Dove—I mean, the Fish Peoples, before the cold season comes this way. Father, when will we move again?"

"Son, we have new baby mustangs, and more will soon come. We cannot move any faster than the slowest animal."

"Perhaps I should leave and go ahead then—"

"Your mother would skin and tan *me* if you did. Maybe your grandmother would come after me with her skinning knife also! Your mother has told me she will decide matters when it came to you and Dove."

He held up his hands and crossed his arms. "When I told her my people called you a man, she cried and refused to accept it. She nods in understanding only because she has to. Our bands do not hold the same ideas on approaching life. If your band had been larger, we would have had to accept your ways, and you would have become a man after your Vision Quest. Men in our band have tried and failed their Quests, but they are still men. They became one after their first humpback hunt.

"In the eyes of our people, you are a man. You can make your own choice, but you must remember your mother's heart. It would tear to pieces if you were harmed in any way. Do not think of doing this, and please say nothing to her."

His stern stare held Singing Stone in place. "Already she yelled when you raced past her on Spirit Eyes only five sunrises ago. She glared me at, not you. She did not know you had been riding him. Your mother is a strong woman, one I love with all my being, but still a strong woman with her own mind. Women have a Power over men. Yes, we are the warriors, but once a woman looks into your eyes and smiles, you forget who you are. You think Dove will be different?"

Falcon Storm jumped off his mustang and motioned Singing Stone to do the same. "You and I need to walk and speak of things you have still to learn."

***

The 'talk' did nothing to change Singing Stone's mind. He loved the mustangs, and now they had protection. No harm would come their way if he left.

He slipped out of his lodge and left with a gentle old female mustang who followed Spirit Eyes. She could carry his robe and pack while he rode the male.

Spirit Eyes responded to his low whistle and trotted up to him. The old female stood beside him.

"Boy, I do not need the nose rope with you, but with the old one I will. I wonder why she follows you. The other band left her as if she had no worth. That is why I still hold anger against our new band choosing to trade with them. One day, I will lead this band and will not allow people I do not know to take our mustangs!" His voice carried. He put his hands across his mouth, but it was too late.

Listens To Wind came out from their lodge's flap. "Grandson, you sound like a grunting humpback pushing his way through shrubs." She put her finger across her lips. "I knew your heart. I am packed and ready."

As quiet as a soft breeze, she dropped her pack and made her way to the herd. A nearly black female and her new baby, the same color, followed her back. "These people use the young ones as an excuse to move slowly across the grasslands. Anyone who knows mustangs knows the young ones can keep up. Nature made sure they were ready to run within a short span of being able to stand."

Singing Stone smiled. His grandmother's Power shined across her face in Sister Moon's light. "I am happy I do not leave alone."

She held two well-made packs lashed together in such a way as to fit in comfort over a mustang's back, with the back edge made to hold a humpback robe. She tossed him one like it. "Inside one of the packs you will find new leggings with the middle thick for the inside of your legs, as we used to wear when riding. Some things *we* will teach this new band of ours."

Her voice stayed so low the camp dogs did not stir. She cocked her head as the sprawled out dogs whimpered in their sleep. "No one watches the herd this night, Grandson. The people relax and do not worry. One day, this will be a bad choice. But who listens to me? They think they are strong enough in numbers. They do not share my worries."

Sister Moon drifted in and out of the scattered clouds this night. No one would know they were gone until after the morning meal. As his grandmother and he moved away from the sleeping camp, so did every mustang not tied to a lodge.

The lead female trotted to the front of the herd, and the male pushed them forward from behind. Little ones trotted next to their mothers as the adults' hooves glided across the soft green grass. Singing Stone's dogs raised their heads, tumbled around and ran to catch up.

Not a human stirred. Tiny embers from campfires spit upward in reds and oranges, rotating their direction as if to point and say, 'they go!'

Both Singing Stone and Listens To Wind stretched on their mustangs and twisted back toward the lodges. No one responded. Not even a baby woke. They vanished silently into the darkness, and left the band behind.

***

Father Sun lit up the grasslands, exposing the rich green land of rolling hills. A colorful canvas of white, yellow, orange-red and purple flowers poked their heads out of the grasses to greet the warmth. The mustangs had slowed down. Their young ones hung their heads and trailed behind.

"We must stop and hope the band will take time to gather itself. Only now do they realize the herd did not just move off to graze." Singing Stone hopped off Spirit Eyes, whose own head drooped.

"I did not think the whole herd would follow! How are we to protect them all, Grandmother? We are but two and if the Likes To Fight find us—"

"Stone, Grandson, do not worry so. Somewhere in the darkness, the young men who slept on the hill above the herd were not so sleepy. We thought we were alone, but we were not. They follow way behind, back so far that I had to squint hard to see them.

"I think they wonder why we left, and as young as they are, I am sure they seek adventure. We did not hear them jump on the straggling mustangs, so intent were we on hearing the movements of men in the camp. They will ride up after their own animals have rested, and we have your dogs, who followed you to warn us of anyone who approaches in the darkness."

She shrugged as she unloaded the mustang who carried her packs. "Perhaps this will make the camp realize they need to move faster... or anger them enough to move faster. Either way, we must stay one day ahead of them. Water Lily and I spoke—"

"Water Lily knows of this?" He plopped down flat on the grass, too tired to stand and argue. "I am glad the dogs came along. We can rest better. Why did... how did you know to speak to Water Lily?"

She rolled out her humpback robe and stretched out. "She is a Holy Woman and already knew of your plans. She told me to follow, to keep you out of trouble. This is your destiny, boy, and you may be a man, but you have much to learn before any man will allow you to take his daughter as your mate. I need to sleep."

She pulled the robe off her mustang, laid it on the cool grass, and curled up inside it. "For now, we are safe. Rest while you can. Not all days will be as pleasant."

She stretched out on her side and spoke a silent prayer. *Forgive this child for not greeting Father Sun in prayer. I have forgotten how tired I could be. Please guide us to where we are going. We enter unknown lands of unknown people, and Sister Wind whispers of dangers I do not understand.*

***

Spirit Eyes pushed at Singing Stone's head and nickered.

Stone stretched his arms above his head and yawned. "Why did you wake me? Oh, I am careless!" He sat up to the smell of cooking.

Seven young men, most about his age, a couple older, and his grandmother ate. The young men chatted among themselves and poked each other's arms as they spoke about young women.

He rolled over and stared their way, and Spirit Eyes nickered even more. The animal rolled his lips over his teeth and bobbed his head up and down, sending spit into Singing Stone's eyes.

"Hey, I am awake, mustang!"

He rubbed the spit out of his eyes and realized his grandmother and two of their companions stood over him, grinning. "I... heh, slept very hard. My mind was... so overrun with worry—"

Two hands reached for his and pulled him up. "I am Four Arrows. Do not be red-faced. We know you worked hard to plan this for several sunrises. Your grandmother spoke of it to us. Your mind must have used up much Power. Come... eat. Your grandmother is a fine cook."

Four Arrows turned to grin at Listens To Wind. "Perhaps she would like a young man to keep her warm?" He dropped Singing Stone's hands when he was about halfway up from the ground.

"Four Arrows, I am old enough to be your mother! You have maybe seven, eight winters over my own grandson." She waved him away, trying to look offended, but a grin crept across her face as the young man hurried off.

"So you like him, eh?" Singing Stone grunted as he sat up. His grandmother shoved him back to the ground, and her foot barely missed him as he rolled and jumped up. "Maybe I am not so hungry!"

She waved a hand over her shoulder. "Good, the last piece will not go to waste. Though dogs have eaten their fill of these fine rabbits the *men* hunted, I am sure they could eat more!"

Eyes downcast, he sat next to her, his hair a woven combination of his own and horsehair.

"When you meet Dove, your hair will make her think she stares at the wrong end of a mustang. You must either work out that mustang hair or I will cut it out!"

"Grandmother, I am a man! You should not speak to—"

"A very silly looking man. The young men with us asked if your father was a mustang. No, do not glare their way. I agree with them. If you must wear animal hair, hang it in braids from your legging's tie-on."

When they reached the fire, she handed him the last big piece of rabbit on a small, thin hide. "It is hot. I do not wish you to burn your hand. Take my carved bone comb and start working on that... that hair of yours, Wild Boy. You will need it to find your own hair. Do you wish to terrify Dove? It is a good time to move on. We have much daylight and all the animals have rested."

"Thank you, Grandmother, for your food and the kind words about *my* hair." He turned and smiled at her. "You really are good to look at, for one so old." He jumped backward before she lunged at him, and raced away with the meat in one hand and the comb in the other.

***

Listens To Wind's animal pranced in circles as she tried to jump on. "What is it, girl?" She let her mustang go, closed her eyes and stilled her body. Sister Wind carried a smell—not the food, not the mustangs, but... something bitter.

Sister Wind, this smell has a sound. But what? How can a smell have a sound?

Her mustang nickered and backed away from her.

Mustangs have much in smarts. She calls to the one the last boy rides, but why? Ah, he holds his animal tight and he himself is tense and... it is him! The bitter smell.

He is too young to have hair on his face, but he has the look of a hairy-face. Why did I not see it before? Do I turn him away? No. I need him where I can watch him. His movements will give away much. How it is he is a member of the band? I will drive my mind crazy if I do not be silent and watch. Just watch.

As the boy passed, her mustang came back to her. "What is it you feel, old friend? Does he have the heart of a hairy-face? Is he the kind to give no respect to your Mustang Peoples? How can the hairy-faces not understand that you give a great gift by allowing us on your backs? You and Dog are the only Peoples to have attached yourselves to humans, though Singing Stone says wolves are part of the band Dove belongs to."

She jumped on her now-calm mustang. "Heh, as a child, I had Hawk as a companion. I found him injured, with no feathers to fly with, too young, so I cared for him. One day he flew away, but not before he dipped over the head of the boy who was to be my mate. I knew what he showed me and thanked him. He was meant to fly the skies, not sit on our lodge. Yet when I sat outside at night, he would fly down from the top of our lodge and stand before me, stare deep into my eyes, past them, and into my Spirit. He gave me his ability to listen to Sister Wind. I saved his life and he gave me mine. I speak to you more often than to my own kind and you understand. He protected and warned me, as you did now."

She patted the mustang's neck and scratched deep into her neck hair. "You are a beauty. You have the same colors as did your mother—rich black and browns with black stripes up your legs, and small splashes of white in your neck hair." She leaned in. "You know, that is why I called you Snow—your small white specks."

She raised her head as the boy trotted away from the herd into a dry gulch. After he came out the far end, she took her mustang to the gulch. She leaned sideways over Snow and followed the other mustang's hoof prints, which only partly showed in the bent grass. They came back onto the flat land. Nothing.

She returned to the gulch and again followed the boy's path. *Why did he take his mustang down there?*

Ahead, no one turned back to see where she rode. Sister Wind blew a strong gust of cool air past her. Loose hair whipped across her face, smacking her hard enough to sting. "Sister Wind, what is this message you have for me? I see nothing."

Her mustang bobbed her head and moved once again toward the gulch.

Listens To Wind, like her grandson, never used nose ropes. They used shifting of their bodies, tightening and loosening of their hands and legs, and light taps of their heels to guide the animals.

Her mustang snorted and tossed her head, so she let her animal go the way she chose. The mustang retraced their path and stopped near a flat stone.

She jumped off and scratched the mustang's head. "I do not understand."

She paced past a patch of white flowers with exposed yellow centers, then stopped and turned. On one side, nearest the stone, the flower tops were mashed and several stems broken.

"The stone. It has been moved." She knelt beside it and brushed at an exposed a bare spot. A small piece of tanned leather showed itself and she moved the stone. A thin hide lay covered under a layer of sprinkled dirt. She brushed it clean.

"Sweet Mother. It is a painted arrow pointing the way we are moving."

***

"We will catch up to them, River Song. Do not worry so. I did not know your son would do this!"

"*Our* son, Falcon Storm In Clear Skies! You took me—you took him as well. We stayed longer than we needed to in this spot." She jumped on her mustang and headed toward the trail the herd left behind.

"Woman, we are only a sunrise behind! Allow the rest of the band to prepare. They are not so happy that most of their mustangs are gone also, but we are a band, and a band stays together."

She turned her animal around and faced the people. "I am ashamed Singing Stone and my mother left. I know she left to keep him safe. Seven young men have left also. I do not think *our* son knew the mustangs would follow them. We will catch up to them and the band will know this is true."

She stretched her arms wide, palms up. "He is a young man who follows his dream of a girl called Dove. As any young man, he wishes to know his mate sooner than the parents wish it. Man or not, he will always be my son, and I wish to know Dove before he takes her as mate." Her arms dropped and relaxed when one of the elder women chuckled behind her.

Falcon Storm reached for her. "Woman, no one is angry. You need not feel shame. Come, eat, and we will allow everyone to gather their belongings. It may take a little while longer since every animal not leg-tied left. The people believe he has a Power over these four-leggeds. Ha! Even his dogs left! Come eat and we will soon be on our way."

Out or breath, Water Lily ran up to Falcon Storm and River Song. "Last night, I dreamed a vision of danger that comes our way. It was good to leave our old camp, and we have Singing Stone to thank for this. The ancients did not show him the paintings of the Fish People only so he could find his future mate. They showed him the paintings to also save our people."

Water filled her eyes. "In the vision, I saw our old camp is no more."

Ruby Standing Deer

Chapter 17

"Fire, be still! I cannot reach Sandstone's back if you keep pushing me." Dove steadied herself on the stump. She reached over Sandstone's back and grasped the wide strap that circled her belly and would hold her pack. She tightened it as best as a girl her age could and tied it. "Sandstone, I know you do not need a nose rope when Father rides you, but I must use it until I know you will follow. Soon, Father Sun will wake and we must be gone. I do not worry about traders because White Paws and Moon Face are here with us and they will follow me."

"Girl, you cannot leave on your own. Others will follow soon." Wanderer leaned against a small tree opposite of her. Several mice scurried up his chest and into his hair.

"Wanderer!" She slipped off the stump.

"Good thing the grass is soft. Your backside would be broken, and I would have to lay you across Fire's back and your head would bounce up and down."

She stood up and rubbed her sore bottom. "Why are you standing there?"

"Because you are standing there. I could not stand in the same place as you."

She smacked her head. "No wonder my mother says you are a Great Holy Man full of Power, but you are also full of—"

"Oh my, your mother is wise. I am full of Power, yes, but we all are." He walked to the mustang. "You are too young to do this alone. Child, I have watched you for several seasons and understand your young heart. Dangers outside the forest are more than you understand." He undid the pack and it slid off Sandstone, dropping to the ground. He laid a hand on top of her head, lifted her chin and stared into her eyes. "Though you are nearly as tall as I am, your leaving would kill both your mother's and father's hearts." He tilted his head. "I know you promised your father you would not leave without him. Have you forgotten?"

She lowered her head and remained where she stood.

"A promise is more than words. It comes from the heart. If you tear a promise apart, it does much damage, little one." He put his arms around her as a tear slid down her face. "A promise tells if your heart is good, if you can truly be trusted. I have heard many people say they promise something just to get another to let them be. This is wrong, as it causes pain for both—the one who believes and the one who now carries an empty hole in their Soul for not keeping that promise."

He hugged her even tighter. "That empty hole grows until it becomes so big the person dies inside. It may take a short span, or it may take most of their lives to feel it, but when they do, it is a death that all share, because the person changes, becomes bitter. Who wishes to be around a bitter person?"

"Wanderer?" She wiped the wet from her face. "I promise to keep all my promises for now and always. I promise to love you always and forever as well. I need to go speak to Father."

***

"But Father, I have a great need to go to him." Dove sat against a rolled up hide in their lodge, her arms crossed. "When you were a boy, I wonder what you did when you had a great need." Her lower lip drooped as she turned her head toward her mother.

"Daughter, you speak to your father, yet you make sad faces my way." Animal Speaks sewed a pair of new footwear for Hawk Feather. "Your brother's feet are growing faster than the rest of him! I do not remember your little feet—"

"Mother, he goes without his footwear anyway. Why make him any? He wiggles out of them and you need to hunt for them every day. If I was a mother—"

"You would be making footwear and disagreeing with your daughter, as I do."

Shining Light chuckled under his hand. "I never wore footwear and do not see why he needs to, either. You gave up on Dove long before she was two winters old, yet you still try with our son. Children need to feel the Mother beneath their feet. It helps them to connect. You know this, woman. Bare feet can feel the Energy, feel life. Covered feet cannot, and that is why before the mustang, the runners who went from band to band with news never wore footwear. They needed that connection to know if danger was near. I never understood why anyone should disconnect and wear—"

"You, man of mine, would wear nothing. What do I say! You only wear a breechclout in the warm season and no footwear." She tossed the footwear aside.

"As do all men." He grinned. "That way you can see how strong I am, how brave I am. How much strength is in my legs, how big my chest is, how—"

He wiggled his brows and grinned again, then ducked, barely missing a wad of hide scraps she threw his way.

"Sweet woman, caring woman, why do you throw your sewing at me? In the warm season, children do not wear anything... except a little boy from our lodge, who as soon as he is out of your sight races away with nothing on."

"You change from speaking of our son, to you, then back to our son." She squinted her eyes at him. "Do you say our son will be as you? Just as silly?"

He raised both hands in the air. "Would not another as me be a fine catch for a young woman?"

"If he did not run away and leave the girl of his desires to wonder if he had any of this fine bravery you speak of."

"Mother, Father! Please stop speaking of such silly things. I need you to listen to me."

Animal Speaks nodded toward Dove. "Let us listen to our daughter's needs, not the bragging of a man. She sounds so deep in her pain."

A bare-footed Hawk Feather crawled over her lap and out of the raised bottom of the lodge. The beginning of warm season brought a welcome breeze inside their lodge, and a good escape for a boy who wished to play.

Dove pulled her long, loose hair and twisted it into a single wrap. "Is anyone in this lodge ready to hear my words?"

"Daughter, I, your mother, am. Come sit on my lap while I finish weaving this basket. You can help me work in the pine needles."

Speaks waved her over, but Dove sat and played with the shells at the bottom of her dress, lips tightened into a pout once more.

"I will put aside my basket for now, sweet Dove. Come sit by my side, not as a child, but as a growing woman."

Dove freed her lips from the tightened pout and grinned as she slid past Shining Light to wrap an arm around her mother.

Speaks hugged her. "We women do understand each other. When there is a love in our hearts, a man cannot understand the need as we do."

"Dove, little one—" Shining Light scooted closer and rested a hand on her knee.

"Father, I am not a little one. I am almost a woman. Mother knows my heart."

Animal Speaks stiffened and pulled Dove's chin up to see into her eyes. "What does this mother know?"

"How love can make your heart hurt, can make you walk in circles in your mind. And make you almost not keep a promise."

Shining Light stared hard at his daughter, and she shivered in response.

She grabbed the unfinished basket and her mother's hand stopped her. She gripped her mother's hand and shifted her legs toward the lodge flap. "Perhaps I should look for my little brother. He is sure to get into trouble—"

Shining Light held her leg. "There are many mothers who are watching over your brother. Everyone in camp—mothers, fathers—everyone knows where every child is all the time. Even a Great Elder such as Wanderer knows where little girls go at sunrise."

She cocked her head and dropped her jaw. Just as quickly, her mouth closed and she scooted next him. Teary eyes stared up at him. "Why did you not come get me when you knew?"

"Children must be allowed to make their own decisions, and sometimes they need guidance from elders. I could have gone after you, but you needed someone—not your parents—to speak to you. Children do not always have big enough ears to hear the ones they are the closest to. Your Mother and I were there, too, watching you." He hugged her and his own tears fell.

Animal Speaks scooted against her other side to hold her hand. "We cannot allow you to leave on your own. You are too young. Who would look after you? Feed you and keep you safe?"

"But Mother, Singing Stone has left. His grandmother knew, and she was packed and waiting. I had hoped the both of you would know I was leaving, pack and follow me. I am a child in your eyes, in both of your eyes, but my heart feels for another. You say I am too young, but my heart tells me another thing. Why cannot a girl who pushes toward ten winters feel the love of her one-day-soon-to-be mate? Soft Breeze will be mated in another cycle of seasons, and I am not so much younger than her."

Shining Light bunched her up in his lap and rocked her. "Soft Breeze, as you say, pushes toward fourteen. She has learned much in her soon-to-be four winters that are ahead of yours. She knows the Powers of plants, how to use them, and already knows her future as a healer. She learns well and has great skills for making clothes and baskets. She had her woman making ceremony the last warm season." He held her back and stared into her dark, deep eyes. "Tell me, Daughter, what prepares you to be a mate to someone?"

"Love, Father, love." Dove ran her palm across his face. "Love is the greatest Power of all. I have watched Gentle Wisdom and Sparkling Star, Falling Rainbow and Night Hunter. I have watched Mother and you. I see the smiles that make the other's eyes full of love. I can feel that love. I know that love. Now, I wish to find it for my own. Know Both Sides, Gentle Wisdom's brother, tells me love knows no age, and I know his words are truth. I wish to leave very soon. I know how to sew, and I know the plants—maybe not as well as Soft Breeze, but I can learn. I can clean a hide, and make food too. My woman ceremony will make me a woman for all to see, but the true woman is inside of me, waiting for my mate. And when he comes, the flower within me will bloom." She pushed away and ran outside.

***

Animal Speaks and her man turned toward each other. "Woman, where did such a little girl learn words like that? 'The flower within me will bloom'?"

"Light, Dove is close to Knows Both Sides and he will soon be thirteen winters. She played with Soft Breeze until she became a woman. Our little Dove has felt the changes in both her cousins. She feels left behind. Her mind hurries to catch up."

The soft rumble of thunder made them hurry outside their lodge. Rain would soon fall.

Bright Sun Flower waddled toward them carrying Hawk Feather upside down, giggling as he swung on her dress. "I bring you a squirming little boy who just caught his first fish with Hawk Soaring. Heh, their names are too close." She flipped him over and sat him in front of Animal Speaks. "The sky speaks of rain and soon you would be looking for him."

She laughed as he tried to climb back up her dress. "We will all share in his wonderful catch at my fire before the rains come! He had some help holding the fishing branch, but I was there and claimed the fish to be his. Past two winters! He will not be one to sit still for long."

Speaks laughed, pulled him up, and rested him on her hip.

He giggled and pointed to a small group of doves flying over them.

Doves. Not so soon! The birds landed on one of the poles coming out of the top of the lodge.

Wanderer's voice came from behind her. "Speaks, it is the young who help push us further, help guide us even though we may think it is the other way.

"Many mustangs within the forest are restless. Some left in the night. The Spiral changes as the Circle shifts. You know this from your own childhood. Everything changes to become whole again."

She turned to look up at the cooing doves, then back to Wanderer. "How do you know what I think?"

White Paws reached up to her. "White Paws, where did you come from?" She heard Bear's growl, and it made her shiver. She turned toward the sound, but the forest held only trees.

Chapter 18

The Counsel Lodge held much chatter. Excitement and worry filled the air. Shining Light's voice mixed with the many voices who also wished to speak. "I do not ask anyone to follow. Yes, these are the dreams of a child. Was it not the dreams of a child that brought us here? As Wanderer says, children guide us even when we think we, the adults, make the choices." He raised the talking stick up high in one hand and waved with the other while he stood in the Counsel Lodge's center.

"Has it been so long since we gathered that we forget what this stick means? It was only last cold season when we gathered to decide which path to go hunting outside the forest, and I do not remember such disrespect! I will not have it now."

His voice calm, he cleared his throat and continued. "I do not ask that anyone leave with my family. You all have heard our daughter's own words, and every one of you know she is a young dreamer, as I was. At first, her dreams only spoke of a boy and his family for over a cycle of seasons. Now they show her a band of people with him. Last night she dreamed of a hard wind pushing them and their herd of mustangs. The wind carried many arrows, and this worries me. I ask for only a few men to follow, not the whole band." He waved his arms in opposite directions.

"Many of you would not be here safe, and living a good life, if not for others willing to help when I asked. Many now have families who have never seen the canyons and are eager to go, but I will not take untrained warriors. Your families will be the ones to decide.

"My father is a Holy Man and will stay. The Wolf People will not be without a Holy Person. My mother will stay as Storyteller and to help the young ones who have had dreams that call them to become healers."

The chatter quieted and people nodded in agreement. Young people gathered and whispered among themselves.

Knows Both Sides stood, cleared his throat and waited for Shining Light to nod his way. "I wish to go. I have been through my Vision Quest. My name stayed the same because the Great Holy Woman, Blue Night Sky, knew I was a Two Spirit before I even moved in my mother's belly. I have much to learn about who I am and have done what I can here. It is true I am not a warrior, but I am a good hunter. My father taught me much about what a warrior's life holds. He taught me to use the bow and fight as two men might if they met on the ground. My father taught not just me, but everyone who watched us and wished to learn. These are things we younger ones have not known in our lives because we live in peace here. My father saw this as a need.

"I can make a fine robe and quill as good as any woman. My mother has taught me well. I make good meat, can speak to the Spirits, and I am both man and woman in my heart, which everyone knows means I can speak for both sides because I have two Spirits." He turned toward a couple who argued. "And I can settle arguments." He sat back down with a nod toward the now-silent couple and a quick glance at his mother.

"I would welcome you to come on our journey. I am honored to have one as special as you are. We may need your guidance, and I will not ask that you be a seasoned warrior."

Many young hands shot into the air. He raised his hands once more. "Speak among your families, those of you who have yet to see any kind of battle." He lowered his head. "One thing about living in the Forest of Tall Trees is that we do not see what life, the dangers, can be like."

He raised his head. "Since so many of you wish to go, I will say this. For the next seven sunrises, we will have pretend battles. All of you have trained with your fathers, your friends, but this *'pretend'* battle will not be without wounds. We will use blunt knives and wide flat arrows, but they will still sting.

"I count thirty-seven hands who wish to follow. Even the women who raised their hands must be part of these pretend battles. If, after you have 'battled,' shown yourselves able to hold your own, and you still wish to go, Wanderer will lead you out."

Wanderer shot up in surprise. "I will lead them out?"

Shining Light turned to face him. "Yes, Great Holy Man. I can think of no one else who I would trust to lead our young people out of the forest. My family and a few others are packed to leave and will do so in two sunrises."

Wanderer cleared his throat and stood waiting for Shining Light to nod his way. "I must leave with the mustangs who this very sunrise leave. Thunder will not allow me into her mind. I have no idea why they leave, but I am certain it is of great importance. They head toward the canyons. I had wished to leave with her."

"Great Holy Man, we will be but two sunrises behind them."

"Who leaves with you, Shining Light?" Wanderer stood and swept his arms wide to take in the gathered people.

"My woman, our children."

"You leave with children, yet—"

"Forgive my interruption, Great Holy Man, but I also leave with Gentle Wisdom Who Rides A Flying Horse, a warrior woman, her mate, and their two sons. My cousin has taught them much about battles. Even at only pushing ten winters, their sons are cunning. My woman can fight if she must. My grandfather, Hawk Soaring, goes."

Bright Sun Flower twisted her neck around faster than a snake ready to strike. Hawk Soaring ducked her glare.

"I leave now to allow talks among all of you. I must go speak to others—"

"Shining Light! I, One Who Wanders, say this: you will not leave in two sunrises with only a small group of people. I now see that we must leave together. Thunder will do what she must on her own for a few sunrises. We will teach the young ones who wish to go for many days before we leave, and more as we travel. You will wait. I am older, wiser than you, than anyone here." He turned to see any objections. Not one person stood.

Shining Light lowered his head. "I will do as you say, Great One. You have the wisest voice in this Lodge of Council." *What are we doing? Taking all the young ones with us?*

***

Flying Raven caught up to his son as the young man headed into the forest. "Shining Light, you take on a burden you do not yet understand." He stood in front of his son, blocking his path. "I truly wish I could help you to understand. Your mother and I must stay." His lips tightened and he squeezed his son's arms.

"I wish to follow, very much so, but the people need me, as you said. My dreams tell me to stay. All you need to do is call out to me and I will respond. Know this. You take many young people with you who have little memory of the canyons, if any at all. They will be eager, undisciplined. You must make them aware of the dangers. Ask for adults who understand the dangers to follow." He squeezed his son's hands.

"I wish to go... so much so." His head dropped. "I love you, my son." He let go of his hands. "Listen to Wanderer. Listen well. You will need his counsel. I know of no other man who has been as many places as he, experienced as much as he has. He has lived a life I do not envy. I believe in his words and trust him more than anyone I have ever met." His eyes watered. With a quick turn, he left him. *One day, we will be together again.*

Moon Face and her four pups fell in beside Flying Raven. She rubbed against his leg and pushed him deeper into the forest. "You know, but Shining Light does not. The Spirits told me to say nothing." He knelt next to the wolf, hugged her and cried. "Please watch over my son."

Ruby Standing Deer

Chapter 19

Listens To Wind lifted her head and stopped her mustang. The sky had few clouds to block Father Sun. Sister Wind's cool breath blew softly across the grasses and the colorful flowers. The only sounds came from birds and moving leaves in the sparse trees that grew along a small stream. Few boulders remained. She took in air, and allowed it to come out, her eyes closed. "There is peace here. No danger. Singing Stone, what do the stones tell you?"

He jumped off Spirit Eyes and reached in the pack where he kept the stones he took everywhere with him. "Grandmother, I have felt a humming on my back from carrying them this day. This is good. The stones are calm and sing, not vibrate any warning. It would be a good time to allow the band to catch up. I am sure my father is not very happy with me, and Mother must be spitting fire for what I have done."

She lifted a hand to her brows and stared in the distance. "I count six of the young men who came with us. One is missing. He was not with us when Father Sun woke. While danger is not so close, this is a good place to stop. I fear the missing young man may bring us trouble. It will be good for the band to catch up with us. We are in the open and need to stay alert. Two must always be awake and on guard."

***

River Song pushed her mustang to keep going. "If my own mustang had stayed, I would have caught my wayward son by now."

Falcon Storm rubbed his eyes. "We need to get down and walk, let the mustangs be free of our weight. Do not glare at me, woman. You know we push them too hard. Most of our band is a half-day behind those of us lucky enough to have an animal to ride. Your anger pushes you. Anger will not get you there faster."

He jumped off and motioned her to do the same. "The band is not angry as you are. Many understand young love, how it takes a person's mind and makes it crazy. I know this one well." His grin stopped her from giving him a tongue-lashing as she slid off her animal.

"My heart is heavy with worry for both my son and mother. I know your people call my son a man, but in my heart he will always be my little one. And my mother! Agh! She should have come to our lodge." Her hands flew upward and her animal jerked in response. "I am sorry." She reached out and patted the animal's neck.

"If your mother had come to our lodge, you would have said no. This way she did not have to honor your words." He ducked as a hand came his way.

"Maybe I might have said to wait until the band is awake and speak of this to everyone."

"I am sure you would have. We have elders who cannot move as fast. I told our son the young mustangs needed rest. Perhaps my words were not chosen well. I did not mention our elders as I needed to. I thought speaking about the new mustangs would settle his mind. I was wrong and now take blame as you do. But not the anger."

He turned and placed his hands around her waist. "Anger is as a deep sickness. It makes a Soul slowly sicken and die. Only you can feel the crushing pain it causes. Others around you can feel waves of it, but you are the one who will suffer if you do not release it, push it away before it becomes alive and eats away at you.

"A very long time ago, a Holy Man came to our band and stayed for a short span. He spoke these words. I did not hear them. I rested in my mother's belly. My grandmother told me about him when I became angry at something long ago.

"He told my people he wandered the lands. Before he left, he told them a story about a man who could not let go of his anger. One day his body woke, but his Soul was gone. He was but a shell. There are still a few in the band who remember him. They are the elders who cannot keep up. The ones we must slow down for."

Chapter 20

For many days, all Shining Light could do was shake his head. He twisted around on Sandstone.

Too many young ones follow. And why did Grandmother and Grandfather have to come also? I remember Grandmother saying she would come if I left again, but I thought she only said that because she missed me.

I understand the men, yes. We will need hunters and warriors, but most of the women who follow have never held anything but a skinning knife. And so many children!

My mother. I have never seen her eyes water so much. I do not understand. I am coming back. We are coming back. She made me this shirt with the quilled rainbow in the waterfall. It had to have taken the entire cold season to make! Even I did not know then that I would leave. How is it that she knew?

Eagles drifted in the air currents above his grandmother. "If she comes, there is a reason. But what?"

"Father? What is this you say?" Dove held onto Fire's neck hair. The mustang wanted to trot, not walk. The shells in her small side braid caught Father Sun's light as they bounced with her body. "Do you ask why I come?"

"No, little one. I see many who follow, who needed to stay in the forest, my grandmother among them. Many have come. I feel I am leading the Fish People back home, not leading a rescue."

"Father, you do not—"

Gentle Wisdom bounded up on her mustang. "Cousin, Sparkling Star asks that you teach our sons to throw a spear better when we stop this day. They had pretend fights in the forest, but more is needed to make Sparkling Star relax. She fears for our sons."

"Spears? Wanderer is the best I know. I will speak to him." Shining Light stared at Wisdom's small animal. "Why did you not leave Brown Dog behind and choose a faster mustang? He cannot keep up with even my woman's dog, Blue Waters."

"He can keep up. And he passes your woman's dog with great speed. Do not speak to me of keeping up. We have been out in the grasslands for fifteen sunrises and move too slow. Brown Dog could have gone much further if we did not have so many people with us! And... and small children. Your son is one. He is too big for a backboard, and he squirms so much that Speaks had to tie him to herself. He is the only child who is this way. All the other young ones sit still and do not act as if they are sitting on a burning log." She whipped past them and caught up to Sparking Star.

"Burning log? Not my son."

"Yes, Father - your son, my brother. He is full of burning logs."

"Hawk Feather has maybe a small burning log inside him, as do all children, Daughter."

Dove squished her face. "You have much to learn about how to be a father." She tapped her mustang and raced after Gentle Wisdom.

He cupped his hands and yelled, "My children do not understand me!"

Dove waved over her shoulder and kept going.

Wanderer pulled up beside him. "You must be a child in your heart as the vision you had spoke of."

Shining Light's neck jerked fast enough that he had to rub it. "How do you know of that vision?"

"*I am* an elder, Holy Man. I know many things you can only wonder about. I come to teach you more, and perhaps you will learn if you do not ask so many questions." Mice jumped from a pouch he wore at his waist. One came up and sat next to his ear, and he nodded.

"Mouse says many things will change now. Not one thing will return to the same, but yet everything will become the same as it once was."

Shining Light stopped Sandstone. Her dun-colored young one ran ahead to play with another mustang. "What do you mean, nothing will return to the same?"

"But will become the same, as Mouse said. You need to carry mice. They tell me much. Nothing is ever the same no matter how much you wish it to be." He shrugged. "Life is that way. When you are so sure you have everything understood, things change. Nothing stands still, not even our Mother which we walk upon. You, my young one, you have grown used to stillness. Not as Bear teaches, but as in every sunrise and sunset ending the same."

"You make my head dizzy, Great Holy Man. We will return and bring these people to safety, bring Dove's friend home with us. And our mustangs who have stayed a day ahead of us will come also! I do not understand why that crazy mustang, Thunder, leads so many away from the forest."

"She leads them away to a new beginning. Even *she* knows nothing stays the same." Wanderer jumped off his mustang and walked. "Come, walk with me. No, do not worry so about Dove. Your woman watches her." He waved Shining Light down.

Sandstone trotted to catch up to her young one. Wanderer walked away from the mustangs and people, motioning for him to follow.

"Where do we walk?"

"Away from the others. Let them pass. You think we go to rescue people. Do we? Maybe they will rescue us. You say the Spirits have been silent more these past few cycles of seasons." He pulled a water bladder from his shoulder, offered it to Shining Light, and then took a long drink.

"Let us sit by that small hillside." He pointed at the stream. "It is so clear I can see tiny fish darting about. They keep looking for better places to hide. They do not understand they keep going to the same places every time. We go where we are meant to, where the Spirits lead us. Some may not follow if they knew what was to happen. Like those fish, they follow the one in front, even though that one has no guidance. I am happy we know where we go."

"So, you know where we go and what is to happen?" He sat and waited for Wanderer to sit.

The Great Holy Man leaned forward and stared into his eyes. "Of course I do." He turned and walked away.

"Wanderer!"

He did not turn back. With a wave of his hand back over his shoulder, Wanderer whistled for his mustang.

White Paws, Moon Face, her four pups, and the other eleven wolves who had followed him out into the grasslands settled next to and around him. White Paws put his head in Shining Light's lap.

"Wolf, I was going to get up and follow the band. Who knows where they go? What do I say? Wanderer is leading them. I only follow him and my daughter!" He dug his hands on both sides of the thick neck of his companion who stared deep into his eyes. "Where do we go? I feel as if tiny crawling feet climb up my back, and my belly tightens. Perhaps I worry too much for my people. A Great Holy Man comes with us."

Dark clouds moved in and the land quieted. The moving band vanished into the thick air that formed and left him alone with the wolves. The air vibrated. Stones hummed. He turned to find the stones, but only small ones lay about and inside the hill.

White Paws stretched and stood before his Human Brother. *'Yes and no. Humans make their own minds up about things, about what will be. This we cannot change. Each Human will do what he or she needs to do to find happiness. We cannot control their lives any more than we can control Sister Wind.*

'You worry for your people, and this is good. You are their guide, but not their master. Offer your wisdom. Offer your advice. Love your people as they love you, and in that love you will find peace... if you try.

'Know whatever happens will be for the good. For the good of the People, for all living. Never doubt yourself. I know you have heard these words before, but you need to hear them again. Doubt causes mistrust. If you mistrust your choices, take a few backward steps in your mind. Think. What is the reason you made these choices? For you or for another? You may think they are for another, but you had to make the choice, so the decision was also for you.'

He squeezed the big wolf to his body. "You know something, too, do you not? I wonder still how is it that you can speak to my mind, know what I think?"

Amber eyes sparkled as the wolf stared into the deep, endless dark eyes of his Human Brother. Blue danced at the edges of the wolf's eyes. *'Brother, you have a keen sense for a Human. You know more than most, except for Wanderer. Never doubt his words, even if they sound crazy to you....'*

"I miss my father and mother. I am a grown man, yet right now I wish for my parents to hold me. I know something changes, but not what."

A woman walked out of the fading fog with a boy dancing circles around her. "Here is my lazy man." Animal Speaks handed him Hawk Feather. "Your son needs you." She grinned and walked away.

"What have you done to your mother, my little Hawk Man? I am sure I was not so silly as you. Do you ever slow down? Ever sleep for more than a short span?" He held him high, swaying him back and forth. "Ah, so you want down, eh? Perhaps a walk will do us both good. I see my grandparents. We can walk with them."

White Paws bit into his breechclout and pulled him in a direction away from his grandparents. The other wolves circled him together with White Paws and led him around the hillside. Fog moved back in.

"Why do you wolves push me away from my band?" He tossed his son onto his shoulders and allowed them to lead him. The other side of the hill looked much like where he sat before. Grasses blended with flowers, and the stream flowed around the back of it. The same type of fish scurried from hiding place to hiding place in the waters.

"How can this be? Everything is the same. I even see the same stones on the ground." Above, Hawk called to his mate. They both swooped down and landed on the grass away from him and the wolves.

"Wan' down." Hawk Feather squirmed so much Shining Light allowed him to slide down his arm to the thick grasses.

"Do not wander, little one. You must stay near. And why do you not have footwear on?"

The boy giggled and ran over to a stone that jutted higher from the ground than the others. He grunted as he tried to pull the stone from where it rested a long time. He plopped down next to it and waved his hands in the air, making scolding sounds.

"Son, why do you worry over that stone?" He knelt next to him and ran his hands over the rough surface. "It is warm from Father Sun. And it vibrates! I can feel it through my hand, through my arm—"

White Paws and Moon Face settled beside them. The rest of the wolves circled them and the stone. Sister Wind brushed against his body, chilling him. Shining Light turned his attention to Hawk Feather. "Son, you must be cold."

The boy lay curled next to Moon Face, asleep. She had wrapped herself around him. Her thick, bushy tail covered his body.

Blues swirls appeared above and as they came down, engulfed Shining Light. *So, Light Which Shines, I see you have brought part of your band back out into the grasslands. This is good. They will be needed.*

You have a son who will be good to look at and will become a strong warrior, admired by many. Many young women will look his way. He will prove himself worthy to be a leader of warriors.

You must be wary as Thunder. She takes her own band closer to the canyons.

"I greet you, Blue Night Sky. Many sunrises have passed since you last visited me. I should know by now that when everything changes, but remains the same, it is you. I miss your counsel, Great One. Only my ears hear you, so I know I am not within the Spirit Land."

His son stretched in his sleep. "My son will be a warrior? What is this you say about Thunder? We go to the canyons to bring—"

'Heh, you still spill words as you did as a boy. Pay attention. You are in the Spirit Land. Close your eyes.'

"My son, I cannot—"

'He has the best guardians anyone could wish for. He is safe. Let go, come to me. I wish to show you some things. Things you must pass on to your new Peoples.'

"New Peoples? I do not understand. Oh, you mean new Peoples who will follow us to the forest."

'How ever you see them, Shining Light. How ever you see them. Close your eyes, boy. You cannot see with your outside eyes. Has not Mouse taught you this many, many times?'

Eyes closed, he set his mind free. Swirling blues drew him in, wrapped around him as comfortable as a warm robe. Somewhere, the ancients chanted. Mustangs nickered.

Deeper... deeper. The land changed. *So much grey dust!* He coughed as his body tried to take in clean air.

Men shouted. His eyes opened to a huge, flying winged one above him. The creature's wings spread, widening in large circles as it dipped above racing mustangs. The noise terrified the galloping animals. They stumbled over each other, their young ones lost in the dust behind them.

Another noisy winged one joined the first. Both worked together to chase the mustangs into something made of wood, a trap they could not escape. Eyes bulged from the terror-stricken animals as they ran in circles, rearing high, sharp hooves coming down on smaller animals. No escape. Men on the ground aimed sticks at them that let go with loud blasts. Mustangs fell. Young and old dropped.

Someone laughed. "Useless animals. Now they will not eat the grass my cows need."

The rumbling sounds of big creatures came to a stop before the once-beautiful animals that now lie mangled in blood. "Dog food factory, here we come!"

A scream tore from Shining Light's mouth. "No! What is this horrible thing you show me? This is not right. What is this, I ask? What are cows? What is dog food factory? Why can they not share the land? Is this the future, or some nightmare I cannot push away? Blue Night Sky, why do you do this?" His body shook violently. He lost the food his belly held.

"Sandstone. Where is Sandstone? She has taught me how smart her kind is, how much they understand humans and can love us, guide us. Sandstone!"

'Be at peace, little one. This has not happened... yet. You think your destiny only lies in saving people? Telling stories of the grey dust that will choke future humans? You will tell the Peoples you go to meet of what I have shown you. This is their destiny... and your daughter's. Yours... is what you choose it to be. Your daughter's

children's children will have children who will become guardians of the Mustang Peoples, of the young four-leggeds yet unborn.

'There will be a future where humans only think of themselves, what they can gain by having more things than others have. Some of these people may be our own. Some of these future humans will kill for what they can gain from it. Animals will be pounded into the grey dust because of human greed. Humans will even kill their own kind and take what they wish from them. Entire Peoples will vanish from our Mother.

'Many animals will be thought of as wasting the land that humans could have. They will be killed. If our own people think of the mustang this way, they will lose their way.

'The stories of our mustang relatives must be told. If the stories are lost, our people will forget the gifts the Mustang People give to them. As many times as Father Sun rises the stories must be told. Shining Light, you must help save the mustangs. You must help save the First Peoples.'

His fists tightened in rage and water from his eyes flowed as free as a river. The fog was no more. Birds darted about the grass, and a cool breeze swirled past him. Hawk Feather slept, curled at his side. The wolves were gone, save one. White Paws raised his muzzle and howled with such pain he sounded like a human screaming.

Hawk Feather jerked awake. Instead of crying, he crawled closer to the wolf.

Chapter 21

"I see the band catches up. Grandson, we may have upset the peoples who adopted us. Perhaps I should go and speak to them before they reach our camp."

Next to Listens To Wind, Four Arrows swallowed the last bite of his food and stood. "My... our people do not carry anger with them. That is not our way. Everything happens as it should. Like a young man's love for an older woman." He wagged his brows and grinned at her.

"It is impolite to look at a woman as you do, boy. Keep your hungry eyes from me. I have no desire to join with one so young. I will grow older and then you will not like what you see."

"I will always like what I see. I see inside, too. You are beautiful both ways... pretty woman."

Singing Stone rolled his eyes. "Stop it. I see both of you make big eyes at each other. Stop being silly. Age means nothing to those who care for one another! We have our band who comes, we do not need silliness. I will go ride out and speak to them. It was my choice to do this, and I must explain."

He whistled for Spirit Eyes. The young mustang stood a distance away from him and flicked his ears at the coming animals. He bent his neck to stare at him, then flipped his tail and raced toward the band.

"Spirit Eyes!"

"Heh, Grandson, you better start running." Listens To Wind and Four Arrows bent in laughter as he raced after his companion.

Four Arrows faced Listens To Wind. He grinned at her. "Pretty woman, I am not so young as you think. I am twenty-six winters."

"You are yet a child to me!"

***

"Singing Stone!" River Song jumped from her mustang and ran up to him. She stopped short of hugging the grown man. To do so would embarrass him. "Why, why did you do this? You terrified me." Her voice was a whisper. "You may not live with me, but a mother never stops worrying, not even when her son takes a woman. Do not do this to me again." Her fists balled.

He lowered his head. "I feel great shame for what I did. The others who followed me are not to be shamed. Only me. I will face our Holy Woman alone."

"Water Lily holds no anger. No one of the people holds anger. Perhaps you need to speak to the whole band, or at least the elders who had to take turns riding the old mustangs that did not race after your Spirit Eyes!

"We are tired, son, and must go back with mustangs to the walking elders. Many refused to ride. They said they would not take any animal from the young people who must always be ready to defend the band. These elders... they guide and advise the band as it should be, but they have put themselves in danger form being so far behind.

"We have hunted and carry meat. Allow us to set up camp and we will speak, Stone. We must speak more of this Dove girl. The mustangs are tired as well. They had to drag the poles, lodge hides, and though we did not have many, people had to pull some also."

"Mother." Singing Stone raised his head. "I am very much shamed and will never do this again. I am thought of as a man but acted as a boy." Instead of walking away, he took his mother's animal and headed toward the herd.

She smiled as Falcon Storm rode up and jumped off his mustang to stand beside her. "I think I understand. They allowed him to leave, did they not?"

"They did, woman of mine. Our son has learned what it is to be a man. Now, responsibility to our band will always be in his front thoughts."

River Song turned toward the sounds of mustangs. Singing Stone had gathered the animals and headed toward the elders. "He will not ever again allow an elder to walk. You are right. He has grown with wisdom in these past few sunrises."

Falcon Storm gently slapped his animal's rump and sent him after the herd. "How is it that he can whistle and make sounds like a mustang? The animals know and follow him. Never have I seen such a thing! He really is part mustang."

She stood close enough to bump into him. "He is of my body. And perhaps I should know more, but I do not. He hears stones sing. I pick one up, feel their Energy, but not their song, nor their vibrations as he does. My mother hears Sister Wind, and I can feel the waters. Each one of us has gifts just for us. I am sure you know this." The fringe on her short sleeve swayed as she pulled him away from the others.

"I know we will rest here." She reached for his face. A slender finger traced a scar that disappeared into the hair above his forehead. "How did you come by this?"

"Long ago. I learned you do not jump on a mustang who has never felt weight on his back. The jagged stone I fell on left a reminder on my head."

She separated her fingers and pushed them through his hair. "How far back does it go?"

Listens To Wind rode up on Snow and cleared her throat. "I am sorry to come your way and stop you, Daughter, but we must speak. We are in danger. Not only does Sister Wind carry messages, but I have this." She raised her arm. She waved the leather with the arrow painted on it in front of River Song and Falcon Storm. She looked directly at him. "I know your people do not always talk to the daughter's mother. I have seen the other women stare my way when we speak."

"Mother of my woman, it was not your custom to never speak to me, as it is ours. Your new people honor you instead of scolding. Do not worry so."

He turned the leather over. Red paint from the leather scrap had smeared, but the arrow stood out. "What is this that you show me?"

"The sunrise that Singing Stone and I left with the young men, one rode into a dry wash for a bit, then came up. I followed to see what he was doing. A stone had been moved, and it was there I saw the leather. The red arrow pointed in the direction we headed. I grabbed it so whoever was to find it would not. The boy who put it there disappeared before Father Sun woke again. I fear we are being followed by the same people who have hunted our mustangs even when I was but a girl. Back then, our people were strong. There were many battles over the animals, but also over our women. They had more warriors than my people." She lowered her head. "We became few. Too few to win the last battle. It was then I was taken captive. I fear these are the ones who follow now." She trotted away on Snow and did not look back.

***

"Song... River Song. How did you and your mother lose your mates?" Falcon Storm put the red painted arrow under a stone and pointed it another direction, away from the way they traveled. Sadness in her eyes pierced his heart deeply.

River Song's eyes held emptiness. "Arrows." She shuffled away.

Why did I ask? Now I have opened a wound that had maybe healed. She is my heart. I must learn to not bring forward things that are buried. I must learn to love her as she is and not be so worried about who she was.

Ruby Standing Deer

Chapter 22

Coyotes howled. Wolves gathered around Singing Stone.

Where did Coyote hide? The grass bent to Sister Wind's will. Dark clouds roared their fury as lightning struck where it pleased.

No place to hide. Wolves nudged him, pushed in on his body. Spirit Eyes pranced before him.

'Human Brother, do not fear Coyote. There is no trick here. Many call him trickster, but for you, he is not. Coyotes warn and Wolves protect.

'I, your Animal Brother, will be by your side, offer you my power. Protect the children, the elders. Protect... protect.'

Singing Stone bolted upright. The campfires in the sky burned bright in the clearness. The mustangs moved about and... and Coyote!

The sound echoed around him. He slept outside of out habit, his dogs with him. They lay stretched out, some kicking in their sleep. They dreamed their own dreams. Warm night air greeted him on his walk around the herd. The dogs woke and followed him, sniffing the air.

What was this that I dreamed? I do not dream such dreams. Only Grandmother does. Where are these wolves who gather and protect me? I have only been near the pup I raised. He left long ago to be with his own Wolf People. These wolves were of many colors, the biggest one, grey and white. He looked into my eyes with eyes even more yellow than Father Sun's.

Spirit Eyes snorted and left the herd. He followed the mustang. His dogs followed him, sniffing the air as Coyote still howled. Sister Moon, large and bright, stretched Singing Stone's shadow out behind him and the mustang. Crickets chirred to one another, seeking mates. He kicked into a stone and stopped to pick it up.

"Stone, what message have you for me?" Vibrating and silent in his hand, the stone warmed. He walked on. Many lodge lengths from camp, a small fire burned. As he came closer he slowed. Smells of Sage and Cedar met his nose, and he inhaled deep the Sacred scent.

"Come, boy-man." A robe fell from strong, well-rounded shoulders.

"Water Lily?"

"You expected someone else? Perhaps your Dove?"

"Great Elder, I woke from a dream and needed to walk, to think about the meaning. I expected no one."

"Always expect someone to be near, boy. It may save your life. Never walk and be in your head at the same time, unless you know how to do this." She waved him over. "Your dogs are welcome always at my fire. Spirit Eyes also, if he chooses to be near."

"How did you know I would be out here?"

"I did not. Your dream pulled me from my sleep. You did not know that I, too, slept away from the band when I felt the need, did you? Many nights I slipped past you and you did not stir. Your dogs do. But they are devoted to you and only watch as I move away."

Sister Wind sent a cooling breeze, and chill bumps rose on his body. He rubbed his arms.

"Perhaps, young one, you need to remember the air chills in darkness. You wear only a breechclout. Do you have need of my robe?"

"I would never take a robe away from an elder."

"Ahh, I understand. You think me weak." She threw the robe toward one of the dogs. "Let her rest on my robe. Her belly grows with pups."

"Water Lily, Great—"

"Hush, boy. Weakness only finds those who *allow* it to. Remain strong in mind, and the body will listen. If I had allowed my body to lead me, I would feel the cold, the ache in my bones. I instead tell my body that I am strong." She held up a fist. "I will not allow my body to control me. Remember this well, young one. Time comes when you will need to ignore your body, push beyond it. You will find the strength you need only if you ignore the protests."

Her wispy, grey-white hair hung loose and fell to her elbows. The neckline of her tunic dress, worn with age, laid uneven, paintings across it faded. Her eyes sparkled with the campfire's light. A hint of blue circled the edges of her eyes creating an illusion of wide doe eyes. She tossed a stick in the small fire with her gnarled hand. A spark came to life then died down.

"Always, elders will be needed, but one day young ones will turn away and not learn the lessons they will need to stay part of the Circle of Life. Youth is but a short burst and then is gone. So little time to learn, to teach the next children who will take their place. I have been gifted to see far into a future where a dark grey dust settles on every living thing. This dust is ignorance, thoughtlessness, hatred and greed."

"Thought less ness? What is this word?"

"It means, boy, no one will care about another unless they gain by it. They must be given a reason to care. That care will not be out of love. Love will no longer be the reason for being with someone." She shook her head. "Sad days come. They will come to us all. Only the strong in Spirit will find a path through the grey dust. Look up to the sky, to your stones, even the trees to ask for guidance. It will come to those who truly seek it for the good of the people. The whole of the people is important, not just one person, but everyone, boy. Always have the good of all living in your mind, and the Peoples will stay whole. When you feel them slip, pull them together. You, Singing Stone, have this Power. You may not be a Holy Man, but you are as important." She waved him away.

"Go, let this old woman sleep. And take your dog who now sleeps on my robe. I need to be alone."

***

"What comes our way?" The dogs spread out in front of him as he walked deeper into the grasslands. The cricket's chirring helped him put a beat with his steps. His kept the same rhythm. *What sounded like Water Lily's drum kept a balance.*

The stone warmed in his hand and coyotes howled. Far away, a night bird called out. The stone's heat intensified. "Stone, again, what have you to say?"

No words came. Chanting from the ancient ones pulsated in the distance. All but one of his dogs backed away. The waist high, brown female who carried pups stayed at his side and sniffed the air. She stepped ahead of him and faded into the darkness.

"Dog? Where did you go?" With silent feet, he moved forward. The stone burned hotter and he shook himself free from the heat. The chanting stopped. He bent and picked up the stone, holding it in his breechclout. The ancient ones showed themselves ahead. They faded in and out as they danced around a fire. The grass came alive with singing. The ancients glowed a bright, intense blue. The female dog sat with them, inside their Spirit Land. She turned toward her human companion.

From behind, Spirit Eyes nickered. The mustang nodded her head toward the blue glow. *'Human Brother, do you understand? The blue is the Spirit of all there is, and ever will be. You are part of it, part of their chant. Every living being has a sparkling strand from Grandmother's web that attaches them to you, you to them, to the ancients. Grandmother Spider weaves her web for us all.*

'Your Dove is blood related to these old ones. Since before you came to be part of your mother, the Spiral wove you and Dove together. Do not worry so. You will be mates when her moon time comes. There is a great need for your joining.'

Dog stepped his way. *'I am loyal to you, and will be always. My pups will one day carry their own young who will be there to watch over the mustangs. We, with your help and Dove's, will keep the four-legged Mustang Peoples safe. Go now. Your people need you...'*

"Need *me*?"

In the distance, coyotes howled.

Ruby Standing Deer

Chapter 23

Dove twisted around on Fire many times to find her father walking. He let Sandstone and her young one wander where they pleased. Soon they would camp, and he had walked since sunrise. The wolves had spread out and faded into the grass, except White Paws. The two of them shared too strong a bond to separate for long. Sadness crept across his face.

She turned to Gentle Wisdom, who rode next to her. "He must carry many burdens, Gentle Wisdom. Some days he is happy and silly. Some days he walks with his head down, his shoulders slumped, as if he carries the lodges of all our people on his back."

"These are the ways of a Holy Person, Dove." Her mustang was at least two spread hands smaller than Dove's animal, but he had much muscle, more than many bigger mustangs.

Gentle Wisdom patted Brown Dog's shoulder. "I wonder what burdens mustangs carry. I do know they feel our worry."

Dove stopped her animal. "Of course they do. They can feel our movements. They can feel if we are full of worry, or if we relax. Singing Stone told me this in a dream." She nodded toward Sandstone. "She could go be with her kind, but she chooses to stay near my father. He told me when he was a boy, Sandstone chose him and seldom followed her kind. Even as her young ones were ready to be on their own and followed the herd, she stayed with him.

"Some mustangs are very special, as is my Fire. She knows when I am tired and slows her walk. One sunrise she pushed her head into our lodge and woke everyone! She wanted me to wake up." She bent over Fire and laughed, and then her face grew serious. "In a dream, I watched Singing Stone wave at me and point toward the edge of the forest. He yelled at me, told me to bring Fire."

Gentle Wisdom's brows rose. "How is this so, young one? I have dreams, but not as you. Does Singing Stone speak to you that much? This is hard to understand. Even when I went on my Vision Quest, I only saw things. No one spoke to me. You have visions and dreams as a Holy Person does."

"I am not a Holy Person. I do not think I ever will be. My life will be different." She trotted away from Gentle Wisdom.

After a while, Dove slowed and jumped off her animal. Many of the band passed, leaving her behind.

How can I tell Father and Mother? I had thought maybe Father already understood. That the Spirits had spoken to him. She drifted farther away from the band. Abundant flowers in the swaying grass attracted her. Face down, eyes focused on the many colors, she tripped and fell.

***

'Child, this is not the usual way to come into the Spirit Land.'

"Who are you and why do I only see darkness?" Dove's head spun and her eyes could not focus. "I see nothing! Who *are* you? Where are my mother and father?"

'Here, Dove, reach out and take my hand. Do not fear me. You know who I am, even if you have never met me. Much depends on your future, little one.'

Blue swirls wrapped around her and the campfires in the sky burned brightly. "Blue Night Sky? Is this who you are?"

'Yes, girl. I know you well. I have watched you since you were welcomed into your band. Your father learned much from me and has taught you what he could. Sometimes you seek answers to questions when there are no answers. Even in the future, when you become wiser than you are now, there will be questions that have no answers.

'This does not mean to give up hope, but to become stronger. Never give up, never quit. You will be a strong woman one day. Your family yet to be born will have their own choices to make, just as you will very soon. You will not be alone. Even if you think you are, you are not.'

***

'Dove, wake up! It is I, Singing Stone. You must be all right. You come to me? You come to me! Wake, please. Please wake.'

She opened her eyes to darkness. "Mother? Father, where are you?

'Dove, you are safe. Do not fear. I watch over you and your father comes.'

"Singing Stone? Where are you?"

I am not alone. Never alone. Blue Night Sky says this.

Fire nuzzled her face and whinnied. The mustang circled her, pushed at her back, and called to her again. She pawed the ground beside her and snorted.

"What happened? Why did I fall? Where are you, Blue Night Sky?" She pushed herself up on unsteady feet, stood and leaned on Fire. The campfires in the sky blazed and sparkled. Sister Moon, past her full time, offered a little light. "Hold me up, Fire. Mother and Father must be near. They would not leave me. Someone had to have seen me leave and follow the flowers. Why did I do such a thing? Ah! My ankle hurts!" She pressed her foot down. "I must have twisted my leg as I fell. Not broken, only sore."

The mustang nudged her forward and would not stop pushing her though she could not clearly see where she stepped. Dove stopped. The mustang nickered and kept going.

"Wait! Please do not leave me. I am scared." She limped faster, guided by Fire's call to her. She bumped into her mustang's soft side and stumbled into something hard in front of her. She bit her lip, her heart pounding. Children were taught not to scream if they were alone unless they knew danger approached that they could not hide from.

What did I hit? It does not move. Hands in front of her, she hesitated then reached out to the dark shadow in front of her. "A big stone! I can climb on this stone to jump on your back! You are a smart mustang to stop beside it. Without you, I would have had to walk on my hurt ankle. How is this so? How did you know to do this?" With care, she scooted up on the stone and slid back to the ground.

"Ahh! Now I have scrapes on my knees." She limped around the stone, feeling her way. "The stone is lower here!" Grunting, Dove climbed up the lower side. Fire softly called to her. "I can feel you, girl." She reached out and grabbed the animal's neck hair.

The mustang did not move as Dove scooted across her back and sat upright. "Can you take me to the others?" She tapped Fire's sides. The mustang moved forward and stayed at a steady pace. The land was alive with crickets chirring in the grass. Somewhere, coyotes sang together and night birds cooed.

"How do you know where to go? I cannot see enough to know where we are, but I trust you."

The animal took small steps and nickered as she did. Every few spans she called out. At last, she nickered and stopped. Another mustang called back and Fire trotted toward the call.

"Dove! Where are you?"

"Father, I am here!"

Sandstone pulled up beside Fire. On the other side, Thunder crowded close. "Daughter, I am so sorry I did not know you had fallen back. After we set up camp and you did not come to our fire, I called and called for you." He reached across the small space between them and squeezed her. "You are all right? Your mother was on her way to find you. I told her to go back and be with Hawk Feather. She told me she knew you were hurt."

"I am fine. I hurt my ankle when I fell. All I remember is waking and finding myself alone... but not alone. Blue Night Sky was with me, and Singing Stone called out to me! Is he here? Blue Night Sky told me I would be a strong woman one day and she said I might think I am alone sometimes but will not be."

"Daughter, Singing Stone is not here. His mind must have found you. Come, camp is not far. On the way to camp, perhaps you might wish to speak about Blue Night Sky?"

He reached out to Fire and patted her neck. "Thank you, mustang. You are truly a Sacred animal. Our lives became rich when your kind appeared. Thank you for helping my daughter. Our lives would never be the same without the Sacred Guidance from your Mustang People."

He sat up and nodded toward Thunder. "Thunder must have turned her herd. I wonder at this. Perhaps she knew we were nearby and came looking for us. As soon as she saw Gentle Wisdom and Sparkling Star, she raced through camp to nuzzle Sparkling Star, excited to see her. These mustangs. I will wonder about them always. Their loyalty to us is something I do not understand."

Dove gasped and pointed up at the campfires in the sky. "Father, a campfire just fell!"

Head up, he laughed. "Someone will be born soon, maybe even to our people. I never thought about you not seeing one fall in the forest. The trees hid them. Do not worry so. It only means one of the people is ready to be welcomed into a band again. Some choose to come back when they are needed.

"Perhaps even one never born, but who has been waiting comes. We never die, girl. Only our bodies go back to the Mother. Our Spirits always remain."

"Even animals?"

"Yes, even animals. Each time one returns, they bring back knowledge their Peoples need, be it a human, animal or even a plant. Perhaps they come back to tell their Peoples' stories.

"Our people do not fear death. To die is to join the cycle of life and death and life again. I am sure it is the same way for all beings, be they two-legged, four-legged, or winged ones, even those with no legs, such as snakes or the many-legged who race across the ground. Trees have messages to share with other trees." He shrugged. "Who knows what they share when they come back. The Circle of Life. Every living being has their own cycle. Their own reason for being."

"As do we, Father. As do we."

Chapter 24

"Singing Stone, why did you sleep up on that big stone instead of on the ground or in your lodge? And why do you have a smile that spreads across your face so wide any big bug could find its way in?" River Song raised her hand to her brows and stared up at him.

"Mother, I helped Dove! She fell and I watched over her until she woke. Her mustang is a smart one! She led her to a stone, and she climbed up it and got on her back. Her ankle hurts, but she is safe. Her father found her. I led him toward her by calling his name. They come our way!" He stood and slid down the slick grey-brown stone.

"Slow down and breathe. What do you mean *they* come?" She handed him some fresh cooked meat. "An elder said to give this to you in thanks for giving him a mustang. He was about to sit and end his journey because he could walk no more. His woman is happy he did not and made you something special. You are loved by more people than you know."

He lowered his head. "I put my feelings ahead of everyone else's. Grandmother came with me and now I understand why. I may be called a man, but I have much to learn before I am truly one. My face is red because of my shame."

"You have learned something you will never forget. The band comes first, before your own feelings. You showed the good in you by helping the elders, and they will not forget. You honor our new people."

"I am of the Big Sky Mustang People." He stretched and pulled his shoulders back. "Mother!" He reached out and hugged her. "Dove comes! Dove comes with her family and many people. Mustangs, they have mustangs to make our herd strong!" He pulled back. "I should not have hugged you in front of people. A man would have known better than to hug his mother."

"They show their pride in you, little one. I mean, my son." She brushed away a stray hair from his face. "We must go see Water Lily and tell her of what you saw. How many come?"

He fell in step beside her. "Many come. Maybe her whole band! Mother, I can tell her mind is strong. I hope she finds me as worthy as I do her. What if she does not? Maybe she will not want me. What do I do if she turns away?"

Laughter spilled from her lips. "Slow down. Dove will find you worthy, silly one. How could she not? You are my son. I am happy to see you have only your own hair now!" She walked around him and nodded when she faced him again. "This is better. Why not take the mustang's hair and make it so if fits around your waist?"

"Yes, I will do that and make one for Dove as a gift. I can make another binding rope as well." He turned toward the herd. "There is much color to choose from for it."

"You are young yet. Be young first. You have much time before you take a mate! Your Dove is still very young also. You two have connected in a way I never knew possible. Allow yourselves to grow, to know each other. You have many cycles of seasons before you are mates!"

"That is too long, Mother. I cannot wait so long. I love her now."

She stopped and faced him, her voice gentle. "Give your love time to grow. Learn who she is, who she may become. Allow her to learn these things for herself as well. Slow down. Father Sun will wake many times. Many, many times before you truly know each other.

"Falcon and I learn new things every day." She coughed and cleared her throat. "I... ah have not told anyone yet, not even Mother."

The grin on her face said many words that Singing Stone did not need to hear. "A baby! You have a baby in your belly. I saw your belly growing a little. I thought you were getting fat." His words too loud, everyone nearby chuckled, but with quick glances at each other, the people turned away. Her man should hear these words first. The people moved away and acted as if they heard nothing.

"Fat! You mouth is as big as Elk when he calls for mates. My belly is just now showing. I am almost five moons and need to go tell my man before the whole band knows! And you need to go and speak to Water Lily."

"Mother, you said we would—" His mother hurried toward her lodge and left him to grin after her. *I love you so much, Mother. I hope Dove is as you.*

My mouth is big. "Ha!" He raced to where Water Lily sat sunning herself. She held a small drum and gently patted it. Her medicine drum made of wood and animal skins as all were, called upon the help of the spirits of the tree and the animal's hide used to make the drum.

Maybe I should leave her alone. Stop, silly, you do not approach a Holy Woman like this. He ran back to his lodge and pulled out tobacco a trader had come with two moons ago. Tobacco represented the ebb and flow of life. When smoked, Eagle carried the prayer to Creator. Very Sacred. He shuffled toward her.

Water Lily turned from her drum and called him over. Her smile lit up as he took small steps toward her. *Dark sparkles from her eyes make her still look full of fire. Perhaps age has nothing to do with what a person feels inside.*

"No, age has very little to do with how the heart feels. The body may slow us elders, but not how we feel. Inside, I am just as full of youth as you. Come, boy. Sit. Do not look as if I will eat you. I am not so hungry. You are safe. Besides, I like my children fat." Her many paths through life gathered on her face as she smiled. Her two lower front teeth showed. She patted his bare leg with a well-weathered hand. One long, thin, white braid fell across her shoulder to the middle of her waist.

"Your sweet Dove will enjoy looking at your well-formed body. You are tight with muscles. Your face is good to look at and will be more so as you grow older. Most of all, you have a strong Energy around you, one I am sure she will feel. Who you are will always be more important than how good you are to look at. The outside is only a faint reflection of who you are inside. A person who is good to look at may not always be so inside. Because true beauty is found inside a person, we must not judge anyone by what they look like... ever."

She leaned closer. "If I were young again, your Dove would have competition. Ha! I made your face red. We elders can get away with more than you younger ones. We can speak our minds and are still respected." She sat with her bare feet flat on the ground.

"The dirt and grass feel so nice. It is good for your feet to touch our Mother, for you to lie without your clothes on and press your body against our Mother. The dirt is soothing. It cleanses, heals, and gives you strength. You will see many of us elders walk with our feet bared." She pointed to her head. "We old ones are smart." As she put her drum aside, she ran her hand across the surface and she whispered to it as if it was truly alive.

"We communicate our emotions, worries, pains, and sometimes thoughts we are not aware of as we touch the ground. Even as they spill from our minds, she comforts us. I try to teach this to everyone and say it often to the same people so they will not forget. You, too, need to do this. Both experience it and speak about it. Pass on wisdom always, even if you think someone is not listening. Somewhere in their minds, they hear it."

"Holy Woman, I bring you tobacco. I wish to honor you and speak of—"

"Of your Dove, who comes. I thank you for the tobacco, young one." She took it and placed it in a pouch around her neck. "I will enjoy this later. Perhaps you will join me? You and I need to walk right now. There are things you need to know before we meet up with you future mate."

Ruby Standing Deer

Chapter 25

Water Lily led the way across the grasses, her hands wrapped around a pack she carried filled with things Singing Stone could only guess at. Her walk held no limp, no stressed movements. Power followed her. Taut muscles showed on her legs and arms. A woman who worked hard all her life, she stood straight, not one part of her body bent with age.

"I feel your eyes on me, boy." She stopped and turned with a wide grin. Her eyes held mischief. "Perhaps you find me good to look at? Do you desire me as your mate, hmm? I am a good cook, very good. I would make you fat."

He stumbled over a stone and barely caught himself before his knees met the ground. "I... I um... find you good to look at, Holy Woman." He swallowed much air and choked.

"Ha! You must catch your air before I have to drag back a young hunter who our band would sorely miss. I would have to tell them he choked on his words.

"Our elders appreciate the meat you always bring to them after a good hunt! I have grown used to seeing your smiling face as you go to tend to the mustangs. I would have no one as you to watch as you walk, jump on the mustangs. I see the animals, as very much part of who you are, ever will be. Perhaps you would like me to be part of that life?"

Does she joke, or does she really desire me? His mouth found no words and curved inward. He still tried not to choke. "I am honored by your attention, Holy—"

"Call me Water Lily. I hear Holy Woman enough. I desire someone to be my friend and not be afraid to speak to me as a real friend would. Ever since I was young and the band learned I was a dreamer, they treated me different. No longer did girls come to play with me, and boys! All they did was stare my way. Not one would look my way anymore. I had a lonely childhood. My only human companionship was my mother and father. They loved and treated me well.

"Deer followed me as I walked alone, and I would leave the band for days to follow herds of their kind. I would run with them just to feel true freedom. I even sat with their newborns when the mothers left to feed. Deer have much responsibility. So much that at times they forget to care for themselves. Humans think they run out of fear when hunted. Not so. They run to warn others, even stop to stomp their feet to say "warning." To this day, I follow them. They have taught me much, as your mustangs do you.

"Tell me, Young Mustang Man, does your Dove love the mustangs as you do? Does she hear the calling to devote her life to them as you? Your mate will be part of you always, and it is better if you and she share the same needs, desires."

"Dove rides a female who has much Power. When she was young, this female chose her. I saw—" Singing Stone leaned forward, picked up a stone, and tossed it in his hands.

Water Lily put her hand out and stopped him from walking any further." Boy, I know some of what you have seen and felt. I, too, have watched her in my dreams. I would not have dreamed of her if she did not have something the Spirits desired."

She faced him and motioned for him to sit on the grass. "I have felt your emotions and hers also. I have said nothing, worried I might scare you, but things change and now I must speak.

"Dove will show her devotion to you, to the animals. To her wolves."

"Wolves? Wait. What wolves? I have seen one large wolf with her and I forgot about him. Will he not harm the mustangs?"

"Hush. I speak. Her wolves are not like other wolves that we have seen. These are special. One is her father's living Spirit Guide that she, too, shares. The mustangs will shy away at first. But I know things you do not.

"She does not yet understand this about the wolves being part of her, so say nothing." She stared long into his eyes before he looked away.

"Dove will change you much, boy. And yes, you her also. Her first love will be the mustangs. You will work hard to be part of her life. She does *love* you in her own way and comes to find you with part of her band. A dream has shown her an enemy follows us."

"Enemy follows? The painted arrow on the leather! We must go—"

"Boy, you are not to interrupt me, or I will get up and leave." Her brows pinched together as she glared at him with tight lips. "Better, be still and listen well. The Circle moves, and you and Dove are moving with it. Sit back down. Do not stand there with your mouth open. Your tongue could fall out, or maybe your voice maker. How would you talk to Dove?

"Sit. Remember, I wish your friendship, to help guide you. You have not been on your walk, have you? I know you started one, but did not finish. This day will be the beginning of your walk. You need to seek a vision.

"You will go from here. I will be near." She handed him a half-full water bladder. "Do not drink until you have had your vision. Understand?"

He nodded. "Does my mother know I am to do this? She will worry herself crazy. Perhaps I should go tell her."

"The band saw us walk away. They know the flaps to my lodge are tied. Your dogs stay with your grandmother. They know. Now go. Walk until your legs tire too much to keep going. There you will search for stones. The ones who call out to you. Put them in a circle and sit in the middle.

"I know this is a bit different than the way your people did it. They just walked and sat where their minds led them. The stones will protect you as long as you do not leave the Circle of Stones." She pulled out a thin robe that took up most of her pack and handed it to him. "Sit on this, or wrap it around your shoulders. Here is a bundle of mixed Sage, Cedar, and a striped grass called Spirit Grass, or Holy Grass. It is also known as the Hair of our Mother. A trader always makes sure to bring me some of the Grass. It smells sweet as wild flowers do when you burn it. It will bring you healing, peace, and put your mind as ease."

"I am honored that you give me this Hair of our Mother. You say you will be near. How can you keep up with me?"

"Ha! I have left the band behind many times when we moved. Do not worry about this old woman! Now go." She waved him away and began to sort through her pack.

***

I did as Water Lily said and sit here thirsty and hungry with no vision. How long has it been? I have watched Father Sun wake again and again, so maybe three days? Singing Stone fidgeted. The water bladder sat too close, too tempting. He leaned over and tossed it away from him.

I should have climbed all the way to the top of this hill! Perhaps then my vision would have come. Or maybe I should have gone on my walk as our old people have always done. I am tired, thirsty, and hungry! He leaned over and clutched his belly.

Dizziness overtook him as he sat back up, and swirls of blues, reds and purples shifted back and forth before him. The stones he chose to sit within hummed as sparks of energy shot from them. Lightning spread its fingers across the sky as thunder bellowed. Rain pelted him. Somewhere, growling mixed in with the sounds. The canyons shone in their orange-red brilliance. Many mustangs raced along the edge of the canyons, so many that he could not see the end of the herd. *We are in the grasslands. You can I see the canyons? I do miss them. They are in my Soul.*

A white mustang with black specks in his neck hair and tail broke away from the herd, reared outside the stone circle, and ran around it, whinnying as he did. The animal stopped and snorted. He reared high and called out loudly. Purple waves followed the animal. Terrified, he grabbed at the edges of the robe Water Lily gave him. *Did I anger this mustang? Never have I heard such a sound.*

The mustang pulled back, turned, and ran to join the disappearing herd into the canyons.

Grey Wolf appeared, tongue hanging to one side of his mouth as he panted. Wolf's nose felt warm on Singing Stone's chilled skin as the animal moved into the circle. Wolf sparkled for a brief span, then his body flowed into many small strands that went into the stones. Stones shot their Energy into him. Singing Stone's body absorbed their power and vibrated unlike anything he had ever known. Power.

He followed sunrise and sunset with his eyes. So fast! Nothing made sense! *How could it be sunrise and sunset at the same time?*

A brilliant blue took the place of Father Sun's warm yellow. The ancients danced around the circle. One shook a rattle close to his face, yet none entered his circle. One dropped her robe, exposing her face and body. *Dove, she looked like Dove!* Just as fast, she was gone.

The blue turned to Father Sun's yellow. Clouds cleared. Before him, a Doe and her three young ones stood. They showed no fear as they made their way across the grass.

"My sister, Deer, greets you."

Still feeling the stones vibrating within, he spun around. A beautiful young woman stood behind him. Her face, body changed and she became Water Lily, the elder Holy Woman.

"Water Lily? Is my Vision Quest finished? Where did you come from? Did you see—"

"No, I only saw Deer. You must speak of the rest to me." She sat just outside the circle and waited.

Singing Stone told her all he saw and she nodded. "Your name will still be Singing Stone, but also you have gained a Power. Wolf. Guardian, protector, teacher. He has a strong sense of family, one who protects the pack or band. Wolf always shares what he learns with others. Show Wolf no fear and he will become your protector.

"White Mustang is a leader. Power comes from him. He is also a teacher. You must always stop and listen to what the mustangs have to say. They may not always speak in words to your mind as does Spirit Eyes, but you will understand their emotions. Never doubt them. Never. Of all the animals I have encountered in my life, the mustang has brought us the most. Not only is life better, but they have something inside them that teaches us who we are.

"They may walk up to a person, sniff them, and even allow them to touch their bodies, but if someone they do not trust tries to jump on them, they will fight, not allow them on. We see mustangs do this when they have never had a human on them before, but this is different. They can smell a human, know if they mean harm. Once I watched a man, a trader, approach a young woman and reach for her. The mustang she had been riding came from behind him and bit his shoulder so deep he bled. The people chased away the trader.

"His black spots speak of warnings. You will encounter dangers in your life and must be ready for them. Always you must be ready. Danger comes from places we do not always expect. Listen well, boy. The lives of our people, the lives of the mustangs are mingled, our Souls intertwined. To keep the people united, the Mustang People must be a part of them. Without them, we become nothing. And nothing fades away. *Always* speak this part to those who will listen. There will be those who do not wish to hear your words, but tell them anyway.

"Power also comes from your stones. One day, young one, you will lead, and others in Council will listen to you. Dove will be at your side, but you already knew this.

"The canyons will always be your home. You may travel, but you will return to the canyons always."

"But Dove comes from the Tall Trees."

"You are to be a teacher, young one. I have said my words." Water Lily stood with ease and walked toward the band, her feet bare.

Singing Stone stood and stretched. He gathered the stones he wished to take with him. His pack became too heavy to lift. "I knew this would happen, yet I took the stones that I felt connected to anyway. Now I must leave many of you behind."

He glanced around for a place to put them. Not finding one, he placed them close together in the circle that had kept him safe these past sunrises. *One day I will be back, maybe even use the same place for another Vision Quest.* "This is good. Now I will place stones in small circles when my pack becomes too heavy. I will know where they came from, but I wonder what others will think when they see them?"

He walked to the edge of the bluff. "I must remember this place. What is this I see? Do I see humpbacks far in the distance? In a few days, if they continue to follow, we will have much meat!" He climbed higher to the top of the rise. "From up here I can see how many come.

"Oh, Sweet Mother. They are not humpbacks grazing." He clutched his pack. "It is the band that attacked us before. They could be wishing revenge for the wounded warrior, or perhaps it only is an excuse to hunt us?"

Chapter 26

Sparkling Star offered her hand to Thunder. The animal's rich dun color was warm to the touch. The female mustang stepped closer and allowed Sparkling Star to jump on her. "You may be lead mare, but you are also my friend." She leaned forward and scratched her neck.

Sparkling Star's red-brown hair gleamed in the breaking sunrise. It had grown well below her waist. She wore it loose with several small braids at the sides. The once timid woman carried scars on her wrists from ropes, but her heart no longer carried any memories to scar her mind. Her sons carried only a small bit of her red hair, and only when Father Sun shined down on their heads.

Would they have face hair? The names she gave them before they lived in the forest had changed. They were still child names and would change again after their Vision Quests. Her first born, Quiet As Falling Leaves, could sneak up on anyone, even Wanderer. His brother, second born that day, carried the name Finds Reason To Laugh. Both born together, but so different. Still, they stayed beside her and each other in all situations.

"Star, Thunder has a strong will. You must be careful." Gentle Wisdom Who Rides A Flying Mustang rushed forward on Brown Dog. "I would wither away, be no more if I lost you! Thunder has run loose these past moons and... and may not--"

"My Sweet Wisdom, you have mustang Power. If Thunder was going to harm me, you would know. She has been gentle with me for many cycles of seasons. Even when she had young ones, she allowed me near." She continued scratching Thunder all over her back and sides. "I have no fear of her. I am very happy we caught up to them, or is it they who slowed down a few sunrises ago when we spotted them? Matters not. Dove says they lead us, but to where? Dove is so young. How can she know these things?"

"She is her father's daughter. I always thought Shining Light's sister, Soft Breeze, would also carry Power, but who is to say what the Spirits decide? My brother, Knows Both Sides, will one day be a great Counselor. This I know in my heart. The Power of Mustang races through my blood, allows me see things yet to be. My visions are misty but clear enough for me.

"I know the people who followed us will have a great importance... as will you, our sons, and me. I will never be a Holy Woman, but I have many blessings."

"Wisdom, when you smile and sit tall, I know I am safe. Even if your mustang is the smallest of all our animals!" She laughed and raced away.

"You ride jerked meat! I hope she runs off with you and you have to walk her back just like she did every time Shining Light tried to ride her!"

***

Brown Dog could not outrun even the older mustangs, but Gentle Wisdom loved him. Once, many seasons ago, she had spotted a small patch of flowers she had never seen before and jumped off him to pick one. Bright Sun Flower would know what the flower was. As she bent to pick the flower, behind her a rattling sounded, warning her not to move. She froze. She had slowly pulled out her knife in hopes of being faster than the snake. This could have been her last day living on the Mother.

A loud squeal from Brown Dog and hooves stomping the ground did not allow her anytime to think. She spun around. Brown Dog still stomped on the dead snake. He mashed the creature into tiny, unrecognizable pieces.

She would never give up her companion, even if another band out on the grasslands came in to visit hoping to trade for mustangs, as several had already done. One man had eyed Brown Dog and wanted him for his small son. He offered her a very well-made pair of footwear for him. She had shaken her head and the man, frustrated, stomped off.

After Father Sun went to sleep, the man had slinked back into camp and roped the mustang. Brown Dog turned around and bit him hard on his arm. His surprised scream woke the camp. The man was so angry that he demanded the animal. He backed down when Gentle Wisdom came at him screaming, knife in hand. *The thief is lucky Shining Light stopped me, or the man's woman and son would still be grieving their lost man.*

What he did was not uncommon. To take a mustang while a band slept showed bravery. Much honor would have come his way from his own band.

Gentle Wisdom started sleeping near her mustang. The first sunset, Sparkling Star and their sons made fun of her. The next night, everyone agreed the younger men would stand guard over the herd for the rest of journey.

Dove pulled her out of her thoughts as the girl's mustang danced around Brown Dog. "Many humpbacks come our way! Most of the men have already left. I thought you might want to go. We will not hunger for a long time.

"Will you teach me how to tan a hide the way you do? You and Sparkling Star are the best in our band, and I wish to be taught by the best. I already know how to skin and tan, but not your way." She lowered her head. "I also wish to tell you of a dream I had about Singing Stone."

"You wish to tell me and not your mother or father?"

"Mothers and fathers do not always understand. This is about love."

"Dove, your parents know much about love."

"But they are my parents. You are my cousin, also my closest friend."

"Perhaps they have enough hunters. We should sit under these nice trees and talk."

Trees and dense shrubs grew where water pooled. Gentle Wisdom grabbed a dead branch and swooshed it along the ground. "Never know where a snake might be. Always remember this. It may one day save your life." She undid the robe that Brown Dog carried. The animal lay down and rolled on the ground. The day had been long and warm.

"Tell me of your dream." Gentle Wisdom leaned back on a tree and rubbed her back against the rough bark. "Ahh, feels so good. Like Brown Dog, I have places I cannot reach."

Dove patted Fire's rump and sent her trotting. She sat by Gentle Wisdom and cleared her throat. She stared at the people who kept moving past where they sat, as if waiting for them to be alone.

"I saw myself with four children, and Singing Stone smiled at me. He spoke of how much our band had grown and how we needed to split into two bands so the land could heal. He waved his arm toward a large herd of mustangs and said I made this possible. He told me to help him decide which mustangs our band would take when we split.

"I felt sad because the people were going to split and our oldest daughter had chosen a man who would leave with the other band.

"Wisdom, does love mean pain in your heart? If it does, I am not so sure I wish this dream to be of my future." She slapped at her wet cheeks.

Gentle Wisdom stared past Dove, unblinking. "Yes, it can mean pain. For some reason, pain is part of love." She gripped Dove's arm. "Do not let love pass you without allowing it to become part of you. Love, to me, is the most wonderful feeling there is.

"Learn about him as he learns about you. You are so young, little one. You have much time. Let your love grow slow and it will last longer than a fast burning desire." She stood and smiled. "I know the deepest love there is with a mate: friendship."

Ruby Standing Deer

Chapter 27

Days grew warmer as the band traveled deeper into the grasslands. Sky colors changed to a familiar turquoise for Bright Sun Flower. Hawk Soaring, who rode next to her, leaned over and pressed his hand on hers. Home. They were going home.

She sat tall and breathed in the air. "I wish to never leave the canyons again. We have lived many seasons past our time, man of mine. We have seen and done much. Now, I wish to go home. Someday, we will sit at a campfire in the sky with people we both miss. I told our daughter that it was time for us to be the elders we were meant to be. To grow old so we could go home to our family who have crossed over." No sadness crossed her face when she turned to look at her loving man.

"Makes Baskets showed her sadness, but understood. She was happy we left with Shining Light and spoke of coming to see us, maybe staying if Flying Raven could teach someone to take his place."

"You and I, woman, have shared the same thoughts for many seasons. I am happy to see the color of the sky change to that of sky beads. We will miss our daughter, our grandchildren, and her man, but they can come see us if they choose."

Hawk Soaring's smile warmed her. "I know we may not step into the forest again. I feel in my heart this could be a good thing. We face not death, but new life. I had a dream just this last sunset. My aunt smiled at me and opened her arms wide. Beside her stood my mother."

He leaned back on his mustang and stared up at the changing sky. "We do the right thing. I, too, look to the campfires in the sky with joy. My father will be happy to see me so we can have long talks as we did when I was a boy.

"Shining Light is in a hurry to help his little daughter's friend. I am not sure how he will feel when we tell him of our decision. Much will change for many of us. Others who went to the forest long ago now speak the same words about missing the canyons. He must hear their talk of this at sunset as we settle in and camp."

Bright Sun Flower raised her hand to shade her eyes and searched for her grandson. "I have watched him pass by fires, stop for a brief span at each one as the people relax and settle in. He remains silent most times and walks away, his head lowered. He rides away from the band and stays on the edges with the wolves, and he speaks to White Paws often. Heh, perhaps even that wolf misses the canyons."

Knows Both Sides rode up to them. Strands of colorful shells covered his long dress. Leggings with fringe at the ankles peeked from under the dress. The elk teeth woven in his long, shiny hair bounced. The beauty of a Two-Spirit shined in his eyes. "I hear your words. Know I am to live in the canyons also. As a boy, I dreamed about the canyons. I knew then I would one day see them.

"Mother held tight to me when I spoke of not returning. I told her that my life does not belong to me, but to others who will seek advice from me. Her sad eyes hurt me deep inside, but she told me she understood. She had too many young ones to worry over and chose to stay.

"Father only looked on and smiled. He gave me the shells I wear and told me to think of him often. He then turned away and walked into the forest alone. I will find a way to reach my parents. Perhaps I will dream my way to them." He cleared his throat and sucked his lips in.

"I have much to learn before I can offer this advice. A Two-Spirit must know much, experience much, and live much to be able to guide others." He waved his arms in a half circle, looking skyward. His hair fell back over his broad shoulders.

"Life will be very different away from the forest. Dangers are out here that we never had to worry about within the forest. I listened to the stories my parents told, talked to Wanderer, and others who have lived what I have not. My Spirit Guide tells me this is to be my life. I am happy to know I will be part of so much more than I was in the forest." His smile showed the tight skin of youth and his eyes sparkled in excitement.

"I would be proud to call you grandmother and grandfather. Mine, I never knew. My mother told me stories, but I cannot live them, so I wish to live these coming seasons as your grandchild."

Hawk Soaring took his sky beads off and handed them to Knows Both Sides. "Your mother is my niece, so we are blood related, as you know. Even if we were not, many young ones call us grandfather and grandmother, as it should be because we are older. If you wish, you are welcome to live with us. We will teach you what we know, what others passed onto us."

"Then I will be a wise person." He put the sky beads around his neck and handed Hawk Soaring a quilled knife sheath designed with flowers. It held an obsidian blade sharpened to perfection. "Honor for honor." He clucked to his mustang and raced away.

Bright Sun Flower nodded his way. "He carries much beauty, inside and out. Woman and man combined, balanced so well. If only we all had such an understanding."

Wanderer turned and trotted back to them. His near-white mustang bobbed her head and pranced until he reached out to calm her. "I gave my mustang's first son back to Falling Rainbow and Night Hunter. I feel sorrow that they chose to stay in the forest. They were as grandchildren to me. Perhaps I will go back as they are my only family. Knows Both Sides will be needed in the canyons. I will not."

"You do not speak true words, old friend. Wherever you go, you are needed. Otherwise, you would not go to these places." Bright Sun Flower's lowered brows always worked well for her, even toward the Great Holy Man.

He fell in beside her. A mouse peered out from inside his hair. "You remind me of a story once told to me by a child, one that made much sense to me. This little girl, about ten winters old, was part of a band I spent a winter with. She used to peek around trees at me, and if I pretended not to see her, she would come closer. One day, she finally became courageous and sat next to me as I made an arrow point. She asked me if I had plans to stay with her people. I shook my head. 'I am as a blowing wind, I need freedom to wander,' I told her.

"She giggled and spoke words of wisdom to me. 'You are not free. You only think you are. The Spirits, Creator, will decide where you will go next. We think we decide on our own where we will go, what we will do, but we do not. You go where you are meant to go.'

"She jumped up and ran away." He patted Bright Sun Flower's leg. "And now as an adult, you tell me almost the same words you did back then." He tapped his mustang and trotted away.

"What is this you say? Wanderer!" She watched him tap his mustang into a run.

Ruby Standing Deer

Chapter 28

Singing Stone yelled as he ran. He stumbled over clods of dirt and nearly twisted his ankle twice. "Water Lily, where did you go? Where is the camp?"

Dark spots marked where campfires had been in the yellowing grass. One lodge stood alone in the camp. Spirit Eyes trotted up to him along with four other mustangs, but no one came from the lodge. "Where is everyone?" No one answered as he whirled about searching.

The lodge's flap moved in the breeze. No other sound came from within. Dogs barked, and he turned toward the sound. His grandmother, mother and father came into sight. Four Arrows followed close behind them. Their animals kicked up dust as they raced forward. Seven dogs ran behind.

Four Arrows trotted up. "Good, you are back. We need to catch up to the band. I hope your Vision Quest was good."

"Where is Water Lily? I was just with her."

"Water Lily?" Four Arrows cocked his head. "She left with the band five sunrises ago."

River Song jumped down and ran to him, but stopped short of hugging him. He was a man, not a child. "We stayed behind and waited for you to return. We have just returned from a successful hunt." She held up five ground birds. "We need to eat quickly and pack so we can catch up to the band.

"Water Lily showed no fear in her eyes when she told us you were safe and to let you be."

Singing Stone scratched his head. "I spoke to Water Lily only a short span ago. How can she be with the band?"

His eyes widened. "Mother, I saw what I thought to be humpbacks, but they were not! They may be from the Likes To Fight people. We must not stay."

"Son, the band sent young men to find out before most of the warriors took the elders, women and children away from here. We waited for you, and now we wait for them to return. Catch your air and do not worry so. We will know soon who follows, if they do. Sit. Your grandmother and I will cook you a good meal. Was your Vision Quest a good one?"

"Yes." He would say no more about it. No one shared such a Sacred Happening, except with a Holy Person. "Why did no one come get me? We could have left with the band."

"Water Lily did not wish it. We are safe, or she would have not taken you on a Vision Quest. Trust a Holy Person always. They will not guide you the wrong way."

Several young warriors stirred up the midseason dust as they trotted toward the lodge. Falcon Storm reached for his bow. "They bring mustangs!"

The young men stopped before the lodge and jumped off their own animals. The youngest herded the new animals toward a small stream while another of the young men walked toward Falcon Storm. "It is the Likes To Fight. We counted eleven men. They wandered in wide circles searching the ground. One leads them. When they camped and the dark took the land, they slept foolishly. No one watched over their camp and we took their mustangs. They heard nothing!" He turned and waved his hands toward the new animals.

"Three got away. It does not matter. They will need those mustangs to go back to their main camp before they can again hunt us, if that is what they do. We could not understand their words. Two of our warriors stayed to watch them. They do not wish for us to wait. They will catch up."

Listens To Wind joined the others and eyed the young warrior. "Do not think you have stopped them. If they want us, they will still come. You have slowed them down, and this is good." She motioned them to the fire where food waited. "When a hungry animal stalks a deer, he does not leave until he has his meal."

Singing Stone held his meat in one hand and touched the pack on his back. "Grandmother, the stones. They still sing to me. When they no longer sing, I will warn you. It is when they vibrate that it is time to pay heed."

"Still, Grandson, it is better to be with the band. Eat. Sleep this night and we will leave at sunrise."

***

Listens To Wind followed her grandson as he slipped out of his robe. Neither liked sleeping inside a lodge unless the air cooled, so they offered it to the young men. River Song and Falcon Storm stood guard this night high on a bluff that overlooked their camp.

Singing Stone turned as Listens To Wind caught up to him. "Nice to see my grandson's own hair did not suffer the change." She nodded toward the mustang hair that swung at his waist.

He reached up and touched his hair. "I did this to please you. Dove would not have minded."

"For the first time that you meet her, it will be better if she sees you as all human. A girl, or woman, always remembers the first look. When you two are old, she will speak of her first memory of you, what you looked like. Make that memory a good one.

"I still see my man as a young boy who ran from angry small winged ones as he raced away carrying a chunk of their sweet home with him. He yelled as some of them caught up to him. Yelled good, too. He had red welts all over his back, chest and legs! Heh. That is still how I see him. By the time he came into camp, the dogs were all over him, licking his hands. He had nothing to show for what he did other than many red welts. He was twelve winters old, and I was sixteen winters—"

"Grandmother, you never told me you were older! Ha! And now you and Four Arrows—"

She placed a hand across his mouth and glanced back at camp. "Your mouth carries as far as thunder as it rumbles on and on! I am not... not anything to Four Arrows. He is too—"

Four Arrows appeared out to the darkness. "Young? You call me too young, yet I see you as the beautiful colors of the rainbow as it crosses the sky after a rain."

Listens To Wind twirled around to see if anyone in camp stirred. "Four Arrows! Do you follow us?"

"Yes, I do. How do we not know a hungry animal is not hunting nearby? I would not allow my future woman to be eaten—"

"I am not your future woman, young pup." She turned to her grandson, but he had already vanished from her side.

Four Arrows slid closer to her. "We do not need to pretend anymore. I care much for you. I know you watch me. To me, as to many others, age means nothing to two people who have walked into the Soul of another as we have." He wrapped his arm around hers.

She twisted to be free for a short span and stopped. "I... why do you wish an old woman as mate? Will you not miss the giggles of young girls as they whisper among themselves about how they wish for you?"

"I would miss your laughter after a long day as you settle in next to the night campfire. I would miss your sparkling eyes when your face fills with joy from simple things. I watched you one sunrise as a new mustang stood for the first time. It was as if you had seen it for the first time. You laughed as a girl, not the old woman you say you are.

"A yellow and black baby bird fell from his nest. You climbed the tree to put him back! You do not think I see these things, but I do. An old woman could not have climbed that tree. You even freed a fish from a tangle of small twigs in a stream we passed. Another would have made a meal out of him."

She pulled away. "I was not hungry that day. And the baby bird, his mother may not have found him. I only helped to save the next generation of their kind."

He reached out and pulled her close again. "You are a strong woman with a soft heart. I love this about you. When we reach camp, I am going to ask Water Lily to bind us."

"Ask me first. I am not a girl to—"

"You *are not* an old woman, either."

She stopped and turned to face him. "I must think on your words. I still bleed. We could have a child maybe."

"Listens To Wind... Wind, my woman... I do not wish children from you. I wish only your love." He grabbed both her hands and tapped his head against hers. "I will be good to you, always and forever. Please, do not say no."

Chapter 29

"When a seed falls to the ground and becomes a big plant, that plant will grow to make more seeds, which make new plants." Knows Both Sides sat next to Dove when the band stopped to eat. He pointed at a single flower peering out of a bud. "The ones next to it have made their seeds already. They have set free their young ones, and now they will find their way, grow into more flowers."

Dove handed him part of the rabbit she ate and licked her fingers. She leaned back against an old log and relaxed. The breeze felt wonderful, and many people rested in the welcome shade of the trees. Water splashed as children played in the cool stream. The cloudless, hot day made it hard to want to leave. Many spoke of setting up camp. Some unpacked and did just that. They would go no farther this day. Smells of cooking filled the air, as did the laughter of children and barking dogs. Wolf pups joined in the excitement.

"I do not understand what you say. You speak as Wanderer does." She moved away from the log, stretched out on the grass, and put her arms behind her head. Her tunic dress showed off her mother's painting of a rainbow and Dove's yellow and orange quilling of Father Sun. Her footwear was plain like everyone else's when they traveled.

Knows Both Sides stretched out next to her and turned her way. His face always made her smile. He had a glow about him that spread to anyone near him. His tunic had the finest quillwork of anyone's. Detailed flowers grew along the top and across both shoulders of his tunic dress. Tiny shells made up the centers of the colorful flowers. Below them in several rows hung small flint beads, each one rounded with a hole worked into it. His necklace of sky beads added to the artful beauty.

"What I mean is that *you* are as the seed. You grow and learn. What you learn you will pass onto others, and those seeds will grow, and more seeds will be planted. It will never end as long as seeds grow. Good things come from the right seeds."

"Why do you tell me this?"

He shrugged and stood. "I have no real reason. When I saw you, the thought came into my mind. It was meant for me to say these words." He smiled and moved toward a new couple who faced away from each other.

Wanderer trotted up on his mustang. The Holy Man jumped down and nodded Knows Both Sides. "Smart. He reminds me of my own self as a boy. Perhaps I do have a reason to stay. Heh, we could live in a cave in the canyons. I do know where there is one. I could teach him much in one cold season."

Dove started to respond that she did not think a cave would be such a good idea, but Wanderer, hands behind his back, muttered to three mice who sat on his shoulder as he walked after his mustang.

"Mice? Why mice?" Two ran down his shoulder and skittered away. "How does he... how do they know where to find him again? He has *me* speaking to no one. Perhaps I will grow up to be like him!"

"Daughter, you would be blessed to be like him." Animal Speaks Woman plopped next to her with Hawk Feather in her arms. "You have found a nice place to rest. Wanderer is not so crazy. He is gifted. Yes, sometimes he does make me feel crazy, but I care for him. Many times, he has left me to try to understand what he says. I may think about it for a short span and understand, or think about it for as long as a moon, maybe longer, but then I understand. When someone tells you things that make you think, they also help you to grow, stretch your mind." She did her best to hold onto the squirming little boy.

"I see my brother wears no clothes again. I wonder if Wanderer was like Hawk Feather?" She pulled on the boy's toes as he fought to get loose. "What is it like to be a mother?"

"Ahh." She leaned back and tickled her little son. "To be a mother is the greatest joy there is for me. I am teacher, caretaker of the next generation. Both parents are this, but a mother spends much time with her little ones. We see deep into our children's hearts and feel their wants, what they need. We share a connection that no matter how far away our children may be, no matter how much they grow, and become part of another's life, we are still connected. We watch a tiny seed that started in our bellies grow and bloom.

"I still seek advice from my mother. The sunrise we left for the grasslands, Mother and I spoke about many things. She gave me much advice." She reached for Dove's hand, and the boy managed to get loose and chase after other children. "As I will do for you even when you are a mother yourself. Never think you cannot ask me for advice, little one, no matter where we go. I will be there for you. One day, you will come to me and ask the same questions I asked my own mother about men, children and much more."

"You know then." Dove squeezed her hand. "I think I understand what Knows Both Sides meant by seeds. One day I, too, will plant seeds."

"Yes, I know where we are to go. And yes, girl, you will plant seeds that grow, and perhaps one day will be carried by Sister Wind to a faraway place." Animal Speaks stood when Hawk Feather landed on top a pile of children who screamed and laughed as the pile grew larger. "One day, I will be chasing my grandchildren."

***

Shining Light stood away from Dove but close enough to hear what everyone said to her. *I am beginning to understand, little one. White Bear has spoken of my changing future in nearly every dream I have had since we left the forest. I now wonder when we will see the forest again.*

He walked to the edge of the camp. "Nothing but grasslands. No forest in sight. Mother, Father, will I see you again? Or only in my dreams?"

A small tug on his breechclout made him turn. "White Paws, you pull me away from my thoughts. Perhaps you also pull me away from the forest?"

Moon Face came and stood at his side. She raised her muzzle, eyes fixed on him.

He sighed, turned around, and shuffled back toward the laughing people, his heart filled with sadness.

'Boy, do not worry so. Stand tall. You go to your future as you have always done.'

"Blue Night Sky?"

The stones around his neck warmed. Before him, the camp of his people was alive with activity. "My people. Will we go back to the forest or into the canyons? Blue Night Sky? Speak to me, please."

The stone necklace became warm and he ran his hands over it. "I go to my future... my family's future."

Chapter 30

The stream had started to grow into a river and more shrubs appeared beside it. Wispy, grey-silver plants with yellow flowers waved in the breeze and Sacred silvery Sage grew above Dove's knees. In the shorter grass clumps, white and orange flowers stretched their stems as if trying to see over the grass. Soil took on a light brown yellow-orange color. Larger tan and red-orange stones dotted the landscape under the turquoise sky. Eagles called to each other as they floated in and out of the clouds. Even the air had changed. It took on the aroma of the grasses and the Sage.

Dove used dry grass to rub down her mustang until Fire's coat shined. "I will never forget how you helped me when I found myself alone." She leaned in close and inhaled. "How is it you smell so sweet?"

Fire turned her head and rubbed it against the top of Dove's. She reached out and hugged the animal. "How could anyone not love you and your Peoples? Father told me what it was like before you came to us. He was young, but remembers how hard life was. It was risky hunting the humpbacks on foot. He told me hunters were hurt, even lost their lives while trying to make sure their families had food. Then you mustangs came and changed everything, made life easier.

"He told me the elders could not have made the journey to the forest if they would have had to walk. Many would not allow others to pull them on drags. They did not wish to slow down the people." She let the mustang loose and scratched the animal's side.

Fire bobbed her head and let out a small moan. She moved forward to get Dove to scratch another place.

"Feels good, eh? I bet that is why I see you and another mustang scratch each other with your teeth. At first I wondered if you bit each other, but I watched as the two of you moved from one side to the other still doing it." She walked around and scratched the mustang's rump.

"I see some of the mustangs stay in groups and even sleep together. I wondered what would happen when Thunder brought her herd and joined the one you are part of. She walked up to the lead female with her head raised tall and pushed herself against the other female. Father pulled me back, worried they might fight, but nothing happened. The other female turned and walked away. He explained that even your kind have leaders, and Thunder is a lead female and respected. I am happy you are not a lead female. I would worry about you getting hurt." Footsteps from behind made her turn.

"This is good, that you speak to her. She knows your heart, and even if she cannot understand your words, she understands your touch, your voice." Wanderer reached out and scratched Fire's back. "She will be there for you if you are there for her. Always treat her as *you* wish to be treated. Mustangs have emotions, needs, and want love just as we do. My animal has followed me since we became companions and has even waked me by poking her head in my lodge when she thinks I have slept enough."

Dove cocked her head and smiled. "I wish to ask why you always have mice." Dove patted Fire's rump. The mustang moved off and joined the herd, but not before she turned around and nickered to her.

Four mice jumped from a pouch tied to Wanderer's side and vanished into the brush. "You ask about my mice. They are not mine. We share the same space is all. For many cycles of seasons they have been with me, generation after generation. They warn me of things."

"What do they say?"

"Nothing. Mice do not speak." He grinned at her.

She scrunched up her face. "Father warned me you would say that, yet I asked anyway. How do they warn you? May I ask?"

"You may ask me anything, little one." He smiled, clicked for his mice, and headed for the growing stream.

She fell in behind him. "Anything?" She reached the small river's edge as he knelt down to fill his water bladder.

"Anything. I may not have the answer, but you can ask anyway."

A mouse jumped from his shoulder to hers as she, too, knelt. "Um, one of your mice—"

"I see she wished to meet you."

"How do you know if they do not speak to you?" She leaned back and held out her arm to allow the mouse to jump down. He did not. "Do they bite?"

"Yes, but only when they feel scared or threatened. They taught me not to become angered at someone unless I was sure they meant me harm." He took the mouse from Dove's arm and put him on his shoulder.

"But, Wanderer, if they do not speak, how do you learn from them?"

"One way is by watching how they respond to things."

"But the ones who are too scared to move become a meal. This I have seen." She leaned back and sat.

"That is why I do not stand still if I face danger. The mice showed me what not to do." He lifted the water bladder and drank. "So cold." He handed her the water.

She swallowed deeply and then gave him the water bladder back. "How else do they guide you?"

"They whisper in my ear."

"You... wait, they whisper in your ear? You said they do not speak to you!"

"They do not. Heh, I have had to explain this to too many people." He tied the water bladder, took off his footwear, and walked across the waters.

"Where do you go?" She jumped up and put one foot in the cold waters.

"The same place you go." He sat on the other side and put his footwear back on. "Better hurry. Father Sun will soon go to sleep."

Dove took off her footwear, raised the bottom of her dress with her free hand, and splashed across to his side. "It comes up to my knees. Ah, cold!"

"You drank it and found it was cold, so you should have expected that, silly. Put your footwear on now that you are across. The smaller stones are sharp." He chuckled and moved on ahead. A short way from the river, the land began a sharp ascent.

The steep climb had Dove grabbing for handholds. She slid down once, scraping her knees. *Again I scrape my knees. Not going to act as a child! The pain is nothing. I am big enough to scrape myself and not speak about it.*

"These stones are so different from the ones we have in the forest. Why are there orange and tan stones? We must be near the canyons." Partway up the slope, she climbed faster, passing him.

"Girl! Slow down or you will slide all the way to the bottom and I will have to explain to your parents why I bring you back in pieces. They maybe will be angry with me when they learn I cannot sew you back together, silly girl."

"You cannot sew me back together! I am not a dress. Who is silly now with such ideas?"

"Slow down before we find out." She slid back on loose dirt and grabbed his hand before she slipped anymore.

"You have strong hands for one so old."

He pulled her up even with him. "I am old, older than you understand, but weak I am not! You are as the fluff of a feather."

She frowned. "I will not always be small! Mother says I will grow much more."

He held her hand tighter and pulled her the rest of the way to the top of the hill. "Yes, Dove, you are small. You are not yet ten winters old and you must remember this." He scooted small stones to the side and sat on the bare spot. "Sit."

She put her hand above her brows and gazed toward where Father Sun woke. "More grass. I hoped to see the canyons."

"They are there." He pointed toward something small and deep purple on the far horizon. "Those are the beginning of the canyons."

Dove's eyes rounded and she gasped. "We must go tell the others!"

He caught the bottom of her dress before she could dash back down the hill.

"Slow down, or I *will* have to pick up your pieces. The canyons are far away, maybe ten days, maybe more. The ground will become rockier. We will have to go around deep drops so we can take the lodge poles and hides. Without the mustangs to ride and help pull drags, it would take twice as long."

She propped her hands on her hips. "Why did you bring me up here?"

"Because you needed to come up here."

"Your words mix up my mind. Why did I need to come up here?" She pinched her brows and crossed her arms.

"Why do you still stand? Sit, girl." He patted the ground beside himself.

She pushed aside smaller stones with her foot and sank gracefully to the ground next to him. "Does Father know I am up here? Is this a Sacred place? How long will we be here? Soon darkness will take the land. Are we going to stay up here?"

"We will be here until we leave." He stared across the valley, cross-legged with his arms draped over his legs.

"Grandmother told me I have my father's mouth. Perhaps I should give it back to him." Her head drooped.

"Ha! Now you make me laugh!" He wrapped his arms around his sides. "It has been many seasons since I have laughed so hard." He reached out, flung an arm over her shoulder, and continued to chuckle.

Red reached her cheeks. "Mother would say I am acting as a child who does not know when to hold her tongue." She grinned shyly at him. "You live with mice all over you. This, too, is something a child might do. Perhaps we are father and daughter."

He pulled her tighter into a hug, then let her go. "All of us have a child living within us. Yours has much growing to do. Do not force growth. You push your winters to come too fast. They will do so on their own.

"One sunrise, you race across the camp and play, a child of the band. One day, a young man makes eyes at you. Before long, you are a mate and mother. Not much time will pass before you watch your children do the binding with the one they will spend their lives with, and they leave you. Soon, grandchildren sit at your feet to hear stories. Another sunrise passes and, as you sit up, a pain will hit your back, maybe your hands feel as if you quilled far too much. Stardust will have found its way into your hair. The elder in the band is you.

"Now that we leave the forest, the mystery of it leaves us. With each sunrise, stand and give thanks for the beauty. With each sunset, remember the day and speak of it to family and friends who come to sit at the fire. Many things we do will be forgotten if we do not keep them alive with the stories." He twisted sideways so he could see her better.

"What we do now will be told in stories. We are doing good things by going to meet Singing Stone. The mustangs have much to do with this journey. Our names will be forgotten, but that does not matter. What *we* do is all that matters. Perhaps the things we do will create a future that would not have been."

Dove jumped up and started to slide down the hill. "I must go tell Father and Mother what you have said. I must tell everyone!"

Wanderer stood and called after her. "Girl, slow down. Allow me to help you back down before you *have* to be sewn back together. Your mother would take any skin you need from me!"

Mice jumped from his pouch around his neck and scampered down on their own. "And I do not allow mice to live all over me. They allow me to live with *them*. It was they who wanted me to take you up the hill."

"They do not speak to you, remember?" Dove called over her shoulder as she reached the bottom and ran toward her family, hair flying behind.

Chapter 31

The Big Sky Mustang People's scouts returned with news. Their enemies had sent some of their men away, probably to a bigger camp to get more mustangs. Until they returned with the animals, the Likes To Fight People would not be able to follow and cause problems. The band had a few sunrises to put distance between them and their enemies.

Singing Stone relaxed on Spirit Eyes and rode behind the last of his people. A pouch around his neck carried four small stones that sung to him, calming his mood. No need to worry about danger.

Now and then, Listens To Wind turned her head Four Arrow's way and urged her animal faster. For a few steps, her mustang outpaced Four Arrow's animal. He laughed and caught up to her. She would glance his way and, for a bit, ride by his side before she pushed her animal out ahead of his again.

"I will have a young grandfather if my grandmother does not try harder to get away. Ha! Spirit Eyes, look at her glancing back to be sure she has not gone too far ahead of him!" A grin stretched across Singing Stone's mouth as he leaned over to pat Spirit Eyes' neck. "We are close enough to see the smiles on both their faces. And Mother and Father have moved away to allow them to be alone.

"In my pack is the binding rope I made for when Dove and I become mates." He tilted his head and thought of the Great Elders' words to him. "Perhaps it would be wise to listen to Water Lily's words, give Dove and me time to learn about one another, to allow us to act silly as Grandmother and Four Arrows do. Yes, it is not time for Dove and I to worry about a binding rope. I will give the rope to Four Arrows when we camp. One day, I will make another for us." He touched the binding rope around his waist. *Someday, me sweet one, someday soon.*

"Ah, Spirit Eyes, my dreams tell me that one day our bands will become two, maybe three bands. That many mustangs will come to be with us." He reached sideways and scratched his animal's side. "We will have our own herd."

He frowned and turned his head to listen more closely. He slowed. *Someone follows! Why do my stones still sing as if nothing is wrong?* He twisted around on Spirits Eye's back and stared hard at the flatlands around him. The birds had stopped singing in the shrubs that dotted the land.

Yes, movement in the grass! He urged his animal to move a bit faster. When he reached Falcon Storm, he placed a hand on his new father's forearm and whispered, "Someone follows. The grass moves where there is no wind." *My stones did not warn me. Why?*

Falcon Storm moved his mustang sideways so he could glance behind him without appearing to do so. "Where? I see nothing." He stretched tall on his animal and raised his hand to his forehead pretending to look all around.

"There. Did you see?" Singing Stone tilted his chin toward a patch of grass. "I am going to see—"

His father touched Stone's shoulder. "Not on your own, son. No one in the band ever takes a chance like that. We go together." He reached behind his shoulder, pulled out his bow, and readied an arrow. "You do the same. We will approach from different sides. Keep your bow low unless you see movement. Do not trot. Ask Spirit Eyes to walk slow. We must pretend we hunt, so do not stare at that place."

River Song, Listens To Wind, and Four Arrows rode close to Falcon Storm and Singing Stone. "What makes you ready your bows?" River Song stared into her man's face as she reached for her bow.

With a slight tilt to his head, he pointed toward the grass that now swayed in the still air. Four Arrows and Listens To Wind readied their bows and spread out as if they helped in a hunt. Several young men noticed what they did and followed. By the time they surrounded the spot where the grass moved, it no longer moved.

River Song closed in on the spot. She slid from her animal and landed lightly on the ground. She bent, staring as she motioned the others closer. In a quiet voice, she spoke. "These footprints are small, and there are two sets."

On silent feet, she crept closer to the thick shrubs that were along the bank of the nearby stream. With a darting movement, she reached into the leaves of a shrub and pulled out a screaming boy. Another boy charged out, screamed, and kicked at her legs. A bow in one hand, she could only whirl around and try to dodge the attacking boy while hanging onto the other one. "Will all of you stop staring my way and help me? I am bitten!"

Falcon Storm leapt from his animal and grabbed the boy before he landed another kick on River Song. "Aii! They are only maybe nine winters old, and by their clothing, they are Likes To Fight boys."

Listens To Wind rode closer and spoke some of the Likes To Fight's words that she learned when they had held her captive as a girl while signing meanings for words she did not know. She turned to Falcon Storm when she finished. "The boys are ten and eight winters old. They wished to prove themselves and did not return with their warriors who went back to their camp to get mustangs, nor did they stay with the ones who must wait for the animals."

The larger boy spit her way, raised his chin and pushed his chest out.

"He demands we give him our mustangs. He says he and his cousin will take them back to the waiting men. They will praise him and his cousin, maybe make them warriors."

"Warriors!" Falcon Storm laughed and gently shook the boy he held. "Tell them the Likes To Fight men will hang them upside down for what they tried to do and leave them behind."

She signed to the older boy that he was but a child in body and mind to hide in the grass with no idea, no plans. His cousin and he would be shamed for being captured. She nodded at River Song and Falcon Storm. The two adults shoved the boys to the ground as she scolded them. "Go back to your people so you may grow up to be men and warriors."

The youngest boy glared at Listens To Wind, turned to his cousin, and whispered to him. After much head shaking, the older boy stood. The younger one stood as well and puffed out his chest, mimicking his cousin. He sucked in his belly and his ribs poked out, giving him the look of a hungry baby bird.

The older boy lifted his chin and narrowed his eyes as he signed that his cousin and he would not return to the Likes To Fight People. His hands and words flew like a flock of startled birds. "Without mustangs, we cannot return."

He crossed his arms and stood as if awaiting punishment. Eyes forward, chin up the younger boy crossed his arms and stepped forward.

Listens To Wind signed, "How are you called?"

The older boy, still staring forward, uncrossed his arms. "I am called Fire Keeper. My father gave me this name before we left."

She cocked her head at the younger boy and signed, "How are you called?"

The younger boy dropped his eyes, but did not uncross his arms.

Fire Keeper signed. "He is shamed. His father did not give him a new name before we left. He still must carry the name his mother gave him, Big Moon, for his round face.

Singing Stone walked slowly toward Big Moon. He reached out his hand, palm up.

Listens To Wind threw her arm in front of him. "He will not understand your sign of peace. He will think you wish to fight him. They expect to be killed."

"Killed? But, Grandmother they are only boys. I do not understand." His hand fell to his side. "They are children!"

She shook her head. "They have heard many stories around campfires, ones used to frighten them so they would not wander off or try what these two did." She shifted her eyes toward the boys and signed, "Welcome. No harm will come your way."

Singing Stone glanced from his grandmother to the boys and back again. "Now what?"

***

A scout brought an old female mustang over, and Listens To Wind signed for the boys to get on. After they mounted, the scout handed the nose rope of the old animal to Fire Starter. Listens To Wind signed, "You are free to go. Return to your people."

Everyone mounted. With one quick glance at the boys, she clucked to her mustang and caught up to the others.

They had not gone far when the old female caught up to them. Listens To Wind twisted her animal around. Both boys stood in the grass, arms crossed, unmoving.

Singing Stone threw his hands up. "Grandmother, why can they not understand that we willingly send them home?" The old mustang trotted up and nuzzled Spirit Eyes. "I did not wish for them to have Spirit Eyes' companion anyway. I think she loves him and, if she was human, you would not even think of sending her away because she is old."

His grandmother reached over and patted his arm. "I know, Grandson, but we chose her because she is old, gentle. No matter. The boys want two good mustangs to return with so they do not lose face, but we cannot allow the men who hunt us to think we make gifts of our mustangs to them."

Falcon Storm turned back toward the boys and the others followed. He pointed to the old female who stood next to Spirit Eyes. His scolding voice was enough to get them back on the mustang. He picked up her nose rope and trotted up next to River Song. "We have no choice but to keep them with us. Perhaps they will be a good trade to get their warriors to leave us alone, if they catch up to us before we can get back to the main camp. We need to pick up speed. Once they realize their sons are missing, they will begin to search. At least, if I was their father, I would hunt down those who had my children." He held onto the rope and motioned for everyone to trot faster. Even the old female picked up speed, leaving a trail of dust behind her.

Chapter 32

By the time Father Sun rode the middle of the sky, the small group rejoined the main band of The Big Sky Mustang People. The band followed the ever-steepening ridgeline until it leveled out. To the side that Father Sun rose, the bluff dropped away without warning. Below them lay a small valley filled with trees. Pine trees dotted the landscape, and trees that gave up their leaves to the cold season hugged tightly along the bank of the small stream. Now and then, the people spotted a flat, wide bed of what once had been a great river. Father Sun glinted off the trickle of water that followed the edge of the old river's path where the trees lined the edge. Thick shrubs competed for a place alongside tan-brown boulders that looked as if they fell from the sky and landed in no planned placement.

Falcon Storm and a scout rode back to where the land widened slightly. He jumped off his mustang. Tired elders and the children swayed on their feet. The people needed rest. Elders who had made sure the warriors rode, and not walked, now sat on the ground. "This is a good place to camp. If we make small fires, the enemy will not know we are here. We have trees along the rim that grow in between boulders. Trees in some places are so thick no one will see us through them."

Many people glanced around and nodded. Water Lily stepped beside him and pointed toward a copse of trees. "We will have a good place to remain invisible after sundown. The Likes To Fight People will not see us up here."

He made his way to the side where Father Sun would dip down and sleep. The land dove down sharply. That side of the bluff was dangerous, with wide swaths of slick rock and areas of small loose stones that would slide beneath the hooves of mustangs and under human feet. A few good warriors could keep watch there.

Ahead of them, toward the place where the one campfire in the sky that never moves, a single line of mustangs or humans could follow a deer trail to the valley below. The trail looped and wove along the hillside. Jagged walls rose on one side and sudden drops to the valley floor on the other side. It would not take much to guard this pathway.

The narrow path they took to get up there wound upward and had soft sides where one wrong step would make a mustang or human tumble to their death among the boulders on the hillside. Only the best hunters and warriors would guard that area.

After the guards had been set, Falcon Storm headed toward Water Lily's campsite. The boys were huddled in front of her lodge. He knelt beside her small fire that barely licked up toward the sky. "Great Elder, what will we do with the boys?"

Behind him, the people had gathered. The boys' shoulder length hair and strange clothing made of something other than leather caused many of the people to reach out and touch them. The boys edged closer to Falcon Storm, one on each side. Their actions gave away their youth. He pretended to not notice them clinging to his arms.

Water Lily stared into Fire Starter's eyes until he looked down. Big Moon kept his eyes to the ground and fumbled with a small pouch that hung around his neck.

"I know one of the stories they were maybe told is that some enemies eat children. Heh, they are too thin for me." She clapped her hands to gain their attention. Her bent, withered hands moved rapidly when she signed.

"You will not be harmed. Our people will treat you with respect. You are brave to try to steal mustangs." She signed words that would put them at ease and handed each boy a cold piece of rabbit. They tore into the meat as if they had not eaten in some time. She handed them more, and they ate it as ravenously as the first piece.

She turned her attention to Falcon. "Perhaps when their bellies are full they will tell their story. Listens To Wind will know enough of their words to speak to them, if she will do so again. Hearing words they understand will calm them."

With a shake of his head, he looked down. "Listens To Wind has avoided them since we made camp. I worry memories of being a captive of the Likes To Fight people have caused her pain." He lifted his eyes from gazing at the fire. River Song and Singing Stone walked into the firelight, and he stood to go with his family.

"Can the boys stay with you, Great Elder, until we know what do with them?"

Water Lily cocked her head and studied the youngsters. The boys ripped the meat from the rabbit. They broke the bones and sucked out the marrow. They tossed the cracked bones in the fire-pit and looked at the water bladder.

Water Lily dipped her chin in agreement and smiled at the boys as she offered her water bladder to Fire Starter. "He is the oldest, and out of respect, I give it to him first." Her eyes met Falcon Storm's. "Find Listens To Wind. She is needed."

***

Listens To Wind walked deeper into the trees, away from camp to seek solace as Father Sun changed the color of the sky to deep blue. Memories pushed up from the hidden places in her mind. Voices of the past rose like a screech in her ears.

"Look at her! She is so ugly. Her people must have been shamed by her! She has no worth. Too weak to even skin a hide the right way. Little baby, little baby!" The children danced in a circle around her, taunting her. She charged at them, fists tight and swinging. They ran backward, scattered and laughed. Not long after, when they returned and threw stones at her, a jagged one cut deep across her cheek, barely missing her eye. The adults stopped what they were doing to watch, no one intervening. Finally, the children tired of tormenting her and ran away to play another game.

Why did they have to beat on me? I was a child! I did everything asked of me and more. I do not wish to speak to those boys, and I will not!

Darkness started to steal the warmth, and she rubbed her arms to ward off the cool air. Two boulders nestled against each other. She curled into the middle of the cold boulders and cried as more memories ran endless, cruel circles in her mind. She cried until her body numbed and the sounds of taunting children faded. Her arms fell to her sides and she pushed herself up on shaky legs. The light of the moon drew her eyes upward. Her tears dried. She took in a long breath, and her mind let go of the torture of long ago pain as she exhaled.

Sister Wind moved through the woods. Sapling leaves rubbed together, whispering secrets to one another. A rustle in the branches of an older tree caught her attention. A large, dark shadow leaped from a high branch, and the sounds of large wings melted into the darkness.

Hoof falls crackled leaves and twigs. Her mustang, Snow, nipped at her clothing and nuzzled her hair. Listens To Wind placed her hands on either side of the animal's face and leaned her forehead between Snow's eyes. A sigh wove its way out of her, floating away in the darkening night. "Snow, my friend. You and I share the same mind. Did you feel my pain? I know your movements, and you know mine." She rubbed under the mustang's chin. "As soft as a breast feather."

Sister Wind cooled the air with her breath as small clouds drifted over the moon. "Snow, do you ever wish to be as a cloud, drift where Sister Wind pushes you? I wonder if clouds have thoughts, memories to burden them. Do you, my friend, have memories that burden you? Or is it only we humans who burden ourselves with such?"

Snow's whinny brushed across her face, and Listens To Wind jumped when a twig snapped. She stood, still straining to hear. The nearly-silent movements came closer. "Ah, Four Arrows followed me. Snow, his heart calls to mine. But I am older, perhaps too much so. He rides as if he was born on that mustang of his. The black-brown of the animal and his own skin and hair color blend well. His well formed body moves with the muscles of his...."

She blinked hard and shook her head. "Why do I allow myself to see him this way? He *is* a man." She exhaled as he stepped in the pool of moonlight. His breechclout-covered body moved as sinuously as one of the great mountain lions. She looked away as her heartbeat made her breath come faster.

Four Arrows stood close enough to shadow her, yet she did not look up. Snow backed away and went out into the deeper grass, leaving her alone with him.

"Woman, look my way. I have things I wish to say. Perhaps we could sit on that log under the bigger tree?" He waved his hand.

She stepped away from his warmth, moved to the log and sat down. The branches entwined above their heads. *Even the branches mingle with one another, seek the caress of each other.*

"I came out here to be alone."

"No, you did not." His voice firm as if he spoke to a stubborn child. "You came out here to avoid the boys, as you did all the way to this campsite. I know your story. Your grandson told me that the Likes To Fight People attacked your camp when you were a child." He turned sideways to face her and leaned against a boulder. Compassion filled his words and softened their hard-edged truth.

Her eyes followed a tree trunk whose branches arched out, untouched by human fears and memories. Her belly ached from all the sorrow she held inside.

He ran a hand lightly down her arm. "These young boys are not the ones who mistreated you. They know nothing of what you went through. They sit with eyes wide and faces terrified. Each clings to Falcon Storm, the only one they do not fear. Or, perhaps it is because he is the only one to show them kindness besides your daughter and grandson. You are the only one who can speak their words, woman. Fire Starter, Big Moon... those boys need you."

His hands shook when he took her face and turned it toward him.

Love, I see love in his eyes.

She reached up and brushed his chin with her fingers. She pulled away, but his free hand caught hers. This time, she did not pull away.

"Memories can cause scars so deep they go all the way to the heart." This time she did try pull away, but he held her hands tighter.

He cleared his throat. "I may be younger, but you know I feel much for you. I know you are loving and that you care much for those who need your help. Before we left the canyons, you helped a child who could not keep up with the older ones as they played. You showed her a shortcut through the many winding turns in the canyons, and she beat them to the top of the peak. You stood back with joy on your face. Yes, I watched. I have watched you often since the first sunrise I saw you. I knew your heart then. Wished to be with you."

She felt his warm breath as he leaned closer. She met his eyes with her own. "I am confused with my feelings. You make my mind and heart speak differently." She pulled away, stood by a tree, and placed her hand on its rough bark to lean into its steadiness.

Four Arrows followed. "We must speak of the boys. Yes, they are of our enemies, but children just the same, Woman. You know many of their words." He side-stepped around her when she tried to move away and made her stop.

"Was there not one person who helped you?" He offered his hand to her.

She took his offered hand and raised her eyes to meet his again. "There was. One girl made sure I had food. At night, she would bring me something she had hidden from her parents. She would slip past the family who kept me tied outside their lodge." She ducked her head and whispered, "I had forgotten about the kindness and only remembered the bad."

"We have both memories, but it is often the bad that rises above the good. Always leave room in your heart for the good to fight off the bad so the bad does not win and blacken your heart."

"I speak of my age again." She leaned close to him. His body felt warm, welcoming. Unsure of herself, she pulled back. *What do I do? My mind builds walls of stone between Four Arrows and me, but my heart shoves at the walls, pushing them away almost as fast as my mind places them.*

"Forget age. Age does not belong to us. Love does. After you calm the boys' fears, you and I will go speak to Water Lily." His eyes held a question, not a demand.

"I never thought to say this to another man. I care much for you. You are young. Are you certain of your wish? I will age, and my face will look like the outside of an old tree. You will still—"

"Love you. With each passing season, like the roots of a tree, my love will grow deeper, forever in search of the love you have for me. I know you love me, not just care. Come, we go show smiles to the boys and then to Water Lily."

"I do not wish my heart to become cold toward those who have not caused me harm. I will speak to the boys, what I remember of their words. What will become of them?"

"We, you and I, will offer them a kindness. We will show them what kind of people found them. Perhaps, after they return to their own camp, they will remember this and act kindly toward any children they may find in the future."

Sister Wind pushed through her hair, making it crackle with Energy. *Something changes. Everything changes, but this is a Powerful change that comes our way.*

Chapter 33

"Mother, stop pacing. You make my eyes crazy." River Song's belly stretched her dress as she shifted to find a comfortable position. "How is it so many moons have passed? Am I really past eight moons?" She leaned over and tried to reach for the sinew to stitch the last of Falcon Storm's leggings, but gave up and sat back with a grunt.

"I cannot help but pace. I am too... not.... I do not wish to do the binding." Listens to Wind waved her hands as if she could make it all vanish. "I do care for him. Love him. But he is—"

"A good hunter, a proven warrior, he has the elders' respect, and loves you, Mother." She reached for the sinew again with the same results.

Listens To Wind continued to pace. "I do not need a man to have to sew for. To feed. To sew for."

"You said sew two times. I would like to *sew* for my man, if someone would offer me my rolled up sinew that escapes my reach. If you love someone, sewing and cooking means nothing. You work with leather and cook even if though you have no man. You sew for Singing Stone, cook for him as well, and I never hear you complain."

Her mother stopped pacing. "Who will cook for my grandson? Make his clothes? I cannot leave him, he is—"

"A man, as you remind me every time I look his way. He knows how to scrape a hide, sew and cook. He fed himself well before you moved in with him. You spoil that *grown* man with fine clothes, footwear I know others cannot make as well as your skilled hands. He spends much time with the mustangs and his dogs instead of in camp anyway. He is a fine hunter. Look at how fat his dogs are. The one with pups is even fat." She folded her legs under her and stretched for the sinew. She rocked herself trying to reach it.

Her mother leaned over and picked it up. "Why did you not ask me? I would have gotten it for you." She tossed it in River Song's bulging lap. "Why do you mumble, Daughter?" Listens To Wind jumped when someone scratched the lodge flap.

"Mother, please untie the flap. There is no reason for you to have tied it when you came in. The sides are raised. If anyone wished to know if you were pacing, they have already done so." When her mother stepped away from the flap, River Song rolled over onto her knees and used a lodge pole to pull herself up.

"Ah, Four Arrows, there you are. I see you have brought some very nice quills! Please, come inside. I am in need of stretching. Perhaps I will go help the other women hunt tubers. I am not used to living with others and need to learn better manners."

"You have visitors, Daughter. You need to stay here, in your lodge." Listens To Wind crossed her arms and stood in the center of the lodge, her eyes darting from Four Arrows to River Song.

River Song glanced back and chuckled. "I get too lazy now that my belly no longer allows me to see my feet." She smiled at Four Arrows and slipped out.

"Woman, we are to be with Water Lily. To speak of the boys and decide if they will stay with you and your grandson, or," he stared about the lodge, "maybe a newly bonded pair."

"What newly bonded pair? Who has bonded? I saw no ceremony." Listens To Wind turned to face the back of the lodge and fingered a recently smoked hide.

He approached her from behind and put his hands on her shoulder. "Wind, do not deny what you feel. You must stop worrying about your grandson. Not one person in the band sees our union as wrong."

She spun around. "Who knows of you asking me to bond with you?" Her eyes traveled down his muscled chest. A smile played at the corner of her lips.

He laid his head back and laughed. "Only everyone in the band! You think people do not see? I have walked past many campfires to see grins my way. You do not see what your mind does not pay heed to. I desire you to be my mate, and I know you also desire me. I will treat you well. You will have much love from me. I am a good hunter, respect the mustangs as you do, and will never ask of you what you cannot give. All I ask is to always be at your side."

"You do not understand. Our lives are the mustangs. Can you always follow where they lead instead of forcing them to follow the band? There may come a sunrise when the herd chooses another way, away from the people. My family will follow the herd. Could be the band will split, or only my family will leave. Can you leave your relations behind?" She searched his face and eyes.

He stepped closer. "I will follow you, as I will be part of your family. The band will split after a late season hunt. We are too many to stay together. I see no reason to worry. They will be only a few sunrises away, and in the cold season, there is much visiting among our sister bands." He put his hands on her slender waist and pulled her close. "Every person knows how important the animals are. Not one man, woman, or child, will allow harm to come their way.

"Listens To Wind, I give you my heart to do with what you please. All I ask is that you never tear it to pieces." He let her go and handed her a basket with cleaned and sorted quills. "I spent much time sorting these for you. I am skilled with quills also. When the days become cold, you and I will sit and quill together. I have dyes I have waited to try, and we will do it together."

She wanted to pull away, but this time her body responded to his touch and she remained where she stood. *He has the scent of a... a man. So long since I have smelled a man.* Her legs trembled.

"We will always do things together, if you wish. I know you hunt and are a good warrior. Our women do not fight, but you can teach them if they wish it. Stories of your family reached our campfires from other bands. You may think you are alone, but bands you do not know about chased your enemies away from your family. Yes, they have. Do not shake your head. Many in the canyons and beyond know your family. I must tell you, the boys you spoke to wish to stay with you until—"

Singing Stone burst in since the flap was open. "People and mustangs come!"

Ruby Standing Deer

Chapter 34

Dove slowed Fire down and fell back. "Oh, Mother, where are you? I was excited when we started out. My whole body shakes, but with worry. What have I done? Did I force a future on everyone who followed? I wish to go home!" She swiveled sideways on Fire and glanced back toward where they had traveled this day.

"You are home, girl."

"Wanderer! Where did you come from?" She twisted around and found him in front of her and Fire.

"I came from the forest, just as you did." A single mouse jumped from his mustang to Fire's neck hair and hurried onto Dove's arm.

"Heh, you have been chosen. My mice have never left me for another before. Allow her to climb up on your shoulder, sit by your ear. I have a pouch I made you for when this would happen." He reached into his tunic and took off a pouch that rested around his neck.

"Before we left the forest, I made this for you. It is lined with fur that you can remove."

She held out her arm and allowed the mouse to climb up her shoulder and sit near her ear. "How can you hold still? This tickles too much. Wanderer, how did you know to make the pouch? Why did he choose me? What am I to do with him?"

"He is a she, and I have no idea what you will do with her. She chose you. I will teach you how to care for her and her babies."

"Babies! Wait. Is my body going to become a home for *mice* as yours is?"

"That will be for you and the mice to decide. My body is not a home for mice. It is a safe place for them when they choose. Many people do not understand mice are full of secrets, clever ideas. "

"But, Wanderer, what will Singing Stone think?"

"And, unlike humans, mice do not ask silly questions. Does it matter?"

"Yes... I mean, no." She slapped her thigh, and the mouse climbed up into her hair. *Am I to be Mustang Woman or Mouse Woman?*

"I have someone to meet. I will see you tonight around a campfire."

He left her with words still in her mouth that she wished to speak. "Fire, what do I do? Ride up to him with smiles, or... I know what to do. *He* can find me!"

She examined the finely painted, dark brown pouch that spread across her hands. Little white flowers poked through green grass and peered up at a blue sky. Little leather ties held the fur lining in place. Several mice could fit in it.

She put it around her neck and tucked it inside her dress that happened to have the same design done in quills on the top half.

The mouse peered out from her hair. "Now I must explain this mouse to Singing Stone. Perhaps I should approach him first."

Knows Both Sides cleared his throat as he came up from behind. His mustang wore a thin necklace of elk teeth that matched the one he wore. "You should stay with your parents and allow them to meet his. This is the way of our people. Allow him to sit at your fire and speak for himself."

She lowered her head. "I am only a girl in everyone's eyes. I cannot yet cook a good meal without Mother. I do not have the beauty of a woman. I am only me."

"Dove." He stopped his mustang and motioned for her to do the same. "Beauty does not mean only your face, your body. It is what you carry in your heart, how you act, how you treat others and so much more than just being good to look at."

"Another I met... I think I met her... I woke from a dream and was in the lodge, but she showed me a part of the forest only a few have ever seen. She spoke nearly the same way you have. Perhaps she reminded me through you."

"Girl, too many can only see the outside, and that becomes their reality. They see a reflection as if they stare into water, and they never try to go beyond it to find what is real. Too many judge only by what they see first, feel first. True, many have become mates with only a glance at each other because they knew right away. Their hearts spoke to one another.

"Others take their time and learn about one another. My mother did not like my father right away even though she says she did. She told me it was a cycle of seasons before she really knew him, understood him."

She warmed at his smile. "I will always seek your advice, cousin. I am so mixed up and dizzy inside with emotions." She reached out and clutched his leg. "I see him!" She raced off, forgetting his advice to allow Singing Stone to come to their campfire at sunset.

***

Dove leaned back to signal her animal to slow down and stop. "There he is, Fire! I can see his mustang! Is that really him? He is too far away to know. My heart pounds! What do I do?"

White Paws moved in front of her mustang and tried to turn Fire.

Shining Light trotted up beside her. "Daughter, we will stop and camp here on the flat top of this rise. We give space between our bands, and in this way, we show respect. Space can make good friends. Besides, I must gather the wolves and keep them near our camp. Their mustangs will smell them and run. Even Thunder has stopped the herd to show this is her herd. We can learn much by watching her. She paces. I can only guess that there must be a lead female in the other herd, and Thunder knows this. We must be careful what we do." He jumped off Sandstone and motioned White Paws to follow.

"Father, we are so far away from them! I wish to go—"

He motioned her to jump down, but she sat on Fire and squirmed. Her little mouse climbed up on her shoulder.

"Ha! I see Wanderer has finally had a mouse leave him. I know we are too far away for you. Be calm. Before sunset, we will visit or they will. And you can show Singing Stone your mouse!" He laughed and waved at Animal Speaks Woman.

"Father Sun will never sleep this day! What if I ride Fire a little further? I will not go far. I only wish to get a bit closer so I can see—"

He stepped around Fire and pulled her off. "Allow the mustangs to graze, drink water. We have much to do before we meet. Go help your mother set up our lodge, make meat. It would be impolite to not have food ready. I know you are excited. We will all meet soon and speak of returning to the forest. Heh. So there will be two with mice in the forest."

"Um, father... you and I must speak." Dove pinched her lips and stared up into his eyes.

"Light!" Animal Speaks Woman trotted up to the pair. "Where do you wish to have the lodge?"

Shining Light left Dove and followed Speaks, laughing about her having a mouse.

She stared after her father. "How do I make him understand?"

Ruby Standing Deer

Chapter 35

Singing Stone's mother caught him weaving into the herd and leaning over Spirit Eyes to slip past the band. He now sat in front of his parents' lodge, knees up, his head between his palms.

"Son, we have been camped here for two sunrises. Water Lily knew where to wait. Since we camped here first, it is polite for their Holy Person to come greet ours." She raised her hand to her brow. "I cannot see who will greet us yet. Some make camp while others tend to their mustangs. And... do I see ten, twelve *wolves*? They have wolves? How is this so? I think we need to pull the mustangs back some."

"The wolves will come no farther. This I know. My stones do not vibrate. This is a good thing! I am sure the wolves will not cause harm. Do you not remember my telling you of the wolves sitting next to Dove that I saw in my dream? I wish to go see Dove, not sit here and wait. I have waited for so long, mother!" He sat tall. "I am a man. Not a boy to sit—"

"Because you *are* a man, you will sit. And no, I do not remember you telling me about so many wolves! Are you so sure these are the Wolf People of your dreams?" She gripped her skinning knife in the sheath on her side. "I understand carrying the name of Wolf, but to have so many who travel with them?"

"Mother, we have lived a life mostly alone, and it is good to be wary, but we have a band now. You have a man. We need not worry. We no longer are alone."

"Having a man does not mean I will be always waiting for him to do something first." Her voice took on a deeper tone. "I am not like other women who need protection. I protect myself!" She ran her hand across her belly. "I miss who we were."

"So much, woman of mine, that you wish to leave? To leave me?" Falcon Storm pressed his hands into her shoulders and turned her to face him.

"I only speak words, Falcon. I would never leave you. I only wish to be free to make my own choices. Your child will know you always. I am not used to being with so many people. That is all I say. Our lives had been simple, but lonely. Never do I care to be lonely again."

Singing Stone stood and greeted Water Lily. She wore colorful clothing with quillwork in the hues of the canyons that zigzagged across the top of her tunic dress and down the sides in reds, oranges and white. A yellow thunderbolt shot down the middle of the design and vanished into long fringe. Her feet were bare.

He offered her his place and moved to the other side of the fire. He pointed to the food cooking by the fire. "We have good meat cooked with tubers and late season greens, Great One. Mother caught many fish from the river that she wrapped in the tall green leaves of the swamp plant that even grow here! She has a gift for knowing where to find fish." He leaned forward and smelled the fish cooking on the edges of the fire where it was mostly ash so they would not burn. "They smell good!"

Wanderer rode up on his off-white mustang and raised his hand in greeting. "Water Lily, ho! Many cycles of seasons have passed between us." He hopped down and offered her a finely tanned elk skin. "I am still good at some things, like tanning. I greet you, Holy Woman of the Big Sky People. I see you are still greatly skilled with quills. Perhaps I should have brought you quills also."

"One Who Wanders?" She squinted her eyes in confusion as she reached for the hide. "Your voice speaks his words, but you do not look like him. We are now the Big Sky Mustang People. I wish to know how you stay so young when you are older than I am." She cocked her head and raised her brows.

"Perhaps I will tell you one day, show you."

"You do me a great honor with such a beautiful gift, One Who Wanders. We have much to speak on." She rubbed the fine leather. "Come, sit. These good people have cooked food I wish to enjoy. I am certain there is enough for all."

Singing Stone moved so Wanderer could sit next to Water Lily. Three mice jumped from inside of Wanderer's hair and onto the robes River Song had spread on the ground.

Singing Stone startled and leaned back. "Dove told me you had mice as companions. Do they not eat or chew on your things? What can mice do for you?"

"Singing Stone, Dove speaks of you so often that sometimes I think she has nothing else in her mind. She is excited to meet you." Wanderer scooped up the mice and placed them on his shoulder. "My mice offer me much advice, good advice that I follow. Dove has one as well."

"Where is she? I wish to meet her." He jumped up and stood on his toes. When that did not work, he whistled for Spirit Eyes. "I will go and find her!"

Water Lily stood and stopped him from jumping on his animal. "You now act as a boy. You wish to go see her, but you have no gifts for her parents. Be still and allow them to settle in. Father Sun is high, and they need to rest, eat and tend to their animals."

She turned to Wanderer who now stood out of respect. "Wolves. Your band has wolves. Already our mustangs and dogs are restless. I made people tie the dogs to lodges and trees. Look how Singing Stone's mustang sniffs the air. I am sure it is not the new mustangs who make his eyes wide. This is one thing we must find a way to agree on."

Singing Stone interrupted. "I will find a way. Dove and I will take care of this. I know we can. We cannot wait until sunset. The darkness will cause more problems. Water Lily, please." The expression on his face was a mix of wonder and worry. His brows rose above wide eyes.

"You have gifts, young man?" Water Lily stood her ground. "You will not approach Dove without gifts. I know she is very young, too young to take as a mate. Whatever you give them will be only a beginning. What do you have to offer?" She sat back down and motioned for Wanderer to sit.

River Song slipped into her lodge and came out with a smoked light brown dress for a girl. Elk teeth dangled below four quill-worked flowers that made up the neckline. Fringe dangled from the bottom of the short sleeves and edge of the dress. She unwrapped footwear that had a quilled, yellow flower on the top of each one. She also unwrapped four pine needle baskets with white quills that went around the tops of each. Each basket held wrapped, cooked fish.

"You, my son, can offer these to Dove's parents, if you wish." She grinned at his open mouth.

"Mother, these are beautiful! What can I offer you for the fine work you have done?" He reached out and touched the soft leather of the dress.

"I will need much help when our baby comes to be with us. I am not weak and will do much as I always have, but I wish for you to gather wood for me this cold season. That is a good trade."

"I will do as you ask and more. Now that Grandmother will soon be with Four Arrows, I will be alone once again and will hunt—"

"You tell me your grandmother is going to be his mate? She did decide to do this?"

Singing Stone took the dress, footwear, and baskets, then jumped on Spirit Eyes. "I need to leave now." He glanced back at his grandmother who walked beside Four Arrows as they wove their way in between lodges toward them. They smiled at each other and did not look his way. He tapped Spirit Eyes into a fast trot, and they choked on the dust kicked up by the mustang.

Ruby Standing Deer

Chapter 36

Dove sat behind Shining Light and Animal Speaks Woman as Singing Stone stumbled over words. His hands shook as he offered the clothing and baskets to her father. She giggled into her hands as her father also stumbled for words. Her mother offered Singing Stone a choice piece of elk meat, and as he was about to thank her, White Paws raced by and grabbed the food from his hands. Everyone nearby laughed. Dove hid her laughter behind her hands.

Singing Stone jerked back and gasped. "So... so this is one of the wolves." Shaky smile on his face, he stared at his empty hands.

Animal Speaks offered Singing Stone more meat and laughed while trying to hold onto Hawk Feather as he pulled off his footwear. "White Paws, he greets you in his own way. We had nine wolves and eight dogs with us when we left, and seven more wolves caught up to us. Do not fear them. They have protected us, shared their food, and taught us much about many things I am sure Dove would like to share with you. You will learn about what I say the more you are near them. Cycles of seasons ago, they helped to save me and some others when I thought our lives had come to an end on our Mother.

"It took time, but now the wolves and dogs hunt together. They are still separate and sleep with their own, but join when they need to. Our mustangs have grown used to them. White Paws and his pack warn other wolves away from our herd."

She took Singing Stone's gifts from Shining Light and examined the baskets and the contents. "Ahh. Such a good smell comes from these well-made baskets. I have never smelled such good fish. Your mother must be the best cook in your band."

She held out the clothing and smiled. "This is very well made! The quilling is the best I have seen. The stitching is very fine. These are all beautiful gifts. I wonder who in our family can wear these?" She turned her head to a red-faced Dove who still giggled.

Dove pulled at her sleeve. "Mother, may I please see them? I am sure they will fit me." She leaned over her mother and smiled at Singing Stone.

"Dove, perhaps you might get us some water—"

Before her mother finished speaking, Dove pushed her way through her parents and scooped up the water bladder. "Of course, Mother!"

She walked backward until her father waved Singing Stone away, giving his permission for him to walk with her. She turned forward and headed for the water.

***

Shining Light could hold his stoic face no longer. He uncrossed his legs and stretched them forward. "My face did not feel like me! Wanderer told me not to show emotions, and that is not me. Perhaps I still have a burning log inside me as our son does. I still go off alone and dance to the crickets when I hear them chirring. They fill me with Power, make me feel whole, as does being bare footed. Heh, our son will never wish to wear anything on his feet."

He grinned as Hawk Feather raced away, leaving behind most of his clothes. "I am as restless as our child in my mind. I wish to run with White Paws and Moon Face at my side." He stood and grinned at Speaks. "Perhaps I will do as my son and race away."

"Man of mine, you really *are* a burning log. You could not have held your face in place much longer! That is why I told Dove to go get water. You were turning red." She pushed him with her shoulder and laughed until tears streamed down her face.

Animal Speaks wiped her eyes with her hands. "Burning logs. Ha! You will always need to be near water so you do not cook yourself. You are much like the boy I met long ago. I see him in your eyes, in your smile. I see you in our daughter, the same Energy and excitement for life."

He nodded at their daughter and Singing Stone sitting in the small stream, kicking water up in the air with their bare feet. "Our daughter has many burning logs inside her also. I wish to see a few more burn before she becomes a woman and mate. I know she will be with us for cycles of seasons, yet my heart feels pain, worry, and joy as well. I have not seen her laugh so much since we played in the forest."

"You will never lose our daughter. She will grow up, mate, have children of her own. We will watch our grandchildren as they hunt and do things to help the band stay well and strong. We older ones will care for all the children while we sit in the shade and—"

"Old ones? I show you old, woman." He crawled into their lodge, held out his hand to his giggling woman. She climbed in and tied the flap shut.

***

Bright Sun Flower rocked a sleeping Hawk Feather in her arms. "Such a joy, these young ones. I will be happy to grow old holding children." She smiled at Gentle Wisdom and Sparkling Star.

Sparkling Star reached for Gentle Wisdom's hand. "I worry about our sons growing up anywhere but the forest. Wisdom promised long ago to follow Shining Light. My heart hurts with fear. I will never leave Wisdom, and she will never leave her cousin." She dropped her hand, stood, and headed for the herd.

Gentle Wisdom stared after her. "She needs to ride Thunder, maybe race the wind. I asked Knows Both Sides to follow her, but to stay back. He will watch over her as we speak." She stared around at the camp at the people getting ready to meet the other band. The air smelled of cooking. She replaced her frown with a grin at the sounds of children chasing each other while running with the wolves and dogs.

"I love to watch so many people happy. Outside the forest, this will be harder to do. To just relax and enjoy life without worry. In the forest, we made sure to stay strong, practice our fighting skills, but that was with each other, not an enemy. If Dove is right and the Likes To Fight band is after the mustangs, I do not wish to stay. Our sons say stay, but they do not understand. They were not raised in the ways of the Fish People. All the way here we have had pretend raids on each other, but none of the young ones understands how serious real raids are."

She gripped Bright Sun Flower's arm. "I will not lose my sons! And I will not leave my cousin's side. I am torn." She jumped up, hurried to her campsite, and disappeared into their lodge.

Hawk Soaring plopped beside Bright Sun Flower. "I saw your smile fade. Why?" He rubbed Hawk Feather's hair.

She hugged Hawk Feather tighter. "It has been too long since I fasted and sought a vision. I need to go off by myself. Eagle always waits for me, sends me dreams, but I have not spoken with her as often as I should now. Her call is strong."

She cleared her throat and turned with troubled eyes to face him. "We spoke of staying, even decided we would not go back. Now I am not so sure. I do not worry for us. I worry about the dangers outside the forest and for the futures of our family and band."

"Woman, we are a strong people. Those who wish to stay will do so knowing what they face. We never ran from a fight. I admit we seldom had to fight hidden in the canyons."

He gripped her hand. "As you said before, we have lived many cycles of seasons past elders who have never seen the forest. Still, it is hard to choose what is right for us, for our family. The band must speak on this together. Perhaps some will stay, and some will choose to return to the forest. Could be part of the Big Sky Mustang Peoples will choose to experience the forest, and part will wish to stay. If they do," his eyes met hers, "will we stay? Should we stay?

"I, too, woman, worry about the hairy-faces and the Peoples Sparkling Star came from. How long before we encounter them? Will they invade and take what they wish? I have had my own dreams. Dreams of a future where our people will not live as we do now. If these dreams come to pass, can the forest protect us? If we stay, are we being selfish by our wishes to go to the campfires in the sky? We have much knowledge to pass onto the young. In the forest, we would have more time to teach, but we need to learn more ourselves and cannot do that in the safety of the forest." He looked up as children ran past, chasing each other, and nodded their way. "I see many children and know there is much they need to learn. How do we choose?

"If we return to the forest, how can we learn more so we can better teach the young out here? And what we learn out here, the young ones within the forest will need to learn. Now, we can pass on the knowledge we have, but to have more to pass on, we must also experience it. Perhaps we will do both and come out onto the grasslands as teachers when we are needed."

Bright Sun Flower nodded past her man. "You see Dove and Singing Stone walking in the stream? Do you think if his band does not wish to follow that Dove will willingly leave him behind and go back to the forest? I must seek guidance from Eagle." She reached out and played with the fringe on his tunic. "I wish you to do the cutting. I know you will aid me."

"Woman, it has been many cycles of seasons since you have done this."

"And?"

"I have a mate's worry. I will do it for you and be near. For now, we must meet the people the boy belongs to, then we will go and be alone. We have much time. When Father Sun wakes you may start your fast. This night, we will join as one band and learn about each other, enjoy good food, sing, dance, and not worry."

"Man of mine, we must all worry for children yet unborn." She smiled at Hawk Feather as he woke. "He is strong willed, this one."

Chapter 37

Once the Wolf People had settled in, many campfires burned. Women passed much food back and forth from the camps. Before long, the bands had settled, bellies full, and stories made their rounds, passing from fire to fire about the forest, the canyons, and the Likes To Fight People. Scouts from all the bands took turns staying alert for any possible attacks.

Listens To Wind chose to care for Fire Starter and Big Moon after seeing tears in the youngest boy's eyes. She sat with them in front of her grandson's lodge. *If their fathers came to camp, they would see their sons unharmed. Perhaps then their fathers would raise a hand in peace.*

Her own emotions flooded forth with the memories of her mistreatment as a captive. To help the boys overcome their fear, she kept them busy learning how to patch their footwear, and she told them stories about her seasons with the mustangs, how much they meant to the people.

Singing Stone glanced around while sitting with his own repaired footwear. "I think perhaps I will go care for my dogs, maybe walk past Four Arrows' lodge." He raised his arms and walked in a circle. "I see much beauty this day. There are wonderful smells everywhere, like cooking and the sweet smell of mustangs." He glanced toward Listens To Wind. "There is the sweet smell of women in the air."

She threw leather scraps at him. "Grandson, I know you well. Do not speak this to anyone, not even your mother. I will decide if I will become Four Arrows' mate, not you."

"Of course." He stretched and cleared his throat. "We men never know what to say about a stubborn woman."

Listens To Wind reached for his foot, but he moved and was gone before she could grab hold. *Men! Four Arrow has the winters of my daughter's man. Does this make me old in my thinking?* "I am not so old!"

Fire Starter and Big Moon dropped their footwear and stared at her, worry etched across their faces.

She smiled and shook her head "Boys... men. Mustangs are easier to understand."

***

Singing Stone jumped on Spirit Eyes and headed away from both camps but still in the cover of the trees. Not far from camp, Dove sat on Fire and waited for him. The tall grass waved as Sister Wind caressed it. He tapped his animal into a trot. They were within four mustang lengths of each other when Spirit Eyes reared and backed up. The animal bobbed his head in irritation and snorted. He tried to turn and run.

"This will be a good thing, boy. You are the first mustang to meet the wolves, not just smell them. We moved our herd way back so they would not run. I need you to meet them and to help the others understand. My dreams tell me they will be part of the future of our band."

Spirit Eyes balked. Singing Stone leaned over and looped a rope from twisted grass around the mustang's neck, then slid to the ground, hugged the animal, and spoke in quiet tones. "Do not fear anything, boy. These are special wolves, mystical." He held onto the neck rope and continued to speak in whispers as he led his mustang one step at a time closer to the wolves.

With White Paws at her side, Dove motioned for her mustang and the other wolves to remain where they stood. From behind her, Fire whinnied and trotted up to Spirit Eyes before they could stop her. She met him muzzle to muzzle. They greeted each other, breathing into the other's nostrils.

From the side, White Paws moved at a slant to the mustangs, curving his body away as he neared. He kept his head turned to one side, away from Spirit Eyes. The wolf kept his head at the same height as his shoulders, as crouching was a sign of a hunting wolf. Before Spirit Eyes could react, the wolf already sat sideways before him, tongue hanging to one side. The mustang snorted and stepped back a half step. The animal's body trembled.

Fire nickered softly as she moved closer and placed her head across Spirit Eyes' neck. The male, eyes still wide, stopped his nervous prancing, turned his head, and touched Fire's shoulder.

White Paws turned so his back showed toward the mustangs. After a short span, Spirit Eyes settled. Fire withdrew her head, walked over to the wolf, lowered her muzzle, and sniffed White Paw's back. The wolf glanced over his shoulder at the mustang, his tongue lolling from the side of his mouth as if he were smiling at Fire.

Singing Stone's mouth fell open. "How does she know to do that? You must have Power, Dove! Do you? You are as a Mustang Woman."

She twisted her head his way. "You called me a name that another has told me will be my name one day. It was not my Power that created Fire's smart mind. She has her own Power. Everyone carries power. Every living being has Energy, and from that Energy comes Power. My father taught me that."

Dove approached Spirit Eyes and reached toward the animal's muzzle. Spirit Eyes blew in her palm, and she laid her forehead against his cheek. "It is all right, boy. White Paws will not harm you, any child, or any other mustang. This I tell you."

The mustang bobbed his head as if he understood her words. One hoof at a time, he edged toward Fire and White Paws. Singing Stone, while singing his calming song, took the rope from Spirit Eyes' neck and stood to one side.

White Paws sat still, only turning his head for brief glances as the mustang approached. Spirit Eyes hesitantly lowered his muzzle and ran it up and down the wolf's back. After a short span, White Paws stood, shook himself and turned his side to Spirit Eyes. The mustang stretched his neck and touched muzzles with the wolf. White Paws lowered his head as if he sniffed an interesting smell and wandered away. The rest of the wolves followed him.

Fire led Spirit Eyes a little ways off and dropped her nose to graze. He grazed next to her. Her muzzle touched his to help reassure the mustang all was well.

"Dove, Spirit Eyes understood you, understood your words! This has not happened with any other. You truly are Mustang Woman."

"I do not know why he understood me. Perhaps he felt my mind and heart. I am honored that he did. "She turned and walked away from the mustangs, and he fell in beside her.

"Stone, I watched you go into the herd and walk up to the lead male. It is you who speaks the words of mustangs."

He turned toward her and smiled. "And you speak with wolves."

She shrugged. "We understand each other. When I was a baby and my people were on the grasslands, Father said if the wolves had not been with us, helped us, we would not have made it back to the safety of the forest."

The wolves trotted toward them. White Paws moved to Dove's side while the others sniffed the ground a little ways from them.

Singing Stone started to reach out to the wolf, but pulled back. "I wish to touch him as you do. Will he allow me?"

"You must ask him. I do not own him."

The amber eyes of White Paws drew him in. "May I touch you, White Paws?" With great caution, he reached his hand out.

The wolf stepped close to him and tilted his head, muzzle pointed away. Singing Stone scratched beneath the wolf's chin as he had seen Dove do. After a short span, White Paws moved to the other side of Dove and sat.

The mustangs walked between the widely spaced wolves as Fire led Spirit Eyes back to Singing Stone. He reached up and rubbed between the mustang's eyes. "I hope we do not have to do this with every mustang!"

She laughed as she nuzzled Fire's neck. "You have the gift of singing calming sounds to comfort the animals. I am sure the others will respond and listen to you and watch Spirit Eyes as a wolf comes up to him. Most of our younger ones have been with these wolves since they were born, so they accept them. We must walk among the mustangs with only White Paws at first."

The mustangs wandered away again. She sat on the grass, and the wolves sprawled out to rest in the warmth. She lay back on her arms, her face tilted upward to Father Sun. Her long, loose hair fell backward and fanned out the grass.

"Dove, where are we to go?" Singing Stone sat next to her, crossed his legs and picked a long blade of grass to twist between his fingers. "To your home, the forest, or will we go back and stay in the canyons where I live, where your people once came from? I wish to see your home, but I also wish you to be in the canyons, to show you the beauty there. My parents speak of following the mustangs, perhaps wandering the canyons and grasslands both. Water Lily and Wanderer speak much on living in the forest."

She leaned forward and hugged White Paws who came to rest at her side, his head in her lap. "Father speaks of going back to the forest before the cold season finds us. I wish to see the canyons. He says we must turn back soon or we could be caught in snow in another moon, maybe two, and it will take over a moon to return.

She turned to face him. "I wish to see the canyons, so much so." She bit her lower lip and creased her brows. "Yet my dreams of arrows filling the air frighten me. My dreams may or may not happen, but could be a warning just the same.

"Father says some dreams are warnings of danger, but do not always mean they will happen exactly as we see them. I worry still because of what you have told me of the ones who chase your people. To me, it is wrong that they want to harm such beautiful animals. I wish for the mustangs to be safe. In the forest, they will be safe. Out here... are they safe, Singing Stone?"

He pulled a small stone from its resting place and felt the smooth edges with his fingers. "The stones are vibrating and have been since our camps met. When they vibrate, it is a warning to be aware. Grandmother has heard warnings in the breath of Sister Wind and has told me not to wander far, that even if we do not see the Likes To Fight, she is sure they mean to find us. We must decide soon, you and I. You know of the two boys in our camp. We have men watching for their people."

"*We* must decide? Both our Peoples have Holy People, elders. *They* are the ones who will decide." She put her head down and snuggled White Paws.

"No, it is we who must decide. We are to be the warriors for the mustangs. My dreams show me this."

"They will not listen to us. I am but a girl to my people, and you—"

"I am a man among our people." He puffed out his chest. "Because the stones sing to me, Water Lily asked our people to listen to my dreams. She has great Power and is respected. She made the people see that I, too, have Power."

He stared into her bright eyes. "I welcomed Power. I have heard there are those who fear Power. Fear the changes it will bring." He reached out and took both her hands in his. "I can see Power in you, feel it. I know you do not fear it."

He leaned closer as White Paws moved away from her. "We are more together than alone. You are me... I am you. I have felt this connection since I saw you in my dreams, and I know you felt it, too. My heart says our Peoples will only listen if we both speak. Side by side, we will stand."

Dove's lips firmed and she lifted her chin. "Then this is why *she* called me Mustang Woman."

"She, Dove?"

Chapter 38

Bright Sun Flower had left the camps three days ago to pray, to cry for a vision. Hawk Soaring took tiny pieces from her arm, her sacrifice, and then left her alone. She sat in the long grass and waited for Eagle to respond. All around her, small white flowers bloomed. The same kind she had used to teach Shining Light about life's Circles. She ran her hands over the tops of the flowers. "Nature teaches us so much if we only listen, watch."

Eagles calling above in the cornflower sky caught her attention. One came back from the hunt with food for their young, and the other called to his mate as he passed her. They both turned and took pieces of the food to tease their young ones. The pair of nearly grown eaglets called and chased after their parents who evaded them.

"Eagles, too, make sacrifices for their young. They feed them many times a day, and then must teach them to hunt for themselves. Not much different from our own people."

'Our duty is always to the young ones. Their future depends on the choices we make for them and ourselves. Those choices become their future and the future of those yet unborn. The guidance we offer will live on in our children — if we have it to offer.'

Eagle gave her no chance to respond. The Sacred bird spread her wings, flew into a cloud, and vanished. Bright Sun Flower sat in silence as Father Sun made his way across the sky and melted into the grass. With a smile, she lay down and slept.

When Father Sun woke, she stood, stretched out her arms and sang her song of thanks. Perhaps things would be different, but with Creator's guidance, everything would be as it should.

"Sometimes we need to be alone to discover just how lonely we can become. How often we blame others for things gone wrong. Maybe blame Creator. But we are responsible for our own choices. *We* are Sister Wind, the trees, each leaf of grass. We are the small stones water rushes over. We are the water."

Arms still outstretched, she raised her head and stared up at Father Sky. "Every strand in the Web Of Life connects us, one to the other. When one strand is broken, it harms all of the Web. If too many strands are broken, we cannot live. The strands connect us, gives us the Energy of life, the Power that makes us who we are. We are Creator, and Creator us."

Hawk Soaring slipped next to her. "Your words.... Forgive me for listening, but they are words we all need to hear. I hope you say them again and again to everyone you meet. Your words have touched my heart and will touch many more, my sweet woman. It has been an honor to have known you all these long cycles of seasons, to have been part of your life. It is right and good that we teach our children how important women are. It is the women who keep the band together, who carry the next generation in their bellies, who bring balance to men. My woman, my friend, I now understand why we belonged in the forest for so many cycles of seasons. We had much to learn about each other and the different Peoples. We could not have done so in our beautiful canyons.

"Your vision? Is there anything you can tell me?" He took her hand and pressed his lips to it. "No matter if you cannot. I heard much wisdom from your words and they will guide me. Heh. I am not so old that I cannot learn from the words of another."

She leaned against him and laid her head on his shoulder. She took in air and let it out in one long breath. "Eagle is the wise one. She spoke of things we can do nothing about, but also told me how we could maybe help."

"What of us, woman? Will we stay or return to the Forest of Tall Trees?"

Chapter 39

With both camps settled in, the people spent time learning about each other. Men met women, and some joined the other's band and became mates. Families passed many gifts to the new couples and between themselves. Every night, the camps grew closer to each other until they were one. Children chased each other and adults talked well into the darkness. The wolves remained along the fringes where Shining Light and his family stayed to be near them.

Father Sun woke and slept many times before the new mustangs settled down enough so they did not race away at the sight of wolves nearby. The lead female still chased the wolves away if they came too close to the herd.

Thunder raced past the older lead female and pawed the ground near her, but raced off when she bared her teeth and started to chase her. Each day, Thunder grazed closer until she settled in far enough away to not be a threat, yet close enough to keep the old one wary. With only one dominant male, problems did not arise.

Four Likes To Fight men came in weaponless and palms forward to speak of getting Fire Starter and Big Moon back. Falcon Storm invited Wanderer, Shining Light, and Water Lily to sit with him. Listens To Wind and Four Arrows sat far away enough to hear, but not disrupt the talk.

Two lodges away, River Song sat with the boys, Singing Stone, Gentle Wisdom, and Animal Speaks Woman. Expressions on the boys' faces stayed stoic and they stared ahead, not at the men who came to speak.

Any warrior not guarding those who spoke to the Likes To Fight men hid along pathways where an enemy might sneak up. The rest of the warriors stood along the edges of the rise where the bluff rose from the valley and trees below where the enemy could see them. The men were careful to stay out of arrow range.

Worry made River Song sew Falcon Storm's new tunic a bit too fast. She poked herself repeatedly and growled her frustration. "I wonder how many of them wait where we cannot see." She rubbed her large belly. "I have never felt so helpless. My belly is too big to allow my mind comfort. I can still fight, but it is my child I worry for if something happens. These men may only be waiting to signal their companions."

"There are few bands who allow their women to fight alongside their men." Gentle Wisdom handed her a wooden bowl steaming with meat and tubers. "Eat. It is good food made by Animal Speaks Woman. She knows where to find the best and sweetest tubers. Do not worry so. A woman who will soon welcome a new baby should allow others to worry about fighting."

She dropped her sewing and took the bowl. "I am honored to have such good food." She breathed in the aroma. "My mother, my son, and I had no band for five cycles of seasons. We had to fight. We followed the mustangs and did our best to keep them safe from those kinds of bands." She nodded toward the Likes To Fight men whose hands moved as rapidly as their mouths. "I would be over there if not for my unborn baby. It is sometimes hard for our new band to accept women who fight next to their men, but I will never change who I am."

After heated words, the Likes To Fight men stood without a glance at the boys as they jumped on their mustangs and raced away. The boys looked down. Fire Starter crawled in the lodge. Big Moon crawled in after him.

Animal Speaks stood as Shining Light stomped her way. "Light, what has happened? Never have I seen such an angry look on your face!"

His glare did not soften as he sat among the women. "Wanderer spit out his words as if he could poison the enemy with them. He asked why they did not bring tobacco to Water Lily as is tradition among all the Peoples to show respect for a Holy Person. They sat with eyes squinted in response. They must think us weak in body and mind to show such disrespect."

He shook his head. "I do not understand them. They show no care, no worry for the boys who wanted to only bring honor to them. They did not even glance toward Fire Starter and Big Moon." Anger tightened his jaw. "How can a people not wish to have their children back?

"Water Lily offered to give each boy two mustangs and other gifts to honor the boys' bravery. The men did not even nod their thanks. They demanded that we give them the woman they sought, half of each of our herds and... and the wolves! When I told them the wolves would not follow them, they laughed and spoke of killing them for their hides. Their hides! They yelled things I did not understand. I stood and left before I did anything to show my readiness to fight. I would have been the one disrespecting Water Lily for my boldness at her fire."

Listens To Wind grumbled as she walked over and sat next to her daughter. "Shining Light, they do not know who we are, but they know we joined the Big Sky People. One warrior claims to have knowledge about us joining this band. I understood their last words well.

"The man, I believe to be the lead warrior, spoke of his son being badly wounded by a 'wild woman.' That the boy nearly passed over from his heart nearly being pierced." Her eyes narrowed. "I am the woman who wounded his son. He tried to pull me off my mustang and I sliced only his chest, and he was not so bad that he would have passed over. He hit his head on a rock and fell into a deep sleep. Their tongues are dirty, heavy with lies." She leaned forward and raised her hands to her face. "How can a people do this?"

She dropped her hands. "Holy Man, they only make such demands to force the people to give me, my daughter and grandson over to them.

"They have no interest in the boys. They stole them during a raid on another band three cold seasons ago. When Fire Starter and Big Moon's people offered many gifts for their return, they attacked them." She held up her hands, palms out. "I wish to speak of this no more. The boys have no family to care for them. I will be their family." Listens To Wind crawled inside the lodge. River Song followed her in.

Animal Speaks crawled inside, pulling Hawk Feather with her. "Light, Singing Stone, go find Dove. Tell her to not leave camp. Who knows what such people would do. I feel I am needed here. River Song holds her belly too tight."

***

Listens To Wind sat next to River Song as her daughter shed tears. "Daughter, we are safe. No one will tell who we are. I told the enemy that the ones they seek had been here, spent two nights, and vanished into the darkness. I did not tell them the herd they chased is now among the other mustangs." She held River Song close. "I have never seen your eyes make so much water. Not even when we lost our men."

River Song pushed away her tears. "I went to be alone after we sang them to the campfire in the sky. You did not see my grief. I do not fear for myself. I fear for my baby, Singing Stone, and you. Perhaps once the baby is welcomed into the band, I will go hunt these men down!" She pounded her fists on her thighs. "You must care for the baby and watch out for Singing Stone if I do this. Maybe the forest is not so bad a place."

"I, your mother, refuse to allow you to do such a thing!" She held River Song's shoulders and gently shook her.

River Song laid her hands on her mother's arms. "Mother."

Listens To Wind held her close again." Daughter, you must relax."

A sharp pain shot though River Song. She jerked and pulled away. "I feel pain I should not. The baby comes early. I wish to stay here, with you, and not use the birthing lodge."

Concern clouded Listens To Wind's wet eyes. "How long have you been in pain?"

"Since before sunrise. Now that Father Sun is high, the pain sharpens. I feel the wetness that comes before the baby." She gripped her mother's arm. "For the first time since Singing Stone's first father went to the campfires in the sky, I am afraid. I am a strong woman. Some say a warrior woman, but I feel as a lost child."

Animal Speaks Woman began a song for the baby to come fast, for the child to be strong. Listens To Wind added her voice to the song.

Fire Starter and Big Moon made their way outside and sat close to the lodge's flap.

***

Every warrior in both camps readied for what would come. The people herded the mustangs together, but each time, Thunder squealed a protest at the other lead mare until a space separated the two herds. Shining Light roped Thunder and led her to Sparkling Star.

Though she tried to tie the mustang to her lodge, the animal yanked away, rope falling to the ground. Shining Light raised his hands in exasperation as Thunder once again enforced a separation between the herds. "As long as they are not too far apart, perhaps that crazy female is wiser than me. The herds may need a little space between them to ease their minds." He walked away to make sure the people stayed close together.

The children and many of the women gathered in a tight circle of lodges near the center of the bluff. Warriors, mostly men, but a few women, too, scattered to guard all pathways up the hill.

When Listens To Wind poked her head outside the lodge flap, Fire Starter stood tall, head raised. "You are our family now. My cousin and I will stand outside the lodge and protect you women." The boy held up a small skinning knife.

"Boy, you understand our words?" Listens To Wind's jaw fell open.

"Yes, we understand your words, but feared that you might be as the others who captured us, maybe harm us." He looked down. "Though they killed our band and changed our names, we tried to show bravery so they would accept us and allow us to sleep inside their stick huts. Nothing we did was good enough. For three cycles of seasons, we tried. Still, they made us sleep on the ground. We huddled with the dogs for warmth. As we lay on the ground, we spoke our own people's words to each other so we would not forget who we came from. Our people's words were not so different from yours." He glanced up. "If you will have us, we will fight for you."

Listens To Wind nodded. "You are smart boys to first listen and learn. When this is over, I will go in front of the Council and claim you as my children. It will be an honor to do this. For now, it may not be safe for you to show yourselves. Stay low. The Likes To Fight warriors did not act as if they cared what happened to you. I must care for my daughter now." She nodded and went inside to River Song's side.

Crouched on the other side of River Song, Animal Speaks Woman sat her son in the middle of a pile of hides. "Hawk Feather, listen well to me." Her eyes met his. "You are not to move."

Hawk Feather sat wide-eyed and silent.

"So, little one, you can listen. Good." She handed her son a strip of jerked meat to keep him busy.

River Song tried to sit up. "Where is Singing Stone? I must find him!"

Listens To Wind gently pushed on her daughter's shoulders. "I heard him leave and go to the Wolf People's side of camp to find Dove. You have no time to worry for him, only time to worry for your baby. I know you have a mother's worry, but Singing Stone knows how to care for himself."

"Mother, they call him a man! He has never been in a battle like this."

"We taught him well. He is smart and knows what to do to avoid danger."

River Song fell back. "He is my baby."

"No longer. Your *baby* is the one you are about to bring into this lodge, not the one who joins others to protect our band."

Animal Speaks Woman and Listens To Wind began singing again. River Song rocked herself and sang with them.

Ruby Standing Deer

Chapter 40

Water Lily sat in front of her lodge with Shining Light and Wanderer in a well hidden position behind saplings and thick shrubs that grew mixed in with the young trees. "Our leader of warriors is still gone with his scouts. Falcon Storm takes his place, but has many concerns in leading the warriors who defend the camp. Both he and the elders of the Big Sky Mustang People have asked me to speak for them. I know the Wolf People trust you both. We must decide our actions soon. I value the words both of you speak."

Wanderer remained quiet for a span. "We must protect our people who cannot fight, pull them back. The Likes To Fight must not know we do this. I must think." He stood to leave.

She also stood and lit her Sacred Sage. She ran it over their bodies, both front and back, while she sang a prayer of protection over them. "You must both go, think about our people and how to keep them safe. Before you go, know this: I can and will fight. Only our women with young children and the elders who can no longer battle will leave. I am sure some of our women, such as I, will fight."

She held up her hand when Wanderer frowned. "Do not waste breath and time, old man. I will not—cannot sit by and not be part of this."

***

Wanderer sat next to Shining Light, who crouched on the edge of the bluff, close to some of the warriors of the Big Sky Mustang People. "Soon darkness will take the land. If they are like any other band of people, they will not fight until Father Sun wakes."

"Wanderer, I fear we may be wrong. The stones around my neck feel very hot. I have come to know this as a warning. Never before have they burned my neck. We must move the children and women while darkness hides them."

"My young friend, you are truly becoming wise. Many times, while sitting at our band's campfires, I have heard the story of how my sister, Blue Night Sky, helped to move the captives of the hairy-faces through the darkness when your dreams told you about Peoples in the grasslands who were in much trouble." Wanderer shook his head. "Still, I fear our women and children will be helpless once they leave the flat top of this hill."

Singing Stone crawled out of the shadows of a nearby boulder and stood. "We can use the mustangs. We will use the deer trail on the side away from the Likes To Fight People. Our people can hide within the herd, and the mustangs' hooves will hide their footsteps. They will not know where our people went."

Wanderer raised his head and looked at the young man. "What if one animal becomes frightened? The whole herd could spook and run. Any of our people caught in their path could be trampled or pushed over the edge of the narrow trail."

"Great One, I, Singing Stone, have a gift Creator gave me." He lowered himself beside Wanderer. "I will walk among the mustangs and keep them calm. I can sing to them, soothe them. Maybe even that crazy one you call Thunder will listen." He reached out and touched the boulder he sat near. "The big stone is hot. I worry for all of us. My mother, grandmother... Dove.—"

Wanderer clutched his arm. "Boy, if you can really do this, you must try. If the mustangs move slowly, our Peoples can vanish as a fog on a clear sunrise."

Singing Stone nodded. "I leave now."

Shining Light touched his own necklace. "I know your people call you a man, and I will honor you as one. When the people are far away enough from here, have them ride the mustangs. If there are not enough animals, they must ride two to a mustang. Ask our four-legged relatives to do this for our people, to take them to a safe place."

He nodded to Shining Light. "I am honored by your belief in me."

Shining Light crawled away from the bluff's edge. "I will go speak to my people, tell them to listen to your words."

Wanderer pushed up from the ground with a grunt. "Singing Stone, you have a sister who just greeted the band. Go to your mother first. Your mother is strong but will need help moving as soon as you can get to her." A mouse ran up the Great Holy Man's sleeve and sat on his shoulder. He smiled and stroked the tiny grey creature. "Hmm, what is it, little one? Oh, yes. Tell the others." The mouse scampered back down and jumped off him.

Singing Stone's eyebrows gathered tightly. "What did that mouse say to you? How do you know my mother—"

Wanderer leaned in closer. "That mouse has his own plan. I know things you do not understand. Your mother, go to her. I wish to speak to Water Lily. I know she spoke of fighting, but I worry for her safety."

His words had barely left his mouth when Water Lily and Gentle Wisdom stepped out of the trees' shadows.

"I find it amusing that the Great Holy Man did not hear us." Water Lily grinned. "I go where I am needed, and I am needed here. Gentle Wisdom is faster in her mind than you men are. She has already sent her mate and the others to gather their animals."

Wanderer held Water Lily's arm. "Gentle Wisdom is a warrior woman. You are—"

"Here, old man, as you are. Let go my arm or I will have to defend myself. Can you not feel the strength in my arm? I am not an old, helpless woman."

The defiance in her voice challenged him and he let go. "When last did you hold a bow, old woman?" He squeezed his lips into a thin line.

She lifted her chin. "Just this sunrise. I hunt my own food to stay strong. And I never miss. Yes, I took a risk hunting this day, but I do not fear the Spirit Land. I will go there when it is my time, as we all will." She squeezed her brows into one line. "I am not some hairy-face's weak woman who cannot jump on a mustang without help.

"Ha! One of their men tried to take me down from my mustang three cycles of seasons ago, and I kicked him hard enough to break his nose. He screamed like a terrified rabbit! His other two companions were too busy laughing to keep me from riding away. I am strong." She bent her arm. "Feel my muscles, if you wish." She grinned when his eyes locked on her.

"Never doubt that Power of the mind keeps the Power of the body going. Any doubt, and your body will falter. Never doubt, Holy Man. You are strong if you listen to your mind and throw doubt into the dirt behind you as I have done. You and I will speak more on this when we are safe." She leaned into his shoulder. "Perhaps we will speak of even more, Man Of Power who has mice on his shoulders. Mice. Do they also sleep with you?"

Singing Stone grinned at the two elders. "You have eyes for each other as Four Arrows has for my grandmother."

Glares from both Wanderer and Water Lily made him shuffle backward. "Perhaps this is a good time to leave."

Shining Light chuckled, then silently moved away and headed toward his people to speak to them.

Water Lily turned toward Singing Stone and waved him away. "Tell your mother I dreamed of a fawn dancing. Now go save your family. Help get our people to a safe place. Have the elders ride so you can move faster. Once you are on the grasslands, go toward the four campfires in the sky that make a straight line. There are canyons there in which the people can become as hard to find as dry grass in a thunderstorm. This is the way you need to go."

"I hear your words, Holy Woman. I go to help my mother and new sister, then I will lead the mustangs." He followed the way Shining Light had gone.

Gentle Wisdom cleared her throat. "There is much, I, too, need to do." She moved away as quiet as Butterfly's wings.

After Gentle Wisdom left, Wanderer reached for Water Lily's hand. "When Father Sun rises and we fight, stay at my side. When we have ended this, I wish to take you to the Land of Tall Trees. I have not loved a woman in so long my heart may be too old to stand the pain of loss. I do not wish to lose you now."

She squeezed his hand. "I have never loved before. I do not have any desire to lose this feeling." She started to pull her hand away. "What are we doing? We are beyond the age of... of love. Are we not?"

"I thought I was, and refused all women after I lost both my women and sons to the hairy-faces long ago. Now I know different." They sank to the ground, sitting so close that their arms touched. He leaned over and rubbed his face against hers.

"We could both take our last breath when Father Sun wakes." She laid her head on his shoulder.

"I would be happy to breathe my last in your arms, woman."

Chapter 41

Knows Both Sides crawled out of River Song's lodge flap carrying the new baby tightly bundled in furs. Listens To Wind and Animal Speaks Woman each held one of River Song's arms and helped her outside.

"Daughter, we cannot wait." Listens To Wind whistled low. "Snow is nearby."

Knows Both Sides untied his mustang from a slender tree. "Snow was not tied. Would she not have moved on to be with the herd?"

Listens to Wind whistled low again. "Snow would not leave me any more than Spirit Eyes would walk away from Singing Stone."

A soft nicker sounded from the deep shadows of the darkness. Another nicker answered it from a bit farther away. Snow came forward and nuzzled her without hesitation.

The crackle of a dry twig sounded loud in the stillness. Spirit Eyes followed behind Singing Stone over to the women and Knows Both Sides.

Listens To Wind placed a hand on her grandson's shoulder. "This is Knows Both Sides. He is a wise man, a Two-Spirit, who has come to help us. He comes with Dove's mother."

She took the new baby from him. "Please, help my daughter onto my animal. Snow is the only mustang I trust to carry my daughter and her new baby."

"I am not so weak that I cannot walk." River Song protested as Knows Both Sides lifted her.

"Take your new daughter." Listens To Wind reached up and handed her the tiny bundle. "She is small, but strong. You will ride Snow. If you need to get away with your baby quickly, you can do so." The sound of her voice left no room for argument.

After Knows Both Sides jumped on his mustang, he nodded toward Animal Speaks Woman. "Give Hawk Feather to me." Speaks handed the unusually still child up to him.

Singing Stone wrapped his arms around Spirit Eyes then pushed the mustang toward his grandmother. "You and Animal Speaks ride him. He will allow you to do so. Since we must ask the animals to walk slowly, we will not have to worry about stepping into the ground animals' homes. We may not be able to see very far, but the Mustangs know where they are and you will be safe.

"I must go to help the others of our people and the Wolf People mix the herds and to ask the mustangs to accept one another and carry the elders so we may move quicker." He pointed to the campfires in the sky. "The people need to follow those four campfires, go where they lead so those who stay behind can find everyone when the... the battle is over."

"Son, I will not have you leaving me! I do not know where Falcon Storm is."

The panic in his mother's voice made him stop. "I am not a boy. I am a man, and I have responsibilities to the whole band."

He firmed his lips and met his mother's frantic eyes with a steadfast gaze. "I learned this lesson when Grandmother and I left ahead of everyone because of my own need. I did not think of anyone else. A shame I will never forget." He glanced about in the darkness. "Where are the boys?"

"They were sitting outside the lodge and... I... I thought they were right behind us!" Listens To Wind whirled about and stared into the darkness then slapped her head. "Those silly, brave boys! I fear they have gone to fight! I must find them."

Before she could run off, Singing Stone reached out and grasped her shoulder. "It is dark and you cannot know which way to go. You have a new granddaughter to help protect. I will try to find Falcon Storm and ask him to look for the boys. Now, please go."

River Song stared down at her son. "Singing Stone is truly a man now." She tapped Snow into a walk and moved off behind Knows Both Sides.

Listens To Wind and Animal Speaks Woman leapt onto Spirit Eyes and followed.

***

The way from the bluff was a steep, winding trail animals had used for some time. The mustangs traveled in single file with the people scattered along the path. Sister Wind picked up and hid the sounds that might carry in the darkness as Listens To Wind whispered to her for help. Like Spirits that make no sound, the peoples' footsteps glided across the rough ground, kicking no stones loose to rattle down the hill. Hooves stepped softly. Not one mustang nickered to another. Only crickets chirred as the lone, low voice of Singing Stone's song blended into Sister Wind's own song.

When they reached the area where the land flattened, Shining Light touched Singing Stone's shoulder and whispered, "Dove... have you seen Dove? I thought she was with my grandparents, but they told me she never went to them."

"Dove is missing? I must go find her!" He stopped and spun around, desperately searching for a mustang who would not mind carrying him.

Shining Light pressed his hand against Singing Stone's chest. "You must calm yourself. Breathe deep and feel with your mind. Hold tighter to the stone you wear around your neck and think of my daughter. I can feel my own stones connect to yours. I feel only cold stones that do not vibrate when I think of her."

Still, Singing Stone's eyes darted over the mustangs. "But I worry!"

Shining Light grabbed his arm and shook it lightly. "Make your voice low! We are not far enough away. Our voices may carry above Sister Wind. I worry as well, but the stones tell me she is safe. Listen to yours. It is because of you that I understand my stones. You are to keep moving and keep the mustangs calm. Only you can do this. If they panic, our Peoples will be in danger, maybe trampled."

A shove from behind made Shining Light whirl around. "Thunder!"

The animal shoved him again and nickered softly, her hooves dancing in place.

"I need go with Thunder. She has never sought me out before." He placed both hands on the young man's shoulders. "Will you stay with our Peoples and the animals? See them to safety?"

Singing Stone tensed under his hands. "Yes, Holy Man, I will do this. You must find Dove, please! And, Holy Man, the two boys my grandmother wishes to adopt are missing and she might try to go find them. I know her well. She is strong in her will and will do what she must to protect them, even risk her life as any mother would."

"I will find my daughter and watch for the boys. Do not worry so. The mustangs feel your Energy. You must stay calm and sing your song. You will do this?"

The young man nodded, turned and moved away with the herd, his voice lost beneath Sister Wind.

Shining Light spoke soft words to Thunder expecting the mustang to back away. She stood and allowed him to jump on. She turned around and headed back toward the empty lodges. Before she reached the path that lead up the bluff, she swerved away and picked up a faint trail that looped around instead.

Shining Light's eyes grew large. Was she taking him to the Likes To Fight camp? His heart drummed in his head. He loosened his thighs from around her sides, leaned low on her neck, and whispered, "Thunder, what is this that you do? Stop!" *Creator, protect us please!*

She did not stop. The mustang kept moving with quick, deliberate steps. She slowed as she came closer to a small group of trees. A low whinny called out in the darkness. Thunder moved toward it. He could see a roped string of mustangs tied between two trees. A young boy slumped over a log facing away from the animals. His head bobbed in sleep.

How can these people leave only a boy to guard their mustangs after the Big Sky Mustang People captured them before? Are they so sure we would not try it again? Quiet laughter stopped the breath he meant to let go. Off in a group of trees, a small fire burned. Four warriors played a game with small round stones. They sat away from their animals. *They are careless! Our people would never be like this. Do they think we fear them too much to try again?*

Ahhh... I see they pass something around to drink. Their lead warrior will be very angry! One leans against another. Do they drink the red drink of the hairy-faces? I have heard that it makes a man's ears deaf and even his eyes cross. Is this why they are so careless?

He slid off Thunder, sneaked past the laughing men and pulled ropes off the mustangs' necks, letting seven go before someone brushed against his legs. He yanked out his knife, but stayed his hand at the last moment.

White Paws let out a low growl. The wolf's amber eyes shined red in the darkness. Shining Light knelt in front of him and whispered, "I had no idea you followed me, wolf. How it is that you are everywhere?"

The sounds of mustangs moving off drew Shining Light's attention. Thunder wove in between the slower moving animals and shoved them with her nose. She nipped lightly on one's rump and started to guide them away.

"White Paws, I must let the others go before they call to the loose ones. Stay and watch for the enemy." Silent as a feather drifting on the breeze, Shining Light backed away. One eye on the men, he quickly released the rest of the mustangs.

Thunder pushed on the last freed mustang, forcing her toward the path Shining Light had ridden in on, and vanished.

Shining Light shook his head as Thunder disappeared behind the other animals. *Thunder, I wish I understood your mind. You have an ability I have not seen, except in your mother, but even she is not as you.* He held still for a short span, listening. He cupped his ears, but heard no one. No sounds of anyone coming. Two of the men argued in words he could not understand. They stood and staggered for a span before they sat back down. One man offered them more to drink, and they slapped each other on the back as if there had never been an argument between the two.

He backed away and whispered to White Paws to follow. Too dark to know how many mustangs there were, or know where they went, he allowed Thunder to push them and he followed on foot, running with White Paws.

Chapter 42

Listens To Wind stopped Spirit Eyes and slid off. She tugged at the bottom of Animal Speaks' dress and frowned. "Lean over, I wish to speak to you."

"What will you do?"

"I must go back and find the boys. I fear for their lives. If they are captured again, who knows what they will do to them? In the darkness, their souls could be lost. Please watch over my daughter and the baby for me." She slipped into the stream of mustangs and people and disappeared back up the trail they had just come down.

She crept along the shadows and emerged next to her lodge. How many moons had she worked on those hides, and to have to run away and leave them! Her face flamed hot with anger, but she swallowed it down. *The boys are more important than all the hides on all of these lodges! I must find them.*

As she stepped around the side of the lodge, a dark shadow darted out from the lodge and grabbed her. She kicked and flailed until a voice hissed, "It is me, Four Arrows!"

Her body stilled and he set her feet on the ground. She spun around to face him. "Why are you here, in this lodge? My heart fell into my belly!" She pushed him away, then pulled him to her just as quickly and hugged him. "I thought my life had come to an end."

He held her, let her go, and motioned for her to sit, then took her hands in his. "We do not need anyone seeing us. No matter who we are, someone would maybe think we are the enemy. Shining Light spoke of the boys missing as he left to find his daughter. He found me and asked that I remain here in case they return. I realized if they were out here in the darkness, you would soon follow in search of them."

She trembled beneath his hands. "When I was... captive, the hairy-faces came often to the Likes To Fight camp with the red drink that makes men crazy. They would give this... poison of the mind drink to the warriors. The warriors would become crazy, and they would offer their own women to the hairy-faces to get more."

She stared into the darkness. The fear from her childhood crept over her like ice before sunrise on a cold morning. "When I would see the hairy-faces come, I would run, hide. One day, I was not fast enough and a warrior saw me, drug me out and threw me to the ground."

Tears gathered in her eyes, and Four Arrows fingered one from her cheek. "My shame is great. He held me down and poured the sweet, sticky drink into my mouth. I fought, but the harder I fought, the more he laughed. Other men came and held me while he forced the drink down my throat. One man did more than hold me down...."

"You are safe here in my arms. I will never look upon you with shame in my eyes. Ever." He brushed her hair from her face and smiled. "I see you for the woman you are now, not then. My heart is yours, always. Go on and speak to me. Get it out from where it hides deep in your mind. Let it out and let it go. Sister Wind will surely take it with her."

With a shudder, she continued. "They became tired of me and left me where I was. I lay out in the heat and no one cared, except one girl. She pulled me into the shade of a tree and stayed with me until my mind came back to my body. I was so sick I could not hold down water for a sunrise. She vanished before I could thank her. I do not even know if she was part of the band or with the hairy-faces."

Her jaw hardened. "The red drink kills the mind, but it also steals the Soul. I fear for the Souls of Fire Starter and Big Moon should they be forced to return to the Likes To Fight People."

He pulled her tighter against his warm chest. "We will find them, woman. We will find our sons, and they will stand with us at the binding ceremony."

She arched her neck to see him better. "Yes."

He tipped his head to one side. "Yes?"

"I will be your woman forever and always. Come." She stood and held out her hand. "Let us find our children."

He stood, reached for his bow and quiver of arrows, and swung them over his shoulder. "Where do you think they may have gone?"

She shook her head and picked up her bow from where it fell when she fought him. "I think the boys maybe believe they are the cause of this. It is not they the enemy searches for, it is my family. And that is only because they crave to fight. They use my family as a bear uses a tree to scratch. To help their itch to fight. If someone is at fault, it is me."

"It is no one's fault! The Likes To Fight men are who they are. The hairy-faces, with their greed and gifts to our enemy, give them much reason to fight, attack our people."

She pulled away, stared into his eyes, took his hand, and laid it against her cheek. "Now I understand the words Sister Wind spoke of the future. I see it was this future. Even the burning of my lodge and the loss of everything we had has been turned into a good thing, maybe a Sacred Happening. If it had not burned, we would not have joined your people, River Song would have never let go of her grief of losing her first man, Fire Starter and Big Moon would still be slaves... and I would not have found you. All is as it should be. We *will* find our boys, I feel it!"

He rested his chin on the top of her head. "You have a Sacred gift, to be able to understand Sister Wind." Arm around her shoulder, he gave her a squeeze, then let go. "You have never spoken so freely about yourself before. Our boys will have a good life. We go now to find them."

They moved silently through the edge of the trees, looking and listening for any signs of the two boys. They had gone halfway across the top of the bluff when Four Arrows stopped and pulled his knife from the sheath at his side. "The hair on my neck stands! Someone comes."

She took an arrow from her quiver and readied her bow. "I can fight. Never doubt that, future man of mine."

Standing back to back, they scanned the darkness. A great wolf stepped from the deeper shadows of the shrubs in front of Listens To Wind. Four Arrows reached out an arm as if to push her behind him.

"Is this a wild wolf, or one from the Wolf People's band?"

She ducked beneath Four Arrows and darted for the wolf. "White Paws? I am sure I know you. You follow their Holy Man." She knelt and reached out to him.

"Woman, are you certain of what you do? He may bite your face!"

"I am safe. If he wanted to bite me, he would have done so." She offered her hand for him to smell. As the wolf moved closer and sniffed her fingers, she looked in the wolf's nearly all white face. "Ahh! You are Moon Face, White Paws' mate."

The wolf sat and cocked her head at Listens To Wind.

"Woman, do not be so ready to touch a wolf! And... and I see more shadows coming our way." He moved up beside her and held out his knife.

Before either human could say more, two other wolves appeared before them.

"Do not fear them, Four Arrows. These wolves will not cause harm to us. They come to us for a reason. We must follow them. I feel this is what they wish."

A wolf mixed with grey and brown fur bumped his head into the warrior's thigh. With great caution, he offered his hand. The wolf rested her chin on Four Arrows extended hand, and he scratched under her chin. He raised his head, eyes with wonder. "Never before have I touched a wolf. I can feel the Power in this one. Her Power mingles with my own. I feel stronger! How is this so? The hairs on my arms stand up. Wolf Power."

He lowered his head to see the wolf's face better. Brown eyes stared into amber-brown ones. The wolf did not look away. "They do come to guide us." He sheathed his knife. "Lead us, wolves, and we will follow."

Chapter 43

"Dove!" Singing Stone picked up speed as he spotted her walking past a few mustang lengths away. "Where have you been? Why do you turn around? You must stay with the people. Your father and I searched for you."

Before he caught up to her, she stopped beside Fire and wrapped one arm around the mustang's neck. "I went back to my mother's lodge to get some dried pink flowers for an elder whose chest hurt. The flowers are full of Power and stopped his pain. I do not fear darkness, Singing Stone." She stretched herself tall. "My father is here? Where? I must let his know I am safe."

"I do not know. That crazy one you call Thunder trotted up to him, shoved him in the back. He jumped on her and left. You must stay here. When the people are a bit further from the bluff, I will go back and find your father, let him know you are with our people." He reached for her hand, but she jerked away.

"I must find my father." She hopped on Fire and started around him when he caught hold of the mustang's neck hair.

She scowled. "You will not force me to do something I do not wish to do. Mother is safe and so is my brother. If you see them, only speak of seeing me on Fire." She tapped her animal's sides and tried to get past Singing Stone.

"I will not allow you to leave alone. You are only a girl, Dove, and I... I love you. I must stay and keep singing to calm the mustangs until they are further away, then I will hurry back. Please, do not leave. Your father does what he must. You must not leave. You are only a girl, Dove."

Dove lowered herself to stare into his eyes. "It may be impolite to stare as I do, but know this: you are my heart. I may be only a girl, but I have known your touch in my dreams. One day we will be mates, but listen well. A man does not own his woman. A woman will always follow the Spirit's guidance and her own heart. Even when we are mates and I hear your words, the choices I make must be my own." She tapped Fire to go forward and left him standing alone.

As she rode further from the herd and the people, the eerie silence made Dove's heart thump. Even Sister Wind's light whisper had fallen silent. Shadows danced as the moon peeked from behind clouds. Each movement of the shadows made her jerk her head about as if the Likes To Fight might jump out and grab her. Her heart raced each time until she saw it was only grass moving or a stone hunched half hiding in the ground. The closer to the trail, up to the bluff and their deserted camp, the more her eyes saw what was not there.

Every loose stone Fire stepped on became the enemy ready to pull her off the animal. Her breathing came in short gasps, and she leaned down and clung to Fire's neck hair. With a quick glance around, she tapped her mustang to move faster. *'Be brave Dove, you are never alone.' Father spoke these words to me... believe.*

Fire stopped. The mustang's ears twitched in opposite directions. She snorted and bobbed her head, then nickered.

"Fire, no! Shhh."

A mustang somewhere in the surrounding darkness answered. Fire moved toward the sound and ignored Dove's pleas to stop. From the blackness, a mustang with two figures sitting on the animal approached. She sat up on her animal. "Fire Starter? Big Moon?" She signed to them. "Why are you not with the people?"

"Why are *you* not with the people?" Fire Starter slid down off his animal and went to her side.

Dove's mouth gaped. "You speak our words? I thought you were Likes To Fight People."

The boy grinned. "No, we never were. We were captives and are now free. We will have much time to speak of this. We saw an enemy creeping behind the herd as the animals started out into the flatlands. Big Moon and I waited in the darkness of a shrub and I jumped him. I hit him in the head with a stone and he fell into a deep sleep." He puffed out his chest. "Big Moon found where the enemy had hidden his mustang and see...." He waved at the animal Big Moon sat on. "Big Moon and I go climb the bluff to help fight." He held up a small knife.

That knife is too small. He cannot fight with only a knife! "Do not leave, please. I wish to find my father and ask your help. It... it will make you look good to our Peoples."

Fire Starter put his knife away and moved to their mustang's side to whisper to Big Moon, who leaned down from atop the mustang.

"We will do this for you. Where do we go?"

Fire shifted under Dove and pawed the ground. "I cannot feel his Energy. He is not on the bluff."

Fire Starter shrugged. "We would not have known you were out here if your mustang did not call out. With only half the moon awake, it is hard to see much." He jumped back on the mustang.

Fire pawed at the ground again, this time snorting and backing up.

"Fire, what is this you do?" She tried to squeeze her legs and lean forward, but Fire kept backing up.

Laughter in the shadows made Dove's belly clench. *Sweet Mother, is it the Likes To Fight?*

Two mustangs with riders showed themselves. One spoke and laughed as he grabbed the neck hair of the boys' animal. Before the man could throw a rope around the mustang's neck, Fire Starter jerked his knife from its sheath and stabbed the warrior's chest. The warrior's animal reared and he tumbled to the ground.

The second warrior charged at Fire Starter.

Arm raised, knife glinting in the dim moon light, Fire Starter slashed downward. Blood welled from the man's chest. The first warrior's animal danced close to Big Moon and he leaped onto the mustang.

Fire Starter cried out. "Dove, leave! Go to our warriors!"

For a short span, the second warrior nearly caught up to them, but then he clutched his chest and slumped over on his animal's neck. The mustang raced along, but then turned away from the boys and Dove. Panicked, Big Moon and Fire Starter's animals galloped headlong into the darkness.

Dove held on as Fire did her best to keep up, but the boys soon disappeared into the darkness. The dust their mustangs pounding hooves left behind filled the air.

She could taste the dust. *Sweet Mother, the enemy is near!* She tapped Fire, urging the animal to run faster. She found herself alone, lost. Fire stopped.

Her heart thumped in her ears and sweat dripped into her eyes. She leaned over and rubbed the animal's neck. "Fire, you helped me once before. Please help me again. So wrong that I left. What makes me think I am old enough to do such things? Spirits, help me please."

'Sometimes we get our minds headed on a path, and we think we know more than we do.'

She jerked up and stared into the darkness. "Who... who is there?" She wrapped her arms around herself.

'Me, girl. Mouse who sits on your shoulder. You forgot me, forgot I was with you, did you not? I held on with my claws to your tunic. You ride well.'

"Mouse? You speak!" She felt for her companion and rubbed the tiny body.

'Of course I speak. Just not your words.'

She turned toward the shoulder Mouse sat on. "Then why do I hear your words as if they were spoken by one of my people? Are you going to help me?"

Fire moved past a silhouette of large boulders and stopped.

'Only you can help yourself. I can only offer guidance. You hear my words because you need to. I could have spoken sooner, but destiny leads us all before anything else. Dove, you have come to where you needed to be. I know your fear. I feel it. I smell the bitterness in your throat, the sweat on your face. You are a little girl who has known only the safety of your parents, the forest. Your father told you that you were never alone, and his words are truth.'

Fire whinnied and turned her head. Dove crouched and leaned to the animal's side to hide herself.

"Dove?" A low whisper called out.

She sat upright. "Singing Stone? I thought you were guiding the mustangs and the people to a safe place. How did you find me? Why do you not ride Spirit Eyes?"

He rode closer and Fire greeted the mustang he rode with a touch of her muzzle to his. "Stones. As long as they vibrated, I knew I went the right way. When they stopped, I moved around until they vibrated again." He jumped off his animal. "Grandmother and Animal Speaks ride Spirit Eyes and follow my mother and my new sister on Snow. I needed to know they would be safe.

"Your father returned with more mustangs. Thunder, the crazy mustang, she is crazy smart. She leads the other mustangs your father brought and the people follow her. I told him Thunder would lead the herd and I would find you. We are not to go to the warriors, as there is much danger. These are the words of your father. We must hurry to where the herd and our people go."

"Mouse told me I am where I need to be. I stay." She slid from Fire's back and took Singing Stone's hand. "I think we are to wait here."

Brows furrowed, he stared at her. "Mouse?"

Chapter 44

Listens To Wind and Four Arrows came across the Likes To Fight warrior that had fallen from his mustang. They rode around him, then jumped off their animals.

Four Arrows knelt next to the fallen warrior. "This one will move no more. He bled from a wound to his belly. Too many hoof prints scatter from here. One set is heavy, as if a man rides. Three sets are light, maybe carry children." Head down, he followed the hoof prints as best he could. He stopped and pointed in two directions. "At first, all ran together. One animal turned and went alone, leaving three running together." He continued to track. "I cannot see where they may have gone, too much darkness.

"The adult could have been another Likes To Fight, but why would he stop chasing the others? And who are the three children? I have no answers."

"Three children?" She glanced about, then jumped off her mustang and knelt beside him. "Sweet Mother. What do we do?" She stood and stared across the empty land. "We can see nothing beyond our own animals."

"Yes, and it is too dark to split up. We must stay together. We do not know if other enemy warriors are about, maybe on foot. I see human prints mixed in the hoof prints." He stood and reached for her hand. "I will not lose you to an enemy arrow." He squeezed her hand. "I will not lose you!" He pulled her up and held her close. "You should not even be out here. And I brought you."

"I brought myself. You followed. Allow me now to walk alone. I need guidance. Do not worry so. I will whistle if I cannot find you. We both need to move away from this man, far away." She pulled herself away from him. "I do not get lost in the darkness. I follow the campfires in the sky as any person might, as I know you do. Take the mustangs and go follow the brightest campfire that never moves. Go toward our camp and wait near my lodge. I will come to you. Do not open your mouth to tell me no. I must try to hear what Sister Wind may say and I need to be alone to do so." She turned to leave, but reached out to touch his face. "Know that I love you."

***

Listens To Wind moved on silent feet into the darkness that lay close to the bottom of the bluff, near where the trail came down from the flat top. Sister Wind caressed her hair. The sounds of crickets chirring became part of her mind. She stopped and danced to the beat, twirling in circles, arms raised and moving as wings, a silent song in her heart.

Sister of mine, Sister of all that is cleansing, hear me.
Hear me call to you.
I become part of all that is. I become part of all that will be.
Without you, Sister Wind, life could not exist.
Hear me call to you.

She repeated her song four times and then became still.

Sister Wind teased at her hair before whirling around her body. Deep blue colors sparkled with tiny specks of even deeper blue around her. Eyes closed, she danced and whisper-sang her song once more.

'Human Sister, I feel your needs, know your desires. Become part of me.... Lift your mind from your body and move with me.'

Listens To Wind stilled herself and willed her mind free from the burden of her body. She relaxed her head and allowed it to drop. Shoulders slumped, arms hanging loose at her sides, her body released her mind.

"I am here, Sister Wind, I am within you. I am you."

'We go.'

"Where do we go?"

'Where you need to go.'

Darkness melted, and though Father Sun did not shine, the land lit up.

She looked down as if from a great height. "My grandson is out here with Dove? The boys! They are about to reach them."

'This is what you needed to see. This and your daughter.'

"My daughter? She is with the band, with her new baby."

'No longer. She comes with women from the Wolf People. Some of the Big Sky Mustang women also come.'

"Why? She only welcomed her baby—'

'She is strong like you were when you had to run with her in your arms while your band fought the hairy-faces long ago. Your daughter was not even a sunrise old and you ran with her.'

"Why do they come?"

'To help their men. Their children are with the elders of the Big Sky Mustang People.'

"I am torn! What do I do? My family... split, not together."

'You will know what to do. You always have, Human Sister.

Chapter 45

Shining Light rode back on Sandstone toward the bluff where the Peoples' warriors watched for danger. White Paws trotted with him a ways, then vanished. "That mustang daughter of yours has the knowing, Sandstone. If not for her, the Likes To Fight would still have their mustangs.

"They are twice bested. They will see their mustangs have been taken again. Too much shame for them to bear. They will be dangerous. I only wish I knew how many there are." He urged her to go faster.

Sandstone moved at a fast trot up the narrow, rocky trail. On the flat top, he turned her toward the abandoned lodges. He smelled smoke. Bow ready, he rode toward the lodges. Sandstone whinnied a greeting to the mustang tied outside.

He cupped his hands and called in a low voice. "Ho, who is there?" As Shining Light raised his bow, Four Arrows stepped from the shadows on the far side of the lodge.

"I greet you, Holy Man. I wait here for Listens To Wind to return. She has gone to find a place to better hear Sister Wind. The boys from the Likes To Fight People, Fire Starter and Big Moon, our soon-to-be-sons, are missing. Listens To Wind's grandson may be out there... and there may be another child out there. We found an enemy warrior that will ride no more. Four sets of tracks led away from him. One set showed a mustang carried an adult, but those tracks turned away, back toward the Likes To Fight camp. Two sets of tracks that were light, as if children rode the animals, soon bent away from a third set. Those tracks were light also. Maybe another child is out there and alone."

Shining Light's belly clenched with fear. "Soon, Father Sun will wake. We do not know what our enemy will do. I must go find the children. My daughter may be with them." He spun Sandstone around to leave when another mustang called out of the darkness. He dove off Sandstone and hunched on the ground, bow still in his hands.

A low whistle floated from the dark and Four Arrows jumped in front of Shining Light. "Listens To Wind!"

She called out. "Four Arrows?"

"We are here. The Holy Man, Shining Light, is with me."

The red-brown mustang walked closer. "Good. We must go now. In my vision I saw my grandson, the boys, and your daughter, Dove, Holy Man. They are together, but we must hurry!" She wheeled her animal around.

Four Arrows leaped forward and grabbed the mustang's neck hair. "Woman, where do you go? We must all stay close in this darkness."

Shining Light flew onto Sandstone. "Four Arrows, you go to the warriors. I go with her to find my daughter."

Four Arrows, clearly torn about what to do, froze in place. "I... I ... Listens To Wind is my woman. Soon to be my woman, and the boys—"

"You two may fight over who goes. I go now! Holy Man, Sister Wind showed me the women of your band come, my daughter with them." She squeezed her legs and the mustang sprang away and left both men behind.

Four Arrows flung himself on his animal, bow in hand. "I will go to Listens To Wind."

Shining Light tapped Sandstone and led out. "We both go. We do not know what waits for her. Sweet Mother, there must be a way to stop this! Our warriors of the Wolf People are not experienced. Life in the forest has been too easy. Never again. I will see to the young people's fighting games, prepare them for the life my visions have shown me."

Both men raced after Listens To Wind.

***

"I hear growling. The wolves, are they here?" Dove whistled. White Paws skulked from the darkness, a growl rumbling low in his chest. She offered her hand to the wolf. "White Paws, where did you come from?"

Big Moon panicked and jumped on his mustang. The animal's nostrils flared as the wolf came closer and she reared. The boy slid to the ground as she raced away.

"You do not need to fear these wolves. You are safe with him." She went to the boy, but he remained on the ground and stared at the frightening wolf who stood beside her.

The wolf's growl deepened and grew louder. She searched the darkness." I can see nothing. White Paws, why do you growl? Are we in danger?" She ran her hand down his back. "I have never heard you do this. Perhaps we need to leave this place."

A shiver raced up her back. "It was not good of me to come. I understand this now. Searching for my father has only brought danger closer."

Singing Stone spoke in low tones. "Dove, we will leave now. I came in search of you. Your wolf sees or smells what we cannot. We must hurry from this place."

A voice snarled in the darkness. "You babies go nowhere. They send you to fight?"

Dove's animal pranced around snorting and might have run if she had not been smart enough to put on her nose rope.

"I know you!" Singing Stone yanked his knife from his sheath. "You were the one who disappeared and left a painted arrow on a piece of leather that pointed to where Grandmother and I went!" He jumped and stepped in front of Dove.

A nasty chuckle erupted from the man's chest. "Yes, I am a Likes To Fight man, boy. I learned your words from one of my father's captive women when I was young and used them to become accepted by the Big Sky Peoples. Now I will be a big man among my people when they see I have captured the enemy's children. My father will be proud to know I have found the boy of the women we seek! This means the women *are* with the band. Ha! They will come running to save you, and we will have them."

Dove ducked around Singing Stone and faced the warrior. "Why do you seek to harm our people?"

He leaned down, an ugly grin on his lips. "Are you a warrior woman, little girl? Is that your dog who growls? You think I fear a dog? Fear you little children? We hunt the mustangs for the hairy-faces, and they bring us much that our people wish for. Your people have mustangs, more that I have seen before all together. We will take them and your wolves since your people refuse to give them to us."

The warrior bragged so loud he did not hear or pay attention to White Paws. The wolf slunk away from Dove and circled around the man. He lunged, struck the warrior on his side, and clamped his fangs into the warrior's upper arm. They both tumbled to the ground, but the wolf came out on top of him.

"Aii! His teeth have torn into my arm! Why does he hold tight?" He cowered and held still, too panicked to move.

Dove rushed over. "White Paws, stop!"

"Why does he not tear into my arm? Instead, he holds me still and could cause great harm. He is a killer!"

Dove now grinned. "Perhaps he knows we need you alive. Or maybe he is not hungry."

The wolf stopped, stepped back, but stayed between the man and Dove. Moon Face and several other wolves came out of the shadows and surrounded the warrior in deadly silence.

"We can use him as he wanted to use us. I will bind him." Singing Stone reached for a rope he had tied at his waist. "This was to be our binding rope. Now it has another reason."

Dove stood over the cowering man while Fire Starter held him at knifepoint and Singing Stone tied his wrists. "You are the boy. How could you not know the sound of a wolf? You are careless to not have watched for a little longer. Even a girl would have known better, known the difference between a dog's growl and a wolf's. How can you be so foolish to wish harm on the beings the Spirits have brought to both our Peoples? Are your lives not better with the mustangs?" She stepped back and White Paws moved with her. She knelt and hugged the wolf.

Big Moon held onto the three mustangs left. No one thought to try to stop the warrior's animal who ran when White Paws pulled the man down.

"Who are you? How are you called? If a 'little girl' can best you, perhaps you need to be taught what a warrior does." Singing Stone stood over him, knife drawn.

"I am Eyes On Clouds, son of the war leader." He fought his bindings. "Are you to feed me to your wolves? How is it you even *have* wolves?" His voice raised in pitch.

Fire Starter stepped close to him. Even in the darkness, his sneer showed. "It is a big shame for their family, for a warrior to be bested by a woman."

Eyes On Clouds twisted to free himself. "I am the brother of the one who the wild woman nearly killed. She should have killed him! He was shamed for allowing himself to be caught by a woman. When he told Father it was a woman, he was told to walk away, that he was no longer a Likes To Fight man." The roughness from his voice gone, he spoke slower. "I... Father was hard on him. He was but fifteen winters." He hung his head.

"Eyes On Clouds, I am the grandson of the woman who bested your brother a cycle of seasons ago. She could have ended his life, but she saw he was only grazed by her knife and *she* let him live! He hit his head on a stone and lay there helpless. I may not have been so easy on him. He hunted us! What were we to do? You are going to make words to your father and stop this!"

"He bleeds, Singing Stone. We must stop the bleeding." Dove cut into the bottom of Eyes On Cloud's tunic and wrapped his arm.

"Why would you help me instead of killing me?" Eyes On Clouds stopped struggling while Dove tended to his arm.

"We are not like your people! "Singing Stone's voice sounded much like a wolf growling. "We only wish to be left alone.

"Grandmother, my grandmother worried over your brother! And you wish her life, my mother's life? You may try to take mine first."

Chapter 46

Listens To Wind's mustang raised her head and smelled the air. The animal whinnied and several mustangs responded. The animal's long legs stretched further, and she picked up speed. The animal called again as if using the voices to show her the way.

She bent low over the mustang's back, urging her on. Father Sun edged above the land. *Could it be Four Arrows and Shining Light? Perhaps the children?*

She reached behind her shoulder and pulled out her bow and an arrow. *Father Sun wakes.*

Without direction from her, the animal stopped. "What is it? I wish I had Snow to ride, I feel more connected to her. You, I know nothing about. Where do you lead me? Why did you stop?"

Three mustangs, heavy with riders, showed themselves just as Father Sun's golden fingers reached across the grasslands.

"Grandson! Dove, boys!" She raised her hand and squinted her eyes. "Who is the one you ride with, Grandson? Wolves? What happens here? Moon Face and other wolves started out following me, but disappeared."

"Grandmother, I am happy to see you!" He called out with a wave of his arm. "Wait, why are you here?" He leaned forward on his mustang. "Why are you not with Mother?"

"You tell me first why this one is with you. He is the one who paints arrows on leather to lead our enemy to us."

"I speak for myself. I know you. You are his grandmother!"

"Yes."

"Why did you not end my brother's life?"

"I do not understand."

"You left him wounded seasons ago."

"You are the son of the lead warrior?" She nudged her mustang closer.

He raised his chin. "Sunrise comes. What will you do?"

"First, we must tend to your wound. Singing Stone, Dove gather moss and mud from the stream. It is not far from here. You can see the waters now with Father Sun waking.

"You are the brother of the man who hit his head on the sharp stone. Is this why you hunt us, or is this a trick to hide behind?"

"Grandmother, he is dangerous. I will stay. Send the boys with Dove."

"I ask that you to go with Dove. First, help me to get him down and untie him."

With her grandson's help, Eyes On Clouds slid from the mustang. His face softened as he stared at Listens To Wind. "You could harm me now, yet you wish to help me. I see great honor in your eyes. I will cause no harm to one such as you."

She waved her hand. "Go, grandson, get what I need. We must reach the warriors quickly. " Listens To Wind unwrapped the wound to add the moss and mud to aid in healing his arm. *Spirits, please watch over us and guide my healing of this man.*

***

Shining Light and Four Arrows slowed their mustangs. Father Sun had started to light up the land.

"I can see Listens To Wind and the children." Four Arrows squinted. "There is another person with them. What do we do? They are safely away from where we must fight, but others are not. I hear shouting, maybe from our warriors."

Shining Light lowered his head. "We must return. We have no choice but to turn back, and do so with great speed. Listens To Wind knows what she does." He leaned sideways on Sandstone and she turned. He tapped her into a hard run. Four Arrows did the same with his mustang.

Sandstone raced up the narrow trail to the bluff top, with Four Arrows right behind on his animal. Shining Light stopped his mustang, slid to the ground and stopped. Seven enemy warriors stood staked out. Angry women from both bands milled around the helpless men. He hurried to the rim of the bluff where Big Sky Mustang and Wolf People warriors shouted down at the enemy in the valley. At the bottom of the bluff stood angry, barefooted men.

"Wander, what happens here?"

Wanderer's eyes twinkled with mischief. "Ha! My mice had a plan of their own. Somehow, they understood we faced danger and scampered into the enemy's camp long before sunrise. They chewed the bowstrings of the warriors who did not try to come after us in the darkness. The mice must have chewed on their footwear as well! I did not have many mice with me. Maybe twelve. They either found help or worked very fast to do such good work."

After Shining Light stopped chuckling, he turned around and waved his hand toward the staked men. "These men tried to attack in the darkness? They must not worry about their Souls becoming lost."

Wanderer waved his own hand as he turned around. "They have more than their Souls to worry over."

Shining Light studied the women surrounding the captured warriors. They were a mix of both bands. River Song stood in front, arms crossed and head raised. The other women stood in a half circle around the tall stakes that had been driven into the ground.

Water Lily hooted in laughter. "For so long they have tormented small bands. Now they have been treated as they treat others."

Shining Light became quiet for a span before he spoke. "What will become of them?" Father Sun, fully awake, shone across the grasslands. "The mustangs! They act as if they wait for something. Never have I seen so many four-legged animals stand and not graze."

Water Lily spoke, her voice deep. "Even the mustangs must know their enemy. We cannot allow these... these two-legged beasts to live. They will never allow us to live in peace."

Shining Light reached toward her. "Please, hold your hand."

Instead, she turned and waved her hand down at the waiting women. Women of her band started to place wood beneath the staked warriors while the Wolf People women stepped away. Animal Speaks Woman waved her hands and tried to talk to the other women, but their hearts were full of anger. She even stood in front of the doomed warriors, palms reaching out with her hands up asking them to stop.

One woman yelled out, "Where is your daughter? They kill children."

Defeated, she turned and walked away.

Shining Light called out to her to come to him. "I cannot bear to see anymore. I am a man of peace! Water Lily please, do not do this." He gripped Wanderer's shoulder. "Brother, I know your heart. There must be another way!"

Wanderer stared at him, the blue glow in his eyes brighter than usual. "There is another way. Feel it. It comes our way. It is up to us how we act upon what is to come." He held Shining Light with his eyes. "You have learned much, but I will teach you more. You have yet to learn how to see with your inside eyes. Anger is so strong that it blocks everyone's mind. Watch."

***

A woman yelled, "Stop, we may have another way out of this!" Eyes On Clouds rode behind Listens To Wind. The mustang they shared came up, sweat on her sides. They raced up to where the warriors lined the rim of the bluff. They hopped off the winded animal and ran to the bluff's edge. She signed for her people as she spoke the words of the Likes To Fight People. "Bring the father of Eyes On Clouds forward." Dove and Singing Stone slid off their mustangs and made their way to where Listens To Wind stood. Fire Starter and Big Moon walked up behind Dove and Singing Stone.

"I ask for the father of this young man, Eyes On Clouds." Back straight, Listens To Wind stood defiant. One hand rested on the forearm of Eyes On Clouds.

A man in a painted tunic that fell to his knees came forward and stared up at the top of the rim. "I am Throws High With Spear. Who asks for me? *A woman?*"

Eyes On Clouds stepped forward, injured arm raised. White Paws and Moon Face slipped in beside him. He rested his good arm against the side of White Paw's neck. "This must stop! The women you hunt, one stands with me.

She and this girl, daughter of a Holy Man, saved my life, and they did not have to do so. I stand with them, not against them."

Listens To Wind pivoted to face her people and repeated his words. The women stopped piling wood around their captives.

"Father!" Eyes On Clouds waved his uninjured hand. "One day, we will all have to fight to keep our lands from the hairy-faces. Their greed for the yellow stone will destroy us if we do not. Yes, my mother is a hairy-face and it is in my blood, but I am a Likes To Fight man. I have overheard things from the Likes To Fight men who go to the harry-faces' wood lodges. They ask everyone they encounter where to find the yellow stone they prize. They smile and give us gifts, but their eyes are greedy.

"They promise us that we may keep the best of the mustangs we capture. They tell us to kill the ones we cannot capture so other bands cannot have them. Why?" His voice thundered. "They wish our Peoples to remain weak. I have learned much living between our band and my mother's people. I have heard how the hairy-faces build their lodges, then take the lives of the people whose land they have stolen. One day, they will look to our lands.

"Listens To Wind is not to blame. My father, do her no harm. *We* are to blame. Our own greed has led to this, to fight people who may one day join us in battle against the true enemy as they try to take more land.

"I believe the Spirits made all of this happen to open our ears and hearts to these people." He half turned and swept his good arm wide to include the people he now stood with. "Our Peoples need to speak of peace, not battle."

Dove moved beside him. "I, Turtle Dove, ask you to let us be friends. I may be a girl, and you do not respect women as the Wolf People do, but I say this to you. My father, a Holy Man, has seen the future and shared it with all of our people, even the women. If we are to live and stay strong, we must be as one people!"

The lead warrior roared with laughter. "You insult me, girl. You go back to the other girl children or I will make food for the dogs out of you." Anger jumbled his signing and words together.

Eyes On Clouds spoke. "Father, this girl is right. To keep our lands safe, we must be as one people."

"You, my son, risk much." His father glared at him. "You act as a boy with no mind. You are not my son." He waved him away with a short jerk of his arm. "You have shamed me. I take your name away."

He sneered at his father. "You cannot take a name away when given by the Sprits. But I will no more walk at your side."

The lead warrior raised his head to stare at the people above who stared back at his people. "You have children speak for you. Children? Turn my own against me and still ask for peace?"

Shining Light opened his mouth to speak, but Wanderer tapped his arm and shook his head.

Dove lifted her chin even as she stared down at the enemy. "My people only wish peace, to be left alone. Sometimes children know what is best, but adults do not always listen. I ask you to hear the words of a child and those of your son. You cannot kill the blood he carries." She turned and walked away from the edge of the cliff.

The lead Warrior stared up, looking past his son as if he no longer existed, and into Shining Light's face. "You have brave females who make many words." He made the sign for mouth and laughed.

"We do not allow women to speak to men in such a way. Perhaps you like women whose mouths grow large with words. They think too much of themselves. You give us mustangs back, we give you woman back, if she is *worth* that much to you." He pushed Gentle Wisdom forward. "Too mean and too loud, not make good slave."

"Sweet Mother! How...." Shining Light raised his bow.

"Stop." Wanderer spoke in a calm voice. "My brother, we stare at a nest of winged ones who guard their sweet food. One bad move and they will swarm all over us."

Wanderer raised his hands and called down to the warrior. "I thank you for returning her to us. We will return your mustangs. Send three men along with her to come find your animals. They are mixed in our herd." Wanderer dropped his arms.

The lead warrior nodded and motioned for Gentle Wisdom to leave. "I hear even your mustangs are mean." He waved his men away. "Maybe we return to fight. Maybe not."

Without a glance at his son, he left. As Eyes On Clouds moved away from the edge, his arm started to bleed again. Small streams of blood tracked their way down his arm.

Dove reached out. "Allow me care for your arm. I am sorry your father threw you away."

He gave a shrug with his uninjured shoulder. "I am not the only one who can never return. The men your women bound cannot return either. To them, a captured man is dead in their eyes. And I shamed my father. I spoke to him, defended your people in front of all his warriors. I no longer have a people anymore than the warriors you hold." He pointed with his chin. "Let them go. You will see. We will leave and never return."

"Hold, Eyes On Clouds." Shining Light and Animal Speak Woman both went to his side.

"I, Shining Light, say you are safe among our Peoples. You could have spoken with a dirty tongue about us, but you defended us. Come, we need to care for your wound. Eyes On Clouds... it is a good name."

***

The women turned the captives loose, but not before a few warriors had bruises on their faces. They disappeared on foot without a word or a glance toward Eyes On Clouds. He watched them vanish, then turned to Shining Light. "Give me a mustang and I will also leave. I am a man with no people now."

White Paws and Moon Face flopped onto their sides on the ground in front of him. Pups chased each other past their parents. He shook his head slowly, a wistful note in his voice. "Never have I been fearful for my life as I was when that big one attacked me. Now, he and his mate relax in front of me. I have no anger toward him, only wonder. He no longer wishes me harm. I would have liked to learn more about these wolves who do not make mustangs panic."

Listens To Wind waved her arm. "Come. I will finish cleaning your arm." She offered him dried meat to eat. "There will be good food soon. I can smell fires being brought back to life. I tell you now, what you have done for us, trying to stop a battle, has earned you a place among us."

Shining Light wove through the women and lead a well-muscled near-black mustang who pranced behind him. He tied the animal to a lodge pole. "For you to keep as a man of our band, the Wolf People, or if you choose, The Big Sky Mustang People."

Eyes On Clouds dropped his head. When he glanced up, a glimmer of water sparkled in his eyes. "I am greatly honored, Holy Man." He jerked his chin toward Water Lily, who bent over her cooking fire. "It was not long ago that the Big Sky People took me in, and I had come to them to learn how to best them, not—" He lowered his head again.

"A man can change. I can see in it your eyes, feel it in your heart. Water Lily is a Great Elder and she, too, will be able to see and feel your heart. I call you brother."

Eyes On Clouds raised his head and spoke in a low, humble voice. "I will do my best to bring honor to your people."

"We must know. Will your father make peace?"

"My father is a war leader and has gained much respect in battle. He does not listen to women, and seldom speaks to his own children until the boys have proved themselves in battle. The girls, he gives away when their moon time comes. I cannot answer what he will do. Please send your women away. I do not see elders or many children. You must have a safe place for them. You do not wish any to fall into the hands of the Likes To Fight.

"My father will go to our camp, speak to the elders, and seek advice as your people do, but he will decide once he hears their words. He may choose to listen or to fight. I will stay and fight for your people, if I am allowed to do so." He raised his good arm. "I can still fight."

"As will I." Gentle Wisdom stood, chin high as she approached Eyes On Clouds. "Your father must have Power to have found me. I was careful when I went to turn the mustangs loose. The animals were already gone." Heat reddened her face. "I should not have acted on my own." She shifted her feet and looked away. A deep purple bruise colored her cheek.

Singing Stone approached with a big grin. "The *enemy* came and took their mustangs. I made sure they only took theirs. That crazy mustang, Thunder, bit one of the men on his shoulder, then trotted off with her head held high. Even Thunder knows they are no friend to us."

Gentle Wisdom gritted her teeth. "Why, Light, did you let them do this? Now they have their animals. They laughed as they passed me when they let me loose. One spit on the ground in front of me. I wish to meet that one in battle."

"Cousin, how could I not return their animals?" Shining Light brought his hands together and clasped them. "We are as this. Bound to each other. My heart would fall and shatter into many pieces if anything happened to you."

She pinched her lips closed and stared at him. After a short span, she took in air and forced it out. Anger still vibrated in her words. "Cousin, I thank you for your concern." She opened her mouth as if to say more. Instead, she turned and stormed off.

Eyes On Clouds pinched his brows. "I have much to learn. You treat your women with respect I have not seen before. There is something about her I do not understand. She wears men's clothes, carries battle scars on her arms and an old scar across one cheek. Only once have I seen such a woman. She led her people's men into battle against us and fought well.

"That day, I was too young to fight, but I remember the stories told about her. She reached out and touched three of my father's warriors. To show such bravery is much respected among the Likes To Fight People, even if she was a woman. She rode away untouched."

Shining Light frowned. "She has never held anger as she does now. I need to find out why this is so."

He had taken a few steps when Knows Both Sides came up beside him. The elk teeth on the dark brown, elk hide dress clicked as he walked. He laid a hand in Shining Light's arm. "She goes to clear her mind. I am sure she will be grateful if you help her. Her heart is torn and needs mended in ways I feel only you can do."

He offered Shining Light a new obsidian knife wrapped in very soft leather. "I traded for this knife long ago, when I was but a child. My heart knew it would one day be needed. Wanderer blessed it with Sage and Cedar before he traded to me. I gave him my first attempt at quilling a dress. It was not so good a dress, but he took it anyway. Go to Gentle Wisdom Who Rides A Flying Mustang. If anything happens, I will come get you."

Ruby Standing Deer

Chapter 47

Gentle Wisdom guided Brown Dog between trees, seeking a place to pray. Tall, soft leaved plants with drying yellow flowers waved in a slight breeze that wove around the trees. Late season flowers in white, yellows and oranges stood above the now browning grass. The clouds made little water this past moon, and twigs and leaves on the ground crackled as the mustang walked. She raised her hand to her eyes. *I know I cannot be away long, but I must make myself feel clean again.*

Ahead stood four large trees close together whose leaves still had much green. They formed a safe, quiet place for her to be alone. She nudged Brown Dog toward them just as a pure white mustang with long neck hair and a tail that swept the ground stepped into sight. The animal nickered to Brown Dog, who lifted his head, blew air from his nose and broke into a trot. The white mustang waited, but as they came closer, he whirled and leaped behind the trees.

As Brown Dog rounded the trees, Gentle Wisdom craned her neck and searched for the white animal. She put her hands to her ears. Nothing. "White Mustang, where are you? Why do you call to Brown Dog?"

Sister Wind answered with a strong gust. Eagles called from above the trees. "Brown Dog, I know you saw the White One from my Vision Quest, just as I did. I do not have the proper time to prepare my body, nor my mind. Perhaps the White One only teases." She hung her head. "Perhaps I should go back." She turned her animal around and started to head back to the camps, but the mustang stood in the middle of the deer trail she meant to take.

The White One bobbed his head and whinnied to her.

'The battle you fight comes from within. Only your mind suffered their taunts, not your body. Your body is strong. The marks they put on your body will heal. They cannot touch your Spirit if you no longer allow them to do so. Brush off the anger, as it serves no purpose... you are needed, Warrior Woman. As you said, there is little time to prepare yourself. Go back. Be with Sparkling Star and your sons. The people need you.'
The White One walked into the shadows of the trees and vanished.

"I am a warrior! If I am with my mate and our sons, how am I to fight?"

As Gentle Wisdom rode out from the stand of trees, Shining Light trotted Sandstone up to her. "Cousin, I come to be with you, to help you go within yourself."

She raised troubled eyes to him. "I thank you for coming to me, but I was told our people need me. I do not understand."

He walked Sandstone up to her. "The stones of my necklace have been hot, a sign of danger." He glanced away for a brief span, then turned back her way. His red eyes watered. "I fear for our young, our women, and our elders."

She wrinkled her brows. "They are well away and hidden."

"Still, I feel danger draws closer to them. The warriors must stay here to face the Likes To Fight men. Some of their warriors maybe know where they are. If they choose to attack our defenseless people...." He reached out a hand and laid it on her forearm. "I ask that you take our youngest warriors and go to our people, prepare them to fight if they must. I would trust no other, only you, my cousin, to do this. Will you go, Warrior Woman?"

She grasped his hand and her eyes brightened. "I will do as you ask, cousin. Now I understand why my Spirit Guide spoke the way she did."

His face withered before her. An old man took Shining Light's place. She spoke in voice not quite her own. "Cousin, you will live many cycles of seasons." Wisdom shook her head and blinked several times. "I will ask Speaks to go with me. She is strong and knows how to use a bow as well as any man." She tapped Brown Dog's sides and trotted away.

***

Two days passed. The Likes To Fight lead warrior had not returned, and the warriors on the rim of the bluff had seen no enemies skulking about the land. Shining Light, Wanderer and Falcon Storm sat with Water Lily.

The Great Elder adjusted herself on her humpback robe, eyes downcast. "We must be prepared to find our enemy. We can no longer wait. Our people need to hunt. We sent most of our food with the ones who we sent away sunrises ago." She stopped and drew in air. "Eyes On Clouds will not be asked to go. Even if he says he is no longer part of them, they are part of him, and he should not make war against his own father. I will ask that he stay behind. One of you, bring him to me."

Eyes On Clouds came out from the grey shadows of the coming darkness. "I am here, Holy Woman. Forgive me, please, but I have listened to your words. I must speak for myself. Yes, my mixed blood flows part from my... from the Likes To Fight People. But I am no longer one of them. If I were to go back, my father would turn his back to me."

Wanderer cleared his throat. "A man should not have to fight his brothers, his father."

The warrior shifted and bowed his head toward him. "I know you, too, are a Holy Man. I have heard much about you, about your wisdom, but a man cannot stand aside when his new family needs his strong arm. Never before have I seen so many Holy People in one place. My father never allowed me to sit in Council when the bands came together. I feel your bonds are strong, to be respected. I am honored to be here, accepted without feeling sharp words spit at me for what my *old* people have done. I will fight for you."

Water Lily raised her head. "You are injured, young warrior. Still healing. Stay with the young ones who have refused to leave. You know one is Shining

Light's daughter. She hid when her mother came for her. She and the others need to be protected. I do not say you must. You are a man, and the choice is yours to make."

He smiled. "I thank you for your worry, but my arm will not stop me from defending my new family, Great One. My whole family. My Spirit is strong, but would weaken if I knew any of you were harmed by a people who have little love for even their own when they fall in battle. I have seen a new way to live, and I wish to be part of it."

Falcon Storm stood and looked into the young man's eyes. "Do not look away. I respect you as an equal. Truly, I see you have changed much from the enemy who sneaked into our band. Even your voice has softened. You must listen to our elders. Our Holy People have wisdom beyond us, and it is good to listen. We do not think you weak or an enemy who still must be watched.

"As you know, an injured warrior could bring danger to others during battle. Unlike your old people who would have cast you out, we care for our injured. You are one of those we will care for. I know if you must, you will fight to defend the young ones who remain with us."

Frustration gathered on his face. Eyes On Clouds breathed deep. "I hear you, Falcon Storm." He turned and went into the trees without another word.

"Scouts come!" A voice in the darkening land shouted.

The lead scout jumped off his mustang and went to speak to Water Lily. She handed him food as he sat. "Ho, Water Lily. The land is quiet. Not even a fresh hoof print remains." The scout took the offered food from Water Lily, squatted, and nodded his thanks. "We do not believe they would vanish like this. If we leave, we are on open grasslands. If we stay, we cannot hunt, feed the mustangs. Perhaps this is what they wait for."

***

Father Sun had barely peeked from his sleeping place when Singing Stone yelled from where he sat behind a boulder next to the bluff edge. "Eyes On Clouds comes! He rides hard!"

Wanderer, Shining Light, Falcon Storm, and Water Lily rushed to the rim. Dust rose from the dry land as Eyes On Clouds led men at a gallop toward the bluff.

Falcon Storm turned to Water Lily with a scowl on his face. "Perhaps I was wrong, but I see no bows readied."

"Nor do I." Water Lily stayed Singing Stones' hand as he reached behind for his bow. "Eyes On Clouds raises a hand in greeting. Stay your bow. I believe in him. I know our scouts have their bows ready, but they are unseen by the warriors below. Go tell them to stay their bows as well. I go to prepare a place in front of my lodge."

By the time Eyes On Clouds and his men rode into camp, fire danced across the wood in front of the lodge and Water Lily had laid humpback robes for everyone to sit on. Shining Light, Wanderer and Falcon Storm came and sat near her. All eyes were on Eyes on Clouds as he leaped from his animal and tossed the nose rope to one of his warriors. The other five also jumped down but remained next to their animals. When the young warrior approached, hand in the air, Water Lily nodded her head for him to sit.

Singing Stone and Dove stood a ways off. The Holy Woman waved them over. "Come, sit, learn. Someday you will be the ones at the Council fire." She made room for them, one on either side of her. She offered her hand, palm up to Eyes On Clouds. "I see you come in peace. I offer you peace in return. Speak."

The young man eyed everyone who sat at the fire before he spoke. A new, clean bandage covered the wound on his arm. "I waited until the darkness deepened and left. I know none of you expected me to do battle for you, so I did it for myself."

He faced Shining Light. "You made me one of your Wolf People, made me feel emotions my father taught me were useless and made a man weak. What I felt was not weakness, but love for a people who could have ended my life. My father was wrong to feel others had no worth unless they proved themselves in battle. To throw them away when he decided they served him no more. No one deserves this. All have worth, from a new baby to the eldest in the band. This I learned by watching the Wolf People."

For a long span, he stared down, unmoving. At last, he took a deep breath. "I fought my father and won with my arm is still weak. I held my spear with my other hand. My father's spear hit mine and knocked it away from me. He slapped my head with the shaft of his spear and I fell. I knew soon I would sit at a campfire in the sky if I did not stand. I reached for my knife and slashed his leg. His anger grew and he raised his spear and aimed it at my chest.

"Before he could bring it down on me, a great wolf sprang through the warriors who surrounded us. The wolf leapt, and his teeth crushed my father's arm. He jerked back and fell into the circle of warriors. They moved and allowed him to fall, and the men backed away from the wolf and me.

"Eyes of the wolf bore into mine. I began my death song to tell the Spirits I come, but the wolf—" Tears sprang to his eyes and he wiped them away. "The wolf pushed his nose against my side, then lay beside me with his head upon my chest and watched those around me. I could hear my father scream at the warriors to kill me and the great wolf. None moved. Instead, they turned toward the man who would have killed his own son. They yelled at him, spit on him and waved him away. All my brothers, and even my sisters, yelled at him, told him he was no longer part of the Likes To Fight People. Bleeding, he turned and walked into the trees."

White Paws came to lay next to him, and he reached a hand out and scratched the wolf. He smiled at Shining Light. "I now lead my people. I owe my life to your wolf, my brother. Know I will never raise a bow against your people. We will be two bands, but one people. Your band and the Big Sky Mustang People will always be welcome at our fires."

Shining Light stared deep into the young warrior's eyes. "What will you do if your father returns?"

"I will welcome him home as I have my brother. Some of my people have gone. Maybe to go live near the hairy-faces. I will not allow the bad Spirits from the red drink in our camp. Our Souls will not die from this poison. We will move away from our old camp, become a new people. Perhaps carry Wolf in our new name. I have much to do." He stood to leave and everyone at Water Lily's fire also stood, including White Paws, who slipped away.

Shining Light grasped Eyes On Clouds forearm in a brotherly grip. "One people, but two bands."

As Eyes On Clouds turned to go, White Paws walked in front of him. "I will remember you always, my Animal Brother." He knelt and hugged him. Moon Face and her now-grown pups followed. The warrior cocked his head as two young wolves pushed their way past White Paws. He knelt in front of them, and the wolves licked his face.

"What is this?" He laughed as the two grey wolves continued to lick him.

Dove laughed. "They wish to go with you! As I have heard my father say, this is a Sacred Happening."

Shining Light put his arm around his daughter. "I never thought any of the wolves would leave. This is sad for me, yet I feel joy to know they trust Eyes On Clouds. Yes, Daughter, this is a Sacred Happening."

As Eyes On Clouds stood, Dove offered him a necklace from around her neck made of small cone-shaped shells. "When you come looking for us, know you are welcome."

"Dove, I will be honored to sit at your fire. One day we will speak of the future and how we will help each other. The words you spoke in front of my father helped me to see the wisdom and courage of young ones such as you. Sometimes a child has to be the brave one and make blind adults see." He took the nose rope from the warrior, jumped on his near black mustang and motioned his men to follow. The two young wolves stared at their parents and then trotted off with them.

***

The next sunrise, the people who had hid in the valley mounted mustangs and rode back to the main camps. Gentle Wisdom led the people, her arm held tight against her body by a sling. She rode, head high.

Shining Light pulled away from the dancing and ran to her side. "What has happened? Your arm!"

She leaned forward, held onto Brown Dog's neck hair with her good arm and slid from his back. "Everyone is safe. Do not look at my arm as if it is no longer useful. The bone will heal.

"The Likes to Fight men that the women had let go found us. They tried to take our mustangs by scaring them into a run before Father Sun woke. Brown Dog called to me and pushed his head against mine as I slept on the bare ground. It was my small mustang who charged after the warrior who came at me. I jumped up, and the man grabbed my arm and twisted it behind my back.

Brown Dog reared and brought him down. The fight was brief. Ha! They thought we were weak." She raised her chin.

"The women of both the Wolf People and the Big Sky Mustang People were on them before they could harm anyone. The mustangs ran, but with Brown Dog's help, I turned them and brought them back. The captured warriors were twice bested. As we prepared to bring them back with us, tied and led by ropes by their own people, and Eyes On Clouds came for them. You must tell me how it is that he is now lead warrior.

"I asked him how he knew to come. He said whispers of a woman told him we were in the valley and that he needed to find us. I asked why he would follow the voice of a woman. He grinned and asked who Blue Night Sky was. She told him to remember her name and to never think a woman weak again." She whooped and reached around Shining Light with her good arm.

"Never again will I be shy to hug you in front of anyone. I love you, cousin! I wish to join in the dancing with my mate." She held herself tall and smiled as if her arm did not pain her.

***

Even though scouts still guarded the rim, there was much dancing and singing. Many sat at fires laughing. Wanderer and Water Lily sat alone and had eyes for no one else but each other. River Song worked on a carry board for her baby while Falcon Storm held their new daughter.

Animal Speaks Woman tossed a robe over her shoulder and pulled Shining Light away from the camp out into the darkness. "Bright Sun Flower and Hawk Soaring keep our son. Our daughter stays at Singing Stone and Listens To Wind's fire to enjoy his grandmother's stories. She will stay with them and Four Arrows. Singing Stone wears smiles that will surely stretch out his face as he glances our daughter's way.

"We have much to think about, man of mine." She slipped her arm into his as they made their way into the shadows. "We must soon choose the life we are to lead. Dove may only be a child in our eyes, but she has done many brave things these past sunrises. Some of what she did was not wise, but she is young and learns. She even stood up to a dangerous man, and all the Peoples saw her. It was she who encouraged the other young ones to be brave by what she did." She stared down. "Had I not been sent back, I may have stopped Dove's bravery by being a scared mother, and maybe shot the lead warrior, ruined the peace we now have. Children truly must be listened to."

She squeezed his arm. "Our daughter has met her future mate. We know this and must listen to the words that many speak. The Big Sky Mustang People, some wish to see the forest." She stopped, knelt and spread out the robe. "Here we stay until Father Sun wakes us. I have a great need, as our daughter would say." She pulled him close. "I wish to feel very safe in the darkness."

Chapter 48

Sunrise burst through the clouds. Rays of golden light spread across the clouds, and the land shouted out its beauty. Along the flat top and out into the grasslands, mustangs grazed on the yellowing grass mixed with the fading, yellow flowers of the Sacred Sage.

In the grasslands, Singing Stone and Dove sat on their animals and allowed them to wander where they pleased. A plant with tiny yellow-orange flowers grew tall enough to touch the bellies of their mustangs. On the lower parts of the plant, the flowers had turned into seeds that floated past them.

He tried to make simple talk. "When young, that one is very good cooked. Now it has little stickers on the branches that are very hard to get out of your skin if you get too close." He cleared his throat. Still, she stared somewhere he could not see.

"I see the women make two lodges into one for the Council. You and I will make our words there. Are you worried about what to say?"

She shrugged, bit her lower lip and shifted Fire away from him.

"Dove, when you are in doubt, go off and sit by yourself. Be still. Wait. When doubt leaves you, then speak your words." Singing Stone stopped Spirit Eyes and raised the pitch in his voice as she moved further away. "I can see you are torn. Half of you wishes to be here, to remain. It is the other half I fear." He tapped his animal and moved ahead of her at a trot. His long hair bounced the same speed as Spirit Eyes' trotting. He did not glance back.

"Oh, Fire. I know his pain. I carry it as well. I know where I belong, where I need to be." She tapped Fire into a run, in the opposite of Singing Stone. *How do I choose?*

Fire, breathing hard, slowed down and then stopped. The animal lifted her head as if she listened. The mustang nickered and moved over a small grassy hill. Down in the ravine, a young reddish-white mustang struggled to get up. The animal squealed and fought to stand, her eyes bulged in fear.

Dove flew off Fire and tried to hop-skip down to the bottom, but tripped over a jagged stone. Sister Wind scooped up dust, sending it down on her, and she covered her eyes with her hands. As quickly as it began, the wind stopped. "At least this time I did not hurt myself! I am so clumsy!"

She wiped her eyes with the back of her hand and looked to where the mustang should be. In her place, White Cloud sat on her white mustang. "How is this so? You live in the forest." Dove spun around. "We are not in the forest, but this ravine. Where is the Mustang who cried out in pain?"

'Child. That was you who cried out in pain. I heard you and came to help. Your confusion hurts deep. I can feel it.'

"White Cloud, what do I do?"

'You know, little one. Mustang Woman. You are a child, yes, but not for long. Your moon time will come with the budding leaves, in your eleventh spring. You will have your woman celebration in the time of newborn animals.'

"In another cycle of seasons, I will be a woman?" She reached out to touch the white mustang. "I really can feel him!"

'Of course. He is a real as you.' Her laughter had the melody of a bird who sang for her mate.

'Listen well, young one. Your heart is torn and you feel the pain of one growing up. You wish to be with Singing Stone, yet you still need your parents. I know of your father's desire to return to the forest. He must do what is in his heart, as you must do what is in yours. You must not worry. You will cause yourself pain inside. Think, Mustang Woman, the answer is there...'

"Do not leave. I have much I wish to know!"

As White Cloud faded, she smiled and mouthed the words, *do not worry.*

***

Shining Light kept in step with Sandstone as she roamed over the grassland. Her young one, nearly grown, went her own way as she grazed. White Paws kept brushing up against him as if to give comfort. The air had cooled, and he wore his tunic that Animal Speaks Woman had painted White Paws and Moon Face on with tall trees in the background on the off-white leather. Tiny shells dangled from the fringes and matched the ones on the edge fringes of his plain, light brown leggings. *All reminders of the forest.* He reached for the wolf's thick neck fur and dug his hand in to scratch him as they wandered. "It is time to return. We have found Singing Stone, and with the new lead warrior of the Likes To Fight, there is no reason to stay.

"Some of The Big Sky Mustang Band speak of going back to the canyons, while some wish to stay in the grasslands. Even some have a desire to follow us back and see the forest. Heh, Water Lily follows Wanderer now. Who will be their Holy Person? She has only partly taught a young man, who she took in about five cycles of seasons ago. Knows Both Sides smiles his way and they speak much." He leaned on Sandstone and she stopped.

"Many of the young people in our band took mates and now live among the three bands that make up the Big Sky Mustang People. All make promises to visit their relations in the forest. Some of their people have joined our band. I have yet to meet them all." The sky called to him as Hawk swooped down and flew back into the cloudless sky. Sister Wind blew past his face, lifting his loose hair. *His father voice?*

Sandstone turned and pushed her muzzle against his shoulder until he lost his balance and fell against an old, wide tree. White Paws plopped himself on his lap as he tried to stand. "What do you two do?"

Hawk swooped down again, this time landing on the grass. He called to Shining Light before taking to the sky. Wings spread, he danced on the breeze. Several ravens cawed as they landed in a large tree that stood about fifty paces away. They gathered on a bare branch and waited in silence. Hawk sat on the highest branch, unmoving.

Sandstone trotted toward the tree, and White Paws stood and pushed at his Human Brother. *'We go.'*

"White Paws?"

Sandstone whinnied, reared and pawed the ground with her front hooves as she waited by the tree.

"I go, White Paws. I should have sought my father long before. Now he seeks me." The old, wide tree had warmed where Father Sun touched the bark. It gave Shining Light comfort. Sandstone stayed near and grazed, while White Paws again stretched across his lap. He took in air as deep as he could before freeing it. *Relax. I need to let go....*

He began his song, a song that he had never sung before, one that grew from somewhere inside him. Crickets chirred. Shining Light stood and danced their song while singing. He spun and moved his feet to the rhythm of his heartbeat, to cricket's song. White Paws danced around him and the two became one. Wolf legs replaced his own. Shining Light's body felt covered in grey fur. He stopped. Man and wolf howled together.

Gentle Wisdom slipped in and put small cuts on his arms, and he used the pain to go deeper. Smells came his way from campfires. Voices of the ancients joined his then faded, leaving him standing alone.

A raven lit on his shoulder and eyed him.

"Father?"

The raven flew off, cawing. The rest of his companions flew in seven directions. Hawk still grasped on the highest branch, cocking his head at Shining Light.

"Father, am I to understand that we each have our own path by the directions the ravens took? Dove's cannot be different from mine! I am her father. She is but a child. Or is it my path changes also?"

He sat through the changes of the sky's colors from blue to gold. Bold orange turned to a passive pink just as Father Sun drifted off to sleep. He sat beneath the tree and cuddled with White Paws for warmth. Somewhere in the night, Moon Face and the rest of the pack joined, surrounding him.

He woke to birds and stretched to find himself pinned by wolves. His father sat in front of him.

"Father? How can you be here? Where is Mother? Why do I not see anything past you but trees? Am I home? In the forest? How—"

Flying Raven sat cross-legged and chuckled. *'You are how old? And still ask as many questions as you did when your were a boy.'*

Shining Light reached out and his hand went through his father's image. "I had hoped I was home. I see the forest behind you. The band they do not see me. What am I to do, father? My heart is sick for the forest. But I can feel deep inside I am not to go home to the forest, am I?"

Flying Raven leaned forward, and White Paws crawled over to him. *'You want a good scratch, wolf?'*

"How is this so? How can he touch you and you touch him?"

'Son, have you not learned yet that White Paws lives between lands, as does Wanderer? Your wolf will always be this way. He, Moon Face, and their young will always be this way. They do not need the forest to keep living. They are very Sacred, as is White Bear, her cub and even Mouse. It is we humans who only live in one land until we understand how to live in both.'

"As you have. Am I not in both lands to be able to see you?" He again reached out to touch Flying Raven.

'You are so young yet, my son. You have much to learn and can only learn what you experience. You know where you belong... for now. One day, when lines of every path you have taken appear on your face, come share your knowledge in the forest. We will be here, waiting. Do not fear what you have yet to know.'

He pointed to his head. *'Only age brings true wisdom — only age, little one. Young people think they know all there is to know. You and I know this is wrong. And once you learn, you will teach them how wrong they are. But first you must learn...'*

"Father, I am to stay? Here? Father, you fade." He lowered his head and White Paws jumped up, went to him and licked his face. Moon Face wiggled to get past her mate to lick him as well.

Sandstone nickered, stepped over the wolves and nuzzled his face. *'I also live in-between lands, as all we ones called animals do, but I will be with you as long as I can be before my Mustang People call to me to come to them. We have bonded in ways no other Humans have. Some call us Medicine Dogs and say we have mystical ways. We do.*

'Know you are needed here for now. Your daughter needs you to guide her. The people need you. My Mustang People need you.'

"Sandstone? You have not spoken to me in a long time. What do you mean the people need me? They have Water Lily. Oh. Wanderer. He has offered to take her to the forest and she will go. She loves him. I can feel it."

"What can you feel?" Animal Speaks scooted herself into the menagerie of animals to sit on his lap.

He wrapped his arms around her. "You. I feel you. All these cycles you have never questioned what I do, where I go. Will you understand when I say we will not go back to the forest for a long span?"

She snuggled closer. "Man of mine, I knew before we left we would not return. I will be here, at your side, until I breathe no more." She pulled him away from the tree and pushed him to the ground. "Allow me to show you how much I understand, my love."

Chapter 49

Four Arrows and Listens To Wind faced Water Lily. "I see a deep love connects the two of you like a binding rope. Both of you have eyes that shine with joy as it should be. It does not matter that you come from different ways of life, different in your thinking. One day soon your way of life and way of thinking will blend. You will share the same strand in the Web of Life, forever entwined as you share the dance that is life.

"No matter how many times a boulder is placed in your paths, forcing you to change, you will do it together, forever and always. If one falls, the other must pick them up, carry them if need be, until they are able to walk again. You will share all that is good, all that is not good, and become stronger for it. All relationships have curves to walk before it becomes straight again.

"Remember this well and you will always embrace each other when you sleep, no matter the problem, and find every sunrise a joy when your eyes meet as you wake."

Water Lily glanced to the side, past the couple.. "Who holds the binding rope?"

"I, Fire Starter, hold the binding rope with my cousin, soon to be my brother."

"I, Big Moon, hold the binding rope with my cousin, soon to be my brother." He raised his half of the rope braided with mustang hair as they came forward and offered it to Water Lily.

"I am happy to know this mating begins with the love of two who will be brothers. Family makes life complete." She took the binding rope and reached for Four Arrows' hand. She then took Listens To Wind's hand, held them together and wrapped their wrists to one another.

"May this mating be blessed by Creator, and may you find joy always hiding behind any tears that may flow. You are now mated."

She turned to the boys. "Big Moon, no longer do you carry that name. You are to be called Walking Thunder for the brave boy you have become."

The newly named boy stood tall, chin raised.

"Fire Starter, you have a name you wish to be called. Tell me."

Fire Starter smiled. "The name given to me by the Holy Woman when my mother welcomed me into the band. I wish to carry this name until I am a man. Sun Rising is the name I choose."

Water Lily Nodded. "You are now called Sun Rising."

"Your new parents look upon you with big smiles, as do all of your new people. Listens To Wind and Four Arrows have asked to adopt you. You are both now Big Sky Mustang People."

She clapped her hands. "Much food has been cooked, and I would like to have some. This is a good day to dance and sing for the newly bonded pair... and for our adopted children."

She stood and smiled as Wanderer approached. "I see everything with a clear mind, now."

***

Dove wandered the camps with White Paws and Moon Face in search of Singing Stone. The Big Sky Mustang People's mustangs, still wary, kept moving away but did not run. Much food passed between the camps, and drummers sang as they beat out a rhythm for the dancers. Scouts still took turns watching the rim to ensure the safety of the camps.

She knelt to scratch both wolves. "He does not dance with the dancers nor eat with his family. Does he avoid me? Spirit Eyes is gone."

White Paws turned as Shining Light came up behind them. "Daughter, let him be. I have something to give you. Let us walk."

"Father, I wish to speak to you. You have something for me? May I see it?" She bounced up and down as the young girl inside her came out. "What is it?" Her mouse scurried up into her hair.

"I must not forget my mouse! Wanderer says she will have babies soon." She put her hands to her mouth. "Then what am I to do? Father, I will be covered in mice. What will I do? The wolves! What will they do?"

He laughed and took her one of her hands. "You will always be my little one. Silly girl." His eyes held sadness that his voice hid. She gripped his hand tightly as they walked away from the celebration.

The wolves ran ahead, and the rest of the pack joined in as they jumped in the grass hunting and chasing each other. Shining Light and Dove shuffled through clumps of yellowed grass and late wildflowers, many seeding. The sticky stemmed flowers, once covered in pink blossoms, now formed bright red seedpods. The grasses were full of birds eating seeds. The birds whooshed up in the air as they passed by. In the distance, the reddish-purple of the canyons met the blue-turquoise sky where long stretches of clouds hovered above them.

"Father, I desire to go there, to the canyons. You must know this being a Holy Man. I am so torn that my heart hangs in pieces and I cannot put them back together. Do not call me a child with silly thoughts."

He leaned against a low sandstone boulder and pulled her up to sit next to him as he scooted farther back. His hands ran down her long, loose hair. "I understand and do not call you a child." He reached inside a pouch that hung on the side of his breechclout, but made a fist around what he held. "Soon it will be too cold and your brother and I will have to wear more clothes! Your mother already makes us winter clothing." He reached for the mouse with his free hand and allowed her crawl across his arm.

"You will learn much from this tiny being. They will teach you things others do not see or hear." He put the mouse back on her shoulder, and she ran and hid behind Dove's hair.

"That tickles, Father!" She giggled and raised her shoulder.

"I have never had a mouse honor me as they do you and Wanderer. You will learn much by listening to what she says. They have a hard and fast life, with most other beings eating them, but there is much to learn from this also. They teach us to look within, see with our inside eyes, to feel the Energy around us and hear with both our heart and mind. There is a place for emotions of the heart and for the wisdom in our minds. Combine them always." He fingered the hidden object in his hand.

He cleared his throat. "Wanderer made you something I have kept for you. I did not understand what it meant until you met Singing Stone."

He opened his hand, exposing the carved mustang. "He carved this from a sky stone he carried for a long time. No wonder his arrows fly true. He spends much time on them as he must have this wonderful mustang." He leaned closer as he handed it to her. "Look at the neck and tail hairs. I can count them! Wanderer even made you a rope of mustang hair to wear it around your neck."

She turned the carving in her hands. "This is so... so unlike anything I have seen. Mustang Woman. Father, this leads me to speak of what I must." She lowered her hands into her lap and looked down at them. "I now have the courage to speak what is in my heart. I may be only a girl in your eyes, but I am soon to be a woman." She ran a hand across the rough sandstone. "Feels like home. I am where I need to be. I can maybe live with some of the Wolf People who choose to stay."

Shining Light wrapped his arms around her. "You are going to stay with someone of the Wolf People who choose to stay, daughter. Us, your mother and I, chose to stay." His arms shook. "So you will be with us, who love you more than any others in the band could."

She pulled back. "I see a smile though your tears fall as the waters fall in the forest." Her own eyes began to water. Drops fell down her face. "I will not ask you to stay. You know I will be safe with our people. Go back to the Forest and be safe. Allow Hawk Feather to grow up there. I will come to visit. I promise. Wanderer told me to not promise what I could not keep. This I will. Please understand that I must stay. I knew this before we left and did not tell you." She squeezed the mustang carving in her hand.

"I may not ever be a Holy Woman, but—"

"You are young. You may not have the calling to be a Holy Person, but you have strong dreams, and your mother and my grandmother will teach you the plants as your grandmother taught you in the forest. You already show the knowledge that is born into you."

"How can your grandmother teach me when they will be going back to the forest? Father? She is going to stay? Is this what you say?" He eyes brightened and a wide smile spread across her face. "And grandfather? One day we will go see all of our family together! And they will meet Singing Stone."

"Yes, little one. One day we will go visit the forest. See our sister band." They held tight to one another.

A mustang nickered in the distance. They pulled away from each other to see Singing Stone and Spirit Eyes. The pair stayed back.

"Father, I wish to tell him."

"I need a long walk by myself, little one. I go now."

***

Shining Light glanced back as Singing Stone's mustang trotted up to his daughter. Singing Stone jumped off to sit next to her on the flat sandstone. "White Paws, you follow me, but Moon Face stays with her. She will always have wolves at her side, become Mustang Woman. I wonder at this."

'Human Brother, you will see this for yourself.'

When he was far enough away from Dove, he knelt next to White Paws. "Does it hurt this much when your pups make their own way?"

A cough made him turn his head. Animal Speaks Woman stood with their naked son at her side. She scooped Hawk Feather into her arms and smiled. She let the boy down, and he ran to Shining Light, arms wide. "Fada, wan wak! I saw you wif White Pawz. We wan wak, too. We go... now, fada." Hawk Feather bent and reached with his tiny hands to dig it into the wolf's fur. "I do lak you, see? Now we wak?"

Speaks hurried to his side. "Your son is starting to make more words than his mouth can hold. He tried to tell me about a dream. He is only a baby! How is this so?"

Shining Light stood and a chuckle escaped his lips. "Take my hand, woman. Our son wishes to walk and see this wondrous place of grass. Perhaps he will tell us more of his dream."

"Deam, fada! Mustans run!"

Chapter 50

Gentle Wisdom sat on her mustang, arms crossed, as Shining Light walked further away from her with his family. He had not seen her as she was about to approach, sit, and speak with them. They laughed the laughter of a family that felt much joy. *One sunrise soon I knew this was to going happen. What do I do? I cannot follow like a child and expect always to find comfort in my own needs. To expect nothing to ever change.*

They would stay in the grasslands and move toward the shelter of the canyons before the cold season hit. No pretending they would return to the forest. She slid off Brown Dog and let him trot back to the herd. Her long, ebony hair whipped in her face as she turned back toward camp. She gathered her hair and pulled it forward over one shoulder as she moved away deeper into the grass. Sister Wind had a bite to her that promised the cold season was not far away.

She stared at her footwear as she shuffled through the grasses and clumps of late season flowers. The quillwork Sparkling Star had created for them showed Spider's web, and in its circle she had painted two, small hands embracing. Such love went into the careful, nearly perfect work. The mistake she made, hidden well, was to show that humans were not perfect. That only the Creator could be so. *Spirit Guide, I am lost. Show me the way. Help me to see the direction I am to go.*

What am I to do? I have always been at my cousin's side and never thought life would be different. Oh, Sparking Star, I love you so. I love our sons. Shining Light will stay. You fear staying. I can keep you safe. My life without you would be as the clouds without rain. Empty and with no nourishment from your touch.

Star sat at our fire, and as the stars increased, she covered her hair. I told the people about her story, of her life, and how she came by her dark brown-red hair. Then many people came to visit, brought food, and stared at her until she allowed them to touch her hair. They also touched her arm as if they thought she was not real, but they soon accepted her... and me. These people welcomed us both and said nothing about who we are.

My brother, Knows Both Sides, is loved by all the Big Sky Mustang People. He will stay. Many children follow him, and he smiles in contentment. I wish to stay! She slapped her leggings on the sides. The noise sent birds scattering. She breathed deep the smell of the Sacred Sage that brushed against her knees. "I am home wherever I chose to be! Sweet Star, will you understand? You *must* understand." Her head raised, she spoke a silent prayer, asking Creator and the Sprits to help her chose the right path for her and her mate—and their children, who must come first.

She continued to walk, focusing on her footsteps. "The new couple showed great joy in their binding, as did Star and I when we were bonded. I am sure they thought nothing about the next sunrise, the next time they might encounter any enemy. This is their life out here... not mine." She fought back the urge to get Brown Dog and race away on him. This land had yet to be explored by the Wolf People. Her people.

"It is not as if we will never go back to the forest. We have much family there. Why are things so hard?" She balled her fists and again smacked her leggings. "Even Animal Speaks made peace with the women who showed anger at her for trying to stop the warriors from being burned at the stakes. Women came to her, heads bowed and offered her gifts of quills and the best of their pine needles for baskets. Why, why is my mind dizzy with confusion?" A large spider crawled on her footwear, and she stopped to watch.

"Your mind is dizzy because, you, my mate, carry much in your heart. Too much for one person to bear. Allow me to carry some of your burden."

Sparkling Star startled Gentle Wisdom as she stood in the grass behind her, pulling her out of her thoughts. Gentle Wisdom turned and smiled as her eyes took in the beauty before her.

Sparkling Star wore a light brown elk skin dress with the collar quilled in the deep green color of the forest. Elk teeth sewn in rows fell below her breasts. The bottom fringe had curled some, as all do, but it added to the dress as the long sleeves had the same matching curled fringe. One of the other women must have braided her hair and added fur to the long braids.

"Star, had you been an enemy, I would have surely felt a knife pierce my back. I was too deep within to be a responsible warrior. I will not allow this to happen again unless I have someone to watch over me. Did you follow me, and I, too deaf to hear, did not notice?"

Sparkling Star reached out and took her hand. "I followed at a distance when I saw you leave camp. I knew by the way your body moved that you carried a burden. Deafness sometimes comes with deep thought. No one is near. Let us speak."

Hand in hand, they walked across the grassland to a grove of trees. They sat next to the stream, and Sparkling Star ran her hand through the cold, slow-moving waters before she spoke.

"Wisdom, you worry over your cousin as I worry over our sons. I am here to tell you that I will follow you no matter where we go. We are mates, forever and always. Yes, I have fears, but they are not so strong that I would leave and run back to the safety of the forest without my family... my whole family. You make me feel safe and very much alive." She took Gentle Wisdom's hands into hers.

"You are the sunrise that my body, my Spirit, needs to feel alive. My life belongs to you, as your life belongs to me. When we were bonded, the rope tied us together, weaved our love into one life. We may have separate bodies, but we do not have separate lives. Not once have you mentioned that I am half hairy-face, nor have you ever cared. You make me whole.

"The Big Sky Mustang People will move soon to keep up with their herd. I do not know the wishes of all our people. Some speak of going back, while others say they will stay. Many of our young people have already joined with people of the other bands. Our bloods now mix. I know many have begun to speak of a hunt, so there will enough food for the cold season here and for those who choose to follow the Wolf People back to the forest.

"I will follow whichever band you choose. Perhaps we will become part of the band Singing Stone and his family belongs to for at least the cold season. A large herd of humpbacks have been spotted about a day's ride away. Many are ready for the making of meat." She stood and reached for Wisdom's hand. "Come, my warrior woman. You have a hunt to join."

Ruby Standing Deer

Chapter 51

Wanderer sat near Water Lily as he made new pouches for his mice. Sinew tasted good to them and he worked on repairing their pouches most sunrises. "Ah, yes. I see you have found mates, but you are now too many to live in the pouches. Some of you must form a new band as we humans do and find a pace in the grasslands to live." He stitched new pouches as the mice scuttled about in search of food.

"Mice! If we go together to the forest, will I live with mice?" Water Lily tied the flap to her lodge and placed a log against it worried the mice might find their way in. "Do the wolves not eat your mice? How many babies do they have... and why do you not let them go?"

"I am not their captor. They do as they please." He stretched his legs. "My body feels as an old man again. If not for them chewing the Likes To Fight's bow strings, we would have maybe fought that day."

Water Lily tossed wood on the fire. "What do you mean you feel as an old man... again? You have yet to speak about why you look younger than me." She raised her brows. "I know you have seen more winters than I have, yet your hair only started to show stardust in it a short span ago, and too fast." A mouse hurried across her lap. "Perhaps I need to show you my snake, little mouse."

He jerked up from his sewing. "Snake! You have a snake?" He reached out to pull five mice away from her lodge's entrance. The lump in his throat bounced as he swallowed. "You did not speak of this until now." His eyes widened as he counted his mice.

She turned away, her hand to her mouth. "Ah, yes. My snake. I will get him and show you."

"I do not wish to see your snake!" He scooted farther away.

She wiped away tears of laughter, but could not still her laugh. "Ohhhh... You are a good one to tease! I will enjoy our ride to the forest!"

He frowned and stared at her. "You tease? You tease! Do you not?"

"Well..." She reached behind and undid the flap on her lodge and slipped inside.

"Wait, Water Lily, allow me to call to my mice before—"

A rattlesnake landed in the middle of his lap. He flew up as if he had grown wings. "Snake! You really have a snake!"

Laughter from the surrounding lodges made his face redden. He spun around to see that the snake had not moved. His mice scattered. "What is this?" He leaned closer, and the sound of rattling made him take a step backward.

Water Lily held up the buttons from the snake's tail and rattled them again.

"Woman, you scared ten winters from my life!"

"Good. We will look more like a couple instead of me being with such a young looking man."

"The snake is stuffed, is it not? Heh, it is not alive." He wiped his brow and tried to regain his Holy Man composure as he came closer and sat on the edge of the robe, just not so close to Water Lily and her snake.

"The snake, long ago when I was but a girl, slithered into my sleeping robe. He did not bite me as I scooted out. His belly was round as if he had eaten not long before he sought a quiet, warm place to let his meal settle. Maybe I *am* crazy as you are. I let him live with me and he never once caused me harm. I had many dreams of snakes afterward. I learned from him how to become a Spiritual leader, how to heal. When his Spirit went to be with his kind, I honored him by taking his skin and, while doing that, his rattle came off. I carry it always with me. I will speak to his kind and ask they leave your mice alone... as long as they do not chew my belongings or make a mess in our lodge."

"Our lodge? You will become my mate?" His eyes shined as his smile grew. "I have not wished for another mate in many, many cycles of seasons. Our crazy ways will guide us always." He scooted closer to her and the snake.

She looked away. "I am not so crazy as you. Perhaps. I have never taken a mate, never wanted my Power to suffer by having too much on my mind. I see Shining Light and his family. He is strong and shows no loss of Power, so perhaps."

She grinned and picked up the snake. "I have shed many skins, became many beings in my dreams. Snake bit me once when I went hunting alone. I did not die, but came into my Power instead. I might wish for another snake."

His face dropped.

"I only tease! Unless one comes my way. You understand we cannot turn down Power or we become weak, unsure of who we are. We can lose our way by not listening to the Spirits."

"I am not so crazy as you think, but woman, you might make me so!"

"I cannot make someone crazy who already is so. Do you wish to see my owl?"

"Heh, how did you stuff him?"

"*She* stuffs herself. Maybe with mice. She goes off to hunt alone. I do not know what she eats after sunset."

"Owl! You have a *live* owl? You tease again, woman!"

"Look above you, my soon-to-be mate. She sleeps on top my lodge."

He arched his neck and put a hand to his brow. "Sweet Mother, I do see an owl. Owl speaks of much danger! When they call out in the night, it is a warning to be aware, sometimes of your family or your own self." He whispered. "Her head turns. She knows of my mice. She does not sleep!" He scooped up a young one who had started to wander away from him.

"Yes, I am sure she knows of your little companions. Do not look so worried! Like the wolves, she will leave your mice alone. I have spoken to her of this. Heh, we will have such happy time together, my strong, brave man. Perhaps Shining Light will do the binding before we go to your forest."

***

River Song held her new daughter, Fawn Dancing, and pushed herself against Falcon Storm and chuckled. "I will miss Water Lily, but I wish her much happiness. If those two could have children, I wonder what their lodge would be like?"

Falcon Storm reached for his daughter. "Woman, we could go to the forest and see what mysteries are there. I have heard much happens there."

She leaned away from him. "I will never leave the mustangs. I *am* mustang in my heart. This is where I belong, where my son and mother will stay." Her smile gone, she stared deep into his eyes.

A glint of a smile curved his lips and reached his eyes. "You tease now? Sweet woman, I am as much a part of this land as you. One day, perhaps when Dove takes her children to meet the rest of the Wolf People, we will go and see this place of falling waters. I wish to see if White Bear is only in my dreams or if she really lives there."

"You, too, dream of her? Mother spoke of her as well." She lowered her head. "She and Four Arrows say they will go see this place of Tall Trees. If it holds the magic she speaks of, she will become a mother again. She asked me if I would remain here. She will come back, I know she will. Her desire to give Four Arrows a child is great. Somehow, she feels if they go, she will be able to do this. "She shrugged. "I stay for now. We no longer need to fight to keep our mustangs safe. Eyes On Clouds offered his band for help, not battle. He spoke of being near if another band ever comes our way with greed in their hearts."

Falcon Storm nodded. "We will stay as you wish, woman of my heart. You have walked in my Soul, and I will be at your side, always and forever."

Ruby Standing Deer

Chapter 52

Many tears flowed as people separated to follow Wanderer and Water Lily to the place of Tall Trees. The Wolf People's young stood back with Shining Light, Animal Speaks Woman, Dove, Bright Sun Flower, and Hawk Soaring. Many Big Sky Mustang People had prepared their belongings for the journey and waited for Wanderer to finish his words with those who he would not see for perhaps cycles of seasons.

Singing Stone hugged his grandmother and wished her and Four Arrows a good journey, then stepped back and joined Dove who hung onto her parents' hands.

White Paws and Moon Face sat in the grass surrounded by their pack, and the mustangs moved about to graze. Thunder would stay. The mustangs who followed her brought new blood to the herd, and it would grow strong.

Above the people, blue swirls danced with Sister Wind. *'Circles! Circles, all has come full Circle, my Children.'* Laughter that sounded like Blue Night Sky's echoed in the Wind. Some said she lived with Sister Wind. Others said she was Sister Wind.

THE END

About the Author

Ruby Standing Deer has been a wanderer, and has seen most of the USA. She's the mother of an amazing son, and the wife of a patient husband who indulges her need for animals. She was also the first woman journeyman newspaper pressman in Colorado.

She spent years rescuing animals and learning from them. They taught her that life does not have to be so hard, if you go with the flow and not against it. Forgive today, because tomorrow may not come.

Her life revolves around writing and her family, which includes, of course, her animals. Two car accidents in the mid-nineties changed her life. She resented it at first, until she understood she had simply been put on another path. It was not an easy one, but she accepted it, and while it continues to be a challenge, she now learns with each step she takes.

She writes because she is compelled to pass on knowledge.

Find out more about Ruby at www.RubyStandingDeer.com, or online at Twitter (@R_StandingDeer) and Facebook (R Standing Deer).

Acknowledgements

Many people helped me to make this book a reality.

Among them is Megan Harris, who is my new editor at Evolved Publishing. I appreciate her patience as she and I work to become of one mind—no simple task, as my writing style is difficult for those who do not grow up in the American Indian culture.

I must again thank Lane Diamond, who is my publisher and chief editor, and who has been my mentor and writing coach for years now. He brought my books into the real world.

To the entire team of talented authors, editors and artists at Evolved Publishing, who support me and make this adventure fun even when it's such a grueling challenge.

I owe much to Aya Walksfar, who helped me shape *Stones* in its early stages, and who has been a steadfast friend and guide throughout the process.

And of course, my husband Chuck. Goes without saying.

What's Next?

Ruby is fast at work on her fourth novel, as yet unnamed, featuring a brand new cast of characters from this culture we've come to love in her first three books. We expect to release it in late 2015.

Also by Ruby Standing Deer:

Circles

With much of the world still undiscovered, a small band of people live a peaceful life, until the dream vision of a young boy, Feather Floating In Water, changes everything. Only nine winters old, Feather's dreams turn his seemingly ordinary childhood into the journey of a lifetime. He must help his people face a terrifying destiny from which they cannot turn away. He must find a way to make his people listen.

Bright Sun Flower, the boy's grandmother, guides his beginnings, teaching him about the Circle of Life, and how without it, no life can exist. But he needs a bigger push, and gets it from a grey wolf and a Great Elder. The boy's journey leads him to discover that the Circle of Life involves all people, all living things, and not just the world he knows.

In the end, an ancient People guide the boy in his visions, toward an unexpected place hidden from outsiders.

This story is steeped in American Indian life, in their beliefs and humor, and in their love of family. It shows how we might benefit from the old ways today.

Spirals

A Holy Man, who lives in both this world and the Spirit world, waits hidden in a cave in the canyons, as a newly made woman runs toward him. She flees her would-be suitor, who wants from her more than she can give.

The Holy Man and his constant companions, a colony of mice, accept the woman within the cave. She worries that he may be crazy, but given her fear of the man who desires her, maybe crazy is not so bad.

In this sequel to Ruby Standing Deer's first novel, *Circles*, the main character of Shining Light is now grown and with family. He dreams of the woman and the Holy Man in the canyons, and knows that, after four seasons of calm and peace in the Forest of Trees, he must go to them.

He seeks guidance, but the Spirits tell him only that he must rescue these two people. Yet he need not go alone. Ever Shining Light's faithful companion and Wolf Brother, White Paws senses he must follow his Human Brother. Thus, one Human, one Wolf, and their two families set out for the unknown.

The adventure exceeds all of Shining Light's expectations, and he learns more about his place in this world than the Holy Peoples of his band could ever teach him.

More from Evolved Publishing:

CHILDREN'S PICTURE BOOKS
THE BIRD BRAIN BOOKS by Emlyn Chand:
- *Courtney Saves Christmas*
- *Davey the Detective*
- *Honey the Hero*
- *Izzy the Inventor*
- *Larry the Lonely*
- *Poppy the Proud*
- *Ricky the Runt*
- *Sammy Steals the Show*
- *Tommy Goes Trick-or-Treating*
- *Vicky Finds a Valentine*

Silent Words by Chantal Fournier
Thomas and the Tiger-Turtle by Jonathan Gould
EMLYN AND THE GREMLIN by Steff F. Kneff:
- *Emlyn and the Gremlin*
- *Emlyn and the Gremlin and the Barbeque Disaster*
- *Emlyn and the Gremlin and the Mean Old Cat*

I'd Rather Be Riding My Bike by Eric Pinder
VALENTINA'S SPOOKY ADVENTURES
by Majanka Verstraete:
- *Valentina and the Haunted Mansion*
- *Valentina and the Masked Mummy*
- *Valentina and the Whackadoodle Witch*

HISTORICAL FICTION
Circles by Ruby Standing Deer
Spirals by Ruby Standing Deer
Stones by Ruby Standing Deer

LITERARY FICTION
Torn Together by Emlyn Chand
Carry Me Away by Robb Grindstaff
Hannah's Voice by Robb Grindstaff
Turning Trixie by Robb Grindstaff
The Daughter of the Sea and the Sky by David Litwack
The Lone Wolf by E.D. Martin
Jellicle Girl by Stevie Mikayne
Weight of Earth by Stevie Mikayne
Desert Flower by Angela Scott
Desert Rice by Angela Scott
White Chalk by Pavarti K. Tyler

LOWER GRADE (Chapter Books)
TALES FROM UPON A. TIME by Falcon Storm
- *Natalie the Not-So-Nasty*
- *The Perils of Petunia*
- *The Persnickety Princess*

WEIRDVILLE by Majanka Verstraete
- *Drowning in Fear*
- *Fright Train*
- *Grave Error*
- *House of Horrors*
- *The Clumsy Magician*
- *The Doll Maker*

MEMOIR
And Then It Rained: Lessons for Life by Megan Morrison

MIDDLE GRADE
NOAH ZARC by D. Robert Pease:
- *Cataclysm (Book 2)*
- *Declaration (Book 3)*
- *Mammoth Trouble (Book 1)*
- *Omnibus (Special 3-in-1 Edition)*

MYSTERY / CRIME / DETECTIVE
Hot Sinatra by Axel Howerton

ROMANCE / EROTICA
Walk Away with Me by Darby Davenport
Home Is Where the Heat Is by Amelia James
Secret Storm by Amelia James
Tell Me You Want Me by Amelia James
Tell Me You Want Me Forever by Amelia James
THE TWISTED MOSAIC by Amelia James
- *Her Twisted Pleasures (Book 1)*
- *His Twisted Choice (Book 3)*
- *Their Twisted Love (Book 2)*
- *The Twisted Mosaic – Specail Omnibus Edition*

The Devil Made Me Do It by Amelia James
THE SUGAR HOUSE NOVELLAS by Pavarti K. Tyler
- *Dual Domination (Book 3)*
- *Protecting Portia (Book 2)*
- *Sugar & Salt (Book 1)*

SCI-FI / FANTASY
Eulogy by D.T. Conklin
Shadow Swarm by D. Robert Pease
Two Moons of Sera by Pavarti K. Tyler

SHORT STORY ANTHOLOGIES
FROM THE EDITORS AT EVOLVED PUBLISHING:
    Evolution: Vol. 1 (A Short Story Collection)
    Evolution: Vol. 2 (A Short Story Collection)
All Tolkien No Action: Swords, Sorcery & Sci-Fi by Eric Pinder

SUSPENSE / THRILLER
Forgive Me, Alex by Lane Diamond
The Devil's Bane by Lane Diamond
Whispers of the Dead by C.L. Roberts-Huth
Whispers of the Serpent by C.L. Roberts-Huth

YOUNG ADULT
Farsighted by Emlyn Chand
Open Heart by Emlyn Chand
The Silver Sphere by Michael Dadich
The Sinister Kin by Michael Dadich
THE DARLA DECKER DIARIES by Jessica McHugh
    Darla Decker Hates to Wait (Book 1)
    Darla Decker Shakes the State (Book 3)
    Darla Decker Takes the Cake (Book 2)
JOEY COLA by D. Robert Pease:
    Cleopatra Rising (Book 2)
    Dream Warriors (Book 1)
    Third Reality (Book 3)
Anyone? by Angela Scott
THE ZOMBIE WEST TRILOGY by Angela Scott
    Dead Plains (Zombie West #3)
    Survivor Roundup (Zombie West #2)
    The Zombie West Trilogy – Special Omnibus Edition
    Wanted: Dead or Undead (Zombie West #1)

CPSIA information can be obtained
at www.ICGtesting.com
Printed in the USA
BVHW041930300322
632882BV00004B/292